Legananny Legacy:

The Winds of County Down

By Dorothy MacNeill Dupont

Copyright, © 2014 Dorothy MacNeill Dupont
Legananny Legacy:
The Winds of County Down

ISBN-13: 978-1499341126
ISBN-10: 1499341121

Library of Congress Control Number: 2014915864
CreateSpace Independent Publishing Platform, North Charleston, SC

All rights reserved. No part of this publication may be reproduced, stored in a retrieval system, or transmitted in any form or by any means without prior written permission of the publisher. The only exception is the use of brief quotations for review purposes.

Cover by *Dupont Design*

For Dad, without whose stories
Elizabeth, Maggie and Lizzie,
would be lost to us.

Come, fairies, take me out of this dull world,
For I would ride with you upon the wind
And dance upon the mountains like a flame!
  -*William Butler Yeats*

The Women of the Legananny Legacy:

Elizabeth (Beth) Frazer Cockburn
(The Winds of County Down)

|

Margaret (Maggie) Jane Coburn Heenan
(The Winds of County Down)
(The Self-same Moon and Stars — Spring, 2015)

|

Elizabeth (Lizzie) Jane Heenan MacNeill
(The Winds of County Down)
(The Self-same Moon and Stars — Spring, 2015)
(This Land I Hold Dear — Fall, 2015)

|

Clara (Claire) MacNeill Thayer
(This Land I Hold Dear — Fall, 2015)

PREFACE

Legannany Legacy is written as a fictionalized chronology of real people and their experiences. The stories were brought to our generation by our dad, Raymond H. MacNeill, whose talents for story-telling made this collection of family lore stick in our minds, bonding the struggles of our daily lives with that of the four generations before ours. Through his repetitive, dramatic weaving of stories, we *saw* my grandmother, Lizzie, making soap and candles, going to school in Ireland, venturing to America, being servant and master, raising her incredible family with her husband, living and loving full out, with the bruises and scars, triumphs and defeats, anger, shame, and compassion by which all human life is characterized.

As the stories were written, it became most logical to present the work in several volumes, highlighting Maggie, Lizzie, and Claire. Most of the stories are true, as far as social, economical, genealogical, and political history can testify, and I stand by them. There are completely fictional relationships among this cast of characters and those are enumerated at the back of each book, under the annotation, *The Truth and the Fantasy.*

The Winds of County Down takes place from about 1828 to 1892. It is chiefly the story of Maggie, with her mother, Elizabeth, and her daughter Lizzie. The portraits are painted on a canvas of social and historical events, influenced by the acceptance or rejection of the common beliefs and attitudes of the times.

The three central women in this volume each have a particular strength of their own. A strength as different from the others, as if they had invented the word to have separate meanings when individually applied: Elizabeth strength, Maggie strength, and Lizzie strength. There is a vulnerability laid bare in each woman, against which she wages her personal war. The spoils of that war are strength, dignity, and self-reliance. The consequences of fighting that war too long and too hard, are cynicism, hyper-vigilance, and loss of both compassion and joyful spirit. Each woman finds her own balance in the attributes to which she aspires and discovers the blessings she may have taken for granted.

The writing of this series has been long, sometimes arduous, at most times daunting, but never without a satisfying hope, never without boundless reward. I am eternally grateful for the challenge to record these stories, connecting the events within the framework of time and *mores* of the day. Although this is a fictionalized account, I hope you will see the world in which Elizabeth, Maggie, and Lizzie lived. It is my pleasure to introduce you to our family.

— Dorothy MacNeill Dupont

Prologue

Lieutenant Hon. Hugh Annesley

15 SEPTEMBER 1854 — THE CRIMEA, ABOUT THIRTY MILES SOUTH OF SEBASTOPOL

The young lieutenant wrote in his journal:

After many long days on ship, today we should be able to touch land. The word among the men is that we will make our landing by first light. We can see the French have landed and have an entire division in defensive position on the hills above the beach. We have not yet located the buoy that signals our turning toward the landing area. Not surprising, the officers suspect it was moved in the night by the French to give them an advantage to the battlefield.

The sailors who transport us are rough, but good natured. They eye our kilts and call us 'ladies'. It's all in fun and we use our 'lady-like' status to jibe them a bit in return. If we were on land at home, there would be a broken jaw or two for the repartee we engage in. Since the sea is their expertise, we allow the slight to our manhood.

Truth be told, he mused, *our manhood has suffered greatly in our response to the constant motion of the sea. Our stomachs are emptied regularly and we are pale and rather green of complexion. Our feet anxiously await terra firma.*

His pen hovered over the page as his mother's concerned face gently, relentlessly, invaded his thoughts. *I fear Mother is furious with me since Robert joined the army. I think she believes it is I who convinced him to leave Eton before earning his degree and opt for a life of adventure. In truth, he was never a scholar, but a brawling child who rarely attended classes before noon. In spite of many warnings of expulsion, he continued to flaunt his disgraceful behavior until the bitter end. His only choice of honor was to serve in the Queen's 11th Hassars and hope to buy officer status. God save him, if he has to do more than model the uniform of an officer! God help me if he is injured in any way. He will forever be her child, since her first born of that name died after only two days.*

Poor Mother! I suppose we are each a disappointment to her in some way. William has refused marriage, and is not inclined to change his mind on the matter. I, for my part, am hoping he lives a long life of political service to the Queen. Still, eventually, I will have to marry some suitable cousin, I suppose. How could the handsome Annesley men have so plain and dull a group of female cousins? He hurriedly began writing again as he became aware of a shift in the activity around him.

There is an increase of noise on the deck. They have spotted the buoy, but as we turned to the landing spot, we are faced with a sandstone cliff. Now, the ship is moving further south to where the beach begins again. It is almost nine o'clock and we are still in limbo, anxious to get off the Agamemnon *to solid ground. A signal gunshot from the prow... We are about to land!*

"16-19 September 1854.

Owing to the severe rain and having no shelter the first night, and due to the business of trying to organize our men and supplies, I have not taken the chance to open this journal for several days. The landing was unholy chaos! Men were everywhere trying to find their regiments. Supplies dumped on the beach with no regard to their destinations. We must have lost a dozen panicked horses and the boats that carried them in transport to the beach.

He put his journal down, and closed his eyes, succumbing to the worry churning in his gnawing gut. *They say the* Kangaroo *has three times as many sick or dying men in its hold and the dead on the deck outnumber those! I have not found Robert. I don't even know if he's here. He was not with his regiment on land. Perhaps his orders were changed and he will not have to be here.* Heaving a sigh and trying to clear his head, he wrote:

"*Today, the 19th, we marched ten miles across level ground, until we saw the enemy occupying the hills above us. We will take shelter here tonight.*"[1]

His thoughts drifting to his men, he decided, *I will have mess with my men, despite the disapproving looks of my fellow officers. I need them with me, come tomorrow. Scouting reports the enemy is tending its dead. Tomorrow, although we are at a desperate strategic disadvantage, we will engage the Cossacks. Heaven help us!*

"Hold that line steady, lads!" the young lieutenant shouted through the penetrating rain. "Wait for my signal!" *This is disaster — God save us!* Remembering the squabbling among the rigid and pompous field officers, he muttered to himself bitterly, *Curse those indecisive old men, drawing battle plans equal only to their stupidity!*

It was as if he was outside himself, calmly watching the impending slaughter. He stared at the backs of the men clamoring up the slippery hill. He stood poised with his men, anticipating the moment the front line reached the summit.

---

[1] Details from the field of Battle, quoted from a letter by Lt. Hugh Annesley to his mother, Nelson Examiner and New Zealand Chronicle, Volume XIII, Issue 711, 17 February 1855, page 4, retrieved from *paperspast.natlib.govt.nz/cgi-bin/paperspast?, Nov. 30, 2013.*

"Charge!" he hollered. *What! O God, spare me!* Time slowed by the incredible sight, he stared at the horror played out before him. *Was that a bugle?* The front line snapped, reversed direction and was scrambling down *toward* his men! Bullets bursting through their uniforms from behind, their faces twisted grotesquely with sudden pain and abject fear, their arms flailing uncontrollably. The color standard broke in half as it was torn by merciless Cossack bullets. The remnants of the flag were still hoisted by Lieutenant Robert Lloyd-Linsay who miraculously escaped injury while bullets whizzed by him.

The enemy crested the ridge. The Russian line fired down at the chaotic mob rushing towards his men. *"Forward, Guards!"* He could not hear his own voice. The catastrophic din swallowed up his order.

The clamor of battle assaulted his ears, rendering their function useless. Acrid smells of gun powder, sweat and fear attacked his senses. But it was the blood, the sickening sweet, metallic scent of life spilling out that caused the violent lurch of his stomach. *Hold on,* he thought darkly, grimacing with sudden pain in his gut, *The Scots Fusilier Guards won't follow the Lieutenant Hon. Hugh Annesley into hell if he pukes on his boots like a frightened child!*

His own line split by the panicked front line, the lieutenant desperately tried to keep his men focused on their objective. *Almost there*! He turned toward his men. A white hot flare screamed through his brain, and blackness slammed into him.

A short time later, sporadic gunfire punctured the low moaning of mangled men strewn across the sheltered face of the misty, smoke-fogged hill.

"God save us! Look, Will," whispered the crouching young man, busily tying up his brother's dangling arm, "It's the young Lieut. Aye-ee! Half his face's shot off!" Suddenly, the lieutenant's chest heaved, as gasped a bubbling, liquid intake of air and blood.

"He's alive, Will! Help me with him. He's the only officer here worth his salt." Seeing his brother hesitate, he pleaded, "He ate wit' us jes' las' night, *fer heaven's sake, Will!*"

"Petey, m' boy, ye canna save the whole world," the Scotsman pleaded. "They'll come get him. Yer hurt yerself." A rain of bullets accompanied another roar of orders on the hill.

"We canna wait, Will! He won't make it. He'll drown in his own blood. 'Tween the two o' us, we kin do it." Peter Fraser raised the young officer's body onto his sturdy shoulder, gingerly avoiding his own bloodied hand, wrapped in the rags of his shirt. "Hold him steady, Will! I dinna need drop him." Together, they careened through the carnage of wounded and dying men, crossing the raging river under the hail of bullets, over the ridge to the sheltered side.

When the fog in his brain began to lift, Hugh became aware of someone trying to give him water and listening to a distant, steady groaning. His right eye searched wildly around and the moaning seemed to stop. As his mind filled with vile cursing, it occurred to him, *that mewling noise is me!* His face seemed weighted down like a cannon. He moved his fiery tongue in thirst and searched for teeth that had abandoned him. He was conscious of low, ecclesiastical words surrounding him like a smothering blanket. As he clawed for his precarious purchase on reality, sweet blackness enveloped him once again.

Hours later, alert and feeling some of the pain subside, Hugh tried to write in his journal what he remembered after the battle, *"The doctors gave me some water, and then were obliged to go to others; so when they left, I sat there for above half an hour before I could find out where hospital was. At last, an officer of the 10th, though wounded himself, gave me his arm and took me to the Fusilier hospital where I got some water and sat down to bathe my face. There were six or seven of our fellows there — one with five balls in him, another three, and a third with his leg broken. A servant got me some blankets, then we found a half burnt out stable cleaned out and five of us lay there for the night, very wretched, with operations going on all around us. Some weak brandy and water and some tea were all we had. The shed we were in was a horrid thing — the heat, the dust, and flies intolerable; so in the morning, four of us came down to the fleet and I, with two others, am on board Her Majesty's Ship* London.

Poor B— came to see me in the hovel we were lying in, and burst into tears when he recognized me, I was so altered. Of course, one cannot have an ounce of lead through one without swelling and my face is like a good sized turnip; my mouth much larger than I have any desire to see it in future. I do not suppose the ball could not have hit me in any other part of the head where it would not have been attended with much more danger. [2]

Sometime later, the fog of fever lifted, along with his spirits. Hugh had visitors. Some of his fellow officers were seated quietly near his hammock as he slept. They were horrified at the barely recognizable appearance of this handsome lad of twenty-three. Talking quietly among themselves, they were unaware their comrade had awaken. Hugh reached for the slate and chalk at his bedside. "*A most summary dentist the ball was, to take out all my teeth at one smash, except four grinders; there was a decayed one, which I hope is gone with its brethren, but I can't make out, if it has or not.*"[3] Exchanging nervous glances, his fellow officers smiled, then laughed raucously. Their clown prince was back from the dead.

Later, writing a letter to his mother, he tried to prepare her for the face he would bring home, but still he tried to make light of his injuries. He added, "*There is a good bit of tongue gone also, but the doctors say that will not signify, and that I shall speak as plainly as ever, or at worst with a becoming lisp; so altogether, I think even*

---

[2] *Ibid.*

you must allow, I have every reason to be thankful. I hope you will not allow yourself to fret the least about me."[3]

The days were blurring together now. His commanding officer sent an ensign for his report of the battle. Hugh could speak little as yet, so he had written down a semblance of a report as best he could. There was not much he could recall. *I know it was a pitifully disorganized mess of a landing six days before. We slept in the blasted rain with no tents! My bearskin with a packet of biscuits under it made for a fairly comfortable pillow though. I barely saw six minutes of that miserable massacre, four of them holding for the charge!* His humor failed him at the memory of the fear-ravaged men who suddenly turned from certain death, split his line and laid his men open to Cossack sword, pistol and cannon. *Did they hear a bugle call retreat?* His soldiers held steady in the face of that travesty, for the precious few minutes he was even aware. He was astounded to hear the allies had won the day.

Hugh rubbed his forehead in agitation. After the sudden retreat of the first line at the top of the hill, he remembered only the charge of his men. Hugh hoped there were officers who could recommend his soldiers for valor, but he was shot before their engagement with the enemy. He had fallen at the very moment his men needed him most! Suddenly, overtaken by unreasonable shame, he began to shake violently. With an anguished groan, he dismissed the ensign, turned to the wall and wept.

That afternoon, Hugh learned two men had brought him to the hastily organized triage area. They were both wounded, though not as gravely as he: Private William Fraser, shot in the arm, and his brother, Private Peter Fraser, bayoneted in his hand. *Where are they now?* He asked everyone about the two men, 42nd Regiment,

---

[3] Ibid.

Highlanders, he learned. *"Find them! Send them to me. Now!"* he commanded.

Later that week, two nervous men stood at the foot of his hammock, regimental headgear in hand, sheepishly switching from foot to foot. One soldier scowled at the younger, taller man with obvious distain. *Now yer did it. 'Take care o' yer brother,' says Ma. When did he ever listen ta reason?*

Hugh could see they were not experienced soldiers, probably conscripted, making the best of what the government decided was their destiny. He wrote on his slate, *"Be at ease. If you would be so kind, tell me what happened."*

The elder of the two took the slate with a nod of his head and slid it over to his brother, "Petey, what does it say?" Peter Fraser read it, set the slate down and began their story. He omitted William's reluctance to participate, but in his soft Scottish burr gave an otherwise full accounting of their actions. He told the lieutenant that they tried to see him the next day at the field hospital, but were refused admittance because of their lack of rank.

"I wannet ta thank you, sair, fer breakin' bread wit' the men, the day afore the fightin'. It gave us courage ta knae there was one lieut' cared if his men lived or died. A' times, it's hard ta tell who the foe is, sair," Petey admitted. William kicked him in the ankle. His brother whispered out of the side of his mouth. *"Are yer a complete fool?"*

Hugh raised his hand, laughing he wrote, *"God's honest truth! How came you to the 42nd?"*

Peter looked at his brother warily, "Times are hard fer farmers in the lowlands, sair. Will an' I made a plan ta gae ta America. We saved fer a lang time, but we was green as grass. We went down ta the ship an' were fleeced by pickpockets on the dock. Wit' no money ta e'en gae hame agin, we enlisted. The 42nd Highlanders... We've been well treated, sir. We've food and clothin', which is more than they we left b'hind." Petey hung his head. "We were s'posed ta send fer m' sister an' her family when we made our fortune in America."

The wounded officer wrote, *"Tell me about home."*

The private answered, slowly warming to his tale. As his brother joined in, they began interrupting each other, sometimes joking then, waxing sentimental. "Our sister is married ta a farmer. He's forced ta be a shepherd, 'cause raisin' sheep is more gainful fer the laird. I swear James Co'burn kin grow roses out a' rock, sae good a farmer is he. Beth rules the roost. She's a clever girl. They haf' a wee child o' eight years. She'd break yer heart she's sae fair, crippled though. Canna walk, no' since she was four, maybe five years."

Hugh watched as the words about home tumbled from their mouths. *They're desperately homesick.*

"Gentlemen, I could buy you out of the army, if you wish." he wrote.

"No gentlemen are we, sair. And nay, they's no work ta hame. Besides, 'twas our honor an' duty ta bring ye ta safety. We haf' all we need." The men looked at each other and nodded in agreement.

"I'll see what I can do for your sister's farmer then. I will write to you soon."

Erasing quickly, Hugh wrote, *"42nd Highlanders?"*

"Aye, sir, we're bound ta Sevastopol."

It was as if they just remembered they were talking to an officer and nobility. They visibly changed their demeanor back to the enlisted soldiers they were. Hugh elicited the details he needed about the soldiers' sister and her husband.

"You have saved my life. Let me be worthy of that honor, or how shall I raise this pretty face in public?" With a coquettish tilt of his bandaged head, he set the men at ease again. The brothers grinned. Then snapping to attention, they saluted and left.

Lieutenant Hon. Annesley sent once more for pen and paper.

September 26, 1854
Dearest Mother,

I hope this letter finds you and my dear brother well. I hasten to assure you, your son, Hugh, improves daily. God willing, I will be at Castlewellan within a few weeks time. You may find it difficult to recognize my charming visage at first, but I am, indeed, the same rapscallion, with which you have ever been burdened.

I hear my brother Robert is well and is with the 11th Hussars. I am sorry not to be meeting up with him. Second Lieutenant Hon. Robert John Annesley — I'm sure he'll carry the rank with honor. He's always been a scrappy lad.

I have an odd request for you and my dear brother, William. I have incurred a serious debt of honor and it is imperative I balance the scale in some small way. I will forever be grateful to you if you graciously assist me with my quest . . .

Margaret Jane Coburn
Scotland and Ireland 1846 —1892

Chapter One

Elizabeth Jane Fraser wed James Cockburn of Scotland in the cold gray mist of a late lowland winter. "Wit'out a penny or a prayer o' gittin' one," said her husband's ma, shaking her head. Still, Elizabeth was a pretty little thing and his heart was lost to her, so marry they did.

It was late in November of 1846, while the first snow was still in the air and frost coated the thatched roof of the little cottage, when Elizabeth bore a fragile, sweet bairn — Margaret Jane Cockburn. The Gaelic blessing said over the child, *May you, little baby, be healthy, upright and happy throughout your whole life* did not betray its secret that only two of the three blessings would be hers. Though tiny, she seemed perfect in every way.

Elizabeth's husband was a tenant farmer like his da before him. Such was his reputation, the neighboring tenants claimed, "He's charmed the earth into giving up twict the harvest." The laird, like so many before him, was clearing his land of farming tenants, replacing them with sheep. More predictable and profitable than farming and lower in maintenance, herding sheep required but a few workers to maintain high profits from their wool. The laird plied his evicted families with factory jobs in cities already overcrowded with workers or with ship's passage to America. He kept the young Cockburns farming for longer than the others, owing to James' talents, but it was too impractical to last.

James' father seemed to wither like untended crops as more and more fields went to grazing. Soon, farming in the lowlands perished and his da with it. Gone was his da, gone was his work and there was no help for it. James tended sheep with the laird's regrets, earning enough to keep them warm, or eat, but hardly both, it seemed. James and Elizabeth stayed in the little cottage, watching the fields grow over, now spotted with the cursed wooly animals.

James' brothers went off to America, while his mother moved with his sister and her husband to Glasgow. Elizabeth's brothers were headed for America too, although their most recent letters revealed they had enlisted in the army instead. Elizabeth anxiously awaited the next letter to explain the confusion. With talk of war, she both wished for and feared the missive's arrival.

Their families torn asunder, James and Elizabeth clung to each other, having lost all family but themselves and their wee bairn. Elizabeth watched James staring pensively into the evening fire, her heart aching for a glimpse of joy in his eyes again. His black hair grew thinner and grayer with each year of the penance he paid for unknown sins. The child with sunset red hair could still coax a smile from him, fleeting though it was. Elizabeth saw the prideful man she loved fading a little more each passing day.

Sweet-tempered Maggie was the mister's darling. He doted on her, taking his wee faerie princess everywhere. He sat her up on the bar in the local pub and drank to her health. *A lot o' good thet did her*, Elizabeth thought darkly. *By the time she were five, she walked like her da. Limped like him, she did - him, who broke his leg when he was a lad, felled by a skittish horse.*

Still, Maggie followed him all around then, slower and slower, until finally, he caught her up in his arms to get to where he was off to, sooner rather than later. James put her on his back, prancing down the road, still proud of his failing Maggie. The few remaining old men at the public house, delicately asked after her health, so as not to raise his temper. "She'll be fine," he'd say, his mouth drawn in a stubborn line across his face. "She'll be fine." *But she wasn't. She seemed healthy enough, but couldn't walk straight.* Soon after, she stopped walking altogether. "No matter, I'll put her in the cart. She'll be fine."

She's the only ray o' sunshine thet keeps his dark an' solemn days from swallowin' him up entire, thought his wife.

On the last day of the year, Elizabeth pulled her red-brown hair into the bun she wore every day, tied her kerchief over it and set about preparing her day. Humming an old tune, she busied herself getting ready for Hogmanay (Scottish New Year's Eve). She spread juniper and mistletoe over the doorway and windows. There was a Yule log in the fireplace on which she threw some herbs for pleasant aroma. Outside, she had holiday cakes baking and an extravagant stew with a rare bit of mutton. Tonight, if the light snow stopped, they would celebrate by visiting the neighbors. Tomorrow, they would head off to the crossroads, where she hoped to meet friends at the pub. *That'll depend on James' ability ta be a' tall cheerful,* she grimaced. *Talkin' ta him las' night, seemed ta brin' him up short, when I told him the child needs ta see him smile* onct *in a while. The child shouldn't hafta think thet his dark disposition is* her *fault! I'm gettin' weary myself, but ye canna raise a child ta be afeared o' ye growlin'!* As if to admonish herself for her own demeanor, she smiled at Maggie and began to hum again as she worked. Her eyes blinked as she realized, *Oh! My shortbread! If I let it brown 'twill be no good ta give! Better check on the black bun too.*

"Kin I do som'thin' ta help, Ma?" begged Maggie brightly from her chair at the table.

"You, m' bairn, kin wrap the salt. Take just these squares o' cloth an' pour a wee bit o' salt in each one then, tie 'em with string. Make four of 'em fer *'first footin','*" she said. *When she's done wit' thet, I'll haf' her do a lump o' coal fer each o' them, too. If I can't git James ta gae first footin', I'll gae m'self wit' Maggie,* She determined resolutely. *Good thin' the cottages are fair close t'gether or Maggie an' me would be in a ditch gittin' from one t'other. All there are left are shepherds an' shopkeeps nae.* Elizabeth sighed, remembering the old days. *Used ta spend half the night goin' from farm ta farm. Nae they're all gone. Oh, I hope he'll gae, if only fer Maggie. 'Twould do him good ta see his neighbors, too.* Elizabeth threw on her wool and bustled outside to tend to her breads.

As the evening wore on, Maggie settled down for a nap before the festivities. Elizabeth watched James carefully, seeing his shoulders stooped, his handsome face drawn down, looking older than his years. She hoped he wouldn't imbibe too much to take Maggie out at midnight. It was to be her first sojourn of *first footin'* and she was so looking forward to it.

"*A ghràidh,* will ye be takin' Maggie out t'night, then?" Elizabeth whispered, hoping she wasn't too late to remind him.

James gave her a tired smile then, his eyes brightening a bit, he replied, "O' course, missus, she won' wan' ta be missin' thet, eh?"

"'Tis sae, Mister Co'burn, I thought she'd ne'er sleep." Elizabeth sighed thankfully, "Ye will be takin' the cart, then? I'll hafta add my plaid ta keep her warm enough. It's clear nae. The snow is stopped."

"Nay, I'll put her ta m' back an' wrap her up tight. She'll be fine. I'll not keep her out too lang. Jes' lang enough, ta let her haf' a feel for it. Jes' a wee sip against the chill then, on ta the next, an' hame agin." He pantomimed drinking a pint. "Ye haf' yer bundles, then?" Elizabeth nodded. Touching his hand, she went to work, gathering the little good luck bundles in a cloth for each neighbor. Soon, they'd be off and she'd wait for visitors at her door. *If he hasn't chast 'em off wit' his sad an' sour countenance, thet is. When they're off, I'll make up a bundle fer us. I'll hafta change the cloths. I wan' Maggie ta think someone wished good luck fer us, too.*

Soon they were on their way. James pretended they were off to a great adventure and it was almost like older, happier times.

With her counterfeit bundles wrapped, Elizabeth sat waiting for the knock on her door she didn't think would come. Mesmerized by the fire her weary head nodded, lost in long ago dreams. Slowly, climbing out of her fog, Elizabeth became aware of a banging at the door. *Oh, goodness me, someone did come ta us, Well hurry! Answer the door, woman, afore they decide they made a mistake!* There in the dooryard was a gentleman. Not the laird, she noted. *Who can he be?*

"Are you the wife of James Co'burn, the farmer?" the stranger asked, waiting for an invitation to enter.

"I am, sair, Come in. He'll be here any minute." *Good Laird, save me. He knows my James?* Her mind was racing with thoughts from good to evil, *It canna be good news, comin' in the night like this.* "Haf a seat by the fire. What is yer business wit' us, sair?"

The well-attired stranger nodded and remained standing. "It's New Year's Eve. I hope you do not take affront, my arriving this late. I bring you news." Seeing the panic race across her face, he smiled. "Good fortune brings me, do not fear. If you'd allow, good woman, I'll sit by the fire and wait for Mister Co'burn?"

Elizabeth, remembering her manners, offered him tea or a draught of something stronger. He accepted the tea and removed his cape. She carefully hung it on a peg. *James, please hurry hame!* Elizabeth studied the stranger, not knowing what to make of him. He was tall, wearing a well-tailored suit with bright silver buttons. A slender man of about thirty-five, he looked ruefully at his polished, but wet boots and the damp spot on the floor. He carried a letter of some sort tucked under his arm, as if he were afraid it would fly away if he set it down.

The stranger smiled and as he spoke softly of the chill in the air, of celebrants he had seen going from house to house, shouting greetings to him, Elizabeth began to calm her fears. He identified himself as Thomas Harden, a courier of Lord Annesley of Castlewellan, throwing Elizabeth into a new set of fears. *Wha' is it? Our Laird dinna send him? What could he want wit' a shepherd? Where could this Castle be? My heart is beatin' lak' a dozen horses racin' down a cobblestone road! Come hame, Mister Co'burn, afore I faint dead away from lack o' knowin' wha' this man's Laird wants o' us! Is all this ta do wit' Will an' Petey?*

After conversation finally reduced itself to uneasy silence, the interminable wait was over. The rustic door to the little cottage pushed gently open. Elizabeth rushed to close the door against the sudden cold. Maggie was sound asleep and James, his cheeks ruddy from the bitter night air, was bubbling with his night's adventure. He looked up suddenly realizing there was a stranger standing in the room. As he laid Maggie in her cot, his eyes narrowing, he asked, "Beth, what's *this*?"

Elizabeth hastily introduced the men. Warily, James shook the man's hand. "Sae, wha' brin's a stranger ta m' hame in the dark o' night?"

"Sir, I have a letter that will explain my mission. Because it is New Year's Eve, I had hoped you would receive me at this late hour. I was told not to delay the message, but to deliver it with all haste directly to you."

"I kin read, but no' sae fast as I kin understand, sae if yer read it ta me, I'd be grateful," said James.

"Of course, I hope I can do the reading justice... *Lord William Richard Annesley of Annesley, Viscount of Gerawley, of*

Castlewellan, County Down, Ulster. To James Co'burn of Culter, Lanark Shire, Scotland..." Thomas Harden continued, while Elizabeth and James stood rapt at his recitation. Lord Annesley wrote of the wishes of his brother, Lieutenant Hon. Hugh Annesley, of the Scots Fusilier Guard, severely wounded at the Battle of Alma in the Crimea, on behalf of his rescuers, William and Peter Fraser. *Elizabeth's brothers*! James and Elizabeth looked at each other in amazement.

"James Co'burn with his wife and children," Mister Harden continued, *"If willing, are asked to remove themselves from their present situation to two plots of land in Legananny of Drumgooland and one in Slievnaboley, in the lower half of Upper Inveigh Barony, County Down, Ulster. They have leave to lease the land from Lord Annesley for as long as they continue to work the land. All fees and taxes due to be paid by the Annesley estate May 1st and November 1st of 1854. Subsequently to be paid by James Cockburn. Other stipulations will be designated upon their arrival."*

"W-wha'?" James was speechless. Elizabeth was not. Whatever reticence she had shown while she and Thomas Harden were waiting, was gone. Questions poured out of her almost faster than Mister Harden could answer. They talked through the night. The stranger answered all their questions, as best he could. The Lieutenant was recovering at his brother's home in Castlewellan and would meet with them before they went to the land. There were fourteen acres in James Cockburn's name and seven acres with cottage and offices in Margaret Cockburn's name, *in Maggie's name? Kin thet be true?* "It will all be explained by his Lordship when you see him. If you agree to his proposal, you will have to be on the land for spring planting."

The tall stranger stood, reaching for his cloak. "If you would permit me, I would like to give you some time to rest and talk between yourselves." I have a room at the pub, and will come back tomorrow, say at two hours after noon? Then we can draft a reply to his lordship to be signed by your mark." With a nod, James Harden took his leave.

These are strange tidings, indeed, thought Elizabeth. James drew her into his arms and held her. When she began to speak, he put a finger to her lips, pulled her head to his shoulder and stood quietly, barely moving, staring into the fire. "No more t'night, Love. We'll rest an' talk in the mornin'." *This may save us,* Elizabeth thought. *James will work the land again!*

Maggie rose with the first light, excited about her adventures of the night before. She dressed under her quilt to stay warm. Crawling to the end of her cot, she scooted herself over to her chair. She glanced over at her sleeping parents and smiled. *Oh, there's som'thin' on the table! It looks fancy.* Stretching across, she snagged the paper to read it. Although she read it well, she wasn't sure of its meaning. *What's this Legananny? Is Da not a shepherd? Do we hafta leave?* Spying her name, she tried to understand what it was about. *We are ta gae ta different places? I canna be wit' Ma an' Da?* Maggie's bright face crumbled as she started to cry.

Elizabeth woke in a start. "Wha's the matter, sweet bairn? Wha' are all these tears about?" Her heart nearly broke to see Maggie in such a state. Maggie's words, tumbling out through hiccoughs and gasps, told her worries to her mother.

"No, child, you'll al'ays be wit' us. Ne'er will anythin' come between us." Elizabeth took her child in her lap and rocked her as if she were still two years old. "We don' knae ever'thin' yet, but we do knae we'll never be separated from our sweet Maggie."

James was now awake, asking what the commotion was. Elizabeth hastily explained Maggie's concerns. James touched his little girl's nose and tickled her chin. "Ye are a clever child ta read sae well, Maggie. Are ye no' clever enough ta knae how much we need yer right by us ev'ry day? Who would make yer sour old da smile? Who would make yer ma sing songs all day lang? Indeed, why would the sun rise ev'ry morning, if not fer our Maggie?" Her eyes cleared of tears now, Maggie giggled with delight. Her fears abated, she held her questions for a later time.

James and Elizabeth talked all morning in whispers, at times fast and serious, punctuated with arguing, other times slow and smiling, staring into each other's eyes. For the first time in a long time, they were dreaming of a future and it felt good. Maggie watched the exchanges with excitement. Whatever was happening, the *first footin'* last night seemed to bring good luck! *Happy Ne'er's Day!*

Elizabeth's hopes rode high on the news all morning, refusing to see any negative possibilities in it. Fast on the heels of Thomas Harden's arrival, however, her panic resumed. *I near jumped out o' my skin when he knocked! I daren't breathe over much fer fear my heart will fair leap from m' breast! Calm down, foolish woman! Ye will call down the banshee upon yer.* Maggie grinned with delight seeing her mother so animated.

The courier sat at the table and smiled at the charm of the winsome child. As he spread out another document, Maggie wiggled in excitement. As she looked up at her da, he winked and pursed his lips in a signal to be very quiet.

"This is just a note to tell the Earl you have seen the document, Mister Co'burn. I ask you to sign it as proof I have completed this task." Elizabeth read the note aloud, and handed it to James.

James signed the document and said, "This is fer a new beginnin'. If all is well, we haf a chanct ta gae back ta the land."

Mister Harden folded the note, closed it with the Earl's seal and slipped it into his pocket. "I'm to tell you, Mister Co'burn, I'll return the 22nd day of February, to escort you all to meet with the Earl's brother at Castlewellan. His Lordship will pay the fares for the crossing and will see to your comfort while you are there. If you agree to his terms, I will take you to the land and cottage. Depending on the weather, it could take about five, but possibly up to twelve days, if they delay the crossing. The ferry to Belfast only runs on Tuesdays. If all is to your liking, you will return here, pack your belongings and move into your new home, ready to plan for spring planting. Will that meet with your approval, Mister Co'burn?"

James and Elizabeth nodded, smiling. Shaking hands with James, Mister Harden took his leave.

"Oh Da, this will be the best kind o' adventure, won' it!"

"Aye, it surely will, my angel. Nae it's time ta celebrate our Ne'er's Day! Elizabeth, are ye ready ta gae ta the pub? We've got som'thin' ta smile about!"

"James, we surely do. I think fer nae, 'til we see the land an' we're ready ta be leavin' this place, we should keep this good fortune ta ourselves. No sense in callin' the devil ta our door by talkin' about our good luck! 'Sides, this penny's no' in our pocket yet."

"All right, Ma," he said with a wink to Maggie, "But I'm fairly burstin' ta tell good news fer a change. We kin tell 'em we heard Will an' Petey are doin' well an' in the army!" Bundling Maggie up, Elizabeth wasn't sure stretching the truth to cover up good news was any way to fool the devil, but it was better than having the folks feel they were lording their good fortune over them. They would have to come up with a reason why they would be gone for so long though. *We'll hafta blame thet on Will an' Petey too, I ken. The folk 'round here pro'bly would no' even knae we'd gone.*

Elizabeth was almost ashamed to be so happy. Shaking the gloom off like a heavy cloak, the grin of good fortune she thought would never leave her face earlier, returned as she walked with James and Maggie to the public house. She watched her husband chatting happily with her child and all was well with her world. *Fer t'night, I'll no' think o' wha' could gae wrong in this happenstance. Fer t'night, there's only hope, my angel child an' havin' my husband back — no' as a shepherd, but as the farmer God made him.*

Time in the next month and a half advanced at break-neck speed, as Elizabeth struggled to prepare for the journey to Ulster. Maggie kept up a steady spate of questions well beyond her mother's patience. "James, *please* take her ta the pub, sae I kin git som'thin' done."

"I will, Beth, in a while. I wanna gae through me journals. Maggie, come help me an' don' be plaguin' yer ma." James had taken to studying his farming journals as he did most winters, but now with greater interest, born of hope. As Maggie and her da bent their heads over the collection of old books, James explained the mysteries of a year's crops and expenses. He made a few notes in the margins as he analyzed his figures. His head was full of plans and thoughts of what the new landlord might ask of him. He looked in the corner where Elizabeth had her herbs hanging from the rafters, *I'll hafta take seed from them, fer her new garden, afore we leave. Some o' those plants are from when her mother grew them. It'd be a shame, if she canna git 'em in Ulster.* He knew they were about the only things she had from her mother except for the set of flat irons and her old chipped great dish. The fire that took her mother nearly took her as well, with all their worldly goods. James was already prepared that Elizabeth would leave nothing behind when they moved.

His wife carefully hung their best Sunday clothes for the trip. She inspected every inch of them when she took them out of the trunk. She made a note to re-sew the buttons and checked Maggie's hem to see if she needed to let it down or add to it. The child seemed to have grown over the early winter. She brushed James's jacket front and smelled it to see if he spilled his pint on it when he wore it last. *I canna haf' the new laird thinkin' we don' take care fer our appearance. We canna be fancy as they, but we can be neat an' clean wit' wha' we haf'.*

"Ma?" The little girl's voice broke into her thoughts. Startled, Elizabeth stopped in the middle of what she was doing.

"Wha' is it, Maggie? Oh bother, look at the light! Yer a hungry wee rabbit, aren't yer!" The gathering gloom that heralded the winter evening, told her time had slipped away and her family must be ravenous. *"A bheil an t-acras ort"* Are ye hungry?

Her husband, bent over his books on the table, looked at his wife saying, "We were sae busy we didn't e'en notice. But since ye mention it, we could pro'bly eat one o' those African elephants Maggie talks about." Maggie dissolved into giggles.

Elizabeth looked in the larder and threw ingredients in a bowl. "James, would ye git some water fer tea an' set it on the fire in here? I'll be back in jes' a moment." Grabbing the bowl, a pan and a pot of leftover soup she hurried out the door to the low burning fire outside. Nestling the iron pan on the revived coals, she dropped batter into the larded pan, and sprinkled some herbs on the white mounds. James brought more fuel for the fire and headed back to the house with the water. Elizabeth turned her pan biscuits and lifted the lid on the soup pot to check its progress. While she waited for the fire to do its magic, as she had done since she was a child, she prayed in Scots Gaelic a blessing for the bounty God gave them and the humble hands that prepared it.

Her meal ready, she carried the pot and pan into the little cottage, surprised to see the table set and her family eagerly awaiting the repast. She laughed as James showed his appreciation by taking a deep sniff of the soup, rubbing his belly dramatically. Smiling, Elizabeth took his hand and Maggie's, signaling her daughter to say grace. "The Sacred Three, my fortress be, encirclin' me. Come an' be 'round, my hearth an' my hame. Amen."

"Amen. Verra nice, Maggie. Nae, let's eat." The little group chatted quietly, hungrily downing the hastily-made meal. Elizabeth sighed contentedly. *It's been a lang time since we've been sae peaceful, sae full o' wha' t'marra may bring.*

Thomas Harden returned the afternoon before they were to start their journey. Elizabeth invited Mister Harden and the driver in for tea.

"'Tis most kind of you, Misses Co'burn," Mister Harden replied, "But we must be on our way. I did want to give you some details for the trip before I take my leave, if that would be permitted?" Elizabeth nodded. With that, he turned his attention to James. "We have a carriage which will take all of you, your tickets for the crossing and food enough for the journey. All you will need to bring is warm clothing, a light heart and the assurance that the Earl's brother is very pleased to be meeting with you. I suggest you eat a hearty Scots breakfast and we'll get started early tomorrow morning. Are there any questions?" James and Mister Harden conferred for a moment, then the courier and driver were on their way.

As the door closed, Maggie nearly burst with her questions. "Da, how lang will it take? Wha's it lak' ta ride in a carriage? Where do we cross the sea? Where will we land? How lang will the crossing take? Will we see a big city? Where is Castlewellan? Will the Earl lak' me? Does he live in the castle? Is he verra old? Wha' will we eat? How many horses are there pullin' the carriage? Wha' do they look like? Wha' are their names?" She finally paused to take a breath.

"Hush nae, Maggie. Ye will find out all thet, startin' t'marra, *one* answer at a time. If you haf' all yer answers t'day, we might jes' as well stay hame, eh?"

"But, Da-a!" she cried plaintively.

"The fun o' an adventure is ta watch it unfold one surprise at a time. There's always som'thin' 'round the corner ta delight or amaze you!"

Elizabeth laughed and knew it to be true. They all had so many questions. Her head was buzzing with them. She wondered about Petey and Will and the adventures they were having. *God, keep them safe! ...and God, keep us safe!* She felt like they were sailing off the edge of the earth. *Wha' will t'marra bring,* she wondered. Her da always said, *He who gains much, hae much ta lose.* Elizabeth shuddered at how their lives might change. All the warnings from her childhood popped into her head. *There's a deep an' narrow valley between joy an' disaster. Which side were they climbin'? Perhaps we should stay wit' the devil we knae?*

Haf' some faith, Beth! She could hear her husband's voice in her head. *Wha' e'er befall us we will make the best o' it.* She smiled again. *At the very least, James will be a farmer agin! Ta see him work as God intended, how can thet be wrong?*

The little family ate breakfast in their nightclothes to save their best clothes from spills. Elizabeth bustled about, happy to be doing something to keep her thoughts quiet. Having hung their clothes outside to air them out, she brought them in to warm them before they had to dress. *What am I fergettin'? Maggie hae her prayer doll. We're all dressed. I packed a cloth wit' biscuits jes' in case. Make sure Maggie uses the pot afore we leave. Haf' James put out both fires. I cleaned the table an' put breakfast away. I put a note on the table ta say where we've gone.* Elizabeth looked wildly around the room. *Wha' else?*

"'Twill be fine, Beth. I sent the goats ta Drummond yesterday. I'll tend the fires an' the lamp. There's nothin' else thet won' keep." He held her gently, stroking her back until she quieted. "We'll be fine." Elizabeth looked at James and nodded.

Maggie was dressed, combed and bonneted, sitting in her chair. Her fitful night beginning to show in her tired eyes, her head nodded then, she was asleep. James scooped her up and laid her out fully clothed on her cot. Elizabeth shivered to look at her dear sweet Maggie all dressed up and laid out as if in a coffin. *Stop it, Elizabeth! Ta haf' sech thoughts! Ye'll brin' the devil down upon us!*

As if to lure the beasties away, she smiled broadly at her husband, all dressed in his best, handsome and eager. Just then, she heard noises outside. "Quick! See ta the fires, James."

"Yes, *Mother*," he teased. "Better get Maggie up. We mustn' keep Mister Harden waitin'." The last minute flurry had begun.

Soon, they were loaded into the carriage and staring in wonder at the interior of the opulent conveyance. "Oh Ma, it's beautiful!" Maggie gushed, irrepressibly. "Look at this…, an' this!"

Elizabeth saw Maggie's bonnet was knocked off getting into the carriage. She hastened to fix it, but Maggie was turning her head this way and that, bubbling about all the interesting items she was finding.

"Maggie! Hold still a moment!" her mother barked impatiently. Maggie was startled and stared at her mother, her eyes threatening tears. Elizabeth gasped. "It's all right, Maggie. I'm sorry ta be sae sharp wit' ye. Let me fix this an' you kin look 'round some more." Instantly ashamed at her own behavior, Elizabeth bowed her head.

"We're all a wee excited," said James to Mister Harden, as an apology. Their escort just waived his hand to dismiss the moment. Smiling, he looked out the window at the passing view.

Mister Harden talked to Maggie about the countryside, naming the villages, hills and rivers going by. He patiently answered her many questions and soon the rocking of the carriage lulled her to much-needed sleep. Elizabeth felt her own eyes grow heavier and heavier.

Chapter Two

The elegant carriage was beginning to feel part of their battered bones now, rattling from rut to rut over deeply grooved roads, little more than cow paths. Elizabeth and Maggie were now awake and curious about the passing scenery.

Mister Harden accommodated them with a running narrative about their surroundings. About an hour out, the road followed on the north side of the river Clyde. To their right, was a hillside clustered with trees. Snow huddled around the base of the trees hiding from the unseasonable warmth of the sun. "These are the orchards of Hazelbank. In a month or two, this whole hillside will be covered with blossoms from apple, pear, and plum trees."

Maggie leaned forward to see the trees as they approached the village. Elizabeth held Maggie around her waist, thinking she'd fall from the seat stretching to see everything. "Oh, Mister Harden, I wisht I could write ever'thin' down, sae I would ne'er forget it. Da, kin I sit wit' yer fer a while ta see the river?" James switched her over to his lap and pulled the curtain aside for her view.

"Ye knae, child, we're lucky it be sae bonnie t'day or ye would freeze thet little nose right off yer face!" Elizabeth watched them together, *If only it could be lak' this fore'er, her a child, an' him sae happy.* She glanced at Mister Harden and saw he was looking at them wistfully, too.

"Beggin' ye pardon, sair. Is yer family at this Castle Wellan?"

"Alas no, Ma'am, I had a wife once, but she died in childbirth along with the child. I never could bring myself to marry again. Now, I work for the Earl and it's enough for me."

"I am sae sorry. I shouldn't have been puttin' myself in yer business."

"It's no bother, Missus Co'burn. It was a long time ago." He fell silent after that, lost in his memories. A terrible sadness appeared in his eyes, then his face returned to the calm quiet mask she could no longer read. *Nae, look wha' you've done! Wit' yer bumblin' around, ye haf' reminded him o' things better lef' alone. Still, he seems lak' sech a good, kind man, he should haf' more... Stop it!* She reprimanded herself. *Keep your ain counsel an' let the poor man be.*

After three and a half hours, the carriage pulled up to a coach house in Strathaven. "We will change horses here and continue to Kilmarnock. It will be an additional four hours or more. I don't know what the child's endurance is, or how much rest you need before we continue, but while we are here, please step out of the carriage and walk around. If you wish some tea and refreshment, please let the man in the coach house know to charge it to me and it will be given you. Take the time you need. We will make another stop this afternoon, but we must reach Kilmarnock this evening to make the crossing.

"Tomorrow, we will continue to Stranraer. I promise that part of the journey will be easier. When we get to Stranraer, we will immediately board the ship to cross the North Channel to Belfast. If the weather holds, it should not be too arduous. It will be another very long day, however."

As Elizabeth alit from the carriage, she tried not to show how much she delighted at being on solid ground. She covertly stretched her toes and limbs achingly. Her eyes met James in recognition of the unusual way they were feeling. It was almost as if they had been working hard in the garden for the last few hours. Still, the excitement of the journey made it seem worth the complaints their bodies were making.

After the new team was hitched, the passengers fell to a comfortable silence as they resumed their journey through the rural countryside. Soon Elizabeth and Maggie nodded off again. James and Mister Harden spoke quietly about the land in Ulster, Castlewellan and the Earl. Mister Harden expressed a hope that the weather would be clear for the crossing. "This time of year, the weather is unpredictable and we could be in for it. The current is against us from this direction, so it's slower and any storms are likely to catch us in the open. The ships have both sail and steam so they are powerful, but pray for calm seas in any case. The ships are mostly for transporting livestock, so there will not be much shelter for passengers, I'm afraid. There's more money to be made carrying cattle so they get the best shelter. The company has a good reputation for safe passage, however, so you needn't be overly concerned."

"Twill be a great adventure fer Maggie, I'm sure," said James. "Our lassie's curious 'bout the ship. She's been readin' all about 'em in her books. 'Cause she canna gae about by hersel', she's become verra good at readin'."

Mister Harden laughed, "I can tell! Very soon I won't have answers for her questions. I am delighted to tell her all I know," he quickly assured James. "She has a sharp mind." As if on cue, Maggie awoke, full of questions and observations about the surrounding countryside.

They came to the coach house in Kilmarnock just as darkness was full. Mister Harden took the little family inside for supper and showed them to their room. Elizabeth hoped there were no ticks or bugs in the bedding like she had heard about, but it looked fairly clean. She didn't worry long, because the minute her head hit the bed, it seemed it was morning already. The first light streamed through the window, as she heard a knock on the door. "It's time to get started." Mister Harden called. Elizabeth answered quickly as she roused James and Maggie to get dressed.

"Hurry, little one, we mustn't keep Mister Harden waitin'." She dressed Maggie's half-sleeping body and they went downstairs for a bite to eat. Tea, oatmeal and scones filled their bellies. *The blaeberry jam is a delightful treat,* thought Elizabeth as she wiped the corner of Maggie's smile. *I'll hafta put up some this summer.*

Soon, the travelers were on their way. After a short ride, they were riding on smooth paved roads. Elizabeth marveled at the number of vehicles and people walking near the carriage as they wended their way through villages and noisy towns. She wrinkled her nose at the smells that seemed to assault her nose.

This is all part o' the adventure, Elizabeth thought, trying to convince herself that she was doing this willingly. She noticed the carriage stopped and started more often as pedestrians darted between carriages. Suddenly, the carriage lurched forward and Elizabeth slammed her head smartly on the window frame.

"Beth, are ye hurt, Love?"

Elizabeth rubbed her head ruefully and smiled. "Nay, but I'll haf' an egg ta remember this adventure, fer sure." She was glad Maggie was tucked between them and not near that accursed window. *Her eyes are big as saucers,* she thought. Elizabeth wanted to clap her hands over her own ears as Maggie had done. Soon the sounds of the town's commerce melded together into one variable assault on her ears. Her head was throbbing as she sat back into the leather seats, hoping to shut out the crushing noise, so alien to her.

As they left the town, she watched in wonder at the speed they gathered, freed from the halting pace of the populated streets. Elizabeth escaped into a rhythmic slumber.

She dreamed she was moving slowly through her childhood home. The sunlight streaming through the curtained window bounced sharply off the great dish on the table in the center of the room. The last of the autumn apples were piled in it, ready for peeling to make dumplings. "Ma, kin I haf' one?" she asked in a childish voice.

"Nay, child, they're spoken fer. Nae put on yer coat an' git the eggs, lak' I asked!"

When she started to protest, her mother was stern, "Do it! Nae!"

Elizabeth stepped outside and around the cottage to the back where the hens lay their eggs. She was angry. Ma had plenty apples for them to make her precious dumplings. *Wha' would it hurt ta let me haf' a bite.* She pouted as she gathered the eggs in her basket. She turned to go back when she heard it. The scream burned into her memory in the years to follow was fresh and as harrowing as it was on that day. "Ma, wha' is it?"

As she rounded the corner and burst through the door, she saw a strange apparition. It looked like her mother, yet not her mother, her dress fully engulfed in flame, thrashing about in a macabre dance. Everything in the room was dancing in flames. She stared in disbelief. She grabbed the shelf to steady herself as she began to fall, the floor rising to hit her. She became aware of a crackling sound and smoke filled her eyes and lungs. Slowly, she crawled to the table and dragged the dish to the edge, the apples flying around her. Her foot hit one, but she held onto the dish. It was her mother's dish. She mustn't drop it. *The irons! Git the irons.*

She was outside now. The dish was under her, clutched in her arms. Her cheek on the frost-hardened ground was scratched and bleeding. Beside her in range of her sight were two of the irons her mother prized. Her mother! Looking up, she saw the house waving in the heat of the fire consuming it. She could feel the wall of heat against her feet, her hands, her face. *Ma!* Someone was yelling, but she couldn't understand. Her ma was dying. *Ma-ma!* Elizabeth suddenly awoke to see her daughter's desperate face inches before hers. "Ma, are ye all right?"

As she came back to her senses, the noise, the smell and pain in her head were all still there. She shook herself and straightened her clothes. "Yes," she whispered. "I'm all right, jes' dreamin'. I'm sorry if I frightened yer." *It's been a lang time, since I dreamed 'bout thet day. Laird, please deliver me from these nightmares. I thought I had fergotten it. I dinna wanna remember those black days. Oh, Ma, I'm sorry I wanted thet apple! I take it all back. Ma, I miss you! I'm sae sorry!*

Elizabeth stayed quiet for a long time. James knew the dream. She had it many times in their marriage. *I wish I could take it from her, Laird. It breaks her heart an' mine, ever 'time.*

In two hours time, the carriage reached Stranraer. Elizabeth's head still hurt and now sported a deepening bluish bruise on the side of her forehead. She hoped the journey would be worth the effort of traveling.

The novelty had not worn off for Maggie, however, as she continued her questions and observations. Stranraer was an industrial port with crowds of people rushing about intent on their business. James, Elizabeth and Maggie looked around at this new town. It seemed busier but somehow quieter than the previous berg. There was a more genteel fashion to its people.

Elizabeth frowned at the fine layer of dust that seemed to be on every inch of their clothing. *Wha' was white when we left hame is gray nae.* She thought. While Mister Harden bought tickets for the ship, Elizabeth made plans to shake out their clothing and to make them fresh before they met the earl and his brother. She didn't want her family to be embarrassed. She admitted to herself, she couldn't imagine how this strange fortune had all come about. *I'll hafta wait ta find out the real story from Will an' Petey. Laird, help us! Here we are traveling ta who-knaes-where-or-why on this man's say-so.* She took a deep breath. *Ah well, we'll fin' out soon enough. Think only good thoughts, Elizabeth. The bad ones come all on their ain.*

"Here we gae, Maggie!" said James as he carried her across the boardwalk up the plank to the ship.

"Ay-ee, Da!" Maggie squealed. "It's sae big! Wha' are those smoke stacks fer? Look at the masts! Where does the boat gae?"

"One question at a time, my sweet. We'll haf' time enough ta answer all o' them," James laughed. Elizabeth clung to the railing, feeling the gentle sway of the North Channel below her. She let herself be distracted by the excitement and curiosity of her child. *Bring us ta Ulster. Laird in heaven, bring us ta Ireland an' the land James was meant ta till.*

Mister Harden said the crossing was fair and it seemed so to James and Maggie. Elizabeth was wobbly and pale when her foot touched the dock in Belfast. After so many hours of rocking, she lurched as her equilibrium abandoned her. Their escort deftly caught her as she fell and her face reddened in embarrassment once again. Elizabeth hung her head.

Mister Harden assured her, "There is no one who escapes the awkward walk of being on land after learning to walk on ship. Look there, Missus Co' burn. The elegant gentleman with the cane uses it to balance himself coming down to the dock. It is not a natural way to travel, but a necessary one, if we are to leave one land for another." As he smiled gently to put her at ease, she offered a weak one in return.

"Thank ye, Mister Harden. I'm quite all right nae. Will we be there soon?"

"Tomorrow, Missus Co'burn, we'll spend the night in Belfast then, a few hours by carriage and we will be at Castlewellan by afternoon tea." He led them to a waiting carriage. The city around them seemed to close in on Elizabeth as she struggled to keep her tea down. *Steady on, Elizabeth. Don't make this day worse than it's been already! Hang on.*

Before long, they were at a coach house and shown to a room. They were to meet Mister Harden downstairs for supper, once they were settled. Barely closing the door, Elizabeth ran to the pot beneath the bed and promptly lost her entire tea from the boat. James removed her hat and outer wrap then, gently took a wet cloth, washed her face. James saw the bruise on the side of her face, her pallor and the weariness coming over her. He smoothed her hair back as she curled her body inward against the cramps in her midsection. "Lay down, Beth. I'll take Maggie wit' me ta supper while ye rest." He sighed. *My poor Beth.* James closed the curtains against the afternoon's last rays. Taking a candle in one hand and Maggie in his other arm, he made his way downstairs.

At the courier's questioning look, James said, "Elizabeth is a bit worse fer wear, I fear. She won't be joinin' us fer supper. I'm hopin' thet knot on her head looks a little better t'marra. Yer Earl will think I've been beatin' her, fer sure."

The morning sun was shining, Elizabeth's eyes focused on the window, trying to remember where she was. Slowly, she swung her feet to the floor. Her head was not throbbing, her stomach not heaving — all was right with her world. Smiling, she knew today was the day. All would be revealed. For now though, her immediate thoughts were for food. She was ravenous. She stood quickly, and in the same action plopped immediately back on the bed. Whew! Colored lights clouded her vision as she remembered not having eaten since the day before. She looked around the room. She was alone!

The vertigo passed and she carefully rose. Her dress was on a peg on the opposite wall. She shook it out, hoping the journey's dust would fly away from its folds. She smoothed the back trying to lessen the embedded creases. *There's no help fer it. I will make do.*

They were her only good clothes, her Sunday-gae-ta-church clothes. *I hope James an' Maggie are not too bedraggled.*

Donning her bonnet, she made her way downstairs. James, Maggie and Mister Harden looked up as she entered. Elizabeth noted they had finished their breakfast. Mister Harden immediately requested something for Elizabeth. "I hope you are feeling better, Missus Co'burn?"

Elizabeth nodded and smiled. "Much better, thank ye kindly, Mister Harden. James, you shoulda woke me. Perhaps I should eat in the carriage, sae's no' ta slow us down? I can't imagine sleepin' sae late!" She suddenly realized she was babbling like a child. They were all looking at her, smiling.

"We're delighted yer feelin' better, Beth. We kin wait fer yer ta enjoy yer food. When yer done eatin', we'll all gae upstairs an' you kin straighten us up," said James, knowing she wanted to make sure they were all properly combed and brushed. James stroked her hand. "Ye will get a chance ta fix Maggie's hair, too. Takes a mother's touch, I'll warrant you." Elizabeth smiled her thanks, her heart full.

Soon, they were on their way again, quietly chatting about the places they would see and the people they would meet in only a few hours. Elizabeth tried to soothe her nerves by concentrating on the pale green rolling hills scattered with whitewashed cottages. The hills grew steeper as they traveled southwest from Belfast. The trees stood in clumps with bushes at their bases like elegant gowns on a green-brown ballroom floor. Patches of snow shown in the sunlight, atop blue misty mountains. *Wha' do ye haf' fer us in Legananny, Laird? Kin it be as wonderful as all my imaginin's? How came we ta this fate? Wha' price will we pay ta accept sech favors? If it be sae wonderful, let us work steadfastly ta be worthy of it, all this in Jesus' name. Amen.*

"Look there, Maggie, just beyond the trees," said Mister Harden. "It's Castlewellan. You can see the edge of the town."

James, Elizabeth and Maggie all strained to catch the first glimpse of the buildings.

"It's not as busy today, being Wednesday. Monday is market day and tenants from all over County Down come to do their business."

"There's St. Paul's Anglican Church, built by the Earl and just beyond it, you can see the cottage garden wall. That wall is the outer edge of the Annesley grounds and gardens. We will enter through the back of the Annesley *cottage* by the kitchen. Then we will bring you to the rooms where you'll stay tonight. You be able to freshen up before you meet the Earl." Not one sound by the family could be heard. *Nae, it's real,* thought Elizabeth in awe. *Nae, there's a real hame o' stone an' wood where a great earl lives, behind a wall. God save us. It's no' a dream.*

The carriage relentlessly moved forward. Mister Harden's words could no longer be heard. James seemed to understand what he was saying, but Elizabeth's fears put her world in silence. *Attention, woman! Ye hafta knae wha' he's tellin' ye!* But the frantic buzz in her head drowned out his words. *It's lak' a foreign language! Wha' does he say?*

As they drove up to the back of the large home, Elizabeth looked at James for guidance. Grinning, he touched her hand to reassure her. "It will be fine, Beth. Hae a wee bit o' faith."

In the next hour, Elizabeth was too busy freshening up and making her little family presentable, to worry. She pulled and tugged and brushed and adjusted all their clothing until she was satisfied it was the best she could do. James signaled Maggie to make not a sound while her mother worked. Elizabeth hummed while brushing Maggie's hair, tying her side braids toward the back, letting loose the deep red flames to her waist. James and Maggie exchanged covert looks, eyes shining.

A soft knock on the door, let them know it was time. Elizabeth took a deep breath. *Inta the fire we gae!*

Mister Harden led them through well-appointed hallways to a large room. "This is the salon. Have a seat right here and the Earl will be with you presently." It was difficult not to gawk at the furnishings in the room. Although Maggie said not a word, she took in everything in the room and her incessant questions shone in her eyes. She studied one thing after another. A glass globe on a side table caught her attention. She peered intensely at it, then smiled and clapped her hands. As if shocked that she broke the silence, she gasped and folded them in her lap. "Would you like to hold it, little miss?" said a voice behind her.

"May I? It's sae beautiful! I will be sae verra careful." Maggie looked quickly at her mother and father to see if they would deny her the treasure. Nodding, James gently placed the item on her lap. He tipped his head and looked at her meaningfully, letting her know this was a privilege not to be taken lightly. "Oh, thank you, sair. I will be verra gentle."

"It is almost as beautiful as you are, Little Miss."

Mr. Harden spoke, "Your Honor, may I present James and Elizabeth Co'burn, The Honorable Earl Annesley and his mother, Lady Priscilla Annesley." James and Elizabeth rose and bowed as they would in the presence of their laird in Lanark. The beautifully attired man and woman before them nodded.

"Mr. Harden, where is Hugh? He should be here to explain." Lady Annesley complained irritably. "Ah, there you are, Hugh. We are waiting for you." Mister Harden hastily made the new introduction and they were once again seated. Mister Harden withdrew from the room.

The elegant young man with the military bearing was slender and pale, but handsome. His face was covered on the left side with a black leather patch from his jaw bone to just below the eye and almost to his aristocratic nose. His erect posture was in direct contrast to the Earl who rather languished on the settee with his mother. Unlike the other two, Lieutenant Hugh Annesley seemed genuinely to enjoy meeting them, sitting on the edge of his chair, leaning toward them as he told his story of being rescued from the battlefield by two soldiers, privates of the 42nd Regiment, Highlanders.

Since Elizabeth's brothers, Peter and William Fraser had refused reward, the lieutenant had devised another plan. He spoke softly, his words carefully enunciated, as if he were afraid he would not be clear, softly slurring some of his words, a few syllables causing him to pause, but for the most part, his audience had no difficulty understanding him. His concentration on speech made his story progress slower than normal.

"Before we go into the details, may I also explain why I asked all of you to come to Castlewellan? Usually in these matters, I would conduct this business with Mister Co'burn, but since I talked to your brothers about their home, Missus Co'burn, I wanted to meet the whole family. I appreciate the long journey you've taken and hope you do not think ill of me for asking this indulgence. I was quite taken with them and they spoke so well of you all."

"Hugh dear, perhaps your guests will be more comfortable in the library. I will have Anne bring tea to you there. I do have another engagement to which I must attend. I hope you will forgive me. It was pleasant to have met you. I am most grateful to your courageous brothers for giving me back my son."

"Of course, Mother. S-shall we?" The lieutenant gestured toward the side door of the room. Awkwardly, James took the trinket from Maggie and set it gingerly on the side table from whence it came. He picked up Maggie, following the young engaging man from the room, with Elizabeth trailing behind.

The library was furnished with comfortable dark leather chairs, carved mahogany tables and lined with more books than Elizabeth had ever seen in one place. Maggie was captivated by the walls lined with bookshelves from floor to ceiling. Elizabeth could see she was about to burst with a thousand questions. She put one finger up to her lips in warning. Maggie looked down and held her tongue.

"Mother's right, you know. This has always been my favorite room in the house. Not so much to break in here." Hugh grinned. "I played in here as a child whenever we were in Ulster. We can be more informal in here." Elizabeth began to relax a little for the first time since they arrived.

Hugh pulled a cord near the door and, as if by magic, tea arrived. "Anne, would you stay and pour, please?" The woman, about thirty, bobbed slightly and began to serve tea. "Thank you, Anne," he said. Anne retired from the room.

Immediately, Hugh launched excitedly into his plan. "James, if I may jump right into it, my grandfather started an arboretum at Castlewellan, years ago. I wish to continue his work, with your help. I understand you have the gift of growing in you. I have been many places in service bringing home many plants, shrubs and trees from foreign lands. Because they are not indigenous to this climate, they need to be cultivated until they are strong enough to withstand our soil. I propose, if it meets with your approval, to have you do this work for me, on some of the land I will provide to you. You may have noted the land I have in mind is divided in three parts. One, under Margaret Co'burn's name, has offices and buildings with which to complete the work I need. The other two tracts of land, under your name, you may farm as you need to provide for your family and sell produce on Market Day, as you wish. You will pay taxes and the rents to my brother the Earl twice yearly, starting next spring. He will oversee the management of the property under your name at first, but will allow the work I have described to you on Margaret's land without interference. Is this agreeable to you?"

James cleared his throat to relieve his tension, "Yer honor, it seems lak' a miracle ta us. I would lak' ye ta see my journals, so ye may knae I'll do a good job fer you, an' we're anxious ta see the land, o' course."

"Certainly, we will go there tomorrow. If it meets with your expectations, we will sign a few papers and you can return for your goods in Lanark. I have begun construction of a glass house on the tract for the plants you will tend for the arboretum. I have a couple of men there now, to clear out the house and set it up for you. I'll be able to answer most of your questions when we get there." He turned his attention to Maggie.

"Little Miss, can you reach the sweets, all right?" Hugh picked up the tray to Maggie's delight and offered her a dazzling array of decorated cakes. Turning to Elizabeth, he asked, "So, this is the lovely Maggie, I've heard so much about?" Both Maggie and Elizabeth blushed.

"Yes, sair, my brothers fairly doted on her when last they saw her. Would it be impertinent ta ask how my brothers are? We've not heard from them fer sech a lang time."

"Ah, I apologize for my poor manners. Of course, I should have told you at the first. They are fine, with a few minor bumps of no consequence. Such are the fortunes of war. I do hasten to assure you they are doing well and serve the 42th regiment with honor.

"I should also tell you my mother is usually in much better humor than she has been in recent months. I was injured in September and she lost her youngest son only eight days later. Were it not for your brothers, I would have been gone as well. I am eternally grateful to have her spared her that twice-wrought sorrow."

As he returned to Maggie, the sadness on his face lifted, as if the sun suddenly broke through storm clouds. "So, Maggie, I've heard you have many unanswered questions for me." Turning to her parents, he said, "Perhaps I can take her around the library, while you discuss some questions you may have of your own? When we return, I'll answer your questions as well." When James nodded his assent, Hugh gently picked up Maggie and walked with her on his hip around the room, pointing out the books and small items lining the shelves. James and Elizabeth smiled at each other, watching Maggie engaging in her rapid-fire questions to the lieutenant.

"James, do ye think we kin do it?" Elizabeth whispered. "What do ye know o' foreign plants? We should see if there's a school fer Maggie. Two men are cleaning out a house? God in heaven, help us! A glass house, wha' does thet mean?"

"Easy, woman, don't count yer eggs 'til ye git 'em in yer basket. We'll tak' a look t'marra then, we'll knae wha' we're gittin' inta. He's verra young. He may lose interest in collectin' plants an' trees. Did ye e'er see sae many books? Ye think they read 'em, a' tall?"

Elizabeth could tell he was hoping against everything he knew, that it was the miracle they needed to get back to farming. *He's sae excited he's burstin' his buttons, he is. Me too, an' thet's the truth. Laird, don' let this gae wrong. Let us ride this dream fer a while. We kin survive mos' anythin', if James kin work the land.*

That night and early the next morning, Elizabeth let herself dare to hope without reservation. *T'marra will tell.*

Somehow they slept that night, and rose the next morning with a rejuvenation born of anticipation and a sense of going home. The air was crisp and clean, as they once again climbed into the carriage for the final leg of their journey.

Mister Harden rode with the driver this time. Maggie sat next to the young lieutenant, gazing up at him, while James and Elizabeth watched. *This man can do no wrong in her eyes nae,* thought Elizabeth. *She is smitten fer sure.* She tried to pay attention to what he and James were saying.

"Very soon, I will be going back to the Scots Fusiliers. I have been gone a long time and I am well now. I have spoken to your clan Laird and I have made your leaving right with him. If it doesn't work out for you, which I cannot imagine it won't, I have also arranged for you to return, if that is your wish."

"'Tis more than gen'rous, sair, I canna see how we can be disadvantaged. Is there a school fer Maggie? Missus Co'burn was concerned that she git her schoolin'."

"Legananny has a national schoolhouse and a very capable school teacher, Miss Brennan, just down the road a bit. Maggie should do well there. I will send Mr. Harden back in a few weeks time to answer any other questions you may have about the area. He's quite taken with your family and will enjoy the visit, he says."

"He's been verra kind ta Maggie, answerin' all her questions, an' sae." James raised his eyebrow wryly. "Ye knae, she kin question ye ta death, she kin."

Lieutenant Annesley laughed. "Well, very nearly, it would seem, Mister Co'burn. She's kept me on my toes, I'll have you know. It's a fine mind she has. Miss Brennan will be asking us for more books soon, I'll wager." Hugh smiled down at Maggie and she rewarded him with a grin in return.

Elizabeth looked out the window at the clear sky and the mountains ridges around them in the distance. The carriage seemed to keep climbing and she thought they would reach the blue of the heavens before it started descending again. *What a beautiful land.* Off in the far distance, she heard a hawk scream. She listened to the crunch of the wheels on the dirt road. *I hope there are no big cities near this land, 'tis sae peaceful an' clear. Kin this be the place where we were always meant ta be? Say it is, Laird, an' I will live here fere'er. Amen.*

Chapter Three

Lost in reverie, Elizabeth felt the wheels of the carriage roll to a stop, with the now-familiar lurch of the carriage as the horses strained against the harness for one more step. It was like she had entered another realm of existence, perhaps the mystical deceptive fairie world, as she accepted the young nobleman's hand to step out of the elegant conveyance. There before her, a humble cottage, not much different than the one she left behind, with an attached building on the side, beckoning her to accept it, to make a choice that would change her life. *What mischief is afoot in all this?*

The very picture of aristocracy, clad in his casual riding uniform, every stitch speaking of nobility and grace, Lieutenant Hon. Annesley, turned to her, saying, "Allow me to make sure the workmen I left are out of the cottage." Opening the door, he called out, "The tenants have arrived. Please remove yourselves from the cottage."

There before them, were Peter and William Fraser, Elizabeth's brothers! Elizabeth stared, then as if waking from a dream, she ran to them. She looked back through tears at James to see him grinning wide at her excitement. "Ye knew! How could ye no' tell me," she accused.

"I almost did a dozen times, *mo gradh*. Ever' time ye wore thet sad an' worrisome look on yer face, I wanted ta tell yer, but I was sworn ta secrecy." Maggie nearly leaped out of James' arms to fling herself at her beloved *eme*, Petey.

In their excitement, they had quite forgotten the young officer standing in the background. He stood silently, smiling. *If only I could have done this for Mother and Robert. To see the love in her eyes she had for him, her youngest child.* He sighed. *Poor Bobby died such an ignominious death in a foreign land. How cruel is fate, to take the life of a boy from his mother.* The young man shook his head as if to discard his morbid thoughts. *At least I can do this.*

"Lieutenant Annesley, I do beg yer pardon. Wha' must ye think o' us? Thank ye fer this wonderful present ta my wife. Why don' we all gae inside afore we catch a chill?"

Crossing the threshold, James thought: *In this place, our lives hold new purpose an' promise.*

The room was spare, with few places to sit, but warm, with a fresh laid fire. "How lang are ye here fer, William?" asked James, looking covertly at Elizabeth.

"Only 'til the day after t'marra, then we'll return wit' the lieutenant ta the front. He brought us here ta see ye, but we're bound fer the Black Sea, once agin. We'd already returned after bein' banged up at Alma, very minor fer us, mind ye, no' lak' our Lieut' here. I thought he'd perished when we found him. But here he is, bigger than life itself! He's a great man, James." Will's soft burr was directed at James, but he turned back to Hugh as he spoke. "Thank ye fer this, Lieutenant Annesley, sair. I've ne'er seen my sister sae happy."

"Sair," said James, "Perhaps whilst my family is gittin' reacquainted, we could gae over wha' yer wantin' me ta do? I haf' my journals if ye care ta look, an' I'd like ta see the lay o' the land, if yer a mind ta show me? If yer leavin' sae soon, I haf' a packet o' queries fer yer Honor, if it's not o'er burdensome."

"Quite so, Mister Co'burn, it would be my honor."

They slipped out of the room, with Hugh leading the way. Outside, he turned toward the added room of the cottage. "Mister Co'burn, you can keep your books in the office here. Please, have a seat and let's have a look at your journals." Heads bent over the books James offered, they spoke in low, excited voices, as James explained his numbers and comments to the young man. Intelligent blue eyes bore witness to his interest in James' meticulous notations, "It seems I have the right man for the job, Mister Co'burn."

"Lieutenant, sair, if I may, I haf' a question thet may seem ungrateful, but it is no' intended sae."

"And that is?"

"Why haf' ye put Maggie's name on the land?" James bit his lip, hoping he did not offend his benefactor.

"I understand Maggie will never walk. If anything should happen to you or Missus Co'burn, Maggie will have a home that will not be taken from her, for as long as there is an Annesley to draw breath. It is my pledge to you, your wife and her brothers in return for my life. I have no doubt I have the better bargain, to have you work for me, *and* for me to have my life."

"I am humbled by your generosity ta us, sair," James, choked with emotion, brushed at his eyes, and said, "Please call me James, sair. Nae, if you'll allow, where's this glass house ye spoke of?"

"Out this way, you may call me Hugh in private, James. I prefer my men know me as I am, not as my brother and mother seem to think I should be." Hugh arched his brow, humorously. "Propriety, be damned. I am only a man such as you are, and with not one-tenth your generous talents, I'll wager. The glass house is out back beyond the cook fire and animal sheds."

James looked beyond the out buildings and saw men working on a strange but wondrous structure. "It *is* made o' glass! Won' the glasses break in the cold?"

"We're coming into milder weather now, it's almost March, and once we seal in the glass, the sun will keep it warm in the day and the furnace will force steam inside to keep it humid and warm enough at night. In the summer, you won't need the furnace at all. In the autumn, you'll capture the heat again in the warm days and start up the furnace at the first frost.

"The plants and shrubs I brought from warmer climes can grow in here until they are robust enough to be brought to Castlewellan. I shall return whenever I can, and we'll decide which ones are ready and where we will plant them. What do you think?"

"I mus' say, my head is jes' swimmin' wit' new ideas. Do yer haf' any plants thet are ready fer the glass house, nae? Is the glass house ready ta use?"

"They are glazing the last pieces as we speak. Let me get the plants I have from the Crimea. I stowed them on the back of the carriage, so we could get started. We'll go back to the office and I'll show you what you'll need to do."

James followed him back to the carriage, where Mister Harden and the driver were waiting. "Is this everything, Thomas? I'll take the journal. Bring everything else to the office."

Two trunks and a very large book were brought into the little room. James turned to Mister Harden and said, "Missus Co'burn will be glad ta serve yer an' yer driver, tea ta warm yer up, Mister Harden. She'd be shamed ta knae ye were lef' here waitin' all this time outside, after all yer did fer us. Please, sair."

The two men waited for a sign from Hugh to be dismissed. The lieutenant waved his hand absentmindedly and returned to the trunks on the floor. As the men left, he explained to James, "Now, it is very important to set up each book as a catalogue for these plants. I have a blank one here. I've done the first one to show you what I need. I've taken a picture of the plant, as it was found in its natural habitat. I've taken another of the sample I took with me. Below, I have the Latin name of the plant, and a description of the place from whence it came. What I need you to do, is put it in the soil I've taken with the plant, adding some of our native soil, and place it in the glass house. After that, I want you to write down what happens to the plant while it is in your care. If it should die, see if you can ascertain the reason for it. If it thrives, write that down also. Put in any significant measure of growth while it is in the glass house. Add anything you think will help keep it alive and healthy. I have built a similar glass house at Castlewellan, to house some of the plants which are too delicate to survive outside. Leave room on the page for one more picture, if you have to use two pages to accomplish that, do so. That will be a picture of the specimen after it is transplanted at Castlewellan. These are very valuable plants, James, from places to which I may never return. I trust you will care for them as you would your precious Maggie."

"'Tis a responsibility I'll honor wit' my full attention, sair. I canna believe I haf' the privilege of doin' this wonderful work. I pray I kin meet all your expectations, Laird Annesley."

"I am confident in your abilities, James. If anyone can do it, it is you. I will be sending more samples and pictures by post wherever I am. You'll see I have attached the Latin and common names and descriptions to each sample." With that said, Hugh threw open one of the trunks, displaying layer upon layer of cuttings and soil bags to be catalogued.

"Ay-ee, I haf' me work cut out fer me. I hope I haf' time ta plant the land in the spring! No' thet I'm complainin', sair," James added quickly.

"There will months, James, when I'll be too busy fighting this war to send you anything. Plan your time well, though. If we conquer the Cossacks soon, I will be sending more trunks to be catalogued and put in that glass house."

"Do ye think Mister Harden or someone could walk the land wit' me? I'd no' like ta be plantin' on me neighbor's land, ye ken."

"I have one more day, Mister Co'burn. I would like to do that myself, tomorrow morning. We still have much to talk about and papers to sign. I'll bring two horses and we'll walk the land,

Maggie's and yours. After that, Mister Harden will bring you a wagon and a driver to return with you to Lanark to get your things, if you still agree to stay."

"Lieutenant Annesley," said James with a grin. "If I may be sae bold, an' not call the devil down upon my head, I'd bargain with the devil himself fer this good fortune. I will work hard ta honor ye faith in me, Sair."

"I'm sure of it, Mister Co'burn," said Hugh thoughtfully. "But thank Elizabeth's brothers, as I do, for your good fortune. I'd not be here, but for them." He raised his hand to the patch on his face, remembering. "But for now, let's go back to the house and join the celebration."

As they entered the little cottage, James saw Elizabeth scurrying around setting tea on the table and Maggie holding court, her admirers hanging on her every word. "They dinna even miss us," whispered James to Hugh. "Our Maggie holds them all in her hand." As they became aware of Hugh standing among them, the men immediately scrambled to get him a seat.

How I envy them their honest little family! No formalities, duties to state, no pressure to marry suitably, no pretentious manners that belie true feelings. I may soon be Earl of Annesley, Viscount of Glerawley of County Fermaugh, Baron of Castlewellan, County Down with more land than any man should own, but it is a lonely curse to be born an Annesley. Mother is already making noises to marry me off to any worthy inbred who carries a fan well at court. William shows no inclination to marry, but Mother will no doubt have her way, poor sod. Hugh sighed deeply, smiling quickly when the attention suddenly turned to him. He raised his cup of tea in salute to the gathering, "To the Co'burns and their new home. May they have the best of all they wish for and the devil take the hindmost." A sprinkle of "Here, here!" ruffled through the group and Hugh signaled his men to leave.

Later, uncharacteristically slouching down in the carriage seat across from Thomas Harden, Hugh said softly, "I think James will do well, Thomas. Without being obtrusive, keep an eye on them. See that they have what they need. Especially Maggie, she's such a frail little thing, but she lights up the world when she smiles."

Thomas Harden nodded, seeing melancholy settling like a shroud upon the young man. *He's not the uproarious clown his men know, nor the savior of the blood line his mother wants him to be. He roams the world, chasing battles to fight, daring the fates to kill him, running from the life to which he was born. He's the best of the lot and they wear him thin with their incessant scratching.* As they so often did, Thomas' thoughts turned to his own beloved wife. *If he could find a woman such as mine, he would find the aristocratic prison he fears would have no confines to hold him. If the good Lord wills it, may he survive, if only to find the woman who can make him happy.*

Back at the little cottage, Elizabeth was settling in. "Git yerself outside wit' thet nasty thin', Will!" she scolded, as her brother put a clay pipe in his mouth. He ducked as she tried to swat him with her towel. "Out, I'll no' haf' it in me house. All the food will taste o' tobacco. *Pah!*"

"James, look! They stocked the shelves with provisions. Kin ye believe it? ...An' bowls too. I keep pinching m'self ta see if I'm awake or dreamin'!"

"Here, Beth. Let me help ye wit' thet," Peter teased, pinching her arm. Elizabeth found a new target for her towel. Shaking her head, eyes bright and dancing, she knew she hadn't been this happy for a long, long time. *It's goin' ta be verra hard ta let 'em gae come Wen'sday,* she thought. *Well, they've got ta eat afore then, so ye better fin' som'thin' ta throw in the pot fer supper.*

"James, is the cookin' fire lit? Do ye ken where the well is? I canna tell wha' we're ta eat, but I ken I need ta cook it." James laughed, and headed for the door. *Here she goes. The woman's made hersel' ta hame already.* "I don't see anythin' funny, Mister Co'burn. Maggie, darlin', wud ye gather the cups on the table fer washin', if ye please?" Without waiting for an answer, Elizabeth was already looking in the cupboard, calculating what she could cook. She peeked in the crockery finding flour, a rasher of bacon, lard, potatoes and some leeks…*leek an' tattie soup, biscuits. Oh, some apples, thet should make som'thin' fine. Don't see any herbs or spices, but we'll make do. I've some oats, salt, pepper, and molasses. Good enough.*

"Fire's on," announced Will. "Here's cold water fer nae. We're heatin' more on the fire. Wha' do yer need me ta do?"

"Nothin', Will. Ye ne'er knew nothin' o' cookin', sae I guess ye will hafta learn ta do dishes." Elizabeth smiled at his pulled frown.

"We learnt ta cook while soldierin', Beth. Nothin' fancy, mind yer, but we learnt."

"Ye learnt, did ye? I guess ye won' starve, then. If 'n ye don' mind, though, I ken we'll have some *real* cookin' t'night. Maggie's hungry, aren't ye girl?"

"Kin I make the biscuits, Ma?" Maggie clasped her hands as if to beg.

"Sure, jes' lemme git the makin's. Is thet all ye need, lass?" Elizabeth set out flour, milk and lard.

"An' a *pinch* of salt," giggled Maggie. Following the game they played almost every night, her mother pretended to be shocked that she forgot the salt.

"Oh my, I would ferget my ain silly noggin, wouldn't I?" Maggie lapsed into peals of giggling again, as she did every night. *Someday soon, she'll be too grown up fer playin' wit' her Ma an' I'll be the sadder fer it*, Elizabeth thought. *She probably only plays it fer me, as it is.* "I'll be callin' on ye fer the blessin' t'night, Maggie," she said with a meaningful look. Maggie was pleased with herself. She said grace when there were just the three of them, but tonight they had company and it was a special honor to say it for them.

Maggie thought hard about what she would say. She could just say her regular blessing, but this was a special night. When supper was on the table with chairs and crates pulled up to it, James nodded for Maggie to begin.

"Dear Laird in Heaven, who made all things, bless this humble meal an' yer servants who partake o' it. May we use this food ta strengthen our bodies ta do yer will. We ask in yer precious name, Father, Son an' Holy Spirit. Amen."

"Very nice, Maggie, where did you learn thet prayer?" asked William.

"I read it in a book," she said, beaming. "I read a lot."

"James, yer wee lass is growin' up," said Peter. "I'm verra impressed with this new Maggie. But don' ye be growin' up too fast, child. It makes m' feel a hundert yers old." He made his voice sound shaky and comically aged. Laughing at his pose, the family settled down to supper.

James described the work he was to do with the glass house. He told Elizabeth that the Lieutenant would be back the next day to walk the land with him. "Oh my, James, when was the last time you rode a horse? Ye will be more than lame when yer get hame,' laughed Elizabeth.

"I'll manage, Beth. Maybe it won' tak' too lang. I wan' a chanct ta explore the buildings afore I gae hame ta git our things. Don't worry, Beth. You an' Maggie kin stay here, whilst I go." Seeing Elizabeth's worried face, he hurried to say, "I wisht I could be in both places, Beth, but I'll be back afore ye ken. 'Twill be all right. Mister Harden say the driver's goin' wit' me, sae we can pack up faster an' I won' git lost. The Earl's loaning me a wagon. I should be back in about ten day."

Elizabeth covered her mouth with her fingertips, so as not to voice her fears. *I ne'er bin wit'out him, e'en fer a day.* Elizabeth argued with herself. *Ye will be fine. What are ye, a wee school girl? Ye will be fine.* She forced herself to smile for Maggie's sake. *I canna be scarin' Maggie. Wit'out her Da, she'll be havin' nightmares the whole time.*

While clearing the supper dishes, Elizabeth made a plan for the time when she would be alone with Maggie. She looked around the room that housed the living area. *Let's see...*

"Mister Harden will check on ye, Beth. Ye will be fine. They's an abundance o' peat out back fer the fire. He say he'll sleep in the office, if yer a mind ta haf' him stay."

"We'll be fine, James," Elizabeth said, hesitantly. *I am bein' silly, ever'thin' will be fine.*

Later, when they retired for the night, Elizabeth thought about the day's events. *What a bountiful day it's been. I could nae ask fer more than this. Peter an' William, the house, the young lord, Mr. Harden, ever'thin' I need ta make me happy. They'll come a day, there'll be the devil ta pay, but fer nae, my cup is full ta o'erflowin'.* She watched her husband sleeping and her heart was full. *Laird, keep him safe an' bring him hame ta me. I love him fierce, Laird.*

The morning sun rose and its light fell across Elizabeth's pillow. Her head was still full of happy dreams of their new life together. She saw William at the table, sipping tea. "Why didn't ye wake me, Will? What kin I get yer?" she whispered.

Will raised his hand to quiet her, poured her a cup of tea and motioned her to follow him to the office. Elizabeth quickly threw on a wrap and left the others sleeping. "Wha' is it, Will?"

"I jes' wanted some quiet time alone wit' my sister. Wha's wrong wit' that?"

"No' a thin', Will. Wha's on yer mind?"

"Right ta the point as usual, Beth. I jes' wan' ta say thet though the lieutenant is remarkable gen'rous, ye canna expect the same o' his kin. The Earl is a good man, fer sure, but his mother rules in thet house an' this could be gone in the blink o' an eye, if the lieut' should perish in battle. I dinna wan' ye hurt, Beth, sae be wary."

"Will, if it all disappeared t'marra an' we were beggin' in the streets, I'd be happy fer yesterday an' t'day. We've done nothin' ta earn this, sae if it's gone, it's gone."

"Thet's m' girl, Beth. Yer al'ays had a fine head on yer shoulders. T'day, wha' say we find thet school fer our Maggie?"

"Aye, Will. James will be gone wit' the Lieutenant ta walk the land, sae we should tak' a look around. Fer nae, we better git the rest o' them on their feet. I dinna want ta keep the lieutenant waitin'."

Elizabeth and Will went back in the cottage where the others were rising, talking low among themselves. Elizabeth pulled the little curtain that hid Maggie's bed and saw her hair spread upon her pillow with the sun creating a halo of flames around her face. "Come, Sunshine. Time ta rise and shine, little one. Ye've another day ta bring ye light ta." Maggie stretched and yawned noisily then, smiled. "Come, git dressed. We've more adventures today an' we don't wanna miss a moment o' it."

After breakfast, James heard the Lieutenant and Mister Harden arrive. James went off with the young nobleman and his courier waited with a wagon. Elizabeth called out the door of the little cottage, "Come in fer a cuppa tea, Mister Harden. Isn't it a glorious day?"

"Thank you, Misses Co'burn. But, begging your pardon, we must be on our way if we're to get to the school before it starts for the day." He jumped down from his perch, and entered the doorway.

"Quite sae, Mister Harden, Maggie git yer coat on. Let's no' keep Mister Harden waitin'. Do I need ta bring anythin' wit' us?"

"No, ma'am, we'll just take a visit today and make arrangements to have her enrolled. Your brothers may ride in the back if they wish." With that, Peter picked up Maggie and headed out the door with the rest of them following behind. Maggie was placed in the front of the wagon between Elizabeth and Mister Harden. Chatting merrily, Maggie twisted around to see her two uncles hop up on the wagon bed.

Mister Harden flicked the reins and the two horses jostled into action. "I apologize for the rough ride, but the Lieutenant wanted the wagon to be at your house for the trip tomorrow. I would have preferred to have the carriage for the comfort of you and Maggie, but this is more practical for your brothers' service gear. In the morning, I will ride to the house and your husband and brothers will return to Castlewellan. Your brothers will continue with the Lieutenant to the front and our driver will guide Mister Co'burn back to your cottage in Lanark to retrieve your things. I hope that will all be satisfactory for you."

"Mister Harden, it's all so verra gen'rous an' I am most grateful fer it," replied Elizabeth humbly. "I canna e'en imagine no' wakin' ta find it all a dream."

"It's God's hones' truth, Mr. Harden," called Will from the back. "We're all findin' it difficult ta believe. But we're appreciative, sair." He hastened to add.

The horses were traveling a well-worn road down the mountain bordered by low bushes and a few trees opening up to rolling fields. Ahead was a rude bridge over a brook. The ground was a deep brown boggy expanse of peat. Maggie could see several workers out on the bog in long boots and strange tools. She kept a running stream of questions for Mister Harden who obliged her with the explanations she demanded.

"She'll do well at school. Her teacher, Miss Brennan, will have to stay on her toes to stay ahead of her questions." Mister Harden laughed. "We're almost there, just up there and around the bend."

Maggie stretched herself tall to see. There, set back from the road was a low whitewashed building with a dozen or so children playing in front of it. As the wagon came to the building, the children scattered like leaves before the wind. A tall slender woman of about thirty in a simple blue dress and a gray wrap stood in front of the closed door, watching them come up the drive, the curls escaping from her tidy brown bun framed her narrow hawk-like face. She scowled at the apparent intrusion.

"Good Day, Miss Brennan. I have a new student for you," called Mister Harden, cheerfully.

"Very well, Mister Harden, please come in."

Mister Harden carried Maggie in and introduced her and her mother to the teacher. "Why do you carry her, Mister Harden?" Miss Brennan asked, frowning.

"Miss Brennan, the child does not walk. I trust that will not be a problem?"

"Well, it certainly presents a difficulty. We often take our class outside for natural sciences. Is she teachable?" she asked, irritably.

"Miss Brennan, she is very intelligent and will no doubt be your best student. As far as her not walking, I am confident the Earl and I will reach a solution for that," he said pointedly. He could see Maggie's eyes welling up and her head bowed. Elizabeth's face flushed and her eyes flashed with anger.

"She will begin in a fortnight, when her father returns from Scotland. If you wish to give her work to do at home until then, I'm sure that will be satisfactory. In the meantime, we will find some kind of transport for her in and out of the classroom. The Earl wishes you to provide her schooling the same as you do all of the public students in Legananny."

Miss Brennan's face reddened with the perceived reprimand. "Missus Co'burn, I will need a little information, if you please. Where are you living?" Elizabeth looked at Mister Harden.

"They have taken the McClellan parcel across Ringsend Road toward Drumgooland Road, Miss Brennan." When Mister

Harden answered a few more questions, the teacher turned her attention once again to Elizabeth.

"She is to have a lunch with her, her lessons done and no excuses for tardiness. She will learn lessons of etiquette, English, mathematics, sciences and Latin. She will be tested in each of those subjects before I place her for curriculum. The fee is two pennies per week. I expect to see her on the 12th of April at half-eight precisely."

"Yes, Miss," replied Elizabeth, more meekly than she felt. She did not want to betray the barely suppressed anger that was distracting her from what the woman was saying.

"Miss Brennan, I'm sure I'm goin' ta verra much like attending yer school," said Maggie brightly. The stern woman flashed an icy smile so quickly Elizabeth wasn't sure she saw it.

"I'm sure you will, Miss Co'burn. I will give you two books to review before you come back in April. You will be tested on the first two chapters of those books. Do I make myself clear?"

"Yes, Miss Brennan. I will do m' verra best," said Maggie, her eyes dancing.

"I'm sure you will, Miss Co'burn," the teacher said with an honest smile this time.

Miss Brennan was beginning ta melt afore our eyes, thought Elizabeth. *She's not sae cold as before. Maggie will bring her around, I ken.*

"Thank you for your help, Miss Brennan," said Elizabeth. Mister Harden nodded and turned to leave with Maggie and the books. *Ah, she's watchin' Mister Harden wit' grand interest. Could it be she has placed her heart wit' him?* Elizabeth felt a smile tug around her lips. *She could do worse, I ken. He could certainly sweeten her up a bit, if he hae a mind ta.*

As they left the schoolyard, the teacher rang the bell calling her students to class. Like bees to a hive the children ran from all corners of the yard into the schoolhouse to start their lessons.

Maggie waved as several of the children stopped to stare. Shyly, a few of the younger children waved back then ran to get inside before the door closed.

Mister Harden stopped the wagon at the end of the drive, jumped down and ran back to the door of the schoolhouse. He looked at the closed door, raising his arm as if to measure its width and writing in a little book from his pocket.

"What's he doin', Ma?" asked Maggie.

"I'm sure I don't knae, neither is it our concern, Missy." Elizabeth answered. "He'll tell us, if it has anythin' ta do wit' us, I reckon."

Thomas Harden ran back to the wagon, jumped up on the seat and they were off again. On the way back, he came to a crossroads. "This is Moneyslane Road, to the right is Ballymack Road, to the straight is Rathfriland Road and to the left where we go is Closkelt Road. The townland of Closkelt has a Presbyterian Church, a public house, and a dry goods store. The Church of Ireland at Ballyward is back where we came from and beyond the school. We will take Mountain Road just beyond the dry goods store from Closkelt Road." Seeing the panicked look on Elizabeth's face, trying to remember all his directions, he smiled. "Don't worry, Missus Co'burn, I will write it all down on a map. You won't need the map for long, I assure you.

"We'll go north on Drumgooland Road over Ringsend Road until you come to your cottage. Soon, you'll find out who does what in the area — the blacksmith, the horse doctor, midwife and so on. I'll come by to check on you, so if you have any questions, you've but to ask."

"Ye needn't worry, Beth," called Petey from the back, "Maggie will knae all o' County Down afore the week is out!"

"Yer pro'bly right, Petey," Elizabeth laughed. Maggie looked up at her and grinned, knowing they were teasing about her inquisitive nature. She had already thought to make a map of her own when she got back to the cottage.

Chapter Four

James Co'burn and Lieutenant Annesley rode up the twisted lane to walk the boundaries. James carried his journal to make notes of boundaries, landmarks, and the soil.

"If ye don't mind my askin', sair, what d' ye think the boys will be facin' when they git back? D' ye see lang hardship or a short conflict? I'd lak' ta be able ta tell Elizabeth the truth o' it, should she ask."

"It's difficult to predict, James. In my only experience with this war, our men and supplies were completely mismanaged, but we won the battle. I can say if the engagements are again poorly run, we will not fare as well. Alma was won with great heart and unpredictable actions. I saw very little of it myself." His face twisted in memory of that day.

"Verra well, sair, I will simply tell her ta have faith 'n hope fer the best."

"It's all any of us can do, James. Now, do you have your plan for spring planting yet?"

"Well, sair, I'd like ta knae wha' was planted in each field las' season an' fer how far back, afore I decide which crop will grow there. Kin we stop here a moment?" Slipping off his mount, James bent down to pick up a handful of dirt. The ground was still frozen about a foot down, but he sifted the top soil through his fingers, feeling the mixture of sand, clay, minerals, and decomposed plant life. In his journal, he made note of this location relative to the house, the nature of the soil and Lieutenant Annesley's recollection of the crop history of the field.

Continuing on, the younger man said, "These five acres have lain fallow for several years. The former tenant left to go to America and just abandoned it. I will send word so that you can borrow a workhorse and plow to clear the vegetation you see here. You will be better prepared next year to purchase what you need. Unless you have a horse and plow in Scotland?"

"I haf' a plow, but we had ta sell the horse. I hae some goats an' planned ta buy some sheep onct we harvest. Mister Harden said there's a flax mill here in Legannany, then?"

"Yes, the industry is expanding constantly in Ulster. I think you could do very well with a flax crop on about four and a half acres. You may want to reserve a half acre for home produce as we do at Castlewellan. Of course, the home produce garden at Castlewellan is on a somewhat larger scale, owing to the entertaining of guests throughout the year."

James was impressed by the young man's apparent understanding of the land. "All good thoughts, sair, I will keep thet in mind when I decide. I don't haf' much time, sae the more I find out about the land itself, the better decision I'll make."

They were now at the northwest edge of the land and beginning to descend toward the center division. Traveling along a row of trees and bushes that marked the edges of the plots, James could see the cottage in the distance. The fields ascribed to Maggie, were hillier and had more crop stubble in place than James' fields. *Good,* thought James, *it's more likely ta hold an' enrich the top soil.*

"You may clear most of Maggie's land for crops as well. Although you will not need to reserve much room for the trees and plants I send you, over time they will take over the area. Eventually, I envision the whole of Maggie's partition to be covered with seedlings from foreign lands. Each time I return, those trees and hardy plants that are ready, will go to Castlewellan. We may have to build another glass house at Castlewellan as well for those plants that will not tolerate our winters, else you'll run out of space in your glass house after a while."

"I will shelter each plant you send in the glass house until I can grow another of the same plant, then transplant one of them outside ta test its hardiness. I wouldn't want ta lose any, if it can be helped."

The young man grinned with pride, "I am hoping to make the arboretum my life's work, James. I think together, we can accomplish it."

They rode in silence for a while as they skirted the perimeter of Maggie's seven acre parcel. James stopped, sampling the soil whenever it seemed to change in color or texture, writing his findings, then moving on. The aristocratic young man followed behind watching, yet adrift in his own thoughts. *It's not much land for a man of his talents, but enough to get him started. It will take him a while to work out the seasons and the best crops for the soil. At least he won't be trapped like those wretched souls south and west of here relying only on potatoes to feed their families and exporting all their other crops. Curse the government for allowing the landlords to strip this island of its food! Children starve in the streets and families leave Ireland in droves. At least with William at Castlewellan, our tenants do not starve. So many farms are now run by women whose husbands and sons have left for other shores. We can protect our own, but the others are at the mercy of greedy, absent landlords. They give with one hand and take back even more with the other; then they pretend to take care of the poor they created! I do not look forward to my duties in the House of Lords, if William should go before me. Hah! What am I thinking! It's the same breed of nobility that runs the British Army! What makes me think I could survive another mismanaged battle?* Hugh brought himself back to the matter at hand, as he realized James was speaking to him.

"I beg your pardon, James?"

"I see ever'one is back at the cottage. Will ye join us fer tea one last time?"

"I'll come in to have you sign the final papers, then I must take my leave. Mother will be put out with me if I don't get back early today, I owe her that. I leave with William and Peter tomorrow. But, thank you, all the same." He sounded so weary, James didn't object, but just lead the way to the cottage.

Once inside, Hugh Annesley slipped the papers out of his breast pocket and spread them out on the table.

"Do you want me to read them to you, James?" asked Mister Harden.

"No, Mister Harden. I think I knae the measure o' this man nae." James replied. He took the inkwell and pen Elizabeth offered and signed the papers.

"There is a second set of papers I have signed, so you may read them over at your leisure, James," said Hugh. "If there is anything in it you question later, we will discuss it when I return. James and Elizabeth, it was a pleasure to make your acquaintance. Maggie, you are a delightful child and I look forward to seeing you again. Peter and William, I will see you tomorrow at Castlewellan."

"The wagon will stay here, so you can load your gear and return with James to Castlewellan in the morning." Thomas Harden directed his instructions to the brothers. "Do you remember the way?"

"Yes, yer map is clear an' we'll be there afore noon, Mister Harden," William answered. As the lieutenant and the courier were leaving, Maggie said seriously, "I will pray fer ye, Lieutenant

Annesley, ev'ry day." The young man turned, smiling, bowed deeply in her direction.

"I am most honored, little miss," he said, and went out the door.

The group in the cottage was strangely quiet after the door shut. It was if the door to their old life was gone, and the new one had just begun.

Breaking the silence, Elizabeth asked to see the papers. Everything seemed to be in order. Elizabeth smiled and said, "Well, thet's it, then. There's no turnin' back. We haf' a farmer in the family again." James whisked her off her stool and danced her around the room. One, then the other brother, took over and twirled her around, too. Not to leave her out, James grabbed Maggie in his arms and swung her around.

Elizabeth, breathless and laughing, said, "Well, if you men will stop jumpin' around the room, I haf' tea ta set."

"C'mon, boys, she won't be happy until we're outa her way." James, Peter and William headed for the office.

"Hmm, I like this new house. They wan' be under foot all the time nae, will they, Sunshine? You wanna make the biscuits, Maggie?" The little girl giggled and bobbed her head.

Elizabeth hummed her old tunes all the while she was preparing tea and long after.

A comfortable quiet came over the family as they sat around the table. Elizabeth leaning against James, smiling at her brothers as the sunset dipped below the mountains. James reached over, turning up the lamp. Maggie was safely ensconced on Will's lap, her eyes drooping contentedly. Peter sang an old ballad while Elizabeth whispered, "If it could be like this fore'er, I'd ne'er tire o' it.

"James, ye should write a letter ta yer Ma about all this. Nae thet we knae wha's happenin', she should knae where we will be. She'll be glad ta knae yer a farmer agin. Give her m' love."

"Ye right, m' darlin'. Why don't ye write a note ta her an' haf' Maggie write one, too. She'll be glad fer hearin' from all o' us." Elizabeth watched his eyes grow dreamy, remembering his mother and the last time he saw her. Thoughts of James's mother made her think of her own, gone so long ago. Snatches of childhood memories came flooding in unbidden, before the fire, before her father died, when three children played in fields together.

Elizabeth took the page James had written to his mother and handed it to Maggie. "Write somethin' fer Móraí. She misses yer."

Maggie looked at her mother, proudly. "I shall write about our journey here an' how happy we are," Pausing to think, she added, "an' how much we miss her."

"Thank yer, child. I knae yer haf' much ta tell her, but jes' a few lines fer t'night. It's time fer bed. We haf' an early an' eventful day t'marra."

The letter written, the family reluctantly retired. When James and Elizabeth were snuggled together in bed, Elizabeth said, "James, I canna imagine Maggie an' me alone fer sae lang. How will I sleep wit'out ye wrapped around me an' snorin' in m' ear?" She sighed deeply, betraying the fear and loneliness she felt.

"Yer a strong woman, Beth. I'll be back an' afore ye knae it, I'll be underfoot an' in yer hair, lak' I was ne'er gone. Ye mustn' let Maggie see ye afeared o' bein' by yersel'. Ye will put her in the sel'same state yer in. Haf' faith, love. It'll all work out, jes' fine. I'll be countin' the days till I see my Beth agin. Nae git ta sleep, woman. We've a big day t'marra."

She woke at first light, feeling James leave her bed. She saw him slip out the door to get things ready for their departure. There was much to do. She moved to the spot in the bed still warm from his body, barely gone. She buried herself deeper until the warmth dissipated, then slid out of bed to start her chores for the day.

She could hear the men talking low outside. William and Petey were loading their gear in the wagon, asking James if there was anything they could do to help him prepare for his absence. An overwhelming sadness came over Elizabeth as she thought of them leaving. *It's been a lovely few days*, she thought. *Nae, it's time ta pay the piper, isn' it? Keep them safe, Laird.* Elizabeth brushed away a tear that slipped through her downcast lashes. *Maggie will wake soon an' I must no' be weepin' in front o' her. We'll hafta make another 'adventure' fer jes' us two. What kin I do ta make this right fer her? Together, we'll hafta plan a surprise fer when James comes back hame. I'll think on thet, later. Nae, I've gotta make breakfast an' a hearty lunch ta take wit' them.*

"*Mairéad*, time ta rise 'n shine. Today's an eventful day an' ye dinna want ta miss a minute o' it." Elizabeth kissed Maggie awake and marveled at her deep green eyes and long black lashes.

"I'm up!" Maggie sang as she sat up and swung her legs over the side of her bed. She grabbed the cloth in the bucket by her bed to wash up, all the while, chatting merrily about the day. "Do ye hear the birds this morning? They ken it's the beginnin' o' a bonnie day. Are Da an' Will an' Petey still here?" Elizabeth nodded always surprised at the way the child was able to do so many things for herself from her stationary position. Her arms were strong from pulling herself around, bending this way and that to get things done. *Her legs may be useless, but she doesn't hafta be, does she! Ye are sae much more than people knae, Maggie-girl. I only hope one day others will understan' thet.*

"Tell me when yer ready, Maggie. There's biscuits ta be made 'n lunch pails ta pack."

"Aye, Ma." Maggie chattered on as Elizabeth closed the curtain behind her. She piled dishes on one end of the table, within reach of Maggie's chair. She put out the fixings for biscuits, leaving out the salt as usual. Smiling, she began to hum. Soon, she heard Maggie humming in tune with her.

"I'm ready fer ta make the biscuits, *Ma-mee*." Petey came in the room and swooped behind the curtain ta swing Maggie onto his hip. "Whee!" she squealed.

He plopped her on the bench and said in a deep, gruff voice, "Make me biscuits, woman!" Maggie dissolved into giggles.

"Aye! I will make you wonderful magical biscuits, kind sair. An' ye will turn into a handsome prince an' we shall live happily e'er after." Maggie folded her arms and nodded her head to make it so.

"I would be satisfied, if we had plain biscuits an' Petey could jes' behave himself," said Elizabeth grumpily. Petey pulled an exaggerated frown and pretended to wipe away copious tears.

"Oh, Ma, he's sae sad. Yer hurt his feelings," Maggie said continuing the game.

Petey grabbed Elizabeth around her waist and spun her around. Elizabeth laughed and swatted at her brother. "Gae on wit' ye, I've work ta do, nae, git!" Petey danced out the door and Elizabeth caught her breath. She set the salt on the table before Maggie could ask, and set to work again. *They'll be leavin' soon*, she thought. *I've no time ta be playin'. There's sae much ta do. Oh, my heart will break ta see 'em gae.*

Somehow breakfast was done and lunches were packed, and it was time to go. Amid hugs, tears, and shouts of goodbyes, Elizabeth searched the faces of the men in her life, the better to remember them until they return. They passed Maggie from one to another, holding her tight.

"Come, we mus' be on our way," said James quietly. "The Lieutenant will be expecting us by noon an' we've a ways ta gae."

Elizabeth put on her bravest smile, and said," Sae off wit' ye. D' ye haf' ever'thin'? God be wit' ye an' keep ye safe, 'till yer back ta us again."

With a snap of the reins, they were on their way down the road. Her brothers turned in their seats facing her and waving until they were out of sight.

"Come, m' child, we've adventures of our ain ta commence." Elizabeth whirled back to the door with Maggie on her hip. "We've a whole house ta make aright. You haf' books ta study and letters ta write. We kin plan our own little herb garden, too."

Please come back as soon as ye kin, James. I'm terrible lonely already. Gae wit' God m' love. Laird, watch o'er James, an' Will, an' Petey, bring 'em all home safe ta me. Laird, help me be patient wit' Maggie. In His holy name, I ask it, amen.

The next morning, Elizabeth lay awake in bed going over the plans she overheard the day before. The lieutenant and her brothers would go to Newcastle to sail off to war again. James and the driver would go back to Belfast and take the ferry to Stranraer for the return trip to Lanark. James thought it would give him several days to pack the wagon, sell what they didn't need and tend to business matters before he had to get back for the Tuesday ferry. It would be at least a fortnight before she saw James again. Elizabeth never felt so anxious and alone.

Pulling herself up, she looked over at Maggie still sleeping peacefully. Elizabeth hadn't pulled the curtain around Maggie's bed the night before. She wanted to see every corner of the room before she went to sleep. She hadn't realized until then, how much she depended on James to let her know everything was secure before she went to sleep. With no moon, the world was black as pitch outside the door of the cottage. She wasn't yet used to the sounds of the night in her new home. An owl very close to the cottage sounded off in the night. It was good to haf' an owl near the house to keep rodents away, but she nearly leaped out of her skin at the break in the silence. Later, she heard the wind through the dead grasses nearby and a small animal scurrying through the brush.

Elizabeth shook herself as if to chase away the fears of the night before. *Git dressed an' git busy! Ye don' haf' time ta be ruminatin' 'bout thin's thet gae bump in the night. Maggie will be up an' wonderin' wha's wrong wit' ye.*

She busied herself with her morning chores. The air was brisk, but the sun shone bright and the wind had died down. Elizabeth scurried inside to be there when Maggie awoke.

"Maggie?" There she was getting dressed already.

"What will we do t'day, Ma?"

"Well, let's jes' see how the day plays out, shall we? Firstly, breakfast, then we'll decide wha's next, eh?"

During breakfast, Elizabeth thought of a way to keep Maggie occupied. "Fer starters, Maggie, it'll be yer job ta write a list o' things we must do t'day, an' t'marra. I haf' a paper from yer da's journal. Might jes' as well practice yer schoolin' by scribin' som'thin' we kin use. Finish yer porridge an' we'll git started." Maggie clapped her hands with delight.

"I'll show Miss Brennan how good I kin write. This afternoon, I'll hafta read my books, sae I'll be ready fer school, April 12th."

"Fer nae, m' lass, gather the dishes an' wash down the table. Dry the table good, while I'm cleanin' up. We dinna wan' the paper wet, do we?" Elizabeth tossed a wet cloth and a dry towel on the table. "I'll be right back."

Elizabeth came back wit' clean dishes gathered in her apron. As she put them back on the shelf, she said, "Ye will hafta be writin' sma' ta git it all on one piece o' paper. Let's see, fold yer page in three longwise, so we can haf' three lists on either side. At the top, first column, write 'Herbs 'n Cures'. At the days' warmest, we'll gae out an' see what we kin git for thet column. Over the next two columns, put 'Place' 'n 'Time.' On the other side, put 'Haf',' an' 'Need'. We kin save the last column fer 'Chores', like more shelves and hooks for irons, the kettle..."

"...My books, Ma?"

"Yes, perhaps a place fer ye books. Won' Da be surprised at the chores we think fer him ta do when he gits back?" Laughing, Maggie waited for her mother to give her more to write.

Elizabeth listed the herbs she hoped to find. Later in the year, she knew they would find all they would need, but for now, she and her daughter would have an adventure finding herbs and dry seeds to use for seasoning and curing. Although they may not be ready for picking today, she would know where to look for them when the time was right. She could almost hear her mother's voice telling her: *In the month of April, gather Mead Caileath, or wood anemone, a good plaster for wounds. Later, ground ivy ta cure ringing in the ears, vervain fer wounds, eyebright fer diseases o' the eye an' improving memory, groundsel for headaches, elder-tree flowers also fer headaches, an' young shoots o' the hawthorn fer sore throats.*

There was an old woman in Lanark who had cures for all sorts of ailments. Perhaps Elizabeth could find an 'herb witch' here. Until then, she would find her own herbs to ward off the common ills of spring.

Elizabeth smiled as she remembered the herb jars her mother collected, lining the shelves high on the walls of her childhood home. Her brothers would climb up to steal a pinch or two of each to make pretend 'love potions', hoping her ma and da would stop their squabbling. She and her brothers would run outside when her ma and da would comment how the tea tasted *strange*. They would hide behind the house until they could hear them laughing again.

With the sun high in the sky, it was time to go hunting herbs. Elizabeth tied a string to the pencil and to Maggie's wrist. It was the only pencil she found and she didn't want to disappoint James by losing it. She found a small cart, lined it with a blanket to ease the bumpy ride, dressed Maggie up warm and they were off for their adventure. Elizabeth was careful to keep the cottage in sight as she pulled the cart.

As they found each herb, Maggie wrote down its location, sometimes looking to her mother for a good description. After Maggie's cheeks were reddened by the freshening breeze and the clouds started to cover the sun, Elizabeth decided it was time to head home.

Over Maggie's protest of *'jes' one more,'* she walked the cart down the hill and over a long field to the cottage. As she eased the cart down the rolling hills, Maggie stretched her arms out wide with her fingers splayed. "What are yer doin'?" her mother asked.

"I'm ridin' the wind, Ma," the delighted child answered, "I'm ridin' the wind in County Down!"

Elizabeth smiled thinking, *this child will fin' pleasure in the smalles' o' thin's. If she canna walk, she'll fly.*

Although never out of her sight, the little house was much further away than she thought. She had to watch her footing among ground vines and briars. By the time she reached the door and carried Maggie inside, the long night's wakefulness had caught up to her.

Just as she removed her shawl and plunked down at the table to catch her breath, she heard the clopping of horse's hooves coming to a stop outside. "Oh dear, who on earth...?"

"Mister Harden!" Maggie cried excitedly, "He said he would come."

"Indeed, 'tis," said Elizabeth opening the door for him.

"Missus Co'burn," said Thomas Harden, removing his hat as he entered. "And how is everything this fine day? I trust you spent the night well? No problems?"

Elizabeth admitted to some nervousness about the unfamiliar noises and being alone. *Ye fool! What's the matter wit' ye? He'll be thinkin' yer a child!* Biting her lip, she hastily added, "Nae, I ken wha' the sounds are, we'll be fine. Won' we Maggie?"

"If you want me to, I'd be glad to stay in the office, Missus Co'burn. I have my bedding roll in the carriage." Seeing she was about to protest, he said, "Yes, that would be a solution for the both of us. It would save me the trip to Castlewellan each night. I'm sorry I didn't see to it last night."

"If 'n ye' think ye should, Mister Harden. Maggie an' I wouldn't mind the comp'ny."

"Then it's settled. I'll be able to help set things up for when James comes home. I'm sure there are a few shelves and hooks and such, you'd like to have. I thought this afternoon, if you're willing, you'd like to see the local store and church. With which church would you be affiliated?"

"We'd gae ta the closest Protestant church, I'm supposin'."

"The Drumgooland Presbyterian Church is about a half hour from here. The Church of Ireland in Ballyward is a little over an hour. That's by carriage. A wagon will take a little longer, of course. I could take you there this afternoon, if you wish."

Elizabeth sighed heavily, "Another time perhaps? I must get tea ready. Maggie and I haf' been out searching for herbs since morning and I'm afraid we're spent. It would take too lang to make ourselves presentable, at any rate. Join us fer tea an' we'll add it to Maggie's list o' things ta do."

Noting his quizzical look, Maggie explained her lists to him. Elizabeth invited him to sit and she began preparing an early tea. As she went outside to her cooking fire, Mister Harden feigned great interest in the list of items Maggie proffered. He looked around the room and made suggestions for shelves and cupboards, which Maggie wrote down dutifully.

As Elizabeth returned, she saw the glowing look on Maggie's face. *He knaes jes' how ta make her feel important, doesn't he? What a wonderful father he would haf' been! He seems ta haf' received as much comfort from her attention.*

"Ma-meme says her mother had a shelf up high near the top of the walls ta hold her herbs and other small things. Wouldn't that be good, ta store them out of the way? She could put her irons up there, too."

"I think you're right, Maggie. After tea, I'll look outside to see what I can find left from the workmen that we can use for all these things."

"Mister Harden, I canna be askin' ye ta be doin' all this. It is enough thet ye stay wit' us."

"Missus Co'burn, it is my own comfort of which I am thinking. I have always enjoyed working with my hands and I do not have many chances to satisfy that joy. The Lieutenant would wish me to see you settled in your home with as much help as I could grant you."

Having no argument to that, Elizabeth just shrugged her shoulders and said, "As ye wish."

Mister Harden's presence was more help than they could ever repay. He set up shelves for her spice and herb jars just like her mother had, a shelf over Maggie's bed for her school books and more, and a series of hooks in the rafters for hanging herbs to dry. She now had places for her irons, her pots and pans and her mother's great dish.

Mister Harden appeared to be genuinely pleased to be working with his hands. Every time he completed a project, he discovered another way to keep things organized. He was also working on a secret project in the back shed. He asked that Elizabeth promise not to go out there. It was to be a surprise. He seemed to be very light-hearted and mysterious these days.

Every few days, Mister Harden would go back to Castlewellan to check on his duties there. He always came back at night, with news of the town and the Earl's family. Maggie would be relentless with her questions and he very patiently answered every one.

He took them to the Presbyterian Church, the blacksmith, and the butcher. He introduced them to their neighbors, who seemed more curious than friendly. *There will be time enough ta git ta knae 'em when James gits back,* thought Elizabeth.

One day, when Mister Harden returned from Castlewellan, he brought a book under his arm. "This is for you, Maggie."

Delighted, Maggie immediately opened the book. "Thank you, Mister Harden, but there are no words in this book."

"Ah, Maggie, this is a book that will have only *your* words in it. This is your journal. As often as you have something you want to remember, you can write it in this book. Since it has no lines in it, you can draw pictures in it, too."

"Mister Harden, this is wonderful! I will put my name on the first page, just like Da has in his journal."

"I wanted to talk to you about that. I know that your name is Margaret Cockburn, but sometimes it is easier to spell one's name as it sounds, especially, if you are going to school. I noticed Miss Brennan wrote your name as 'C-o-b-u-r-n' when we were enrolling you for class. If you would like, you could use this new name in your new country. You will want to talk to your father and mother about it first." Turning to Elizabeth, he said, "I do not want to go against your wishes. The name Cockburn is an ancient and noble name in Scotland. People only change their names here to simplify the spelling, not its pronunciation or meaning."

"Mister Harden, I will put in my book, 'Margaret Jane Cockburn of Scotland' and 'Margaret Jane Coburn of Ireland'. What d' you think, Ma?"

"'Tis fine fer yer book, child. When yer da comes hame, we'll decide wha' ta do fer the rest o' the world," said Elizabeth, smiling. *I won' knae till I see his face wha' he'll wanna do, will I? Wit' his family scattered from hither ta yon, will they be able ta fin' us? Will he be willin' ta give up his ain name fer the convenience o' others?*

"Mister Harden, I've been meanin' ta ask, do the folk aroun' here haf' the same traditions as we in Scotland? I've been curious about it, ye ken."

"Quite so, Missus Co'burn, most of the people around here are Scottish born or their parents were, so most of the old Scots traditions are carried on here. There are some who came from England and some who are catholic. You'll find a few more as well. Monday is Market Day. The first Monday in May is a fair day as well as rent 'n tax day in Castlewellan, also, the first Monday in October. They keep all of the Christian holidays according to the church where they are members. Some of the pagan celebrations still persist, but as non-religious festivals. The First Sunday in August is Blaeberry Sunday. Many of the young folks climb *Slieve Croob* to the ancient cairns of the twelve kings. There may be a few who still ascribe to some of the pagan beliefs and superstitions, but they're mostly stories to scare the children on dark and stormy nights." Mister Harden winked at Maggie.

"Sae, we'll haf' our ain, 'n a few more besides. Thet should be interestin', eh Maggie?" said Elizabeth. Maggie engaged Mister Harden with many, many questions on this new subject and as was his delight, he answered every one.

Elizabeth drifted into her own thoughts, and their words no longer had meaning for her. *There is sae much more ta think on than I dreamed, when we came ta this new place. Ev'ry day it seems, they's new discoveries an' changes ta our thinkin'. Kin we e'er feel ta hame here? Will we have new friends in this place? No one hae come ta see us. E'en when Mister Harden introduced us, the people were stand-offish. They said all the polite words, but with no feeling of welcome. Wha' could it be?*

As if reading her mind, Mister Harden said, "Once you are here with James on your own, your neighbors will be more open, than they have been." Seeing Elizabeth's questioning face, he continued. "They have seen you with me, I'm afraid. They are wary when they see the Earl of Annesley's courier, because they think I am bringing them unhappy news. It may take a while to gain their trust, since they believe you have the favor of the Earl. Once you are settled in and are working the land as they are, they will come around. It may take a little time, but I have faith Elizabeth, you will have great friends and neighbors here."

A feeling of homesickness overwhelmed over her and she hurried out the door, so Maggie wouldn't see her sudden tears. *Come back, James.* Elizabeth leaned against the side of the cottage and covered her head with her apron. *Are we doin' the right thin', James?* All the loneliness, worries, and fears she felt in the last ten days seemed to flow out with her weeping. She mopped up her face and blew her nose. *Now, git back ta work, Elizabeth!* She continued to the back yard where her laundry was hanging on bushes, drying in the sun. As she picked up each piece, folded and placed it in her basket, she began to hum again. As she smelled the sun on her fresh wash and batted the bees away, a new calm came over her. *When James comes back, it will be hame. It won' be lang nae.*

Mister Harden was glad Maggie didn't seem to notice how upset her mother was. He kept his voice in an even calm as he answered her curious questions. When Elizabeth came back with a basket of clothes, he was relieved to see she was back to her usual demeanor. He excused himself to work in the shed again.

The sleepless nights, the anxious days watching down the road were nearly over. James could be coming home as early as today. Elizabeth tried not to hope for the earliest arrival, but her heart threatened to burst in the wanting of it. *I mustn't let Maggie think it'll be t'day. She will be sae disappointed if he doesn't come. As will I. Oh, let it be today!*

Chapter Five

James rose early Wednesday morning in Belfast, anxious to get started. He found Robert, the Earl's driver, waiting for him as he entered the livery. Since they did not have to go to Castlewellan, they were headed directly to the cottage in Legannany. They would be home that very day!

The young driver kept a running narration about his experiences growing up in County Down. He talked about Castlewellan's bustling market square and the goings-on at the courthouse. As a coach and wagon driver, Robert heard all the news and gossip of the elite of Castlewellan and the surrounding townlands. He explained he was a mere driver, so they paid him little mind and spoke as if he had no ears to hear. He was careful not to talk directly about the Earl or his family, but he knew who the Earl thought was honorable and who was corrupt among his colleagues in the courthouse and the legislature. Robert seemed to delight in the telling of murders, robberies, and family scandals. As they passed from townland to townland, James knew he would miss the companionship of this tall, lanky young man, barely out of his childhood. He wondered if the long hours of traveling alone contributed to Robert's incessant need to talk.

James smiled at the seemingly haphazard load of household goods they had piled on and attached to the wagon. He had his two goats as well. Elizabeth, he knew, would prefer the goats stayed in Lanark. They seemed to always upset her laundry basket or butt her whenever they saw the opportunity. He would have to keep them away from the glass house, for sure!

I hope all is well with them, thought James. *'Tis only a short while an' I'll be there. How I miss them! Ta have us all leave her ta onct must've been sae hard on Beth. I wonder if Mister Harden chanct to stop by? While I'm listenin' ta Robert's tales o' doom an' destruction, my imagination's fair runnin' wild wit' worry. If anythin' happened ta my two lasses, I wouldn't be worth a tinker's dam. Robert said it would be less than two hours an' we'd be there. Better ask him about his family ta steer him away from these worrisome stories. M' mind kin imagine enough disasters without Robert givin' me more ta think on.*

"Robert," James laughed, interrupting the latest tale of criminal activity. "Would ye haf' me believe all o' Ulster is corrupt an' murderous, except me an' thee? What o' yer brothers an' yer sister? How d' they spend their time? How does yer father ply his trade?"

"Ah, they are ordinary folk, ta be sure, no' as excitin' as the courthouse hounds, but good people. Da's a smithie in Castlewellan an' Joseph works wit' Da. I worked wit' him fer a while, until the Earl hired me ta drive. John ran off ta join the army. He an' Da had a bit o' fallin' out afore he left. He caught Da whilst he were drinkin', an' tol' him he didn't wanna work in the shop wit' him. Whoo-ee, what a quarrel thet was! I was sure they'd come ta blows. Next mornin', John was gone. Ma hasn't allowed any peace fer Pa since. Pow'rful angry, she is. He won't be fergiven 'til her baby boy comes home."

"An' wha' about your sister, Robert?"

"She's o' an age if any boy-o looks her way, they's three Callohans ready ta pluck his eyes out! Da would put her in a convent 'til he kin marry her off, if he had a say," said Robert, laughing.

"My wee lass will be turnin' heads afore I knae it. I wan' be lookin' forward ta those days." James smiled and clapped the young man on the back.

"Da says it keeps him up half the night an' then some. Look, James, we're upon the Dolmen."

"An' wha' would thet be, Robert?"

"Ah, the Dolmen is an ancient cairn, a burial place fer a warrior king. It also marks the road ta yer cottage. Another short while an' we'll be there."

"Ah, thank the Good Laird. I was beginnin' ta think m' backside was bonded ta this board fere'er." It wasn't his discomfort that was on James' mind however, but making his family whole again. Now, he willed the horses to go faster to match the racing of his heart. *Almost there!*

Soon, they were pulling up in front of the cottage. James saw Elizabeth, Maggie, and Mister Harden spilling out the front door to greet them. A whirlwind of tears, laughter, and concern flitted across the faces of the reunited family. They stepped on each other's words and danced on each other's toes in their joy and relief.

Mister Harden and Robert stood quietly to the side, smiling at the excited family. Mister Harden sighed, *I've enjoyed these last few weeks more than I'd like to admit. I'll miss this little family. It'll be sad to go back to Castlewellan, to my routine and my bachelor life. I'd forgotten how much I miss the simple comforts of family. Look at Elizabeth, the light in her eyes as she watches James, and Maggie, her arms flung around his neck like she'll never let go.*

"Oh my, where are my manners!" Elizabeth gasped her face aglow. "Come in for tea, Mister Harden... an' Robert, is it? Tell us about yer journey." They all piled into the cottage, Mister Harden lagging behind.

As Elizabeth set the tea she had been preparing on the table, she asked, "Sae ye had a good crossin', then?" Remembering her own crossing, she was sure it had to have been better than that.

"Calm seas and fair wind, Missus Coburn," answered Robert, somewhat subdued now he was not driving the wagon.

"Come now, Robert. My wee lass wants ta hear every detail, don' ye Maggie! Tell her o' the ship an' the color o' the sea, an' the man on deck who thought he could dance upon the rail," James said, encouragingly.

The young man, now that he had James' blessing, launched his tale of the crossing, turning his full attention to Maggie. Rapt in the story from his first words, Maggie was fascinated with the rise and fall of his voice, and his hands flying through the air, punctuating every phrase.

"Thet will occupy the two o' them fer an hour!" laughed James. Looking around the room, he said, "Beth! You haf' shelves an' hooks all set up fer yer herbs and goods?"

"Mister Harden made all thet fer us. Look there's e'en a shelf fer Maggie's books. He's been sech a wonderful help ta Maggie an' me, I hope ye don' mind?"

"No' at all, Mister Harden, how kin we repay you fer all yer fine work?"

"Have no worry on that account, Mister Co'burn. It's been a long time since I had the pleasure of working with my hands. I'd quite forgotten how much I enjoy it. I used the scraps of wood the workmen who built the glass house left behind."

Maggie looked up from the story Robert was telling and blurted out, "Mister Harden's been making som'thin' in the shed, but he won' tell us what it is. He says it's a surprise an' we were not ta knae 'til yer come hame. He hasta tell us nae, doesn't he, Da?"

James' face flushed with sudden disappointment, *He must haf' been stayin' here the whole time. I wanted ta do all this fer ye, Elizabeth, an' he jes' dances in ta take my place? Wha's goin' on here?* James forced himself to stop his thinking. *Hold on ta yer temper, Jamie-boy. Ye knae Mister Harden is a good man an' Elizabeth is yer ain woman, good an' true. It'll be soon enough ta find out wha' the story is, after these men are gone from the house. 'Sides it were yer idea thet he stay.*

Swallowing his doubt and pride, James smiled and asked, "Sae, wha' do ye haf' in the shed, then? Wha's this *surprise* ye been makin'?"

"Mister Co'burn, I do not wish to tread on your toes, sir. But with Maggie going to school on Monday, I knew you wouldn't have time to make accommodation for her. It is entirely up to you, whether you choose to use it, but I think it may help her at school."

"Well, let's gae see it, Mister Harden," said James, rising. Elizabeth watched her husband closely. She could hear the strain in his voice and the underlying anger. *Oh Laird, don't let him put a cloud on this wondrous day. Mister Harden worked sae hard on his secret project.*

When they reached the outside, Mister Harden raised his hand to keep them at the front of the cottage. "Let me go get it. I'll be right back." He ducked around the corner while James and the others waited impatiently. Maggie, perched on her father's arm, could barely contain herself.

The little group heard a strange noise coming from the back. Light wheels on the dirt path from the shed ground closer and closer.

A collective gasp escaped the group. There around the corner of the cottage came a chair on wheels. It was a caned-back dining room arm chair with three wheels, two large wheels on the sides and one wheel to steer in the back. On the arms of the chair was a tray, hinged on one side. High on the width of the chair back was a bar for pushing and steering the chair.

"Lemme try, lemme try it!" cried Maggie. James lifted the tray to the side and placed Maggie in the chair. Putting the tray back into position, he went around to the back and tentatively gave it a push. Seeing it rolled easily forward, he maneuvered it around to smoother ground. "It's wonderful, Da! Thank you, Mister Harden."

James was overwhelmed at the generosity of the man. Mister Harden stood back to watch Maggie and her father manipulate his handiwork. "How did ye ever come up wit' this chair?" asked James.

"When I took her to the school, I could see Miss Brennan needed help to take her class outside, if Maggie had to be carried. I measured the doorway at the school, so I know it will fit with a little room to spare. I had seen one in London, so I knew how it worked.

"The Earl had thrown out the chairs to this set just recently, so I asked him for this one. It is a small side chair to the set and I hoped it would be small enough to fit. The wheels are from an old pram, the tray is also from Castlewellan. I think it all worked out rather well, if I do say so. I hope you don't mind my presumption in making this for Maggie."

"Mister Harden, I'm 'shamed thet I ne'er thought ta make somethin' lak' this. This'll give her a kind of freedom she would ne'er haf' otherwise. 'Tis a wonderful kindness ye've done fer her...an' Miss Brennan too, of course." The shadow of anger shown earlier on James' face transformed to grateful humility. "I don' knae how ta thank ye properly. She's a thin' of beauty, she is. Yer a prime craftsman wit' wood, sir. I canna tell it was made of different pieces. It looks like it was made from one piece at a cabinet shop."

"No need to thank me, Mister Co'burn. Maggie's face is reward enough. You can keep the wagon to get the chair to school, if you want. You could bring it home on Sundays, perhaps. Or leave it there until school is out for the summer holiday, if you like. Miss Brennan doesn't know about it yet, but I thought on our way back to Castlewellan, Robert and I could stop there for a visit to tell her about it." Mister Harden caught Robert's eye to elicit his agreement. The driver just shrugged, having no reason not to do as he was told.

"Now remember Maggie, on Monday you are to be at the school at half-eight or a little earlier, ready to study. I think that you will be her best student. Oh, there is a box under the seat for books, your slate and such, if needed." Turning to James and Elizabeth, he said, "Until Monday morning, you may want to store the chair in the shed to keep it dry."

"Isn't this a wonderful surprise? Thank you, thank you, thank you, Mister Harden!" Maggie's effusive chatter and delightful grin, nearly broke Elizabeth's heart. *Thank you, Laird, fer sendin' us Mister Harden. Surely he is one o' yer angels. Bless him wit' a happy life. He deserves more than we kin give him. Anythin' Ye want us ta do fer him, will be done in Yer name. Amen.*

"Yer a saint, fer sure, Mister Harden. Please come ta Sunday dinner next. It won' be fancy, but all the same, we'd love fer ye ta come, after all ye did fer us. An' Robert too, if yer able," Elizabeth pleaded.

"I don't know what the Earl's schedule is, Missus Co'burn, but it is surely tempting. Mister Co'burn, your wife is an excellent cook. It is I, who must thank you for making me welcome, and letting me use your tools and shed for this project."

"My tools are in the wagon, sir. Wha' tools did ye use?"

"They must have been left from the last tenant, Mister Co'burn. They were in a bit of a mess, so I should have known. You have some very good tools in there."

"Call me James, sir. The more I look around, the more surprises I find in this place. Well, I'd better take the load off this wagon afore the day gits away from us. Kin ye gie us a hand, Robert?"

"Missus Co'burn, let me get that into the house for you." Mister Harden took a box of dishes from her. "We'd better hurry. It looks like it may rain."

Maggie sat in her new chair and watched her ma and da with Mister Harden and Robert unload the wagon. James directed where each box and bundle should go, and soon it was done. "We'll leave the wagon and one horse. One should be enough, now that the heavy load is off. One of us will be here Tuesday for the wagon. There's feed for the horse left under the seat. That should last you until then. Robert, get it into the shed to keep it dry. Then, we'd better get moving down the road, if we're to make it to the school and to Castlewellan before dark."

Soon James, Elizabeth, and Maggie were alone in their little house. The chair was put in the office, since the goats were in the shed. "No sense in asking fer trouble," Elizabeth said. "Those goats will eat anythin' they can reach. I hope ye put the horse feed up high, or the poor thing will starve."

"I'll check on thet then, I'll be right back. Don't start anythin' until I get back. I haf' som'thin' ta say ta both o' you," he said sternly.

Maggie and Elizabeth looked at each other, wondering what this was all about. Elizabeth was still feeling the effects of all the excitement of the homecoming, the anger she saw on James' face, and Mister Harden's surprise. She didn't think her heart could withstand another emotional moment. She sat down at the table and cradled her head in her hands.

James was back in no time. He sat down beside Elizabeth and gathered her in his arms. "Hush, I jes' need some quiet time wit' my lassies, is all." Elizabeth nestled into his neck and sighed. James reached across the table and covered Maggie's small hand with his. He softly rubbed Elizabeth's back and she began to cry. All of the anxiety of the last few weeks seemed to pour out with her tears. "Wha's this, *mo ghaol*... why the tears?"

"I'm sae happy yer finally hame, James. The bumps in the night haf' taken my sleep. If it weren't fer Mister Hardin, I don' knae wha' ye would haf' found when you got hame. He kept us thinkin' on when ye were comin' hame, instead of bein' alone. I've been sae afeerd o' ever'thin', I'm no good wit'out ye, James."

"Nor am I, wit'out ye, Beth. I put on a cheerful face, but my heart wasn' in it. Poor Robert talked all the way from here an' back ag'in. I'd naught ta say ta him. Jes' lemme hold ye fer a while, 'til we're whole ag'in." They sat in silence wrapped around each other for a long time.

Now that they were together again, Elizabeth and Maggie's lives began to take on a more familiar routine. James spent his days with his journal and out in the field, and his evenings with the Lieutenant's trunk of plant samples. On Monday, Maggie went to school. James and Elizabeth continued to Castlewellan for seed and goods.

After several good years and James' knowledge of the land, the farm was up and running. James sold his flax to the mill, and was able to buy a new wagon and a horse for the farm. The glass house was filled with the Lieutenant's plantings and the catalogue was filled with entries. James added a dried leaf of each sample to the page of its specifications. Maggie became proficient at writing in the details for each plant. To her, each seedling became a new friend and she visited them often in the glass house to see how well they were doing.

Elizabeth adapted to her new surroundings, meeting her neighbors as they traveled to Castlewellan on Market Day. As in all small communities, neighbors depended on each other and celebrated all victories together, small and large.

Owing to her cheerful demeanor and radiant smile, Maggie gained the friendship of most of her schoolmates. The children made allowances for her limitations and she helped many of them with their schoolwork. Miss Brennan was pleasantly surprised at

Maggie's aptitude. With the addition of a small ramp to negotiate the step into the school, she found no objection to having Maggie go outside for class in warm weather. Indeed, with Maggie's knowledge of the plants in the glass house, Miss Brennan was able to expand her class's botanical curriculum.

Mister Harden stopped by the school more often to see Maggie and Miss Brennan. Soon, the news of an impending marriage of the courier and the schoolteacher set the townland abuzz. Elizabeth was satisfied that Mister Harden was finally matched, and delighted that Miss Brennan found many more reasons to smile.

The Crimean War waged on for three years and Elizabeth's worries for the young Lieutenant and her brothers continued with it. They had heard the stories of the rejoicing in Belfast and Castlewellan when the news of the Treaty of Paris reached them. Hugh Annesley came back to Castlewellan unscathed, but weary. He paid them a visit with many more samples for James.

Elizabeth's brothers did not fare as well as the lieutenant. William broke his leg, falling in a ravine, near the end of the war. Peter lost his arm in the same engagement. They were discharged and sent home to Scotland. Once recuperated, the brothers decided once again, to seek their fortune in America. This time, they sailed to Nova Scotia and their letters revealed they were doing well there.

Elizabeth worried about James working so hard, farming by day and working in the glass house by night. In a letter from his mother, James learned that his younger brother was involved in a skirmish with the local constable in Scotland. He sent for John to stay with them in Ireland until the affair blew over. John worked on the farm and appeared content to stay in the office. James was grateful for the help and kept an eye on his brother. James seemed to thrive on the hard work and was happier than Elizabeth had seen him since he was a farmer in Scotland. James was back working the land where he belonged.

As for Elizabeth, her cup was filled to overflowing. Her child grew fairer and cleverer each day. Her husband was back to farming and had John to help him. The rent and the taxes were paid and the North o' Ireland was a truly bonnie place to be.

Chapter Six

Maggie hummed a cheerful tune as she braided her unruly, thick russet hair in the sunlight. In her shadow, she could see the curly tendrils escaping even as she tied the rest of her hair at the nape of her neck. At nineteen, she was shockingly beautiful. Her deep green eyes had bewitched most of the lads in Legannany who were still around. Her heart leaned toward Joseph Heenan, however, who promised to take her to *Slieve Croob* for Blaeberry Sunday.

James and Elizabeth were not in favor of the trip, but knew they could no longer deny her. She had never been, and the girls her age had been climbing the mountain for the festival since they were small children. Maggie had heard tales of the bonfire and the young men who jumped over the flames in daring challenges, for the hand of a maiden fair. Would Joseph declare himself for her tonight?

Maggie had known Joseph since her first day of school at Legannany. Later, she saw him at church and at Market Square in Castlewellan. He always had someone hanging on his arm, and all the while she wished it were she. She dreamed of one day going to the August festival, of carrying a rock to throw on the grave of the twelve kings buried on *Slieve Croob,* and of looking out over the sea to the Isle of Man.

"Will ye' be sittin' here all day dreamin', m' darlin', or are ye ready ta gae ta church?" her father teased, bringing the horse and wagon around. "Maybe we'll stop at the neighbors on the way hame an' stay a while."

"Da, don' ye dare! Joseph will be here right after church. Ye ken he will!" Her face flushed with apprehension and pique. When she saw the twinkle in his eye, she stamped her hand on the table, jarring the dishes on it. "Ooh, Da, yer sech a tease!"

"Thet he is, m' child an' they's no changin' him," said Elizabeth. "Nae James, give her some peace an' git her up in the wagon, or we'll be late ta church."

James winked at his bonnie lass and picked her up. "Ach, I don' know if we haf' a daughter or an elephant." He pretended he was struggling under the load of the tiny woman.

Maggie playfully swatted her father's shoulder. She noted the chair in the back of the wagon with some pride. The chair let her enter the church somewhat more gracefully than being carried like a child. It had gone through several major repairs since Mister Harden first made it, but it was still sturdy and still fit her. *It won't if I wear an extra petticoat,* she thought. As it was, she had to watch the hem of her dress, so it wouldn't get dirty or caught up in the wheels.

John leaned his wiry frame in the office doorway, waving his goodbye. They were used to her uncle not joining them for church. He was generally quiet and subdued, but always declined their invitation to worship. James often spoke of how helpful he was with the farming. Because John didn't talk much, Maggie secretly invented romantic stories of great sadness and intrigue to fill in what she didn't know of his past. One day, perhaps she would know the truth of her father's mysterious brother.

"Church should be interestin' t'day," said her mother. "They's a new pastor, Reverend Willard Crane. Dinna knae anythin' 'bout him, but we'll find out wha' he's lak' t'day."

"New preachers always start out with the Book of Revelation and the Four Horsemen o' the Apocalypse, then they mellow with age," said James with an arched eyebrow. "They go their way backward through the Holy Book from there. First, we're all goin' ta hell in a haybasket, then they're gonna *save* us. Finally, when they are ready to meet their Creator, they tell us of His bountiful love an' how we'll all gae ta heaven."

"James, stop it. Kin ye please put ye mind right afore goin' ta church." Elizabeth's voice was light as she spoke the oft-repeated request, but her warning was clear.

"Yes, Mother." James pulled a long solemn face, so pious, Maggie had to laugh. Although James was not a deeply religious man, he had always shown a comfortable relationship with his Creator and observed his Scottish Book of Prayer.

The bells were ringing as they pulled up with their fellow congregants in front of the small, gray slated church.

"We're none too early," Elizabeth said. "We'd better git inside."

James jumped down, set out Maggie's chair and put her in it, before he helped Elizabeth down from the wagon. Maggie quickly covered her hair with a bit of lace. Elizabeth straightened out her family's clothes to her liking, then they proceeded through the vestibule to the nave of the church. James preferred the back of the church, but Elizabeth, always mindful of what others might be thinking, led them to the front rows, just behind the paid family pews. Maggie's chair sat in the aisle beside them.

A hush fell over the congregation as the new preacher made his dramatic entrance into the sanctuary. His black robes flowing from his stick-like figure seemed to emphasize his narrow face and beak nose. When he first opened his mouth, his voice was barely heard, then realizing his audience could not hear him, he raised his voice to a crackling screech. The congregation, in unison jumped back in their seats at the assault on their ears.

Maggie, once she was accustomed to the sound of his voice, began to daydream about the afternoon's festivities. She was startled out of her reverie by the preacher's scalding indictment of the "Blaeberry Sunday" of which she dreamed. William Crane forcefully expounded on the evils of celebrating pagan rituals, honoring pagan kings on a day that belonged to the Lord. He warned about the dangers of debauchery among the young people who participated in this pagan activity. The devil was lurking, he said, waiting to capture these souls so willing to be deceived by the Unholy One.

Maggie felt her face flush, ducked her head and wished herself to disappear. She furtively looked around the congregation for young people who were suffering as she was. She had never thought sitting in the aisle was conspicuous until now. She thought her torment would never be over. He seemed to go on and on. Across the aisle and a pew ahead, Jamie Simmons slouched in his seat, a smile playing around his handsome face. His mother poked him viciously, making him sit up straight. Maggie's thoughts were frantic. *I hope Ma won't take this sermon ta heart an' change her mind! I've been waiting too lang ta miss this day. Oh Lord, please let me gae.* Maggie gasped with the realization she just prayed to God to let her go to a pagan festival! *Is it wrong, ta want this sae much? Wha's the matter wit' me?*

Her pink face grew scarlet now. She felt as if everyone knew what she was thinking. *Maggie, calm down. Think about som'thin' else.... anythin' else.* The congregation was standing now, concealing her embarrassment. The sermon was over at last. In just a few minutes, they could leave. Maggie tried to concentrate on the words of the benediction, willing her face to turn back to its normal shade. She unconsciously wiped her damp hands on her dress.

As the subdued congregants filed out of Drumgooland Presbyterian Church, Maggie wished Pastor Ried, the gentle ninety-two-year-old former pastor were still alive. She missed the sweet, soft-spoken shepherd of his flock. As she approached the new preacher, she was filled with trepidation. She would have to shake his hand and she could not seem to control them. Next in line, she could feel her heart beating rapidly with both guilt and rebellious anger.

As Maggie's hand reached to shake his, the Reverend Mister Crane looked down from his tall frame and stretched out his hand, placing it directly on her head! He raised his eyes to the heavens and prayed over her. "O Lord in heaven, have mercy on this poor afflicted child, and cleanse her heart from all unrighteousness, in the name of the Father, the Son, and the Holy Ghost. Amen."

To Elizabeth he said, "Bless you, patient mother. It is good of you to bring this unfortunate cripple into the house of the Lord and to His merciful redemption. As the Lord saith, 'Come unto me, all ye that labor and are heavy-laden and I will give you rest'." Elizabeth hastily shook his hand and with head bowed, scurried away. James kept his hands on the chair and didn't offer to shake the man's hand at all. Now all three of them bore red faces.

No one said a word as they boarded the wagon and headed for home. Maggie fumed in silence. *Is it sinful to not be able to walk?* Shocked and frustrated, angry tears slipped through Maggie's dark lashes. Elizabeth put her arm around her daughter and shed a few sympathetic tears herself. James' jaw was tight and he stared straight ahead. The horse responding to his flick of the reins, moved along at a greater speed than was usual with passengers in the wagon.

"If the man were no' sae ignorant, perhaps he could learn from a good thrashin'," James said through gritted teeth. "Elizabeth, I don' think we need ta subject oursel's ta this man's abuse in God's name. If ye still wan' ta continue ta gae ta this church while he's here, I will take yer. But, I'll no' be gracin' him wit' *my* presence anytime soon."

"I don't knae wha' I'll be doin' fer nae, but I don' think he meant any harm. But I'll understand if ye both don't wanna attend. I'm mad as a hornet myself, right nae. But, I'll hafta think on it. Dry yer tears, Maggie. Yer goin' ta the Blaeberry Sunday, aren't yer? Ye won' be disappointin' yer young man, would ye?"

Surprised, Maggie answered, "Ma, yer a wonder d' ye knae that? Thank yer, Ma!" She squeezed her mother joyfully.

Soon, they were talkin' about the festival that afternoon, and the mornin's events were pushed to the back of their thoughts. "I'll hafta talk wit' this boy o' yers, Maggie," James said sternly. "I canna haf' yer stayin' out all hours o' the night."

"Oh Da, the moon is full t'night an' Joey will keep me safe."

"Tha's wha' I worry about, Maggie-girl, the full moon, an' yer strong young man. Why, I 'member when I was jes' a lad an' summer was endin'. There was a bonnie lass I had m' eye on..."

"James...," Elizabeth said slowly and meaningfully. "I'm sure Maggie doesn't wanna hear about ancient times, when ye were a lad."

"Yer prob'ly right about thet, my dear. But, it does m' heart good ta knae *ye* remember it." James winked at Elizabeth, and began to whistle an old tune. Maggie, smiling with curiosity, looked back and forth between them. Elizabeth's eyes were bright with understanding, and her father winked at his wife playfully.

When they were home and the chair unloaded, Maggie went inside to get ready. Elizabeth went around back of the cottage to see how Sunday dinner was progressing. James unhitched the horse and was going into the office when Joseph rode up.

"Come in the office, Joey, m' boy," James said. Joseph dismounted and followed him. "Joseph, haf' ye thought about how Maggie will be able ta enjoy the festivities? Ye hafta be careful wit' her."

"Well sair, I will ride her upon m' horse ta gae up there 'cause there's no room fer a wagon on the road onct ye climb *Slieve*

Croob. I haf' two blankets, one fer sittin', an' one if she gits a chill. My friend hae a 'barrow he's bringin', sae I kin push her around in thet, if she wan's ta move around. I'll tak' good care o' her, sair."

"Ye *better* take care, young man. She's verra precious ta us. We knae ye mean well, but 'twould no' gae well wit' ye if she be hurt in any way, ye ken?"

"Aye, sir," Joseph mumbled with downcast eyes. "I would no' wan' her hurt, mysel', sir."

"Well, off wit' ye, an' bring her hame safe, afore it's too dark."

"Thank ye, Mister Coburn, I will," said Joseph, as he scurried clumsily from the office.

Maggie was outside sitting in her chair impatiently waiting for Joseph. As he burst from the doorway, she grinned in excitement. As was the custom for Blaeberry Sunday, he placed a bracelet of wildflowers on her wrist. She appropriately admired his handiwork, though she suspected his sister fashioned the intricate circlet for him.

James came out of the office and instructed the young man to mount his horse. James lifted Maggie up behind him, telling her to hang on tight. James and Elizabeth watched them trot away until they were out of sight.

"I'll no' be happy 'til she is hame again," said Elizabeth, her tone heavy with worry.

"Nor will I, Beth, nor will I." Together, lost in thought, they went into the cottage.

Out of sight of the cottage, Maggie begged him, "Faster, *Seosamh (Joseph)*, faster! This is wonderful!" Never had she felt such freedom! It was like she caught the wind and rode its current. The horse seemed to be one with her, the rocking motion smoothing out with greater speed. The undulating shadow beneath them and the jostling landscape around them filled her with excitement. *I would ride the wind o'er all County Down, if I could.* Her arms hugged

Joseph tightly. Her cheek felt the coarseness of his home-spun shirt and the warmth of his taut body beneath it.

"Hang on tight, Maggie! Here we gae!" Joseph urged the horse to a gallop up the ever-climbing slope, until he felt her arms shift for a tighter grip.

Maggie's senses were filled with the years of longing to rise from her chair and fly in the wind. *I could ride like this forever!* She lifted her laughing face, feeling her dark fiery hair rise, catching the turbulence as they cut through the warm summer air. To Maggie, it seemed the sun shone brighter, the wild roses smelled sweeter, and even the birds chattered jealously of her daring flight.

Joseph slowed to a trot again. "Thet's enough fer nae. If ye lose yer grip 'n fall, I'll pay a heavy price from yer father an' all o' Legananny will hate me. I'm no' lookin' fer the thrashin' *thet* would bring."

Soon, there were clutches of villagers walking up the path with them, children and adults carrying flowers and rocks, singing as they climbed, giving the horse a wide berth. The higher they climbed, the stronger the breeze, still warm, but persistent.

Maggie looked out over the Mournes to the south. She never saw them so blue nor from so high a stance. The sky was clear, and looking east, she could view the sea and the Isle of Man, sparkling in the sunlight. The mountain was barren of trees, having only low vegetation and mossy rock. In a flat area, at the very top were great mounds of jumbled rock, and among them, long-haired mountain sheep. The children, with blaeberry stains around their mouths and on their shirts, were chasing the nimble-footed sheep and yelping at each other in fun.

Joseph tethered the horse away from the center of the activity. He spread out a blanket on the ground and set Maggie in the wheelbarrow and secured the front wheel with a great stone. He plopped down beside her. From her higher stance, Maggie took everything in, watching and asking Joseph about everything she saw.

There was a bonfire started with piles of wood carried up from below. Families sat around the fire. Pots of potatoes, and separately, cabbage, leeks, and onions were all boiling in preparation of colcannon to celebrate the first fruits of harvest. When the potatoes were tender, they would be mashed with the other vegetables and spices added. Most of it would be scooped out onto a large platter, with a generous hole in the center to be filled with butter and hot milk. Family and friends would eat from the platter. The cook, who wore a fresh white apron for the occasion, would eat her portion from the kettle itself, which was her special honor. Being from the lowlands of Scotland, Maggie had heard of colcannon, but had never taken part in the meal.

"The first wild fruits were a sign o' the earth's covenant wit' her children, sae it was verra important ta gather an' share 'em wit' ever'one in the area," said Joseph, close to her ear.

"Ian brought this 'barrow fer us, an' the blaeberries. Maureen, his intended, cooked some food ta share, as well. I haf' my fiddle wrapped in the other blanket, fer the dancing. Ye kin be our queen. Which only means, we will surround ye wit' flowers an' dance around yer. Would ye be our *Tailtiu*, queen-mother of Lugh?"

"If that's all it is then, of course," said Maggie, her caution coming from the fiery sermon of the morning. From inside the blanket, he retrieved a circlet of wildflowers, fashioned by his own hand for her crown. *I see he was sure I'd be his queen. I'm sure theys others who were hopin' fer it.*

She waved as she saw several women she knew from long ago in school. They came to talk with her and she was delighted to hear the latest news of her classmates. Some of them came with their families and introduced her to husbands and children of their own. As happy as she was for them, she wished she could have been one of them, laughing and dancing with her loved ones, and carrying a child of her own. She had always thought perhaps someday, she would marry and have children, but her heart lost faith in the dream, as she saw nearly all her friends from school paired off.

The afternoon was warm, if breezy, and the children and young people seemed to dance for hours. Joseph played his fiddle with a few of the older men playing drums and fifes, keeping the music lively and cheerful. As the day drew on, and the dancers were beginning to weary, the music changed to soulful ballads and ancient airs. Maggie, sitting in the barrow festooned with flowers, wished she had some time alone with Joseph. In the gathering dusk, the breeze quickly turned cooler. It was one of the children who brought her the other blanket, not Joseph.

Maggie, looking around the crowd of celebrants, finally spotted Joseph, who caught the attention of a dark-haired girl. They seemed to be having a spirited argument off to the side of the festivities. Suddenly, bursting into tears, the girl shouted at him, then crossing her arms, she turned her back to him. To Maggie's surprise, Joseph put his arms around the crying girl, turned her to face him, and kissed her!

Shocked at this display, Maggie sat back on her perch in the wheelbarrow. and the rock at the front wheel was jostled loose. A yelp escaped her lips as the barrow began to roll down the slope toward the edge of the flatten area. No one seemed to see or hear her plight. She grabbed the sides of the weathered cart, as it careened down the hill toward a sharp drop-off. The front wheel hit a small boulder and Maggie flew through the air as the crowd above, now attentive, stared in horror. Something black covered her face, smothering her. The crowd gasped as she was plucked out of the air. She and her rescuer skidded to a stop at the edge of the precipice. The wheelbarrow continued over the edge slamming into the rocks time and again, battered into pieces.

The blackness lifted and Maggie realized it was a heavy black cloak. She looked up and she was staring into the blue eyes of Lieutenant-Colonel Hugh Annesley! On the ground at the mountain's edge, Maggie could feel his chest heaving with hers. Dizzy and frightened, she tried to make sense of what had happened to her. Joseph burst through the gathering crowd, "Maggie, wha' happened? Laird in heaven, are ye hurt?"

Slowly, deliberately, Hugh stood, lifting her in his arms. He wrapped her in his cloak and said coldly, "She will be fine, no thanks to you, Mister Heenan." Maggie could feel the tremble in the man's body against hers, as he struggled to keep his temper in check. "Maggie will take her leave now. Go, enjoy your festivities," Hugh growled in disgust. Joseph's face was red with anger, but his friends held him back. He dare not confront the man whose family owned the land he worked. Maggie was safe enough now.

The Lieutenant Colonel whistled to his horse. "Hold, boy." The horse stood still, as Hugh lifted Maggie onto the animal's back. "Hold tight to his mane, Maggie."

The aristocrat-soldier leapt up behind her and gathered her against him. Maggie's heart threatened to beat out of her chest at the closeness of her childhood hero. He looked at her, slowly smoothed her hair and flowers back from her face. Shaking with her near-disastrous adventure, Maggie put her head against his chest. Gently, he nudged his horse down the mountain path.

A few minutes later, Hugh heard her sharp intake of breath as Maggie released the coarse hair on the animal's neck. "Maggie, show me." She opened her hands to reveal the bloodied splinters caused by her grip on the weathered sides of the barrow.

"Here, let me," he said as he stopped the horse. He drew his knife from his belt and carefully, he eased the wood from her tiny hands. "I'm sorry, Maggie. I know it hurts, just a few more, dear one. We'll have to get the small ones when we have more light."

Finished with his task, he wrapped her hands in his fine silk handkerchief, drawing the ends between them to protect the open cuts. "Your mother should have some salve to put on them when we get you home."

The twilight made the distant Mournes black and there, just peeking above the ridges, was the moon climbing its way to the sky. The yellow orb grew huge as it emerged from the shadow of the mountains. "Look, Maggie," he whispered. "It's the harvest moon."

"Isn't it beautiful?"

"Not nearly as beautiful as you are, my child."

"I'm hardly a child, sir," said Maggie, turning to meet his eyes, irritated.

"No, dear, you're not," he said, and kissed her lips.

You arrogant fool! Hugh screamed in his head. *She's not some Turkish wench, or London hussy you can have your way with and go your merry way! She's entrusted to you on your honor as a gentleman. Her uncles saved your life. Is this how you repay them! You will one day be her landlord. You are a scoundrel!* He turned his head away.

Looking up at him, she kissed the familiar black patch on his face. Nestling into him, she could feel the rapid pulse in his neck. She never felt this way before. Already dizzy with new, uncharted feelings, she felt his arms tighten around her.

"Maggie, I'm sorry. I'd no right," Hugh groaned, his voice husky with emotion. *Fifteen years her senior and you're acting like a confounded puppy! No good can come of this.*

To his surprise and dismay, he sought her mouth again with a deeper hunger than he had felt in a long time. *Send me to hell, now. I have no remorse! I am not in control of my wits. Curse me as a knave. Who am I?*

Breaking away, he suddenly kneed his horse to a gallop, flying through the moonlight at breakneck speed. Maggie was paralyzed by exhilaration and fear. *What is he doing? What happened?* As they approached a crossroad, she closed her eyes and leaned into him for safety.

He slowed the horse down to a walk, then stopped. Sliding off his mount, he commanded tersely, "Maggie, straddle the horse and hold onto the saddle." When she was steady on the horse, he began to walk the horse along the narrow way. In silence, they followed the moonlit road.

He seems to be talking to himself, Maggie observed. Occasionally, he would kick a stone out of his path, or shake his bowed head. Maggie hugged herself in memory of his arms around her. *I don't care if he thinks it's wrong. I will always remember this night. Is it wrong because I'm a cripple, pretty to look at, but useless? That's what Miss Brennan said once. She thought I didn't hear, but I did.* The bitterness she felt when she heard that flooded back to her in rich, angry tears, falling unbidden down her face. She used the handkerchief to mop up her childish tears, but not before Hugh turned to see it.

Send me to hell! Now I've done it. How can I explain this, when I bring her home? I've got to make this right, somehow. Stopping again, Hugh reached up and took Maggie down from his steed. He walked over to a clump of trees and set her down carefully. He wrapped the cloak around her and sat down opposite her, out of reach.

"Maggie, I'd no right to intrude upon your courtesy. I cannot indulge my own desires with no regard for your feelings. I am not a free man. I have many obligations that go with my position. I cannot entangle myself with my family's tenants, regardless of my feelings, nor I will betray my family, my office, my post in the service, and my countrymen. When it becomes necessary, if my brother should die before me, I shall have to marry within my station and produce heirs to the barony. It is not where my heart is, it is where my duty lies. I should not have even been at the festival. I confess I wanted to see you, but I could not have foretold what would happen. I am truly sorry."

Maggie listened to his words, but a sudden spitefulness would not let him make that speech and not suffer for it. Her words were measured and hateful. "So you're just a bull put out for stud, sir? And I ..." she spat her words at him, "I am not a good enough *cow* for you?"

Hugh was shocked at her vehemence. "Maggie! Have I driven you to speak this coarsely? Even so, I deserve it. I curse myself for having hurt you so badly. I cannot undo it, but I need you to know, it is only my duty that makes this impossible. You are more than worthy and far more beautiful than any woman I have ever known. But, I cannot betray my family who gave me life, or your uncles who risked their own to save it. I have already betrayed your trust." Resigned, he said, "Come, I must take you home."

Maggie was immediately ashamed of her words. As he bent to pick her up, she pulled his face toward her and kissed him deeply. With a groan deep in his throat, he returned the kiss with equal passion. "Maggie," he said against her lips. He sat down with her and breathlessly held her to him. "We are in dire straits, my dear," he whispered with great emotion.

"I am so sorry, sir. How could I have said that to you? Please forgive me. I *do* understand your loyalties," she said. Raising her head, she continued. "What I don't understand, is your heart. My heart is not bound by what should or should not be. It is only ruled by who you are right now, here with me."

"There is nothing to forgive. You cannot say anything worse than I have already said to myself as we were walking. But, we must go home now. I must not betray your family's trust for what is in my heart. I cannot throw away my family for what is in my heart. We cannot *act on* what is in our hearts. Please, we must go home." Roughly, he picked her up again and set her astride his horse.

He walked sadly beside her now, but not wanting to release his connection completely, he recaptured her hand.

Softly, she said, "I will let you go, Hugh, but you cannot erase my memory of this night." He smiled sadly when he heard her use his given name and kissed the palm of the hand he held.

When they finally approached the cottage, he reluctantly released her hand. They looked at each other and smiled openly, one last time. He looked over her dress as she sat there and tugged on the hem to cover her exposed ankle. She shook the flowers from her tresses and retied her hair ribbon as best she could, her hands stinging, one still wrapped in the blood-stained handkerchief.

As they stopped at the cottage, the door opened. James, Elizabeth, and John rushed out to greet them. With a forced attempt to be casual, James asked why Hugh brought her home and not Joseph, belying the worry he was feeling waiting for her to come home.

"Why don't we go inside, and we'll explain," said the Lieutenant-Colonel. "We have a story to tell."

They bustled in and Hugh put Maggie in her chair. "Maggie has the beginning of the story and I'll tell the last," he said.

Her hair still wild and her dress a bit disheveled, Maggie told them about the music and dancing, being queen of the festival, and the rock slipping away from the barrow. Hugh, stopping her there, told about her rescue as if it were of no great consequence. He told Joseph he would take her home. Maggie watched his telling of the tale with a light in her eyes, Elizabeth didn't miss. *This smile on her face is a new one. There is more ta this story than this man is telling, I'll wager. She is fair smitten wit' him. Oh Laird, I was hopin' Joseph would stand up better than this. I had plans fer him, I did. If she's dreamin' o' a high n' mighty Annesley, there's bound ta be heartbreak. She'll no' look fer another an' she canna haf' him.*

"Missus Coburn, you may want to look at Maggie's hands. I did the best I could by the moonlight, but she has many smaller splinters and she needs a salve so they won't infect." He seemed reluctant, but he added, "I must be off now. It's late."

Elizabeth got up to get her healing salve and went to work on Maggie's hands. "We'll hafta wait 'til morning fer better light, though the salve may draw 'em out, by then."

"Surely, we don' haf' much ta offer, but I'd feel better, if ye stayed the night here," said James.

"I thank you kindly, but I really must go. I have an early appointment in Castlewellan tomorrow, James. As M.P., I have to make an appearance at County Cavan, and one of the men I am to meet, is the colleague with whom I will travel. The moon is bright tonight and the road is not bad this time of year, so I will fare well enough." Hugh rose from the table and bid them good night.

"Go wit' God, sair. Thank you, fer bringin' our Maggie hame tonight."

Maggie looked up and bid him good night in the calmest voice she could muster. She hoped no one would notice how his eyes softened as he looked at her. She looked away quickly, pretending to study the cuts on her hands, knowing the eyes in the room were all on her. She was glad the room was not too bright, as she felt the now familiar blush rising to her cheeks.

Chapter Seven

In the early hours of the following day, Maggie had disturbing dreams in which Hugh's face and Joey's seemed to switch back and forth in a confusing kaleidoscope of emotions. First, she was laughing with Joseph Heenan, then she was dancing with Hugh Annesley. At the same time, Joey was playing his fiddle with an evil grin on his face. When she woke, she was hugging her blanket, remembering the warmth and nearness of the lieutenant colonel.

She went through the morning hardly aware of the mundane routine she kept. The sky was filled with gray clouds, producing a soft rain that matched her melancholy mood. Near noon, the sun peeked through and so did Maggie's smile. Elizabeth kept up an endless chatter that was unlike her, waiting for Maggie to join in the conversation. Having no success in engaging her daughter, Elizabeth resorted to asking questions, hoping she would get more than one-word answers from her daughter. Her efforts proved fruitless, so she let her alone.

Hearing a knock on the office door, Elizabeth peeked out to see who was there. Joseph Heenan stood with hat in hand.

"Joseph, Mister Coburn's waitin' fer ye in the glass house out back," Elizabeth said.

The unusually serious young man nodded his head respectfully, walking around the corner of the little cottage. Elizabeth hurried to the back door of the cottage to watch him. Maggie seemed oblivious to everything, her head now bowed over a book.

Joseph saw James and John in the glass house and entered cautiously. "Ah, the young man who would take care of my daughter," said James sternly. "I wondered if I would e'er see you again."

"Mister Coburn, I came ta take my beatin', sair. I deserve no less."

"Well, Mister Heenan, suppose ye tell m' exactly wha' yer done ta deserve a beatin'."

Dropping his head to hide his confusion, a red-faced Joseph began his practiced speech. "Mister Coburn, I took my eye off her fer jes' a moment, an' next thin' I knae, the barrow was runnin' away wit' her. I was too far away ta catch her before the earl's brother got to her. Did she get hame aright, sair?"

"Tell me Joey boy, did it occur ta the block thet holds up yer hat, thet ye should've gone wit' her *an' the gentleman*, ta *see* she got hame in one piece?"

"I-I... N-no, sair, him bein' a gentleman, I thought Annesley would do her nae harm." Reflecting on that, he exclaimed, "Oh *God*, Mister Coburn, she *is* all right, isn' she?" The panic that rose in his eyes, told James he was telling the truth of it. It had never occurred to him that she could be in any danger with the nobleman.

"She was *yer* responsibility, Joseph Heenan. Yer fortunate thet Annesley *is* an honorable man an' brought her hame ta us unharmed, but no thanks ta *you*!"

"Yes, sair, if ye wish ta put hands on me, I'll no' stop ye."

"Joseph! Ye may've bin raised ta haf' yer transgressions beaten out o' yer, but I'm not the kind o' man who'd do thet ta any man. I *do* think ye owe m' daughter an apology, though. If *she* kin fergive yer, then I guess I kin. I won' be trustin' yer ta care fer her agin anytime soon, ye ken."

"Yes, sir, d' ye think, she'll e'en see me?"

"Well, she ain't blind, boy. I don' knae if she'll *wan'* ta look yer way, since ye left her ta gae hame wit' another man. Gae knock on the door an' say yer '*sorrys*'. She may be inclined ta beat yer herself, mind ye."

As Joseph, turned to walk away, James winked at John, who was having a hard time keeping his face stern during the whole exchange. The young nobleman said Maggie was never in any serious danger, so James didn't feel he had too much to be angry about. She had a few splinters, but was not injured otherwise. He *was* surprised that Joseph did not insist on taking her home, though. Perhaps there was more to the story than he understood?

Joseph stood at the door of the cottage and knocked. He thought it would be easier to take the beating, than to explain to Maggie why he was not at her side when she rode the barrow to her near destruction.

Elizabeth let him in and took the book out of Maggie's startled hands. She hadn't even noticed Joseph was there, his crumpled hat in his hands, fidgeting with its brim.

"Maggie, I am sae sorry fer las' night. I'm sorry I didn't insist on takin' yer hame m'self. I need ta talk ta you alone, Maggie. Kin ye come outside?"

"I'm not sorry ta gae hame with Lord Annesley, Joseph. I'm fine. What d' ye want?" she replied, coldly.

"Please, Maggie. Come outside."

"Maggie," Elizabeth interrupted. "I'm goin' out ta the fire. Ye kin stay in here. Joseph, let me knae when yer leavin'." Joseph nodded.

"Thank you, Mother. I'm sure he won't be long," Maggie said quite formally. Elizabeth hurried out and went in back to the glass house, burning with curiosity about Joseph's encounter with her husband.

"Nae Joseph, what d' ye wan' wit' me?" sighed the woman-child in the wheelchair.

"I wan' ye ta knae, I'm sorry fer leavin' ye alone at the gathering. Ye were talkin' ta ye friends an' I didn't think they'd leave ye all alone."

"Sae, ye found a chance ta be talkin' ta another girl. She didn't seem all thet pleased wit' ye at first, did she? But thet didn't slow yer down. There ye were, *kissin' her* in front of God an' ever'one. Was she happy, then? I missed her reaction ta yer charmin', when I went *flyin' down the hill*! If it weren' fer the Earl's brother passing through, I would no' hafta bear the embarrassment, would I? I'd be at the bottom o' the mountain, *broken like the barrow!*" Maggie was surprised at how angry she was becoming. She didn't think much of the incident after she came home with Hugh Annsley, but the more she spoke of it now, the more incensed she became.

"Maggie, you an' she haf' every right ta be put out wit' me, but I mus' tell ye the truth. I was thinkin' I was the luckiest man at the festival. Yer by far the finest lookin' girl in these hills an' any man would be honored ta take yer anywhere. I'd haf' asked ye before, if I thought ye'd haf' anythin' ta do wit' me. Nae, I've ruined it fer all o' us.

"Mary, the girl who I was arguin' wit', is a sweet enough child o' sixteen. I was flattered when she showed interest in me. I confess I was in m' cups when I took her hame from the May Fair at Castlewellan, sae I don' remember much o' thet day. I haf' no' seen her since, 'til las' night." Joseph cleared his throat, stalling to think of the words he would say.

"Maggie, me an' Mary was fussin' 'cause she said she's haf'n' my baby, an' at firs' I dinna believe her. She's bound hersel' up ta hide her belly. Nae, her family knaes she's wit' child, an' they've thrown her out. I canna believe ye will e'er fergive me, but there's nae help fer it, I *hafta* marry her. I'll do right by her, but I'm more than sorry ta be hurtin' ye in the meantime."

"Joey, I knae ye will do right by her. It's too bad ye didn't think o' thet in May. Wha's done is done, an' there's no helpin' it, nae. Marry her, but stay away from me hence. I kin fergive ye behavior o' las' night, nae I know the truth o' it, but don' ask thet I forgive yer fer *May*." Maggie's voice was as cold as Joseph had ever heard it.

"I thank yer, Maggie. It's more than I coulda hoped. I'll be gone from yer nae." Joseph's pain evident on his face, he turned and dragged his feet to the door. "Maggie, I am sae sorry."

"God gae wit' ye, Joey," Maggie whispered, humbled by his anguish. "Gae, an' be well."

He left the cottage and rode away without looking back.

Maggie sighed for the two men she adored, lost to her in a single night. They were both to marry women they didn't love, both professing their affections to her. *Laird, they say there's a plan fer each o' us. What could Ye possibly haf' in store fer me?*

Maggie never went back to the Blaeberry Sunday festival on *Slieve Croob*. She went back to her routines a little sadder that year. She heard Joseph and Mary were married and had a son. They lived with Joseph's mother and he still farmed the land. Maggie threw herself into doing the things she did well, pretending it was all she wanted.

"Margaret Jane Coburn," said James, "yer a wonder, ye are! Ye cataloged all the samples o' this crate a'ready. There must've been fifty o' 'em." From the time Maggie was still small, the cataloging fell to her neat hand and accurate detailing. Now, she took even more pride in the work, often daydreaming about the master of the arboretum as she worked.

"'Tis easy enough ta do, an' ye haf' sae much work ta do fer the spring plantin', Da. This is work I like ta do, an' one o' the few things I'm able," replied Maggie.

The Annesley driver had left the crate just a few days before and Maggie was grateful for the occupation of her mind. *The Castlewellan*, the local newspaper, reported Hugh Annesley and his mother had taken several recent trips touring the Mediterranean. As so often happened as she thought of the young nobleman, her thoughts came in his aristocratic speech, and not her colloquial tongue. *She hasn't married him off yet,* she thought with some satisfaction. *I wonder what he'll bring back from there. Most of the mountain plants and trees will survive here, but the samples from the warmer climates will probably never leave the glass houses.*

Two of the samples in the latest group had taken up the full length of an oversized crate, nearly ten feet long. Giant Sequoias, they were called, from California. In his notes, Lord Annesley said they were sent from a cousin who was visiting the United States. The pictures attached to the trees showed a man standing beside a tree trunk, easily the size of their cottage and the office combined. Another picture showed a view from far away with the same man, only a tiny dot next to the tree that stretched high into the sky. Maggie put both pictures in the book, to explain the enormous growth to be expected. *They may have to be planted directly in place at Castlewellan,* she thought. *We don' know how fast they grow and the root system is already larger than we usually allow before transplant. Perhaps he will grace us with his presence for the occasion.*

Maggie longed see Hugh again, if only for him to take possession of the catalogs she painstakingly inscribed for him. Her father gave her weekly notes on the progress of each plant in the glass house, and monthly notes on the outdoor transplanted samples.

In the spring and fall, she led a class in natural sciences for Mrs. Harden, with Hugh's blessing. The nobleman said he hoped someday local families would take some pride in the arboretum, and what better way to instill that pride in them than to teach them while they were yet children. It was his aim to one day make the arboretum a public park for all of Ulster to enjoy the flora of the world in Castlewellan.

The recent catalogs filled one side of the office, even though Lord Annesley had taken most of the nearly twelve years of work back to the castle. The seven acres designated as Maggie's land were covered last fall with hundreds of plantings in various stages of growth. Her portion was being cleared of this year's exotic plants, preparing for the new plantings in the spring. They needed to transplant the samples in Castlewellan well before the first frost, so they would survive their first winter outside the glass house. The samples stored in the glass house this summer would soon be transferred to the Castlewellan glass house. These last samples, excepting the trees, would be cared for in the Coburn glass house for the coming winter.

Maggie tried not to think long on the man who would one day ascend to be Earl of Annesley, Baron of Upper and Lower Inveigh. Such thoughts would lead her to despairing of ever finding someone of her own. She saw him once on Market Day in the autumn when he was passing by on his way to the courthouse. He did not see her, but her heart skipped as he passed by.

On those occasions when Maggie did slump into her daydreaming, Elizabeth worried about her daughter's future. One day, she and Mister Coburn would be gone. Who would care for Maggie? Elizabeth's brother-in-law John, could barely care for himself, and though Maggie could do more than anyone could have predicted, she was limited in so many ways. She was completely vulnerable outside the cottage. The August festival proved that. *She's smart in book learnin', but she canna save hersel' from a world bent on hurtin' her. Joseph was my best hope, an' he turned out ta be worthless! She'll al'ays haf' the land, but she'll need someone ta work it and protect her.*

Early in the year, Elizabeth made up her mind to look around the church on Sunday for another suitor for Maggie. *No' thet she's interested. She's still mopin' around, her mind stuck on thet lang past Blaeberry Sunday.*

One dark April night, while Elizabeth was consumed with Maggie's fate, her husband was taken.

James and John walked down to the public house on a late afternoon, while a storm was threatening. The early spring skies darkened sooner than expected, but still produced no rain. John and James had a pint or two with the local farmers, then set out for home. Though they brought a lamp, the darkness seemed to swallow its glow. Ahead on the mountain road was a band of brash young men discussing an argument with their fists. The battle over the right of way quickly escalated to sticks and stones until someone drew a knife.

John could see the silhouettes of young men in the light of an overturned lamp and began to shake with fears born of distant memories.

Taking his brother's hand, James skirted the fracas by slipping off the road to circle around them. Just as they emerged on the other side, a heavy rock sailed through the darkness and struck James on the back of his head. Paralyzed with fear, John watched the slow eerie dance before him. Arms slashing through the air, James and the lamp bounced hard on the cart-rutted road. John reached for the fallen lamp automatically to set it upright.

Suddenly, at the horror of seeing his brother's crumpled, bleeding body, John dropped to the roadbed, covered his face in his hands and howled relentlessly. Then, feeling James' hand move on his thigh, he screamed in terror.

Startled out of their rage by the banshee-like screech, the young men scattered, dissolving into the black shroud of night.

"James! You can't die! What am I s'posed ta do? Tell me wha' ta do!" A gurgle of whispers escaped James' mouth. John bent his ear close to his face to catch his words, but could not understand.

A torrential rain suddenly burst from the clouds. Cold watery sheets beating his body, John sat on the ground for a long time. Like a child with a broken doll, John held James in his arms, rocking back and forth, until he felt the warmth leave his brother's vanquished body.

Slowly, shifting James' lifeless weight to his shoulder and picking up the almost extinguished lamp, John trudged down the road toward home. Quiet now, but for the rain, he reviewed his tasks. *Take yer brother hame. T'marra, finish plantin' the 'taters an' flax, lak' James said we was gonna. Elizabeth will tell me wha' ta do afta thet.* His head was peaceful now. He knew what to do.

He could see the glow in the windows of the cottage ahead. *Elizabeth will be verra upset with me. Maggie too, I expect. I'll tell them the story, then gae ta bed. In the morning, I'll plant the 'taters in one field, the flax in t'other.*

John began to tremble. *James, wha' am I gonna tell 'em? I don' knae wha' ta say. Beth is gonna be mad at me. I din't do it, but she'll be mad, won' she, James? I'll do like ye said, James. Let 'em talk 'til they run out o' words, then tell 'em the truth an' stay calm. My heart's jumpin' already, James. I'm awful cold James, an' scairt.*

John stood at the door gathering his courage. Resigned, he kicked the bottom of the door with his rain-soaked boot. Immediately, the rude wooden door sprang open. Elizabeth, frantic with worry since the storm started, had her fears realized. At first, he looked like an apparition, John standing in the doorway, drenched with rain. There, on his shoulder, was her James, hanging like a bag of seed. It didn't make sense. She could not make her brain understand. Finally, waking from her stupor, Elizabeth pulled John into the cottage.

"Wha' happened, John? Wha's happened ta James? John! Tell me. Put him down."

John turned and dropped James' body unceremoniously on the table. His head bounced noisily and clattered on the dishes set out for the next day. Shocked, Elizabeth pushed him aside and lifted James' gray and battered head, gently. Angrily, she pushed the dishes out from under him, sending them smashing to the floor. Gently, she set his head down again. She wiped her hands frantically on her apron, as if to remove the stain of death from them. Elizabeth squeezed her eyes shut, to erase the impossible truth before her.

Maggie carefully took John's hand and spoke quietly to him. "John, kin ye tell us wha' happened?"

Startled at the touch of her hand on his, John jumped and began to cry. Between sobs, he spilled out a disjointed story of how James died. The boys fighting, the lamp, the storm, and the lifeless body of his brother, all fought for a place of importance in his tale.

"He *is* dead, isn't he? I thought he was. I haint seen death fer a while." He picked up James' hand high above the table and dropped it. Horrified at this apparent disrespect, the two women yelled in unison, "John, stop!"

John dropped to the floor, raised his arms to protect his head. Quaking, he yelled back, "S-sorry, I thought he might be..."

"Hush, John, it's all right. Take the blanket from my bed an' gae sit down by the fire. I'll make ye some tea ta help warm ye. Ye mus' be verra cold."

"Aye, Maggie. I-I'm sorry," said John contritely.

Maggie and her mother looked at each other, then watched John as he followed Maggie's orders. Remembering how the bloodless hand clunked hard on the table, Maggie clapped her hand over her mouth to stifle an incongruent urge to laugh. *Oh my Laird,*

I'm losin' my wits altogether! Poor Ma will have us both in the Belfast Asylum fer the Insane! Oh Da, wha' are we gonna do nae?

Elizabeth shook her head, sadly. She resumed clearing the table around James' body. Maggie poured tea for each of them. She and her mother sat quietly, sipping tea on either side of James' body. John was nodding off in front of the fire.

Somehow that night, they drank their tea, sent John to sleep in the office, and cleaned the body on the table. They took the blanket John had used, to cover the corpse. They managed to complete the chores they needed and took Maggie's best quilt from the trunk. *T'marra will be soon enough ta tend ta other things*, thought Elizabeth. *I can't send John ta tell the minister an' neighbors. Better send him ta the fields, keep him occupied there. I'll hafta gae myself. Perhaps, if I gae down ta Janie's cottage, her Johnny will gae 'round fer me.*

The two women lay awake, each consumed by their thoughts for a long time. Elizabeth edged over to James' side of their bed to smell his familiar scent and remember the strength of his protective arms around her. Hugging the blanket tightly, she drifted into a wary half-sleep, listening to the discomforting sounds of the dreadful night.

Maggie felt hollow. She seemed to find no position of comfort. She thrashed around, until finally, the tears of loss crept over her. Soon, she had no place to lay her head on her sodden pillow. She flipped it over and new tears filled her eyes. She tried to remain quiet as possible to allow her mother some rest. Sometime near morning, her body spent, she gave herself up to disturbing dreams of death and dying.

The next morning, Elizabeth set out for her neighbor's house. Johnny and Janie Magennis received the news of James' passing well enough, considering the suddenness of it. Mister Magennis, after offering his respects, said the local constable must be informed, owing to the nature of the death.

Her mind on the funeral and viewing, Elizabeth had not considered whether it was a murder or an accident. The loss was no greater or smaller by finding someone at fault. No one had cause to hurt James, so she simply had not considered it. Mister Magennis was right of course, although she did not welcome the further complications informing the law presented. John was hardly a reliable witness and his was the only account she had.

It was decided, Mister Magennis would fetch the constable, talk to the minister, and see to it word of James' death spread about the community. Elizabeth, Janie, and her son Steven, went to the cottage to prepare for the days ahead.

When they arrived to the Coburn home, Maggie was arranging chairs to one side of the room. She had pulled the bed curtains, laid out James' best clothing, and was struggling to stoke the morning fire from her wheel chair, nearly upsetting it.

"Maggie," admonished Elizabeth. "Thet kin wait. Ye will hurt yerself, fer sure."

"I'm fine, Mother," Maggie replied with frustration. "There's sae much ta do an' I canna leave it all ta yer."

"Well, I've brought help fer thet. We canna do much yet, 'cause the constable is comin' ta find out wha' happened. Fer nae, let's move the table ta thet wall o'er there, Steven." Elizabeth and Janie lifted at one end and the sandy-haired lad of fifteen lifted the other, the heavy table made more so by the body on it.

Janie took charge of setting up the room. "The light from thet one window should be enough. The other curtains should be lef' closed while he's here. Thet side table will hold the tea an' bites fer comp'ny. D' ye need another pot or two fer tea? I'll bring thet n' biscuits an' sweets, an' the others will no' come empty-handed. Would ye want ta be openin' the office, then?"

Elizabeth, suddenly overwhelmed with emotion, found she could not make another decision. She looked to her daughter for an answer. "Nay, I think no'," Maggie said. "Our John will need a place ta retreat an' he sleeps there."

"Fine," Janie agreed. "Mister Magennis an' a friend will stay here the night ta sit wit' the body. Elizabeth, why don't ye gae lay down fer awhile, afore my Johnny comes back. Ye too, Maggie, if yer a mind. The boy an' I will work quietly.'

"I'll be fine, Janie." Maggie's weary countenance belied her words. "I'll tidy up the office an' do some work in there." The shadows under her eyes, and the paleness of her face resembled a plaster mask in a play. The eyes that always seemed to hold an amused light had gone dull and melancholy.

"Ye will be sick if ye don' get some rest. Where's yer uncle, Maggie?" her neighbor pressed.

"I heard him gae out early this morning. Mus' be he's in the fields tryin' ta work. He needs ta stay busy. Steven, kin ye bring a pail o' breakfast ta him? I knae he hasn't eaten anythin'. A pot o' tea, yesterday's scones an' butter will do. Kin ye do thet fer me, lad?" Maggie asked. The boy nodded.

"Hae *ye* eaten, Maggie?' asked Jane, gently.

"I had some tea. I'm no' hungry nae, maybe later." Maggie's voice was barely above a whisper.

Janie moved to fill the pail for John. "Steven, see if there's a jacket fer him, too. He pro'bly took off wit'out one."

Shortly after the boy left, there was a knock on the door. Janie answered it and stepped outside. It was the constable, asking where James was laid. The neighbor invited the elderly stoop-shouldered man in, asking him not to disturb Elizabeth. He went immediately over to the corpse, examined the undressed body, especially the skull. Mechanically, Maggie repeated the story John had told them, and the constable decided it was consistent with James' injuries. Then, he asked for John.

Janie took him outside and explained that John was working in the field above the cottage. Following her directions, the constable left to talk to the only witness to the crime. *Fer all the good thet will do him*, thought Janie, *The man kin hardly put two words t'gether*. She tiptoed back into the house and looked around to see what she should do next.

Janie was glad to hear the soft snoring behind Elizabeth's bed curtain. *Maybe I can get James dressed before she wakes up, she thought. Poor James, sech a good man, an' ta die in the road like thet.* Jane tried to lift James' dead weight and decided she would need someone's strong arms to help maneuver the body. She had never tried to dress the corpse of a grown man before.

She was looking in the trunk for a good tablecloth and candlesticks, when she heard a horse and wagon outside. Janie stepped outside again to see her husband. In the bed of the wagon was a wooden coffin. "I guessed at the height, but the undertaker said 'twas pro'bly right. I sent his boy down ta the Presbyterian Church to tell Rev. Crane. I tol' 'em he didn't need ta come afore t'marra. 'Lizabeth will hafta gather her strength fer thet one." John frowned comically and continued, "The boys at the publican were mightily shocked. I sent one o' them ta Castlewellan. Should I haf' done thet? I s'pose thet coulda waited, eh?"

"Pro'bly, but it's done nae. Well, perhaps the M.P. is off to Carvan," said his wife. "Ye canna take ever'thin' out o' their hands, John. I ken yer tryin' ta help, but *sufferin' Joseph*, Johnny, they oughta haf' a say in it," said Jane, more harshly than she meant. Shaking her head, she said, "Well, ne'er mind. Ye kin help me git him dressed. Quiet, mind yer, Elizabeth's nappin'.''

Just as they moved to go back into the cottage, the constable returned. "Where's Miss Maggie, then?" he asked. Janie pointed to the office door and he went inside.

"Beggin' ye pardon, Miss Maggie," said the officer. "I need ta ask a question o' two, 'bout wha' John tol' yer las' night."

"O' course, Mister Smith," she answered softly. The old man, brushing his white hair back with his hand, seemed satisfied with the account of the story she told, admitting he didn't get much from John. When John became overly agitated, the constable decided Maggie would have better answers. "I only knae wha' John told me. He speaks the truth as he sees it, but he does have trouble wit' the telling o' it."

"Well, Miss Maggie, sometimes if a man tells the self-same story a few times, he'll tell it a wee bit diff'rent each time," said the policeman. "Sometimes, I git a little more o' wha' really happened, if I ask often enough."

"Mister Smith, if ye scare him, ye will git nothin' a'tall. His mind is delicate, an' won' abide much pushin'. He's lived through some terrible times."

"I understand thet, an' I'll tread lightly wit' him, but I hafta warn yer, they's others who won't. Sae, if I git as much as I kin nae, maybe they won' feel they hafta tak' a gae at him."

"I appreciate thet, Mister Smith. If Mother is awake, perhaps she'll talk ta ye, an' maybe the men at the pub will shed some light on the hooligans on the road las' night, too."

"Thet's my next stop, miss. Perhaps I won' hafta disturb yer mother or John, jes' yet," he said.

"Thet would be a kindness, Mister Smith," said Maggie, nodding her head.

The constable left and didn't go into the cottage, Maggie noted thankfully. *Ma has enough ta worry about t'day.* Maggie returned to the comfort of sterile numbers and Latin names that didn't require emotional response.

In the cottage, Elizabeth woke up, sad, but somewhat refreshed. She saw Janie and Johnny struggling to dress James and leant a hand. "Where's Steven?" she asked.

Janie was startled to see he was still gone. "He ne'er came back from seein' John. The constable ne'er mentioned seein' him either. Mister Magennis, maybe ye better gae see *where* he is!" She hardly dared to admit it but she was afraid of Elizabeth's John and his strange ways.

"I'm sure he's fine, but I'll jes' tak' a look a' wha's takin' him sae lang," said Mister Magennis.

He lay the body down, and hurried out the door and headed up the hill. He had barely left the dooryard, when he saw his son, leading a bloody-faced John by the hand. "Wha's happened, son?"

"Oh, John got a wee scairt when the constable left, an' banged his head wit' the spade. He's no' hurt bad, but I thought I'd better bring him hame ta Maggie. She knaes how ta talk ta him, sae he's no' too scairt. It looks a lot worse, than it is."

"That's good, son. I think she's in the office. Ye did the right thin', boy."

While the two went to see Maggie, Mister Magennis went back to the cottage to let them know what was going on. "It didn't look bad, Elizabeth. Jes' a scratch, but it was bleedin' a bit. Maggie kin tak' care o' it." To his wife, he said, "Steven's fine. He's a clever an' kind-hearted boy, Janie. Wha' a day!"

Mister Magennis took a breath and continued, "Nae, let's get this job done, afore somethin' else happens."

Together they worked James' clothing onto his body, straightened them and covered him up to his chest with the quilt. Only his head shoulders and crossed hands showed. Mister Magennis went out to the wagon and awkwardly managed to bring the coffin into the cottage. He picked up James, placed him in the wooden box on the floor. Calling for Steven's help, they lifted the coffin onto the table.

With a few more touches, James was ready for viewing.

Elizabeth sat down and let Janie make her a cup of tea. Her mind was a whirlwind at one moment, then empty of all thought the next.

In the office, Maggie saw the blood running down her uncle's face and her stomach lurched.

"Oh John, wha' hae ye done ta yersel'?" She got a box from the desk without waiting for the answer. James kept a small supply of soft linen and salve in the office so he wouldn't have to worry his women if there were a small injury while working. Maggie knew about it from cleaning the office.

"Hush, John. It's fine." Maggie soothed him, as he tried to speak. "Steven, kin ye tell me?"

"Aye, Miss Maggie, when the constable was there, he seemed ta be all right. But, the minute he left, John was all upset an' kept bangin' his head on the spade. I couldn't git ta him afore he split his forehead on it. I talked ta him quiet like ye showed me an' he settled down. I mopped him up good as I could an' brought him here." Steven's story came out all in a rush, excited that he was able to get the tall silent man down the mountain.

"Ye did well, Steven."

Steven, still agitated, bounced from one foot to the other as he spoke. "Miss Maggie, when he settled down, he let me lead him lak' a lamb down the hill. He's no' said nothin' since."

"Ye did well, Steven," she repeated. "Ye haf' a good heart. I think we'll let John rest fer nae."

Steven took John's hand and led him to the bed in the back of the office, where John lay down and curled up facing the wall. "He has bad memories ta haunt him, Steven. Losin' his brother is only one o' many. He'll ne'er be like mos', but he's good man an' a hard worker."

"Someday, I'd like ta help people lak' him, Miss Maggie. I wanna go ta school fer it. Am I foolish ta think I could do thet? Ma says I'm hopin' fer things above my lot, an' doomed ta a life o' wishin', instead o' doin' wha's possible. Is she right, Miss Maggie?"

"Steven, at yer age, ye *need* ta dream the impossible. Ye've got yer whole life ahead ta be practical. Fer nae, jes' do wha' ye kin ta fulfill the dream, study wha' ye kin an' read ever'thin', Steven.

Ye haf' the heart fer it. Who kin knae wha' God has in store fer us?" Maggie's weary voice trailed off into a sigh.

"Thank ye fer listenin' ta me, Miss Maggie. An' fer no' sayin' I'm jes' a foolish boy."

"Were it no' fer dreams, Steven, we'd still live in caves an' ne'er see progress. Let's leave the office ta John. We need ta let him rest."

"Aye, ma'am," Steven said, moving her chair away from the desk and out the door. Maggie pulled her plaid tight around her shoulders as the late April sun went behind heavy, grey, billowy clouds. *The air smells like snow*, she thought.

Janie had tea on the table when they went into cottage. Again, she tried to get Maggie to eat. To oblige her, Maggie ate a sawdust biscuit and weak tea she hardly tasted.

Elizabeth, watching her daughter, hoped she would perk up once friends started arriving. *She looks terrible, but I knew she would, losin' her da lak' thet. I'm barely hangin' on mysel', Laird. I'm no' gonna think about wha' happens t'marra, or when the neighbors stop comin' around. We'll manage somehow.*

Janie sent her men home to change their clothes for the viewing and she would go once they came back. Her daughter stayed home to make supper and bake food for the Coburns. She looked around the room to see anything out of place. The candles were lit; a receiving cloth for food was on every flat surface but the table James' coffin was on. The fire was replenished with fuel, and as many chairs as she could find were set out. Janie remembered she would have to get Mister Magennis' fiddle if he forgot it.

Elizabeth and Maggie had already donned their darkest clothing this morning. Maggie's hair was restrained into a tight bun at the nape of her neck; the familiar unruly curls banished from sight. Framing her face, the short spiral wisps escaping this confinement, only seemed to accent the severity of the style. The brilliant color of her hair was covered by the customary black funeral lace. Maggie and Elizabeth were ready to receive their guests.

The first to arrive were the old men from the pub, shuffling their feet and nodding their heads in respect as they filed past the coffin, mumbling their regrets. They sat across from the family whispering among themselves, telling stories of James, saying what a good man he was and what a tragedy it was to go out like that.

Then, the families came. Mothers and fathers patted the mourners' hands, murmuring stale phrases of sympathy. Awkward, gangly, teary-eyed young people looked soulfully at James in his rude coffin, the brevity and fragility of life beyond their ken.

Lastly, the widows and widowers filed in, weeping fresh tears for their own lost loves. Maggie and Elizabeth comforted them as well as they could. The two women had now joined the communion of *those left behind.* As the last mourners arrived, Mister Magennis' violin sang its mournful song. A flute joined in, and the room silenced its funeral murmurings. As darkness fell outside, the shadows swayed upon the walls of the cottage in a strange dance of funeral candlelight.

Maggie was barely breathing. Lightheaded from lack of nourishment and an overwhelming sadness, she began to shiver. She was vaguely aware of someone throwing a shawl over her shoulders and holding her steady. Another pushed a cup of tea under her nose and she drank. The hot tea was strong and full of honey. It scalded her tongue and throat as she swallowed. The music was further away now, outside perhaps. There came an eerie ringing in her head as she struggled to pull herself above the enveloping darkness.

Bang! Suddenly the door flew open, slamming the wall beyond it. John, disheveled and wild-eyed, filled the portal. He was wearing the same shirt from that morning, covered with dried blood. His head bandaged, John had waken from his sleep in confusion.

"I didn't knae wha' ta do!" he screamed in anguish. "James, I didn't knae wha' ta do!" John threw himself toward the coffin. He fell before he reached James and folded up on the floor. In a dream state, Maggie wheeled her chair toward the crumpled man.

"John," she said quietly in the hush of the room, holding her hand in the air to ward off the men who leapt forward. "Ye did no wrong." She pulled his wrapped head in her lap, and bent over, whispering to him as he cried. "James loved ye, dearly. Ye could do nothin' wrong, John."

The mourners, so intent in comforting Maggie and Elizabeth earlier, edged toward the doorway in fright. They jostled each other, frantic in their escape, spilling out into the night. The noise of their leaving seemed deafening. Steven and his father stayed in the room with Elizabeth, Maggie, and John. The others had all gone. "Whoo-wee, John, ye kin sure clear out a room!" said Steven, ducking as his horrified father swung his hand at him.

Irreverently amused, Maggie started to giggle slowly at first then, hysterically. "Mister Magennis, leave him be. Even Da would appreciate the humor in it!" She could barely get the words out, her mirth overtaking her. Mister Magennis stared at her in confusion, then began to laugh loudly. Elizabeth, her eyes watering in amusement, was holding her sides in spasmodic convulsions.

John looked up from his weeping, in confusion, seeing Maggie laughing, joined in.

"Come, John. Haf' a bite ta eat. Ye haf' no' eaten all day," said Elizabeth. John mopped his face on his sleeve, and rose.

"I'm *awful* hungry, Beth. Kin I haf' some o' those sweets over there?"

"John," said Elizabeth, still laughing, "Haf' what ye like, but haf' a bit o' meat first and save the sweets fer last. Mister Magennis, I haf' som'thin' a wee bit stronger fer ye tea, if ye like."

"Thank ye kindly, ma'am, would yer like me ta play som'thin' special?"

"D' ye knae, *'Scotland the Brave'*? I sae miss the songs o' Scotland."

Mister Magennis launched in a sweet rendition of the old song, and Maggie, sitting back in her chair, fell fast asleep. Elizabeth put a shawl over her lap. John sat on the floor eating cross-legged like a child with his back against the wall. Elizabeth was tired, but sitting dreamily in her chair. Steven sat vigil at James' head, nodding to his father's music. It was an eventful day. *T'marra would be yet another,* thought Elizabeth.

Chapter Eight

Maggie went to bed that night in relative peace. She catnapped until sometime in the middle of the night. She woke with a start. *The furnace! I didn't tell John ta feed the furnace for the glass house! Da al'ays did it or he told John ta do it.*

In her nightdress, she pulled herself from her bed into her chair. She wrapped her plaid around her and slowly wheeled herself to the table. Lighting the spare lamp, she held it in her teeth and wheeled herself to the door. The chair was difficult to maneuver because it had three wheels and was meant to be pushed from behind. The wheels creaked in protest, and several times Maggie thought she would upset the chair and herself. *Be careful nae, one wee step at a time.* Maggie smiled in spite of the torturous labor of exiting the doorway. *Hah! I haven't walked a step since I was five years o' age. I really mus' increase my vocabulary. Inch by inch will make the journey.* Maggie corrected herself, still smiling.

O'er the threshold an' down the wee ramp, o'er ta the office an' through the door. I hope I kin wake John, wit'out scaring the life out o' both o' us. If the furnace goes out, it'll take some time ta git it up ta temp'rature again. I canna lose those samples! I don' knae wha' Hugh will do about replacin' Da. Is he e'en aware? John's too ham-fisted ta handle the small plants and exotics. I wouldn' do thet ta him.

In the office, Maggie paused to take the lamp handle out of her sorely-tensed mouth. Setting the lamp on the table, she turned to her task. John was so peaceful and childlike in his sleep, she hated to disturb him. Tentatively, she gently poked John's shoulder. "John, please wake up. John." She rubbed the long muscles of his arm, "Please, John. Come, John." She was speaking louder now, but still afraid of scaring him. His eyes fluttered. "John! I need your help."

John stared at her, trying to make sense of what he was seeing, "Mother?"

"Nay, John. It's Maggie. I need your help. Will y' git up, please?"

John rubbed his eyes. "Maggie? It's dark out. Am I dreamin'?"

"Nay, John. I need ye ta git outa yer bed right nae an' come wit' me." She spoke sternly now, knowing he would do as she said. The tall lanky man stood, stretching the kinks out of his long body.

"James ain' here, is he, Maggie?"

"Nay, John. He's gone from us, nae. We'll miss him though, won' we?"

"I miss him terrible, Maggie."

Seeing he was about to tear up again, Maggie said quickly, "But, we haf' work ta do, John. James would wan' us ta keep the furnace goin', wouldn' he? Come, John. We hafta go out ta the glass house."

"James said, don' gae in there no more, Maggie. He made me promise. I'm too big an' clumsy."

"John," said Maggie thinking quickly, "He dinna say ye couldna gae wit' me, did he?"

"N-no, Maggie," John replied, child-like, unsure.

"An' he always said ta do as I say, dint he?"

"Yes, Maggie." John seemed satisfied with this logic, and pushed her chair to the door.

"Don' gae too fast, John. Ye hafta watch ye don' bump me inta somethin'."

"Yes, Maggie. I'll be verra careful, like James says."

Maggie sighed with relief. She knew John still talked to James, but she wasn't sure if he knew James was really dead. John talked to him as if he were in the room. *Perhaps, ta him he is.*

Finally, in front of the furnace, behind the glass house, John opened the door and started loading it with peat bricks. The embers were still alive, but had burned very low. Maggie cautioned John not to load the furnace too quickly, or he would extinguish the fire altogether. After the new fuel caught on, and more peat was added, Maggie instructed him to close the furnace door. "Thet should do it. I thank ye, John." she said.

She and John went around the front of the glass house to check its valuable contents. John held the lamp high, while Maggie checked the soil in the pots and trays. *We caught it in time*, she thought. The glass house was cooler than usual, but the temperature was starting to climb back to normal. Near the door and away from the furnace, one of the more delicate plants looked wilted, so she moved it closer to the heated pipes and hoped it would revive. There was no frost anywhere on the glass house, so Maggie thought the danger was averted in time.

"John, we kin gae back ta the cottage nae. I'll let ye git back ta sleep." Maggie yawned loudly. "Missus Harden would haf' a fit ta hear me yawn lak' thet," she said, remembering the emphasis her teacher put on good manners.

John nodded. "She wouldna lak' thet, would she, Maggie?"

"Nay, but maybe she'd fergive us, given the hour an' the work we jes' did," said Maggie. "If ye bring me inta the cottage, John, ye kin gae back ta bed. It'll be mornin' afore we knae it." Maggie pushed the cottage door open.

"There ye go, Maggie," said John, pushing her wheelchair into the middle of the room.

"Thank ye, John, ye were a wonderful help, ye were," Maggie whispered and kissed his bony, veined hand. "G'night, John, sleep well."

Exhausted from her labors, Maggie thought she would drop off to sleep quickly, but not so. Her mind was on the plants in the glass house. She reviewed each plant in the glass house in her mind until she was satisfied they all would survive. *I'd hate for him ta lose one on my account. They come from thousands o' miles away, from places I'll ne'er gae.*

Just a few hours later, the sun shining through the window woke Elizabeth, as she stretched out her hand to the side looking for James. *Will I al'ays wake, expectin' him ta be here? Will my heart al'ays ache fer him this way?*

Elizabeth dressed, and sliding her curtain aside, saw her pale, weary daughter dressed, at the table with hot tea. Maggie poured her a cup, inviting her to sit. She was mixing biscuits as she did as a child. "Ma, kin y' reach me the salt, if ye please?" The memory of the biscuits caused Elizabeth to turn her back, secretively wiping a tear from her eye.

"I imagine we'll hafta contend wit' the Reverend Mister Crane t'day. He'll haf' a donation fer this and a collection fer thet, I'm sure. I'm hopin' he won' stay lang," said Maggie with a touch of bitterness. She had continued to go to church with her mother after their first encounter, but only at her father's request. James had never returned to services, but waited in the churchyard for Elizabeth and Maggie to come out again.

"I'm hopin' he'll allow us ta bury him inside the churchyard cemetery," said Elizabeth. "He must *knae* there will be a mighty hue an' cry if he doesn't. James was baptized. Mister Crane will lose a goodly part o' his congregation, if he doesn't. He'll let us knae t'day."

"Da spent a *goodly* amount o' time in the churchyard. He oughta find his rest there." Maggie smiled weakly.

"Well, let's not decide wha' he's gonna say afore he gits here. They's more than a little work ta do until then." Elizabeth took the biscuit bowl and a few more things to get breakfast started.

While she was gone to the cook fire, Maggie set the table. She looked again at the table to see if she forgot anything, and she realized she had. She had set four places instead of three. She blinked away her sudden tears and rushed to put the extra dish away before her mother could see her blunder.

"Oh Da, do ye miss us as much as we miss ye?" said Maggie aloud, looking at the coffin against the wall. Chastising herself, she thought, *Stop, Maggie! This is jes' selfish indulgence, mopin' around like this. Ma needs ye ta be strong, no' simperin' about like a lady in waiting, flutterin' her fan! She has enough ta worry about. Dinna be another burden ta her.*

Outside, she could hear a wagon and horses pull up. She wheeled herself to the door and opening it, she was taken aback. There in the yard was the Earl's carriage and a wagon draped in black.

Out of the carriage stepped Mister Harden. "The Earl hopes you will accept his humble offering of this carriage for you, and a wagon to transport James to the church. He and his family are heartily sorry for your loss."

Done with his speech from the Earl, Thomas Harden stooped to her level to talk to her. "Maggie, I am so sorry. Your father was a good friend and we'll miss his presence greatly. I will pull the carriage and wagon around the corner of the cottage, out of the way until you need them. The drivers are yours for the funeral. You know I will do whatever you need me to do."

"Mister Harden, we haf' not seen the Reverend Mister Crane as yet, but he should be here shortly. Please convey our gratitude to the Earl for his most thoughtful and generous gesture." Maggie's speech changed from her usual colloquial speech to the very formal, perfected English, as she had been taught by Mister Harden's wife at school. She was happy to know what to say.

"Maggie, is your mother available? I would have a word with her, if possible."

"If you could gimme a minute to let her knae you are here, Mister Harden?"

"Of course I will, Maggie."

Maggie went into the cottage, and directly to the back window, where she saw her mother still outside cooking.

"Mother, please come in. Mister Harden needs to talk to yer."

"Wha', oh Laird, look at me!" said Elizabeth, tucking a stray lock into her cap. She whipped off her apron and straightened her skirts as best she could.

She came around the little house, to let Mister Harden in properly.

Immediately upon entering, Thomas Harden went to the coffin and bowed his head in prayer. Respectfully, he stepped back, turning to Elizabeth. In a quiet tone, he expressed his condolences and told her of the Earl's provision for the funeral.

Elizabeth didn't know what to say. She looked at Maggie questioningly. "Mother, I haf' told Mister Harden that it would be our honor to use the Earl's conveyances for the funeral and requested he express our gratitude to the Earl for his kindness. We will write the family a note of appreciation later.

"Why don't you sit down now Ma, and hear what Mister Harden has to say?" Turning to her dear friend, she said, "Please, Mister Harden, haf' a seat."

"Elizabeth," he said, taking her hand, "I want you to know that James' passing will not affect the contract you signed so long ago. Maggie will always be able to hold the land apportioned to her. She will also be compensated for her work on the samples for the arboretum. Lord Hugh will send a gardener to help Maggie with transplanting the samples, as often as she needs. The land apportioned to James will go to you and John. I understand your brother-in-law is able to do general farming, if he is given instruction? He knows what James had planned for the fields?"

"Yes, Thomas. I think he can. But he does haf' his limitations, ye ken. I canna predict wha' he'll do or no' do."

"For now, we can leave everything as I've outlined, if you agree. I will check on occasion to make sure everything is going as expected, and perhaps make adjustments as needed? If John cannot do the farming, then there is a chance you'll have to give up James' land, or hire someone to do it for you, but Maggie will always have her land."

"I un'erstan', I don' wan' ta disappoint the Laird, so we'll do wha' we kin. We haf' been indebted ta Laird Hugh's kindness since we left Scotland."

"Lord Hugh would say it is he, who is indebted, Elizabeth. When we determine that John can handle the farm work, Lord Annesley will draw up new papers, stating you are responsible for the land. Anything you need help with, please ask me. For now, I must go. I'll leave the drivers here. If you have the funeral another day, you can send them home. The wagon and carriage will stay here as long as you need them for the funeral. The men will return them to the castle."

As he was speaking, there was a knock on the door. "Perhaps, that is the Reverend Mister Crane now. Let me have a word with him. I'll send him in to you, presently," said Thomas, mysteriously.

Elizabeth and Maggie sat in the cottage, curiously waiting.

"Oh Laird," Elizabeth exclaimed. "Our breakfast is burning! I left it on the fire." As Elizabeth rose to go out the back door, the front door swung open and the tall, gawky minister entered.

Elizabeth plopped back down on her stool. She and Maggie watched the black-clad skeleton stride across the room to the coffin. Sonorously, he launched into a long, obsequious prayer over the body of James Coburn. *James mus' be up there somewhere laughin' a' all these fine words spoken on his behalf,* thought Elizabeth.

Finally finished, the Reverend Mister Crane sat at the small table where Elizabeth and Maggie had regained their composure. "Mister Harden says you have wagons to use for yourselves and the deceased. I suggest you have the funeral as soon as possible. There are several matters we will have to attend to first, of course."

"Go on, Reverend," said Maggie, hoping to hurry him along. "We bow to your schedule."

The solemn figure, shrouded in black, explained the usual stipend to the church, where in the churchyard the body would be buried, at what cost, and the number of men required to carry the coffin from the church to the grave.

"Ten o'clock t'marra is the soonest I could possibly accommodate you, I'm afraid." He drew himself up to his full height, as if he were expecting a confrontation about the time.

"Thank you, Reverend Crane. That will do, nicely," answered Maggie formally, as she saw her mother beginning to cringe. "We also have a few requests." She had written several notes, hymns James liked and a list of bearers.

Handing him the paper, she said, "It was kind of you to come so early. We appreciate your time is valuable, so we won't detain you. Good day, Mister Crane. Ten o'clock tomorrow, we will be at the church." The Reverend Mister Crane, stumbling over the chair leg as he rose, strode quickly to the door. He turned, pronounced a hasty benediction, and left.

"Maggie, dear, were you rude ta him?" asked Elizabeth in awe.

"Of course not, Mother. I simply reminded him how valuable his time was. How could he take exception to such a compliment?"

said Maggie, smiling. She reminded Elizabeth, "I wasn't very hungry, Ma, but you may want ta save yer pots an' pans from the fire."

"Oh! My heavens," cried Elizabeth and ran out the door.

Maggie started arranging the food on the shelves and small tables again for the afternoon visitors. She put a few scones and a meat pie in a pail for John, who had gone to the fields long before. Maggie went out to the drivers in the side yard, and told them to return at nine o'clock the following morning. She thanked them for their patience and wished them safe journey. She asked if they would go up the hill to deliver John's breakfast to him before they left and they agreed. *We will hafta gif' 'em somethin' t'marra fer their trouble. I'll git Ma ta divvy the coin among the preacher, the drivers, an' the coffin maker.* She marveled that there was so much business and trappings to burying the dead.

Elizabeth came in from rescuing her pots and pans, having to scrub the char from them. Maggie looked at her mother, her hair straggling out of her white cap, a black streak across her face, and water down the front of her apronless shift. "Ma, ye will hafta wash up an' change clothes afore they come callin' this afternoon."

"Wha'," looking down at her dress and her rough, reddened hands, Elizabeth wailed, "Oh my, what a mess, an' I've no' made breakfast, yet."

Maggie set out a plate of funeral food and sat down with her. "I sent the drivers up ta John wit' his pail, then sent them hame 'till t'marra at nine. The food is set out fer this afternoon. Ye haf' some time ta haf' a bite. I'll fix yer hair if ye like."

"God bless ye, child. I'm no' deservin' a wonder like you."

Maggie and Elizabeth prepared for the second day of mourning, with much more calm than the first day. Maggie decided if someone came with a warm dish, she would put it in the office for John to eat in peace. He was best in the fields until sundown, then in the office where it was quiet. *I hope he didn' scare the callers away.*

Maybe it's jes' as well. Ma's had about all she can take fer t'day, an' all tha's ta come t'marra.

There was a pot of water near the fire ready for boiling, cups set out, tea, milk and sugar, biscuits, scones and sweets for the afternoon, then meat pies and sandwiches for evening guests. Of course, anyone bringing meats in afternoon or light sweets in the evening would have their dish prominently placed among the usual fare. *Thank you, my dear Missus Harden,* thought Maggie, playfully putting her nose in the air. *Your rules of etiquette are not wasted on me.*

Maggie rose before the sun on the day of the funeral. She noticed her mother still sleeping and moved as quietly as possible. *We'll hafta ask John if he'll be goin' ta the funeral. He's no' likely, but we should ask, jes' th' same. Chances, are, he'll head fer the fields, doin' wha' he does best. Poor John, he still thinks this is somehow his fault.*

She made up his dinner pail, adding an extra sweet from the funeral foods. With the pail in her lap, she went outside to wait for him to come to the door. When he didn't come right away, she knocked on the office door.

"John, I haf' yer pail ta take wit' yer ta the fields. Please sit by me, so I kin tell yer about t'day. Were ye thinkin' of goin' ta the funeral fer James? If so, yer welcome an' I'll be tellin' ye wha's expected."

He slowly opened the office door. "Maggie, do I hafta? I'm no good at them thin's. I'll do wha' ye wan', mind ye. But I don' knae what'll happen. My head gits really upset."

"John, I knae ye loved James an' ye don' hafta gae. Stay in the fields an' do as James tol' ye. If ye haf' any questions, it kin wait 'til ye come hame t'night. Bring yer coat, John. Don't git cold. I'll tell Ma ye havin' a good day in the field." Maggie kissed his hand and gave him the pail of food.

"Thank yer, Maggie." John's oversized hand patted Maggie's shoulder, then he grabbed his coat from the hook just inside the door. He took off at a trot up the hill without looking back, glad for his escape from a day of too many people and not knowing what to do.

'Bye John. Say a prayer up there fer the rest o' us. James understands yer heart. She sat in the doorway watching John go up the hill. *We'll take care o' him, Da. He's a good man. Da, how are we gonna do all the thin's ye did fer us all these years?* Answering her own question, she thought, *one task at a time, one day afta the other, we'll figure it out.* Entering the cottage, Maggie looked at the coffin. *I miss ye Da. I miss yer counsel. Please, Laird, git us through this day.*

Elizabeth had risen. She had the funeral clothes for Maggie and herself hanging out in the fresh air. The little table was set for breakfast, hoping Maggie would eat something. The room was tidied up, beds made.

"Maggie? Will John be goin' wit' us?"

"Nay, Ma. He's off ta the fields. He has his dinner pail an' his coat. He'll be fine up there."

Elizabeth heaved a heavy sigh. "It's jes' as well. No sense 'n borrowin' trouble. Canna knae wha' will set him off t'day. It'll be hard enuff ta git through as it is." She looked up from her cup and said, "Maggie, eat somethin'. Ye canna live wit'out sustenance."

All too soon, it was time to leave. Somehow, they were dressed and ready to go, although Maggie didn't recall how it was accomplished. Matt and Steven, Mister and Missus Harden, and the drivers were all there. The coffin was loaded in the wagon. Her chair was lying on its side covered with a sack cloth, so it would not detract from the raised coffin. One of the drivers lifted her into the carriage and Mister Harden helped her mother into the seat next to her. Thomas and Missus Harden were facing them. Maggie was surprised that one of the drivers was Robert, the driver James had fifteen years before, when they had moved to Ulster. She hadn't recognized him the day before.

The horses moved at a slow stately pace, as was appropriate to the occasion. Maggie's mind seemed to retreat from the ritual of the funeral and was unaware of her surroundings until her chair was brought to the burial site. She looked up and saw a circle of town folk, friends and parishioners around the coffin and its waiting grave. Elizabeth stood pale and prayerful beside her. Maggie searched the faces in the crowd but could not remember them.

Finally, one face stood out in the background, the familiar black mask, the strong jaw and straight brow. His piercing blue eyes drew in hers. *Hugh is here!* His presence seemed to give back her waning strength. She returned his gaze until her chair began to move.

The service was over. Mister Harden was bringing her back to the carriage. As she reluctantly looked away from Hugh, Maggie could hardly breathe. When she looked back, she saw him mount his horse and ride away.

Steeling hersel' against yet another loss, Maggie moved devoid of emotion through the rest of her day. Her pale, translucent skin matched the cool demeanor she displayed. The dutiful daughter, the capable young woman, and the proper hostess, were perfect roles in her solemn play. Quietly, she spoke all the proper phrases of courtesy. Those who knew her bright eyes and warm smile saw them turn dim and cool. They suffered the loss of more than a good man. The sunshine that followed him had faded away.

In the long, lonely days that followed, Elizabeth watched her daughter grow ashen and thin. *She eats almost nothin'. She hardly says more than a word or two. I don't think I can bear it much longer. She's makin' herself sick wit' grief.*

"Maggie," said Elizabeth, one Monday, "I'm goin' ta Market t'day. Castlewellan will be busy an' I kin sell some o' the candles an' soap we made. I haf' spices from the fall left ta sell, too. We need ta save fer the rents. The funeral took about half wha' we saved. Yer welcome ta come wit' us, if ye wish. I kin take John wit' me. Maybe I kin git the cobbler ta re-stitch his boots."

"I hafta work on the catalogues t'day, Ma. Besides, I'd be more work than ye need, ta git me there. John kin be a help ta ye. I'll be fine here. I'll pack yer dinner, whilst ye git breakfast, then."

"Are ye sure, Maggie? Ye no' feelin' poorly, are ye? I won' be leavin' ye if ye don' feel right."

"I'm fine," said Maggie, "Nae, gae on wit' ye."

She was an apparition, pale and slight, with deep shadows under dull, lifeless eyes. Maggie's demeanor was as severe as the bun, into which she tamed her hair. She rarely smiled anymore. *I miss her laugh, her curly sunset hair an' her happy spirit,* sighed Elizabeth. *It's like she died with her Da. She's fading away ta nothin', an' I don' knae how ta bring her back.*

"Ye knae Joseph's wife, Mary, is about due. It'll be good ta haf' a baby around ta pick up our spirits. I'm gonna see if I kin git some tattin' silk ta trim a bonnet. Would ye like ta do some fancy work fer me?"

"Sure, Ma, I'll do it fer ye." Maggie had long ago forgiven Joseph for his transgression. *His children, Joseph, Anne, John, who mostly favored Mary, and Elizabeth, his youngest, nae two years, is his spittin' image, with Mary's sweet temper and dark hair. Old Missus Heenan's proudest o' the little one an' well she should be — looks jes' like her Joseph, she does.*

Seeing a hint of a smile on her face, Elizabeth pounced on the hope that Maggie would find some joy in the task. She had a fine hand at tatting and maybe the work would brighten her outlook. *She usta find joy 'n the smallest thin's. Perhaps she will again.*

Later, Maggie rolled her chair out to the dooryard to wave goodbye to her mother and uncle.

She welcomed the time alone, without her mother's worried eyes upon her. *I'll hafta make more o' an effort ta be cheerful,* she chided herself. *Wit' one less person ta worry her, she's payin' a lot more attention ta how I'm farin'. Truth be told, I'm no' my ain self. I sorely miss Da. Food tastes like wood shavings. I'm cold an' tired all the time.* Maggie shook herself to stop thinking and start working.

She went into the office and saw John's bed as rumpled as he left it that morning. She straightened the bedding as best she could, then turned to the desk. John was always careful not to touch anything on the desk. Her most recent catalogue was opened to her last entry and she read it through. She added a note from her visit to the glass house the day before. Another trunk was due to arrive soon, she knew. Hugh was home and she had not received the samples from his latest journey back to the Mediterranean. She read in the newspaper that Hugh's mother stayed in Greece with a family friend, but Lord Annesley returned early.

Her memory of Hugh at the funeral, now several weeks ago, was vague. His blue eyes followed her and his stallion galloped by her in fitful dreams. She awoke almost nightly, drenched in sweat and heart pounding relentlessly. *I'll hafta ask Ma if she's bin puttin' a 'cure' in my tea ta thicken m' blood! It is nae wonder I canna sleep!* Maggie smiled at the thought. *It's either Hugh or Ma, keepin' me from my slumber. I'm hopin' its Ma, cause I kin git her ta stop. I dinna think they's a cure fer Hugh.*

A rap on the door startled her out of her daydream. *Nae who kin thet be?* Maggie rolled herself to the door and opened it cautiously. Steel blue eyes greeted her stare.

"H-hello, Laird Annesley! Come in." Maggie stumbled over her words, rolling back into the room. "What brings you here?"

Hugh Annesley stared at Maggie, shocked at the change in her appearance. "Maggie, are you ill?" He stepped into the room, closing the door behind him. Hugh stooped down in front of her and cupped her cheek in his hand. "Maggie."

Maggie gasped at the sudden nearness of him, feeling his warm touch. The overwhelming sadness of her father's death came rushing at her. She began to cry like a heart-broken child.

Hugh saw a torrent of tears coursing down her cheeks, her mouth open in a silent scream, her outstretched arms begging for him.

Her chair toppled to the floor as he pulled her to him. He sat there on the floor holding her, the sobs wracking her frail body uncontrollably. Hugh thought his heart would burst with her sadness. Unconscious of his motion, he rocked her back and forth until the astonishing grief spasms slowly began to subside.

Obeying an untamed impulse, Hugh tugged her confined hair loose and watched her unruly curls spring to life.

"Maggie." His voice cracked with emotion. As she looked up at him, he wiped her face with his handkerchief.

As she collected her emotions, she became embarrassed at her outburst. "Oh, I am sae sorry. I've made a mess of your fine coat. What a greeting!"

He kissed her reddened nose and eyelids. "Maggie, dear," he chuckled, "My entire leg is numb."

Maggie hung her head. She tried to speak, but paroxysms of laughter shook her frame. The more she laughed, the less Hugh could control his mirth. Finally, completely spent, they stared at each other for a long time. Her lips found his and spoke the physical language they had hidden for years. He shrugged his coat off his shoulders to the floor. He struggled to stand, but to his chagrin, his benumbed leg buckled under him.

She laughed at his discomfort. "We're even now, neither one of us with a leg on which to stand."

"Maggie, you delight me." He pulled her to him again. As a thought came upon him, he abruptly let her go. "Where on earth is your mother? She must have heard this commotion."

Maggie grinned, devilishly. "She's off to Market Day with John. By the by, sir, what brings you to Legannany?"

"I came to pay my respects to your mother and I've new samples from the Mediterranean for you," he said sheepishly.

"My mother would not find you respectful today, sir." Emboldened by his passion for her earlier, she kissed him again, deeply.

Hugh thought, *I will pay dearly for this, but I am conquered. Maggie, though I journey to heaven with you today, its cost is an eternity in hell!* He returned kiss for kiss, passion for passion.

Much later, in the glass house, discussing the winter plants, incredibly, they were shy with each other.

Maggie had the latest catalogue in her lap, telling him of the progress of the plants that wintered in the glass house. She told him about waking John in the night to get the furnace up to temperature after James died. The wilted plant she moved toward the heat was doing well.

"Maggie, don't move." He hurried out to the wagon. When he came back he had a box with an accordion section attached and a stand with three legs. "Just stay where you are. Don't move. I want to take your picture. Now turn your head slightly to the left… ah, just so." All while she followed his directives, the clouds covered the sun. He made numerous adjustments, mumbling instructions to himself. She smiled at his actions.

Just then, the sun abruptly burst through the clouds, bathing her in a luminous glow. Dust particles floated around her caught by the light, and not quite believing his luck, Hugh opened the shutter. Counting to himself, he closed the shutter, telling Maggie she could break her pose.

Maggie laughed, "Do you always talk to your camera?"

"I'm afraid so. There are so many things to remember to get it right. I don't use a pocket watch with a sweep hand like my comrades do, so I have to count to make the exposure right. I won't know until I develop the plate whether the picture will be satisfactory."

"You do this for all your pictures?" she asked incredulously.

"Oh yes, but with the samples, I take them all at one time, so it goes faster. I develop them all together and make prints. It's much more efficient, than taking one picture at a time."

Maggie was quietly taking it all in. Hugh packed up his camera and brought it back to the wagon, leaving Maggie sitting among flowers and greenery. By the time he came back, she had thought of what she had to say to him. Hugh looked quizzically at the seriously pensive look on her face.

"Hugh," she began quietly, "You needn't worry about me making demands on you or your family. You have your life to live up to and I will put no burden on you. I am happy for this afternoon. As much as I love you, I know I cannot keep you," Maggie said quietly.

"Maggie." He stooped once again in front of the chair and kissed her gently. "I wish…"

She put her finger against his lips to silence him. "Don't wish, Hugh. Don't want for more," she said. "I cannot bear to dream with you and live without you. Let this day be enough. Promise me, you'll not think ill of me when I say, you must make your allegiance to the life to which you were born." Her voice threatened to fail her as it grew heavy with emotion. "Do your best with the life you were given, Hugh. Make my heart proud of this day. I'll not betray you."

"I–I don't deserve …" he whispered.

"No one deserves the love of another, Hugh. It's always a surprise, a holy gift."

"When did my Maggie become so wise, so brave, so unselfish? …and when did I become such a cursed coward?"

"It is not cowardice, my love. It is cold duty to be done. If our hearts rule our heads, the world would be in chaos for it, Hugh. People of privilege and power listen to you. Your duty lies in your office and station. We have no right to throw that duty away." Maggie suddenly stopped her impassioned plea, smiling to herself, wryly. "I didn't know 'til now, how much I'd been thinking on it. You have more to give the world out there, than I dare demand of you, Hugh.

"You'd better be off now, my love, before I lose my wits altogether. Send me your gardener to tend your plants. Go, Hugh, marry the girl your mother wants and change the world for us."

"I do this only because you ask it, Maggie. My heart says stay, but you bid me go and I will obey. I dare not let your mother see me look at you. My eyes betray my love for you. Bless you and curse you, Margaret Jane Coburn. Please, take care of yourself. Do this for me. If you need me for anything at all, send a message through Thomas Hardin or the gardener. They will always find me." Hugh brushed back her hair, kissed her forehead and stared into her welling eyes. Maggie touched his mask tenderly and turned from him.

"Go, while I can still bear it," she whispered. She rolled her chair away from him, her head bowed.

Hugh stood there transfixed, heart pounding. Then, he turned on his heel and left the glass house, closing the door without a sound.

Moments later, Maggie heard the office door open then shut and his wagon pulling away. *I've got ta clean up this face afore Ma gits home. She'll think it's because I'm grievin'. She'll be right, but not fer whom I grieve. Da, was I wrong ta send him away? Does it hafta hurt sae much?* Maggie felt James' arms around her again and found comfort in it. She could hear his voice in her head *Yer were right, Maggie, lass. He's manor-born. No' fer the likes o' us. I'd hafta gae a far, far way, ta find a better man, though.*

Maggie wheeled out to the back of the cottage to set a pot of water to boil for tea. She went inside to wash her face and comb her dark red hair. She didn't pull it back into the bun she'd been wearing since her father died. She plaited the sides and pulled it all in back with a ribbon.

The errant curls framed her face, now pink with the afternoon's emotion.

She laughed at her sudden ravenous hunger. She wondered if there would be enough food in the larder to fill her empty belly. *I hope Ma brings hame an abundance o' sausages an' apples from market or poor John will go hungry t'night.* Maggie was surprised at her happy mood, with Hugh gone, probably forever. It was if all her longings were satisfied. There was no more to want, at least for today. *Why spoil such a glorious day wit' mopin' an' sadness o'er somethin' that could ne'er be? There'll be time enuff fer thet when the next tragedy befalls, nae won't there? Ma will knae som'thin's gaein' on, fer sure, if I don' settle down,* Maggie thought smiling. *Sae, she should be happy I'm eatin' an' not weepin'.*

Between bites, Maggie set the table for tea. Just as she thought they should be home soon, Elizabeth and John pulled the wagon in front of the house. Unconsciously, Maggie straightened her skirts, wiped her mouth, and willed the foolish grin off her glowing face.

"Maggie, I sent John around back ta put the water on fer tea. Oh, it looks like yer all ready fer us. Are ye all right, dear? Ye look a wee bit flush. Ye no' been overdoin', haf' ye?"

John came in with the pot of water for tea and plunked himself down unceremoniously.

Elizabeth set the tea to brew and asked John to bring in the food and goods they brought from market.

"Joseph's Mary called fer the midwife this morning. She should haf' the baby by t'night. I bought some tattin' silk, along with a little white linen. It should be enuff fer a bonnet an' maybe a gown. It'll be a pleasant task fer ye, unless ye don' wanna. They's no ill feelin', is there? I'm sorry, I din' think… It was sae lang ago."

Elizabeth finally paused in her babbling and looked in Maggie's direction.

"Nay, Mother, no ill will. I'm glad ta do 'it. Heaven knaes, she oughta haf' somethin' new afta handin' down clothes ta four others. I wonder if this one will be a boy, or girl?"

"Old Missus Heenan was beside hersel' with the news, tellin' ever'one who'd listen. You'd think it were her first grandchild."

John brought in the packages from Market Day and dropped them noisily down on the table.

Elizabeth said, "Maggie, you be 'mother' an' I'll git the rest on the table. As a special treat, I bought some sweets." At Maggie's quizzical look, she added, "I've found a way to make the rent, so I thought we should haf' a wee treat to celebrate our good fortune."

She continued, "I went ta the castle an' spoke ta the washerwoman. Tol' her I would do ironin' fer the Annesley House. At first, she was all a twitter about how she does their laundry and she can do her ain ironin', thank ye please. But I tol' her I could do the laird's shirt collars, fine napkins an' banquet cloths with no crease. I thought I'd hafta bow ta her honor, the washerwoman, afore she'd listen. The Lady Annesley holds dinner parties fer the high 'n mightys nearly ev'ry week. Sae I tol' her I could take them hame on one Market Day an' bring back the next.

O' course, she had ta find the lady ta see if she'd pay fer it bein' done." Elizabeth paused dramatically. "An' she would! Sae, I haf' my firs' load t'day. She say Mister Harden would take it back wit' him, if she needed it sooner than Market Day. What d' ye think?"

"It's a lot o' work, but I knae ye kin do it, Ma. What about stains 'n tears? We'll jest hafta see how it gaes, won' we? I'm proud o' ye though. I knae it wasn't easy ta be askin'."

"Oh, I was tremblin' in m' shoes, I tell yer. 'Specially, when the washerwoman, Missus Bannon, was talkin' like she was sae much more m' better. But, when she went ta her housemistress, her tone wit' me changed. Later, I saw Mister Harden. He says 'hello' ta ye an' hopes yer feelin' better."

Maggie wondered if Mister Harden had anything to do with the change in the washerwoman's manner. She didn't say anything to her mother though, not wanting to spoil her mother's apparent victory.

Elizabeth chattered on about Market Day. John just ate and watched his sister-in-law's animated story, smiling on occasion as Elizabeth reported all the news of the townland to Maggie. Finally, when it looked like she was just winding down, Elizabeth asked, "Well, Maggie, did ye haf' a good day here, then?"

"Aye, Lord Annesley came to look at the books. He said he was sending a gardener to plant the winter samples up on the hill and I think he put new ones in the office. The new gardener will hafta take some o' the samples down ta Castlewellan ta the glass house there. I don't think they'll stand up ta the outdoors," said Maggie, hoping her mother wouldn't ask too many questions. She didn't think she could keep her face calm if she asked about Hugh. Her mother did not share her enthusiasm for the plants, so she was fairly sure the subject would be dropped.

He must be why her eyes are over-bright, her cheeks are bloomin' pink, an' her hair is finally down. An' she's eatin' again. Seein' Laird Hugh brought our Maggie back ta us. Don' ye dare break her heart, Laird Annesley. She's all I have an' I won' lose her to yer, for all yer charmin' ways. I won' spoil her mood by askin' o'ermuch about what went on here. I'm jes' glad ta have her back ta herself. She's much too thin, but if she keeps eatin' like t'day, she won' be fer lang.

Once she stopped worrying about Maggie's health, Elizabeth began again to worry in earnest about her daughter's welfare. *We don't haf' many who would take a wife who canna labor 'lang 'side him. They's hardly any suitable men left in Ulster, as it is. Jes' old* men, married men an' children. Both Protestant an' Cat'lic boys gang off ta America, ta seek their fortunes. More like than no', they'll find the selfsame kind o' trouble there, wit' only the journey ta show fer it.* She thought of her brothers in Canada. Will was in Nova Scotia. Peter went west from there. She had wished they would stay together, but all her wishes couldn't make it so. *Try as I might,* Elizabeth thought, *the people I care about won't stay in the neat little boxes I put them in, with all m' wishes an' worryin'.*

"John, unless yer tired, I'd like ta git started on the new samples. Kin ye help me open the crate?" asked Maggie, suddenly anxious to be working, out from her mother's peering eyes.

John lumbered up from his stool and stretched expansively. "Sure, I'll open it then gae up on the hill ta check the fields afore dark."

"Thank ye, John. If yer needin' anythin', Ma, jes' lemme knae." Together, John and Maggie went to the office. Once there, looking at the trunk in the center of the room, John said, "I thought ye said it were a crate?"

"Sorry, I wasn't payin' attention ta what it was he brought in. I kin open this, if ye'd move it o'er by the desk."

After John left, Maggie opened the trunk. The familiar smell of peaty soil and mold assaulted her nose and made her sneeze. She smiled at how giddy she felt. She put her hand in her apron pocket and found Hugh's handkerchief, still wadded up from this morning. She permitted herself a moment's reflection of the morning's interlude with Hugh. She felt heat rising to her face and her heart's rapid beat in the memory. *Get to work, Maggie. Don't torture yourself. You sent him away and it was the right thing to do.*

One by one, she entered the samples into the book. The photos were there as usual, each attached to its bag of soil with the Latin and generic name of the plant. It was always the same, but she was looking through new eyes, eyes that saw with new understanding. Her brain marveled at the sharpness of the photographs, the technique of placing chemicals on plates, and how it conveyed to her what he saw in the Mediterranean. This was Hugh's work, his passion for beauty displayed by his own hand. Smiling again, her thoughts drifted to other passions she learned about that afternoon.

Chapter Nine

"Elizabeth! Elizabeth let me in!"

Maggie heard the commotion outside the office and uncharacteristically cursed the trunk that impeded her chair. The galloping horse, the banging on the cottage door, and Joseph's panicky hollering, galvanized Maggie's determination to get to the door. Finally, the trunk moved and set her chair free, but not before she jammed her hand against the corner of the desk. When she made it to the office door, she heard, "Missus Coburn, please, wha' do ye haf' among yer cures for childbirth troubles! Mary's dying. Please help her!"

Elizabeth ran back into the cottage. "Joseph, I am no herb witch. Tell me, wha's happenin' wit' Mary! John fetch me those jars over there, no, the next ones over. Aye, put 'em in this sack. Joseph, is the midwife wit' her? Has the baby come?"

"The boy is come, but Mary won' slow her bleedin'. The midwife sent me here, fer the cures an' yer touch. *Please*, we mus' git back."

Elizabeth threw some odds 'n ends into the bag with the herbs. "Let's gae, Joseph."

They ran out the door. Joseph with the sack, mounted his horse. John threw Elizabeth up behind the impatient rider and yelled, "Hang on ta him, 'lizabeth!" The horse tore up the ground as the rider recklessly pushed him to speed and disappeared in the deepening shadows of the gloaming.

Maggie, her heart pounding, absently looked down at her hand which was beginning to sting. She had skinned her knuckles deep enough to bleed. Sighing in impotent frustration, she moved her chair to the cottage. John was inside, shaking his graying head. "She's gonna die, Maggie. Jes' like James, she's gonna die, isn't she Maggie?"

"Let's hope no', John. We won' knae 'til Ma gits back, sae let's no' borrow misfortunes. The wail o' the banshee will find us agin soon enough," said Maggie. "Afore thet comes, would ye set a bowl o' cool water on the table fer me?" John hurried to do as she asked and the cool water felt good on her injured hand.

"John," said Maggie, hoping to keep John's mind away from the death and dying he seemed to address at every turn, "D' ye think ye kin gather some taters an' onions, an' maybe a carrot or two? We'll need a pot o' water on the cook fire. I'll cut up the vegetables while ye git the water started fer me."

John applied himself to the task at hand and Maggie was satisfied that if she kept him busy, she would keep the dogs of melancholy at bay. John seemed to be in higher spirits of late, but it would only take a small setback to send him tumbling back into his former sorrowful state.

As her mother did before her, Maggie resumed humming the songs of her childhood as she prepared the evening meal. Her mother would not be back before morning.

As the darkness enveloped the heavens above her, Maggie thought of Mary slipping into final repose. Maggie shivered and prayed it would not be so. *Poor Joey, he did right by Mary in the end. I ne'er thought Joseph would take ta marriage, if forced by convention. But he carries out his duties ta his wife an' children wit'out complaint. For her part, Mary was good fer him. She genuinely cares fer him, an' from all reports, he fer her. Nae, ta haf' the new babe only at the cost o' her life seems sae unfair.* Maggie stopped her thinking abruptly. *Don' be gittin' ahead o' yersel', Maggie! Ye don' know wha's ta befall Mary. If any kin help, it'll be Ma.*

John and Maggie ate their supper in silence and said goodnight. It would be a long night, she knew. It occurred to her, she'd left the desk a mess, but it was too late to remedy that with John gone to bed. *It'll keep 'til the mornin'.* Maggie tidied up the cottage, checked the fire, and went to bed.

Sleep was still a long way off for Maggie. After tossing and turning for what seemed like half the night, she got up, slipped into her chair and resumed her tatting for the bonnet. *Joseph's child will still need a bonnet.* As she worked the threads, she prayed for the woman who took Joseph's attention on Blaeberry Sunday. *The Laird has plans we canna reason,* she thought as she dropped a thread. Quickly regaining it, she tried not to think of the omen of death it called to her. Then, she heard an owl's mournful call. *I'm gittin' like the old biddies, jumpin' at every chance ta call signs o' misfortune down on our heads. The unexpected sound o' horses hooves, birds peckin' at a window, the cry of the banshee, a black dog, dreamin' o' people who are gone afore us — we sure haf' a lot o' ways ta call death ta our door. Please Mary, don' gae. The children, the babe, an' Joseph need ye.*

After a while, Maggie grew sleepy and went back to bed. The next instant it seemed, the morning sun chased her dreams away and she was awake again. She checked the office and John was gone to the fields already. *He probably couldn't sleep either.*

Maggie busied herself with morning chores. She packed John's pail, knowing he'd come back home when he was hungry. The cottage fire was low and needed more fuel. She could handle that fire, since the peat was cut small and stored nearby. The cook fire was harder for her to handle and she hoped John remembered to replenish it. She silently thanked him when she saw the circle of stones, holding the day's supply of fuel and the pot of water placed near the edge.

As she filled her tea pot, Maggie could hear a rider approach in the front of the cottage. *It's Ma,* she thought. *She'll haf' news of Mary!*

She rounded the edge of the cottage just as the front door burst open. It was Joseph. Maggie went in, set the tea pot on the table and looked at Joseph's face. *Oh Laird, it's true.*

"Oh Maggie, she's gone!" Joseph whispered, as if he didn't believe it. With the signs of the night's strain on his face, he dropped on the stool next to her with his head hanging down almost to the table. "What am I gonna do?"

"Joseph, I'm sae sorry." Maggie put her hands on the sides of the tortured face before her, trying to understand his muffled speech. *Where's Ma? What's he doin' here wit'out her?* "Joey?"

Joseph looked at her finally. His haggard face, streaming with tears, he said, "She knew, Maggie."

"Joseph, what are ye sayin'? What are ye doin' here? Where's Ma?"

"She knew I didn't wan' her. In the beginning when I married her, she *knew*, Maggie! An' nae she's gone an' I need her back. I need ta tell her I *do* love her. I need her ta forgive me. Maggie, she's *gone!*"

"Joseph!" Maggie shook his head between her hands. "She knew thet. In the end, she knew ye loved her. Pull yersel' t'gether fer yer children an' the babe, she's dependin' on ye ta tak' care o' them an' love 'em the way she would, Joey."

"Yer Ma did all she could, Maggie. She's a' hame wit' the babe. The boy is sae sma', Maggie, sae tiny." Joseph abruptly pulled away from her, when he thought of the baby. "I've gotta gae hame,

Maggie. I shouldn't be here. I'm sorry, Maggie. I wasn't thinkin' straight." He strode to the door. Turning back to her, he said, "Fergive me, Maggie. I don't knae wha' I was thinkin'."

He was gone. Although she knew it wasn't so, it was almost like he was never there. Maggie shook her head in amazement. The days that follow would be difficult for him. She remembered the time after her father died, and her heart ached for Joseph. But mostly, her heart ached for the child Mary left behind. *How sad fer him, ta haf' lost his mother afore he knew her.*

Fresh tears of grief came over Maggie, for her father, for Mary and the child who would never know her. Her tears fell on the tatting she did the night before. *The new babe's bonnet washed in tears.* Maggie prayed for the child, wishing his life have special joys in it. She prayed for the child's father, that he share in that joy with him. She prayed too, for the other children to grow strong and protect the little one.

It was two more days before Elizabeth came home. Joseph barely stopped to let her off the wagon. She came home for her funeral clothes, for it was the day of consecration and burial for Mary.

"Who's carin' fer the babe, Ma?" asked Maggie.

"Katherine Rourke's girl, Jenny, she's jes' had a bairn three months past an' will wet-nurse the child as she kin. When she can't, we've given him watered cow's milk an' honey. He's sae wee, the babe. Jenny will stay a' Joseph's cottage with the babe fer the funeral. They'd better baptize him quick, though, fer they'll hafta tak' him ta Jenny's house soon. She canna keep comin' an' goin' from house ta house, with her ain little one ta care fer." Elizabeth kept a running commentary of news as she changed into her good clothes.

"Maggie, d' ye mind stayin' hame from the funeral? I canna git ye inta the wagon an' out agin wit'out John an' he shouldna gae a' tall. I don' mean ta hurt yer feelin's, Maggie, but I jes' canna do it."

"It'll be fine, Ma. Kin ye stop here on yer way back ta Joseph's? I'll haf' the bonnet fer the babe done by then."

"Of course, dear, it'll do them some good ta concentrate on the babe instead o' Mary, fer a brief moment, at least. The babe could be swaddled in a handkerchief, he's sae wee." Maggie's mother finally stopped her motion and speech, dropping heavily to a stool at the table. Maggie poured Elizabeth some tea and waited for the tears that marked her mother's underlying sorrow. "Oh Laird, I was doin' sae well at Joseph's. Nae, losin' yer father is all I kin think of. Well, it won' help Joseph fer me ta be mopin' about, will it then?"

"Ma, Da's passin' is still fresh. While ye give yersel' a moment ta mourn, mourn fer Mary as well. Ye had no time ta git usta one passin' an' along comes another." Maggie rubbed her mother's back and leaned her head against hers.

Maggie raised her head, and smiled wryly, "Tears are the fashion fer fine ladies this spring. Look, even the skies agree." A soft rain began to mist the windows of the cottage and drops gathered to chase each other down the panes.

"Good. Thet means John will come in from the fields an' hitch up the wagon. Take my plaid ta keep yer dry 'till ye git ta the church. I don' want yer ailin' from bein' in the rain all tha' way. Are ye goin' back ta Joseph's cottage afta the burial?"

"Nay, I'll come here, then gae back there in the mornin'. Forgive m' Laird," said Elizabeth, her eyes raised to the ceiling. "I need ta sleep in m' ain bed agin. I'll spell Missus Heenan in the mornin'.

"I've got ta git back ta my ain chores. Market Day will be here soon enough an' I haf' banquet cloths an' shirts ta do. Pray fer two days o' sunshine, Maggie. I've two long cloths wit' stains an' four fine linen shirts ta iron. Lady Annesley has two dinner parties next week an' her guests canna seem ta keep their wine off they shirt fronts." Elizabeth tipped her head sideways and pantomimed her hand raising a glass, with her little finger sticking out jauntily.

Maggie smiled at her mother's mocking, but knew how much the work she would do for the Annesleys meant to her. Even an hour late, could mean Elizabeth's dismissal and a ruined reputation. Even Hugh's intervention would not be able to save the work for her, if his mother's plans were thwarted.

At the thought of Hugh, Maggie willed her mind toward the funeral and Joseph's babe, rather than let it wander to childish fairy tales.

Tears continued in that April of 1871. James and Mary were gone to their reward and the skies seemed to cry for days.

Elizabeth despaired of getting her banquet cloths and shirts done each week. John helped her string lines of cord in the cottage and office to dry the laundry. One day of sunlight meant Elizabeth could spread the cloths and shirts in the yard to bake out the stains with lemon juice. She could not always get lemons on Market Day, however. As a last resort, she could soak them in bleach-water, rinse, and hope it would not weaken the fine fabric or leave a disagreeable smell on them.

Somehow, she always managed to get her cloths and shirts to the Annesley Castle on time, in good condition. She received more shirts as the weeks went by. Houseguests who stayed more than a week could avail themselves of Elizabeth's talents for starched and curled collars. The shirts were laid in the wagon bed flat with rolled cloths to keep the collars from crushing. Her attention to detail was appreciated by her clientele. Maggie and Elizabeth put their heads together to solve each problem as it arose and Elizabeth was able to collect the money she needed for rent by May Fair Day. Market Day on the first of May meant a grand fair, rents were paid and new deals were struck.

One of the sad aspects of the May Fair was the Work Auction. Children of poor families could be auctioned off for six months work with landowners who needed unskilled labor. There were several such children in Legannany working for families without enough children of their own. Some of them were reasonably treated, but more were not. They were rarely schooled and were poorly nourished. When their six months were up, they would be returned to their families again on the November Rent and Tax Market Day. Since the winter months required mostly house help, fewer were auctioned off at that time. It was a shameful system of child slavery with government sanction.

On the Day of May Fair, Maggie stayed at home while John and Elizabeth when to Market. Elizabeth had laundry to return, and herbs to sell. John went to carry the loads and set up the selling table for Elizabeth. It was a good day for Elizabeth. She was able to pay her rent, and anything she made that day was over and above that sum.

Joseph, his mother, and young Johnnie were there. They had nothing to sell, but they paid their rent and hoped to pick up their spirits in the festive atmosphere of the fair. The five-year old Johnnie was restless and impatient to see the games and feats-of-strength contests of the fair. Joseph was negotiating with a local blacksmith to repair a scythe blade. His mother was across the way looking at linens. Young Johnnie saw his opportunity and wandered off. He heard the commotion at the upper square and followed the enticing music. He saw some children milling about in a clump, all older than he, but not much bigger. He was a strong lad for his age and tall, looking older than his years. Young Johnnie was carrying a small parcel, so when he chanced upon the square, he was mistaken for one of the children let out for the hiring fair. He and the other children were roughly pushed into a line, and a group of farmers walked up and down, measuring the potential of each child for the labor he needed done.

Johnnie was beginning to be scared. These men didn't smile like his da. They pushed him, grabbed his ear until he hollered, so they could look in his mouth. He began to cry. The farmers laughed and scorned him for being such a baby.

Finally, an old woman with a worn, dirty apron stopped in front of him and said, "Well, he shouldn't cost much, an' he kin guard a gate, can' he? A few pence nae, an' sixteen when he's done."

"He's no' fer the takin', Missus. He's only five year an' jes' wandered in. Pick another." The woman was furious. When old crone tried to grab the child, Elizabeth raised her voice dangerously. "Pick *another* or I'll haf' the constable on ye." *Where in God's green meadow, was this boy's father? He oughta be horse-whipped, lettin' this child wander about. He's got no more sense than a goose. 'Lizabeth Heenan mus' be here somewhere, frantic wit' worryin'.*

She took the child by the hand and searched for his father in earnest. *He could be anywhere in this crowd o' rowdies.* Being shorter than those around her, Elizabeth looked for something upon which to stand. *The steps o' the courthouse would do*, she thought, and headed to the tallest building in Castlewellan.

"Missus Coburn, what's wrong?" said a male voice close to her ear. It was Lord Annesley.

"Beggin' ye pardon, Laird. I'm tryin' ta git ta the courthouse steps, so I kin find this boy's father." When Hugh looked down at the boy, then back at her questioningly, she added, "Joseph Heenan, curse him fer a fool. This poor thing was almos' auctioned off."

"Let me hold him up high and maybe he can see his father." Hugh lifted the child to his shoulders and grabbing Elizabeth's hand strode through the crowd. "I was on my way to the courthouse anyway," he said. Seeing the new justice, the crowd parted in front of him.

"There he is! There's Da!" the boy shouted happily. "I see him."

"We'll meet him at the courthouse, lad. Don't you worry," said Hugh.

"Oh Laird, look at your coat. The boy's muddy shoes are all over it. Oh Johnnie! I'm sae sorry, yer lairdship."

"I have robes to wear inside, Missus Coburn. Don't fret," he smiled. "Besides, I have a very able laundress who will take care of it, I'm sure. My guests are all a-buzz about the care she gives their shirts, Missus Coburn."

Elizabeth blushed as she reached the steps of the huge granite edifice before them. "'Tis my honor, sair," she said, feeling like a schoolgirl.

Joseph reached the top and was waiting anxiously for them. The crowd was standing below staring at the group to see how the meeting would play out. "Thank you, Laird Annesley, Elizabeth. I lost Johnnie in the crowd." Joseph's eyes flashed, making a falsehood of his gratitude. His deep red countenance was brimming with dark thoughts, obvious to everyone but his exuberant, reunited child.

Hugh just raised his hand as if to dismiss it as nothing. He handed over Joseph's son, turned on his heel and disappeared into the courthouse. Elizabeth was ready with a full barrage of angry remarks for Joseph, but she was left impotent by his swift departure. She followed after him, but the crowd quickly swallowed Joseph and his son. The pair no longer in sight, Elizabeth headed back to her table. Several townsfolk stopped to affirm how just her indignation was, and by the time she reached John, her anger subsided into doubt. *Should I haf' follered Laird Annesley inta the courthouse ta clean his coat? I hope Joseph doesn't take this shamin' out on the child! I'd lak ta take a switch ta tha' Joseph Heenan! He's bin drinkin' too!*

As Joseph strode back to where his mother was standing, the thought of Hugh Annesley rescuing the object of his responsibility yet again was gnawing at him. He was well aware of his standing with Elizabeth Coburn, whose chastising voice still rang in his head. At the memory of her heated, angry face, his own flushed hot again. As he had so many times before, he wished for a time and a place when he did not have to stand before the judgment of the mighty Hugh Annesley, born to riches, to respect, and to power. No mistake an Annesley made would ever be sae great it wouldn't be made right by his noble family's deep pockets.

I love my son! I canna help he's always runnin' off. Nae, there's the babe wha' kilt his ma. What am I suppose' ta do? A man oughta be able ta choose his life, not be stuck livin' wit' his ma all his life, he thought in self-pity. *It should haf' been me wit' Maggie, goin' off ta America, seekin' our fortune. What a life we coulda had!*

"Ma, take Johnnie and don' let him gae runnin' off agin. Take the wagon if ye wanna gae hame. I've bus'ness at the publican an' I'll be hame, when I *damned* well git there." Joseph pushed the boy roughly toward his grandmother, turned toward Castlewellan Road, and stomped away.

He didn't look back to see his mother's disapproving look or the tears coursing down the child's freckled face. His mother gathered Johnnie in her arms and shook her head at her son, now running down the road. *The Good Laird makes ye pay for ev'ry transgression, son. Don' be pilin' 'em up thinkin' ye will escape His wrath fer some o' them. Ye gotta live the life yer haf', no' the one yer dreamin'. An' thet pint yer lookin' fer will drag yer ta ruin quicker than faeries kin fly.* She turned a falsely cheerful face to her grandchild, and hoping to distract him, said, "Look, Johnnie! They've started the caber toss across the field. Let's go over there ta see, an' maybe we'll get a meat pie on the way."

Joseph stopped at the first public house he saw and ordered a pint. There were enough men there escaping the wants of their women at the fair, that he soon found a listening ear for the price of another drink.

After a long while, he fingered the dwindling coin in his pocket, bought a bottle and made his way down the road. With no food in his belly, the drink made his head swim, but the road was empty and his feet trod onward. Stumbling and swaying, he came to the door he was seeking.

Pushing it open, he was dazed and confused. "Maggie?"

"What are you doin' here?" Maggie said, sitting at the desk in the office, staring at an unsteady, frowning Joseph.

"Maggie. My wife is dead." he slurred. "She's gone."

"I knae, Joseph, Mary's gone. What're ye doin' here?" she repeated, hardly above a whisper.

"I don' knae, Maggie. I love yer, Maggie." Joseph pulled her out of her chair and they both crashed to the floor. "Oh, no, did I hurt yer, Mary? I always hurt ever'body, don' I, Mary?" He clumsily gathered her to him and kissed her hard. Maggie struggled against him, but she could find no purchase to pull away.

"Joseph! Let me gae. Yer drunk." She thought she would be sick from the stench of the alcohol on his breath. "Joseph, please!"

"Ye knae I love yer, Mary. A man's got a right ta his wife. Don't fight me. Ye knae yer love me." She struggled beneath him and felt him push her clothing out of his way. Then, she stopped fighting him. Her useless legs would not help her and her arms were not strong enough. *Soon it will be o'er. He'll gae away an' he'll ferget this e'er happened.*

When it *was* over, Joseph pushed himself up on his arms and stared drunkenly at Maggie. "Mary? Yer look strange. Wha'? I-I...." Joseph slumping over her, passed out.

Maggie saw her chance and with a great effort, rolled him off. She sat up, straightened her clothing and worked on getting herself into her chair. John's bed was lower, so she slowly pulled herself up by the bed rail. She jumped in panic as Joseph groaned, rolled to one side and began to snore softly. Maggie pulled John's blanket over him and left the office.

In the cottage, she surveyed her bruises. Between the toppled chair and Joseph's clumsy *helpfulness*, Maggie's arm and shoulder were already showing signs of red and blue mottling. The side of her head was throbbing from her fall. Maggie angrily brushed out her hair and tied it up in a tight bun. She was still shaking. Her dress torn, she pulled her plaid around her aching body, hopeful to block out the chill that seemed to pervade her very bemg. Her face white, her eyes in shadow, Maggie sat facing the door, wondering what she would say when her mother and John came home. What if Joseph woke and found her again?

Chapter Ten

Home from the fair at last, Elizabeth and John entered the cottage. Excited to tell her news, she began relaying the day's events. As her eyes adjusted to the dim light in the cottage, she saw Maggie more clearly. She stopped talking. Nothing escaped her gaze. The blue tinge at the side of her forehead, the shivering pale countenance, her hair back in the severe style of mourning, told a tale of devastation. Her torn dress, her pale, sad face, tore Elizabeth's heart.

"God save us, Maggie, wha's happened?" Elizabeth demanded. "John, stay here." Maggie didn't answer right away, trying to find the words to defuse the madness around her. John knelt by her chair and patted her hand. Looking up at her, he began to rock as he always did, when confronted with intense emotion.

"Hush, John, it will be all right. Stay here by my side. Will ye do thet fer me?" Maggie's voice was inexplicably calm. "Mother, please sit. Be still a moment. I'll tell yer.

"Joseph came ta the office. He was drunk, an' had no idea where he was. He seemed ta think I was his Mary. He's still in the office, I think. He's passed out on the floor. I'm all right, nae. I fell out o' m' chair an' bumped my head. Please haf' John take the wagon an' bring Joseph hame. It's been a lang hard day an' I dinna wan' ta discuss it, Mother."

"But, child...," Looking into Maggie's eyes, Elizabeth grew silent. Turning to her brother-in-law with a defeated sigh, she said, "John, if he's still in there, take the fool hame. Be careful ta no' ta hurt him. I'll make ye some supper fer when ye git back. Ye hear me, John? Dinna *harm* him."

"Aye, Beth. Take him hame an' don' hurt 'em." John answered. He rose, and clumsily patting Maggie on her head, he left.

"If 'twas up ta me..."

"Mother...! It's no'," Maggie said, silencing her mother's words. "No' nae, let's make supper fer John."

Tears of frustration welled up in Elizabeth's eyes, but she kept silent. She knew in a day or two, she would hear the whole story, and she vowed that she would wait until Maggie was up to it. *If I kin keep my ain mind from makin' up the story, I'll be more help ta her. God help us, I hope 'tis no' as bad as it looks.* Then, her mind went to that forbidden place and she could not stop the thought from assailing her. *What man would haf' her nae?*

Before long, John was back and supper was on the table. After a short, barely whispered grace, the three sat in silence, picking at the food on their plates.

"Mother, do ye mind cleanin' up? It's been too lang a day, an' I'd like nothin' more than ta retire." Maggie pushed herself away from the table without waiting for a reply, heading for her bed. With the curtain drawn, she removed her shift and examined her bruises. She was grateful her long sleeves hid the echoes of Joseph's grasping hands from her mother. The bluish blotches on her legs were damning evidence of his intent. *He seemed ta be thinkin' I was Mary in one moment an' me the next. He did love her. Clearly out o' his head wit' drink. I dinna think he meant ta harm either o' us, but took the liberty he thought was his.*

Twict in two months, once more than willing, once without choice. Without warning, the possible consequences of the two events she never thought she would experience, came crashing down on her. *Oh Laird, the very dream I dared ta hope may come true! Poor Mother, her ainly daughter, unwed but nae longer unbed, the maiden's ever-present dream gone awry. Will I pay the price sae many pay these days, of too few men remaining in Ulster an' too many foolish young women? Forgive me, Laird, for no' rightin' the falsehood thet Joseph stole my virgin state. What purpose would thet knowledge serve anyone?*

Maggie was swallowed in dreams of confusion and overwhelming sadness. Her head throbbed, her body ached, and her mind reeled with anxious omens. Sporadically waking, then dropping into deep, heart-pounding sleep, Maggie was grateful to the morning sun for invading her restless cyclical dreams.

Having set about their mundane chores, Elizabeth and Maggie worked around each other in a cautious dance. They did not speak, yet their motions revealed the concern and curiosity of her mother and Maggie's reticence to tell her story. John ate his breakfast silently as he usually did, took his lunch and headed off to the fields.

Later, as they cleaned up, they looked up suddenly staring at each other at the noise of a wagon pulling up. *Oh Laird, what nae!*

Elizabeth opened the door to see the Reverend Willard Crane appear. Upon his tall, stick-like figure hung his customary ill-fitting black suit, whose only relief was the white clerical collar at his scrawny vein-roped throat. Invited in, Mr. Crane stooped through the doorway and barely stood upright under the low ceiling of the room. His Bible was clenched like a shield in his bony hand against his sparrow chest. He arranged his skeletal face to a frightening smile in an unfamiliar attempt at social pleasantries. The ghoulish effect was an almost comic portrayal of pompous self-importance.

"Would ye care fer some tea, sair?" Indicating a seat at the table for him, Elizabeth nervously took a cup from the cabinet. Maggie self-consciously kept the bruised side of her face away from their visitor to avoid his curiosity and judgment.

Ignoring the stool and her offer of tea, the minister drew himself up as far as he could and began his rehearsed speech with a crackling whine. "Missus Coburn, it has come to my attention that you have not been attending Sunday services of late. Indeed, you have been seen washing clothes on the Lord's Day." As he warmed to his condemnation of her, he began to use theatrical gestures to emphasize his points. "It is written in the scriptures, madam, 'Remember the Sabbath day, to keep it holy.' You would be wise to put your house in order. You already have a crippled child, no doubt visited by the sins of the father. Now you are determined to follow his path." His whiney voice began to rise and grow louder with the power of his mission. "Madam, the devil is in your house and you must change your ways before you bring total destruction down upon it!"

Preparing to pour tea in her most prized cup, Elizabeth, in one swift motion changed her delicate grip and flung it with all her might at the minister's head. She grabbed her broom, swinging it furiously, as he warded off the blows in fear. She proceeded to beat him about the head and shoulders, screaming at him, "Yes, the devil *is* in my house and I will thank him to take his leave — NAE! With the help of the Almighty Himself, I cast thee out, Satan!"

The Presbyterian clergyman dropped his holy book in panic, and stooped to retrieve it, bringing more blows upon his back. In his haste to flee the wrath of this wild woman, he bonked his head on the lintel on his way out the door and dropped his Bible yet again. As he scrambled to rescue it once again, Elizabeth landed a few more blows, chasing him out to his wagon. She continued to beat her broom on the wagon as he endeavored to turn it around in the narrow road. His startled horse finally pulled the wagon to the right direction while the minister viciously whipped him to make his escape. With all her might, Elizabeth threw her broom after the retreating wagon. Mr. Warner turned back in fright as the missile hit the back of the wagon with a resounding thunk.

Leaving the broom in the road, Elizabeth slowly went back into the cottage. Her rage now spent, she dropped to the floor and began to cry. Maggie wheeled over to her, pulling her head into her lap and crooning softly to her. "Hush, it will be all right, Ma. Hush, nae."

Still shaking, Elizabeth ranted, "How dare he come inta my hame an' judge *me*! What's he knae o' having ta pay rent an' taxes? It was the first day o' sunshine in three hopeless weeks o' rain! Should I lose m' hame fer want o' one day o' washin'? An' ta say you're crippled 'cause yer father sinned. He don' knae yer, nor yer da! Yer an angel an' I'm glad ta haf' yer. An' yer da... The saints couldn't live up ta the goodness o' tha' man! Well, he won't hafta see the lak's o' us agin, will he, Maggie? It may be a wee bit further, but we'll tak' our churchin' ta them who kin tolerate us. Yer Da was right, Maggie! That man is ...is..." Elizabeth, sputtering, ran out of words. She began to wail again in frustration and anger.

"Hush, Ma. It's o'er nae. Ye don't hafta suffer the lak's o' him anymore. Hush." Maggie knew she had to calm her down. Elizabeth was working herself up to a full rage again and Maggie knew it would take its toll on her body. Her face was deep red, the veins in her neck were distended, and her breathing was fast and shallow. "Hush! Let it go, Ma. Ye knae he's no' worth yer trouble. Hush."

Gradually, Elizabeth's breathing slowed and deepened. She picked up her head and mopped up her face with her apron. Rising, she walked out the door to retrieve her broom. When she came back in, she said sheepishly, "He *did* look a fright, didn't he? He's gonna haf' a great lump on his head 'n the mornin', too!"

"Aye, Ma, ye did a job on him fer sure. He won' be back ta bother ye agin in a hurry." Maggie giggled and said, "He shoulda listened ta the Bible, Ma. 'For they have sown the wind, and they shall reap the whirlwind.' Yer a whirlwind he's gonna remember fer a lang while, Ma."

"Careful, dear, we don' wan' the Good Lord thinkin' we tak' His Word lightly. I dinna think I had it in me ta gae afta a man o' the cloth, though. Well, I guess yer father an' I will be t'gether in the hereafter fer sure nae. He dinna lak' thet man much, neither."

In the following days, Maggie and Elizabeth resolved to leave the Drumgooland Presbyterian Church of Cloghskelt to attend the Church of Ireland services in Ballyward, almost two miles further on rougher road. It would take them the better part of an hour, but it would be worth the longer trip, they decided. Since they could hear the tolling of the Presbyterian bells, they would be able to attend the Church of Ireland in a timely fashion, if they were ready when they heard them.

After nearly two months had passed, Maggie had to let her mother know of the events of May Fair Day. She knew she could delay no longer. *Poor Mother,* Maggie thought. *She's had sae much ta contend wit' this year. Nae her ainly child must give her news ta add ta her burden. The day I spent wit' Hugh Annesley would ne'er be mentioned as long as I draw breath though. My promise will hide in my heart as it did from the day I gave it.*

She chose the time of the telling with the utmost care. After clearing the table from tea, while the late June sun still shone over the mountains, Maggie told her mother to sit by her. John was already in the office and the women were alone in the cottage. As she told the story, Maggie was careful to assess no blame to Joseph. He probably had no idea what he had done, she said. Distraught by the loss of his wife and again at the near loss of his son, Joseph had called her Mary and took his right as her husband. Maggie was not sorry she was with child, but she would do as her mother wished. She had no desire to cause her more pain.

Elizabeth, for her part, was silent during Maggie's calm and emotionless narrative. Shocked, she kissed her daughter gently. As if sleeping, Elizabeth walked thoughtfully outside. *What should we do?* She thought. *There are certainly many young mothers unwed these days whose lovers haf' left them fer war, disease, or the riches of America. I dinna feel shame fer them, nor judge them. 'Tis the times we live in thet's ta blame. But Joseph! 'Twas no' by Maggie's choosin' thet she's come ta this. Did he knae? Could he knae? He asks me about her in polite conversation, an' I kin barely answer him. Wha' would my James do?*

Her last question answered itself. James would ask Maggie what she wanted. Joseph needed a wife, that was certain, but it's not even two months since his Mary died. As far as his drinkin' went, Missus Heenan said he hadn't had a drop since that day John brought him home. Perhaps she should ask her new clergyman, the Reverend McKay, what to do. *Laird, how kin ye let us haf' free will, when all we kin do is make an unholy mess o' it?*

As if she suddenly realized Maggie was still in the cottage, she turned on her heel and returned to her. "Maggie, ye and I will call on Reverend McKay t'marra an' see what he thinks about all this. I canna make these decisions alone an' I wan' ta do the right thin' by ye. Are ye willin' ta do this fer me?"

Maggie sighed and hung her head, then looked her mother in the eye, a weak smile on her face. "O' course I will, Ma. I knae this is no' easy fer ye. What e'er ye need me ta do, I'll be doin'." Elizabeth sat beside Maggie and held her until the sun dropped below the deepening purple Mournes.

The next morning, Elizabeth, John, and Maggie set out to the Ballyward Church of Ireland. Now that she was on her way, Elizabeth began to be fearful of her decision. Maggie watched her mother's shaky hands wringing in her lap and said, "Mother, I kin gae alone if ye wish. I dinna wan' ta visit this on ye. Ye shouldn't hafta tell the tale, when ye weren't there. It will be all right, Ma."

"Nae, child, I'll be wit' ye. Ye shouldn't hafta be alone in this. James would wan' us ta be strong. I'm sorry I'm sae nervous. I dinna wan' the Reverend McKay ta be judgin' ye."

"We dinna knae wha' he'll do, sae let's no' be judgin' *him* afore then. We'll tak' one step at a time, Ma, an' maybe 'tis no' the terrible happenstance we've been afeered it ta be."

"Yer right, Maggie, ye got a lot o' yer father in yer. Yer sensible, no' jumpin' fences afore ye git ta them. Good girl."

As the road turned down toward Ballyward and she saw the granite church loom over the tiny village, Elizabeth felt a calm come over her. She was ready for what was coming. *Of course, if it doesn't gae well, we may be runnin' out o' churches ta claim us. James must be laughin' his head right off his shoulders!* She blushed at the memory of her broom being applied to the backside of her previous clergyman.

John pulled up to the manse, just beyond the church proper. When they were all down from the wagon, John pushed Maggie's chair to the steps of the stone house and waited for Elizabeth. She mounted the steps and knocked at the door. A woman answered. The small waiflike creature with white hair and a bend in her back, introduced herself as the minister's wife. She told Elizabeth her husband was in the church. "Go right over, he's just tidying up."

Elizabeth smiled and thanked her. *So the minister 'tidies up,' does he?* She was amused to think of the distinguished Reverend McKay, with his formal robes and snow white hair, would occupy himself with housecleaning for the Lord.

The little group moved awkwardly to the imposing edifice next door. John lifted Maggie's chair up the stone steps to the landing in front of the ornately-carved arched wood doors. The building stood in sharp contrast to the simple rectangular box structure of the Presbyterian Church they had vacated just weeks before. The massive door groaned in echoed protest when Elizabeth pulled it open. "Come," she whispered to John who was struggling to wiggle the chair over the threshold.

"Hello!" The clergyman greeted them cheerfully. All three jumped as the sound reverberated in the empty sanctuary. "Come in, come in." John pushed Maggie's chair into the aisle, then backing out, bowing as he went, John fled to the outside.

"How can I help you, Missus...Coburn, is it?"

"We need to talk to you and ask your advice, Reverend McKay," Maggie said quietly in her formal speech, when her mother failed to find the words she wanted.

"Oh, I see. Well, come into this little room where we'll have some privacy." The minister took the chair handle and guided Maggie and her mother to a small antechamber. The Reverend Mister McKay pulled a chair next to Maggie for Elizabeth, then walking around a small table, was seated in a worn, but richly upholstered arm chair. "What can I do for you today?"

His quiet, friendly voice and cultured tone seemed to immediately dissipate the nervous energy Maggie and Elizabeth were building. "Mother, shall I explain?" Struck dumb by her surroundings and the elegance of the man before her, Elizabeth nodded. She marveled at her daughter's ability to speak without the country tongue she used with her family. It was as if she adopted a new language for the person with whom she spoke.

"Sir, I am unwed. On May Day, a man I have known since childhood came to my house when I was alone. He had been drinking heavily. He is still in deep mourning for his wife who died in childbirth just three months ago. This sounds uncanny, in the telling of it. He called me by my name *and* his dead wife's name. While he was calling me by his wife's name, he knocked me to the floor and took me as if I were her. When he collapsed from the drink, I escaped. He did not awake until the next morning in his own home, and as far as I know, remembers none of the event. Now, I find myself with child and in need of your counsel."

Mister McKay's face flashed through visages of pity, shock, anger, and compassion during her short unemotional speech. He opened his mouth to say something, snapping it shut again. He tried again, then stopped. Propping his elbows on the arms of his chair, he placed his fingertips together in front of his pursed lips. His heavy white eyebrows drew down and he closed his eyes as if in prayer. A study in thought for almost a full minute, slowly, just above a whisper, he finally began to speak. "Miss Coburn, how do you feel about this man?"

Maggie cocked her head as if she was not sure she heard him correctly, then answered. "He is a childhood friend and we were very close at one time. He is a good man who has suffered greatly. He is not a perpetual drunk, but he was overwhelmed by many unfortunate circumstances that day. From what I understand, he has not had a drink since."

"He has children?"

"Yes. He has four children, plus the bairn who survived her mother's passing in April. He lives with his mother, and his sister is helping out with the infant."

After a long silence, he spoke slowly. "From my point of view, you have two choices. The church will accept your decision either way. You may remain unwed and be silent, which will cause tongues to wag. You and your child would have to bear the shame of an undeclared union. Or, you could marry the man in question and help raise his orphaned children with your own. I will be glad to hold a private ceremony, owing to the recent death of his first wife.

"Only you can make this decision. If you do decide not to marry, however, I charge you to be silent about this man's indiscretion for the sake of his children and the sacred memory of his wife. It will be a difficult life, with only your family and I who know your innocence in this affair. If you have questions or other avenues of conduct you wish to discuss, please let me know. This is not a decision to be made in haste, though time is a factor, of course."

"Father McKay, if I do decide to marry, will you help me tell this man? I believe he has no idea he is responsible for this child. I appreciate your counsel. *If* I decide to marry, I will see you in one week's time. If not, I will continue to see you at Sunday service, as I will need your wisdom and advice more than ever."

The Reverend Mister McKay looked deep into her eyes. Satisfied she meant what she said, he raised his hand over Maggie and Elizabeth, intoning a prayer for spiritual guidance and benediction for them. As they were leaving the church, Maggie was surprised to find her spirit was lighter than it had been since the day she last saw Joseph.

The next week, her decision made, she sent word to Joseph, saying she needed a ride to the Church of Ireland in Ballyward. Joseph and Maggie rode to the church in silence. He had heard the gossip in the village about the Coburn women leaving their Presbyterian church, and there were many theories bandied, about as to the cause of their leaving. Soon, the story seemed to grow legs and walk upright. If anyone knew the truth of it, Maggie and Elizabeth were not saying and no one dared ask John. Joseph was not about to ask them. Elizabeth made no secret of the low regard she held for him since the incident with little Johnnie on May Fair Day.

The summer sun was bright and warm breezes teased the tops of the long waving grasses along the worn rocky road. Joseph made some effort to be pleasant, prattling on about the weather and the local news. With no response from Maggie, he too fell silent.

Although they rode the same horse, Maggie barely touched him. She stared straight ahead without offering a word to ease his curiosity. "Maggie, kin ye tell me nothin'? Wha' are we doin' here?" Joseph stopped the stocky mare and swung down to face his childhood friend. Receiving no answer, he led the horse toward the church, petulantly mumbling to himself as he carefully picked his way down the stony sloping road.

At the manse, Joseph tied the reins to the post in front of the little house, bounding up the steps to rap on the door. Again, the pastor's wife answered. This time, she invited them into the house, as if they were expected. He ran back to Maggie and entered with her in his arms. Spying a cloth-covered arm chair, he deposited his burden gently and took a seat for himself.

The imposing Reverend Mister McKay appeared, stood before Joseph, who rose and shook hands with him, nervously avoiding his perceptive eyes. The minister nodded at Maggie, noting her pallor.

"Mister Heenan, is it?" Joseph nodded. "Miss Coburn is a close friend?"

"Aye," Joseph answered cautiously and corrected himself belatedly, "Aye, sair."

"Mister Heenan, your friend spoke to me last week of a strange and unhappy tale. Miss Coburn, I understand you want me to tell this young man of the occurrence? You are certain?" At Maggie's nod, the pastor continued in a serious but not unkind voice. He revealed Maggie's story of Joseph's visit to her at the office on May Fair Day. "She has been very compassionate about your state of mind after the loss of your wife, and she said you called her Mary."

Joseph became more and more alarmed, as the realization of what this distinguished man of the cloth was saying to him.

"God save me, Maggie!" He leaped from the settee and threw himself on his knees in front of her. "You ken I'd ne'er hurt you apurpose. As God is m' witness, I thought 'twas Mary, in a dream. I didn' e'en 'member I was there. Mother told me, the day John brought me hame, I was passed out drunk. *God in heaven*, help me! I'm cursed ta hell!

"I am sae sorry, sair. I do not mean to compound my sins by cursing. *Maggie!*" Maggie put her hand on his head and smoothed his reddish locks. She raised her misted eyes to the minister to see his reaction. His demeanor remained stern, but a hint of sympathy rose in his eyes as he watched Joseph.

"Mister Heenan, Joseph, please be seated. You are here so we can make this right for Maggie." Quietly, allowing him to recover his composure, the minister told Joseph of Maggie's condition. Seated on the little couch with his elbows on shaky knees, Joseph covered his face with his hands, occasionally peeking up at Maggie as the clergyman began to ask questions.

"Do you have regard for this woman? Are you willing to safeguard her honor? Will you take responsibility for her and the child? You have a lot to account for. You are in mourning for your wife. You have five children by her. You have another child here." Each question and each pronouncement seemed to drive Joseph deeper into his desperation. Finally, Mister McKay was silent. Joseph almost wished for the hellfire and brimstone of the Presbyterian minister, instead of this calm and quietly understanding one.

"Maggie, how kin ye forgive me? How kin ye e'en look at me? I've betrayed ye twict, this time wit'out e'en knowin'. Ye ken I've loved yer since we were children. I'm in yer hands, Maggie. Wha' e'er ye wan', is yers. I'm a worthless excuse o' a man, but I'll spent m' whole life tryin' ta do right by you. Find a tree an' hang me, Maggie. Ye would do well ta be rid o' me." The tortured look on his face finally broke her silence.

Just above a whisper, she said, "Joseph. I'm not a perfect china doll that you've broken wit' your carelessness. I'll haf' ye in marriage an' take yer name fer m' child, if ye would haf' me. I don' hate yer. I don' wanna keep ye locked in a prison o' my makin', either. Ye do haf' a good heart. I've always dreamt o' havin' a husband an' children. I ne'er thought I would be able."

"Maggie, how kin yer haf' me nae…?"

Mercifully, the Reverend Mister McKay interrupted Joseph's impassioned self-flagellation. "It is one of the blessed surprises in life that one person loves another through no merit of his own. We love each other in spite of our faults, not because of our virtues. Why on earth my wife puts up with me, I'll never know." With that, the distinguished minister smiled and stood.

"You two have a great deal to discuss. I will be happy to talk to you again after services on Sunday, if you wish. Do not wait too long before you marry. You must avoid scandal to your other children, as well as to this one." He raised his hand over their heads and offered a prayer of guidance for the couple. Silently, he strode out of the room, leaving Maggie and Joseph alone in the manse's parlor.

Joseph lifted Maggie in his arms once more and walked to the door. Missus McKay seemed to appear out of nowhere, opened the portal and said, "Goodbye. God be with you."

On the way home, Joseph sat astride the horse behind Maggie and wondered at the providence that brought him the woman he had always loved. He held her tight against him as she leaned against the rough linen shirt on his chest. His head and heart were full of the myriad of emotions of the last two months. *The village will ne'er run out o' things to talk about, fer certain. Poor mother! I break her heart daily, just tryin' ta be the man she wants me ta be, an' failin' at ev'ry turn.*

Lost in her own thoughts, Maggie was relieved at the prospect of having a name for her child. She marveled at the thought of having a family. She never dared hope for a family of her own. *Am I doin' the right thin'? Kin I knae the right thin' ta do? 'Tis the best I kin do in the circumstances an' will bring me the most o' what I want: a home, a husband an' a family.* A fleeting thought of Hugh wafted through her head. *This has naught ta do wit' my promise. I must do what is right fer me an' the bairn. What haf' I done? Haf' I veered off the right path ainly ta fall off a clift? I think it'll be fine one minute, then calamitous the next! Hang it! What comes, will come, an' damn these second thoughts! Don't be tearin' down bridges you've no' arrived at yet. Mother won' e'er be happy thet Joseph's my husband, but she kin be satisfied the bairn will haf' a name.*

"Joey, we should tell yer Ma straight away. It's a hard tale ta tell as it is. My Ma a'ready knaes the truth. I've kept nothin' from her."

"*My* Ma is like ta take a switch ta both o' us. You'll bear the brunt of it, ye ken. She thinks all the world is afta her ainly son. She won't be happy on my account neither, fer she's sure I'll be a burden ta her all her life." For the first time in a very long time, Maggie saw the Joseph of the old days, charming and full of wry humor. "She'll be worried about th' neighbors' tongues waggin', but I've always given them plenty o' talk ta spare, haf'n' I?"

Sudden, deep emotion overtaking him, he said hoarsely, "I would haf' married ye anyways, ye ken, in the proper time, but as soon as ye would haf' me — *if* ye would haf' me. I canna imagine how ye kin forgive me, Maggie. Did I hurt yer badly? It musta been terrible fer yer. I'd dreamed thet one day... but knae, I'd ne'er hurt ye apurpose."

"Hush, I knae. Ye were out o' yer head. Truthfully, I was sad, an' scairt, an' jealous, ye were beddin' Mary thet day, no' me. Ye loved her too, Joey, an' ye did right by her."

Joseph buried his head in her neck and held her tighter as they rode along. "Joseph. Someone's comin'." There at the crossroads, a lone rider approached. Lord Hugh Annesley, in his courtly finery, riding a fine black stallion, tipped his hat, his questioning eyes boring straight into Maggie's. She nodded, as did Joseph and they passed by without a word. Hugh stopped his horse to stare back at them. A strange combination of anger, sadness, wanting, tenderness, and jealously were all vying for dominance on his face. *You have no claim on her, Lord Scoundrel. Go your way. She should have someone who can care for her, give her a life. But, oh Maggie, — him?* Viciously kicking his horse into action, Hugh tore down the mountain road trying to outrun the demons crowding his head.

Joseph looked back at the sound of beating hooves and pondered the lord's speedy retreat. Maggie began prattling on about talking to his mother to draw Joseph's attention away from Hugh's curious behavior. It was easy to distract him. His earlier encounter with Hugh was a distant memory, easily dismissed. Not so for Maggie. She pushed her thoughts of Hugh away as well as she could. *My future an' my child's is wit' Joseph.*

Arriving at Joseph's home, young Joseph ran out of the cottage to greet them. "Hello, Miss Coburn. Did you come ta visit?" The boy grabbed his shirt and hopped up and down, barely able to contain himself. "Where's your chair, Miss Coburn? How come…?"

"Joseph, give her a chanct! Ye ask sae many questions. Let's go inta the cottage an' let her sit awhile." He laughed to see his son so excited. To Maggie he whispered, "I hope he's this happy when we make this a more permanent stay."

"From yer mouth ta God's ears." she whispered back.

Joseph's mother appeared at the door holding a wailing baby. "Well, come in, come in. I'm afraid the house is a sight, wha' with this wild banshee an' those frogs o' yern hoppin' about," she said good-naturedly.

Joseph deposited Maggie onto the nearest stool, and turned to retrieve his son. "He has a pair o' lungs thet would put a banshee ta shame, don' he?"

"Let me try, Joey." Joseph set the screaming child in Maggie's arms and with a few crooning notes, the baby stopped and listened. "Hush nae, what's all this noise about, little one?"

Joseph and his mother looked at each other in amazement. The baby raised his tiny hand and touched Maggie's dark auburn hair. His fingers wound around the locks delightedly. Maggie touched her finger to the baby's nose and he responded with a lop-sided smile.

"Ooh look. She's got the touch." Joseph's mother smiled.

"Thet she does, Ma. Thet she does. Young Joseph, gae outside an' play fer a while, an' tak your sisters wit' ye. See if Johnnie's out there. Laird knows wha' he's up ta."

The little round woman called after the boy. "Stay close ta the cottage, we'll be havin' tea, soon. I don't wanna hafta gae huntin' fer ye."

"Nae, wha's this all about?" Joseph's mother face migrated from cheerful to fearful suspicion as she turned from the door to Maggie and Joseph. "Wha's happened nae?"

Joseph's story poured out quickly, without glossing over his guilt or responsibility in it. Maggie admired his forthrightness and honesty in talking to his mother. She, for her part, reserved her words until his story was done. His mother looked down at the calloused hands in her lap, up at her son, then at Maggie. "So it's settled, then? Does yer Ma knae? How does she feel about this son o' mine, wha's more trouble than he's worth?" she said, casting him and angry scowl. "She wasn' too happy about him on May Fair Day *afore* he went ta yer house. And yer content ta *marry* him?"

Maggie took one question at a time and answered Joseph's mother as honestly as she could. It was easy to see from where her son inherited his mercurial temperament.

Missus Heenan said with a long-suffering sigh, "My Joseph would jump in a pool o' mud an' pop up wit' a clean white shirt an' a rose in his teeth. Mary was a lovely girl, if too young, an' yer are too, I expect. When is this belated but all too soon union ta be?"

"I'll hafta talk ta Ma on it, Missus Heenan. We'll talk ta Mister McKay afta services Sunday next ta make arrangements," Maggie replied. "It's no' the way any o' us would haf' planned, but it'll work out." She looked at the now-sleeping baby and marveled at how wonderful it felt to hold him. *It'll work out. It's the best solution, isn't it?*

Chapter Eleven

Sunday services seemed an eternity for Maggie. She was anxious to speak to Father McKay about the wedding. Joseph sat next to her, wearing a silly grin every time he looked at her. He had been over-attentive all week and she tired of his solicitous behavior. She was embarrassed that he could abandon his wife's memory so casually. *But then, he doesn't really knae how he should conduct himself, I s'pose. Ever'thin's piled atop him. Maybe you should show yerself a little happy 'bout the prospect o' gittin' married.* Maggie shook her head, again wondering if she was doing the right thing. *All this folderol will be gone an' fergotten afta the bairn's born. I hope. I'm surprised at Ma, acceptin' this. She ne'er liked or respected Joseph.*

Finally, the distinguished minister pronounced the benediction. Maggie and Joseph waited in the sanctuary while Elizabeth and the rest of the congregation filed out. The Reverend Mister McKay, having greeted his parishioners, came back into the open vaulted room. His soft Irish echoed through the room, "Well, children. What shall we do?" he asked cheerfully.

"We would like to be married privately, on a Sunday afternoon, as soon as allowed, if that meets with your approval," said Maggie.

"You'll have to register your intent immediately with Mister Rowan in Ballyward, Monday morning, if possible. You are required to do so three months before you can be married. I will pronounce the banns starting, let's see, September 20th and you can be married at the earliest Sunday, October 10th. You may still be married on Sunday, if it's a private ceremony you're wishin'."

"We'll git back ta yer after our intents are regist'ed, Mister McKay," Joseph said relieved. "Thank yer, sair." He began to whisk Maggie away in her chair, when she stopped him.

"Mister McKay, we were planning a very small party at the house after the wedding if y' think thet's appropriate. We'd be honored if you an' Missus McKay would join us."

"A party is always appropriate to celebrate a wedding, no matter the circumstances. The Lord blesses the union of all those who are married in His Name. We are honored by your invitation."

Joseph nodded his head toward the minister and proceeded to make his retreat pushing Maggie's chair down the aisle. Once outside and ensconced in the wagon, Joseph whispered sarcastically in her ear, "Well, thet'll put some excitement in the festivities, *won'* it! Mister McKay an' his wee woman should liven up the party."

"Joey, after all he's doin' fer us, ye should be grateful. Besides, it's a party, not a publican brawl!"

"Ye will haf' what ye want, Maggie, don' ye be worryin' about thet. Can't I grouse a bit in the meanwhile?" Joseph grinned his charming best. "Ye ken I love yer, as I al'ays haf' done. I'm doomed ta be trailin' yer footsteps an' doin' yer biddin' fer all time."

In spite of herself, she chuckled at his mocking speech. "Make sure ye remember thet, Joseph Heenan." She stopped in mid-laugh, blushing at the shame she felt at forgetting Mary for a moment.

"Wha' is it, Love? What makes you sae sad, plannin' yer weddin' day?"

"It's Mary, Joseph. I feel sae badly. She's gone from us sae short a time, an' we gae on as if she were ne'er here." Maggie willed her eyes to stop their filling, brimming with burning tears.

"Maggie," Joseph said softly, "Mary is lookin' down on us, laughin' at me. Her husband was an' is always in trouble, always doin' the wrong thin'. She knaes I need someone ta care fer me. Laird knaes, my boys are the same. We need ye, Maggie, an' the bairn does too, an' soon enough another. If she loved me at all, Mary knaes how los' I am wit'out her. I need yer terrible, Maggie, but I love yer e'en more."

Maggie looked at Joseph with new wonder. It was as if he knew exactly what she needed to hear. She turned and kissed his sleeve, hugging the arm on which she was leaning. *This may work, then. It may jes' be the best thin' fer all o' us.* She chanced another peek at her future husband's face, and smiled. Joseph looked straight ahead, whistling a long-forgotten tune, already lost in his own thoughts.

Elizabeth watched them as they emerged from the church and saw her daughter kiss Joseph's arm. *Heaven help us, perhaps she is smitten. Better this, than his honor, Laird Annesley, fer sure. There's hope in this marriage if Maggie is fer it. I wouldna haf' given t'pence for the prospects a week ago, but if she's resigned ta it, they haf' a chance, I 'spose. Ah, Maggie, wha' will I do wit'out ye?* Elizabeth caught herself up short. *Nae don' ye be goin' on about yer ain self, Elizabeth Coburn! Yer gotta do wha's best fer Maggie. Ye will miss her as much as ye miss James, but ye no' the one who needs her. The bairn needs a name, an' Joseph's the one available an' responsible fer it, ain' he? Stay out o' it!* Torn between her feelings of loss and what was right for Maggie and the bairn, she sighed. *Are yer verra sure, Maggie?*

The two were at the wagon now and Elizabeth's argument with herself dissolved into the practical chores of getting home again. Joseph carefully placed Maggie atop the wagon, set her chair securely in the back and mounted his horse. John glared straight ahead, resentful of the young interloper doing his job. The brooding man flicked the reins, urging the horse to the rocky slope homeward.

Joseph rode as close as he dared to the wagon. Bending down, he squeezed Maggie's outstretched hand before he turned at the crossroads. John turned toward home, content that Joseph was no longer with them. *Do they think I don' know wha' happened thet night?* He thought darkly, remembering Maggie's shaking, bruised body, the disarray in the office, and Joseph drunk on the floor. *Don' hurt him, John, they say. Dinna mean I had ta be gentle wit' him. James wouldna haf' been too careful wit' him neither. I didn't hit him, but he sure fell off my horse a time or two on the way hame, didn't he?* John smiled with satisfaction at the memory. *Too bad he didn't break his neck while he was at it, the bastard. Ach, shouldn't say thet, Maggie would be upset ta hear me, e'en if it's true. An' she's marryin' him!* John shook his head in disbelief. *If he hurts her agin, he's in fer it fer sure. When John Coburn's done punishin' him, he'll be no good ta anybody.*

Maggie saw the war being waged on John's flushed angry face. The veins in his neck stood out signaling the rage he usually kept deep within. "John," she said gently. "When we get hame, would you go up on the hill and fetch me some blaeberries? I think we should haf' some blaeberry biscuits fer tea, don' yer?" *Maybe while he's up there it'll calm his spirits a bit.*

"Yes, Maggie," he mumbled. "It's early, but it's been warm. They'll take a bit o' sugar ta sweeten. They'll be sweeter nearer August." His voice became clearer and more cheerful as he warmed to his subject.

God bless his love o' the land, thought Maggie.

Home again, Maggie told her mother what the minister said. They chatted about the chores they needed to accomplish before the October date. Elizabeth was grateful to have a plan and a day by which everything would have to be done. "The day will be here afore y' knae it," she said cheerfully.

"I'm hopin' I'll no' be big as this room. I ken it'll be no secret, but all this is enough ta keep the village tongue-waggers busy, wit'out pushin' m' belly at them, too."

The two months that followed were full of the business of getting ready for the wedding, the party, and the move to Joseph's cottage. Maggie and Elizabeth invited Missus Heenan and the children to tea. They worked on the dress Maggie was to wear for the big day. Joseph came around to bring chairs and linens for the party. Maggie was careful to send John on various errands in the fields when she knew Joseph would be at the cottage.

Somehow, Maggie found time to keep up the record-keeping and care for plants in the greenhouse. Tom Reilly, the new gardener for the Castlewellan estates, appreciated her accuracy and attention to detail, which made his load lighter. Hugh's more tender plant specimens from the greenhouse, had been transported to the castle, and the gardener brought some of the less hardy plants, in from the fields, to the shelter of the greenhouse for the winter.

Mister Reilly was an affable man who loved to tell the latest castle gossip. Lord Annesley, she learned, was engaged to a cousin from London and would be married in the spring. Strange, Maggie thought, she had heard Laird William had been ill, and he was finally marrying after all these years? *Better late than ne'er, I guess.* She had received two new trunks of specimens in early July from Canada. It was a hunting trip, she surmised from the accompanying photographs. In one photograph, she saw Hugh with a black bear twice his size strung up to show his full height. *Poor bear. Why would they shoot such a magnificent creature? How could they be sae proud o' thet dubious accomplishment? He seems so pleased wit' himself in the photograph.* Maggie was shocked at how her heart raced at seeing his face, and the pang deep inside her, just thinking about him. *Be strong, Maggie,* she admonished herself. *He's no' yers an' ne'er will be. Joseph will be yer husband. Ye owe him yer fidelity, an' yer affection. Don' gif' him any reason ta doubt thet.*

On October 10th, sunshine was upon them before any was ready for it. All the arrangements for the wedding and the party were done, but the hearts of all she loved were not prepared for the event.

John and Elizabeth had covered the seats and sides of the wagon with soft muslin, to keep Maggie's wedding clothes clean. John lifted her gingerly to the wagon seat, mindful of the precious treasure he held. *She's more bonnie than ever.* Maggie's shift was soft blue with a gathered neckline. Her loose overdress was cream linen with heavy blue embroidery along the edges of the open sleeves, the hood, and the front. The ribbons in her deep auburn hair, fluttered in the breeze like twenty bluebirds trapped in a wildfire.

When she saw her daughter on the wagon, Elizabeth felt humbled at the beauty of the child she raised. Unbidden tears sprang to her eyes and she turned her back to quickly wipe them from sight. *Oh, James! Kin ye see her t'day? 'So bonnie a child in sight an' heart, a woman the day she doth depart.' Watch o'er her, James. I've los' her.*

Later, Maggie tried to remember what was said at the wedding, but could not recall a word. Joseph, in his Sunday best, looked handsome and nervous. He had to be prompted twice to pronounce his vows, as did Maggie. His bairn wailed heartily throughout most of the service. Soon, it was over and they were at her mother's cottage.

The villagers arrived at the cottage while the family was still at the church. Since it was a warm clear day, they brought the tables and food outside on the wild grass. Those who brought fiddles and *bodhrans* played as the wagon drove up. Maggie was seated in her chair in the shade with Joseph by her side, and the villagers played their music, dancing around them.

Soon, the men drifted to one side where the drink was and the women gathered by the food, each group chatted among themselves. Joseph was dragged off by the men, now boisterous and increasingly rude.

The Reverend McKay and his wife sat with Maggie and Elizabeth. Watching Maggie's look of disappointment, Mister McKay said light-heartedly, "Don't worry. The men will have their fun with him, but Joseph will be yours from now on. It is the tradition of men the world over to isolate the young man from his woman on the day of her wedding." As if on cue, the farmers roared with laughter in answer to a disparaging comment uttered by one of the group.

A group of tittering young girls had surrounded Maggie's feet, fingering the hem of her gown and asking questions of romance. "Haf' yer al'ays known him?" "What was he like, as a boy?" "He's sae handsome. What's it like ta be in love?"

Maggie laughed, finding comfort in Mister Kay's words, and more so, in his wife's nodding agreement. "One at a time me bonnie lasses, I will tell yer. Little boys who pull yer plaits, an' trip yer as ye gae walkin' by, grow up ta be jes' as handsome an' special as my Joseph." Maggie winked and continued, "He had an outrageous mouth, terrible penmanship an' big red freckles. He was al'ays in trouble. He spilled m' books on the floor ever' chanct he got. Then one day, he stopped lookin' sae gawky. He started smilin' an' pickin' up m' books fer me. Jes' ye wait, lassies, it'll happen fer you too." The little girls giggled, running off to talk among themselves about this revelation.

As the afternoon passed into early evening, couples began to find each other and their children again. The music, once joyous and lively, migrated to soft and sadly haunting tunes fraught with the memories of first loves and lovers abandoned by fate. The wagon loaded, and his wife waving from her perch above the crowd, Joseph hopped up to drive them home. The villagers guided the way with lanterns lit, singing the old songs. Maggie leaned on Joseph, tired from the events of the day and the emotional upheaval of the past weeks. She could smell the ale, stale on his breath, his fine linen shirt and his scratchy wool coat against her cheek. *'It will be fine, then. He seems content, happy ev'n. Perhaps I haf' done it right. T'marra will tell.*

As Joseph drove the wagon to the back of the cottage, the followers went on their way, singing the last of their folk melodies for a proper send off. "Joey, wha's this?" asked Maggie.

"This, my love, is our ain room. I built it this last month as a surprise. There is a door to the main room, but we'll haf' our ain home inside the cottage." Maggie looked with wonder at this thoughtful Joseph she hadn't known before. "Jes' wait 'til ye see."

Joseph whisked her off the wagon in a whirl. As he strode through the doorway, he yelped at being struck about the head and shoulders in a clatter of pots and pans. Joseph cursed and stumbled, almost losing his balance and dropping Maggie. "Wha' in the name of...!"

Maggie laughed heartily while Joseph cursed and growled. "Joseph Heenan, did ye think ye could git away wit'out yer friends payin' ye back fer all the times ye did this an' worse ta them?" Maggie continued to laugh and Joseph, seeing her delight, began to chuckle, too.

"Yer right, I do deserve it. I jes' wanted ta make this night perfect fer you, Maggie."

"An' it is, Joey, my love. 'Tis," she answered, gleefully. "The look on yer face was wit'out measure!" Maggie was grateful for the release of tension building in her.

He gently placed her at the edge of the bed and knelt before her. His voice, husky with emotion, he said, "Maggie, I've wanted this moment from the first day I saw yer. Ev'ry time I came close, I saw it all slip away. I canna believe we are here. Ye mus' knae I love yer more than me ain life." With shaking hands, he touched her hair and bowed his head.

"Joey. I'm here. Look at me. I am no' some angel spirit yer conjured up. I am Maggie, with all *my* faults an' demons. I am yers fer better or worse." She picked up his head and brought her lips to his. *I will devote myself ta yer, thet ye may never knae my demons.*

As the seasons changed, so did Maggie. Her confinement was good to her. She grew more radiant with each passing day. As large as she was becoming, it was getting more difficult for her to go to her mother's cottage to visit and to keep the books, but she could not bear to stop. Every week, Joseph would ask her not to go, for fear of her overtaxing herself. The memory of losing Mary loomed heavy on his mind.

"Joey, I need ta see my mother an' the money I'm paid will be helpful 'n the spring. Onct the bairn is born, I won't be able ta gae there fer a while, lemme gae this week."

Every week, Joseph would acquiesce, saying, "I'll hafta hire a man an' a boy ta help me git ye inta the wagon verra soon, my love." He leapt into the wagon, made sure she was warm, and drove to her mother's home. Taking the horse tied on the back, Joseph galloped homeward again, turning on his mount, he shouted. "Haf' John bring yer back ta me, love. Stay warm."

Soon, she would not be able to travel, she knew. There was the smell of snow in the slate gray clouds crowding the Mournes. The near-winter light hid behind a low blanket of mountain fog. Before long, the roadway would be treacherous, covered with patches of ice.

John set her down in the office, on the dining chair left in position at the desk. He pulled the latest trunk close to her and Elizabeth brought in tea. Elizabeth enjoyed this time she had with her daughter. Even though Maggie shed her coat and went right to work, her mother stayed by her side, reaching for the samples in the trunk for her and chatting about the latest news. *Poor Mother, she's sae lonely. She's told me thet story three times nae, jes' ta haf' som'thin' ta say.* Maggie talked to her about Joseph, Missus Heenan, and the children. She loved being around them, but she hated to leave Elizabeth and John by themselves.

Once a week is all she could spare of her time. She was fortunate that Joseph's mother took care of the children. His sister came to spell her a bit too. They both insisted she nap every day. *It's because o' losing Mary,* she thought. *I'm fine, though. It's lak' God is sayin', 'I've taken her legs away, sae I hafta make every thin' else easier.'* Maggie knew most women had some difficulty in carrying babies, but she didn't. She felt healthier than ever. The babe, as if to remind her of its presence, kicked her forcefully under her ribs. She laughed. At her mother's questioning look, she explained it was the bairn's *playtime*.

"What is it lak' wit' Joseph?" asked Elizabeth cautiously.

"He's verra attentive an' content most o' the time, Ma. He hasn't a drop ta drink since the wedding, either. His ma, an' the children haf' seen the change in him, too. Young Johnnie seems ta no' git on his nerves as much anymore. We are gittin' alang jes' fine, Ma."

"I'm glad ta hear it. The bairn mus' be growin' lak' a weed, then?"

"His name is James, Ma, an' he is. He's sittin' up by himself, an' gurglin' lak' he wants ta talk! He's ainly six month. I think I ran over his finger wit' my chair the other day. Oh, what a holler! Missus Heenan straps him in a chair nae, while I'm rollin' about. I felt terrible ta hurt the wee thing!"

"He'll learn ta avoid yer chair, if ye let him on the floor. But if yer tender-hearted about it, he'll ne'er learn."

"Oh, Ma, I don't wan' fer him ta be scairt o' me. When he's older, is soon enough ta be hurt by the thin's around him."

"Well, *ye* will be the one takin' care o' him when he's grown an' afeerd o' ever'thin', won' ye? Sae it's no' my bus'ness, then."

"Well, don' let's fuss about it. I hafta git along wit' Missus Heenan too, ye ken. How about another cup o' tea, while I git this one written up?" Her mother mumbled under her breath, but poured the tea. Maggie changed the subject to the festivities of Christmas Day. She invited her mother and John to the Heenan house for Christmas dinner.

Then, she said, "Ma, I probably won't be comin' here agin until afta the babe's born. The roads will be bad soon an' I am becomin' big as an elephant. Thet reminds me, do ye still haf' my book on wild animals I had as a child? I'd like ta give it ta young Joseph. He's learning ta read already!"

Later, when she was leaving with John, Maggie wistfully looked at her mother in the doorway of the little cottage and thought how rapidly things were changing. *This year, I'll haf' Christmas in a new home wit' five children. Next year, I'll add my ain child. What could the followin' year possibly bring? Dear Laird, give me a minute ta catch my breath!*

Somehow Christmas and January flew by, and Maggie was anxiously awaiting the impending birth of her child. She asked everyone she saw what to expect, but all they did was give her vague words of comfort. "Ye will knae when it's time." "It's different fer ev'ry woman." "Birthin' is easier wit' each baby." "The midwife will tell yer what ta do." "It'll be o'er afore ye knae it." "Ye won' remember the pain, sae jes' git through it." "Next thing ye knae, ye will haf' one in ye arms, an' one by the hand, until it's time for ye eldest ta haf' one o' her ain."

"*If Candlemas Day be fair an' bright, winter will haf' another fight. If Candlemas Day brings cloud an' rain, winter won't come again.*" Maggie looked out the small window and saw a sky of menacing clouds and rain running down the pane. *Spring will come,* she thought, *an' so will this babe. It's a little early, but it jes' keeps* goin'. I hope there's nothin' wrong. It speeds up, then slows down. At this rate, it could be a week afore it happens! The midwife keeps fussin' around, askin' me all kinds o' questions. Haf' I been to a graveyard while I was 'confined'? Did I wash windows? Did I hold a newborn baby? All evidently terrible thin's ta do, an' all o' which I haf' done. She has tied a red ribbon on the cradle an' has one prepared ta tie on the baby's ankle ta keep fairies from stealin' the child. The swaddlin' clothes were put out ta the sunshine on St. Brigid's Feast Day ta safeguard the mother an' child. The cloth was laid across my belly ta protect it until the baby's born. I wonder if she did all this fer poor Mary?*

"God help me!" Maggie exclaimed as another pain shot through her. It wasn't strong, it just surprised her.

"Be careful, Missy. Don' be takin' the Laird's name in vain! Ye will curse the child's whole life, if it survives," said the midwife, sharply.

"I'll not say another word, e'en in prayer," promised Maggie as another pain pushed through, *almost there.*

"Yer ready, let it come. C'mon, Missy, give us a push."

Stop callin' me Missy! You....! Maggie's thoughts were interrupted by her body's overwhelming desire to finally push this child out.

The tiny cry brought a roar from the other room. The midwife crowed, "It's a wee girl, but a strong one!" She quickly made the sign of the cross on the babe's forehead to protect her. She washed her off, wrapped her tightly in the swaddling clothes, and laid her in Maggie's arms.

Responding to the child's crying, Maggie looked at the midwife and asked, "What should I do?"

"Stick yer finger in her mouth fer nae. Ye ain' done wit' birthin' yet." Maggie, subdued and exhausted, did as she was told. As soon as the midwife cleaned her up, and straightened the bedclothes, she invite d her husband to see his little girl.

"What will ye name her, son?" demanded the midwife. I wan' ta mark it down, an' git on wit' it. I've got another comin' in Ballyward."

"Elizabeth Jane Heenan's her name, Biddy," said Maggie.

"Ye wan' another of the same name? Well, its yer bairn." She wrote it down, stuck her hand out for the coin he gave her and she was gone.

"Ye sure, Maggie, same name?"

"We kin call her Lizzie. Eliza is her sister."

"Yer ma an' mine are both named Elizabeth, too. We'll worry about a new name when the next one comes." Joseph beamed proudly.

"The next one…? Don't git ahead o' yerself, Joseph Heenan." Maggie grinned, nuzzling the red fuzz on her baby's head.

On the thirteenth of February, Joseph took his mother to Ballyward to Mister Rowan. This time, it was to mark the birth of Elizabeth Jane Heenan. Joseph waited for her outside, talking to the local men. She answered Mister Rowan's questions carefully: Mother's name, Margaret Heenan, child's name, Elizabeth Jane Heenan. When he asked the father's name, she shook her head and said, mysteriously, "We'll see." She marked her "x" to note she witnessed the birth. *This child was born too early*, she thought. *What if it's no' e'en his? Maggie is a lovely girl, but what if….*

Chapter Twelve

"But Maggie, ye knae I haf' no talent fer farmin'. I barely made enough fer the rent an' taxes last year. They say this year will be wors'! Da's brother, Fergus, has been a peddler fer many a year, an' he say the railroad will make trade even better. He's asked fer my help."

"But Joey, ye'll lose yer mother's land if ye' don't work it. If yer a peddler, ye will be gone fer weeks at a time, an'we need yer here wit' yer family." They had been arguing for the several days that Uncle Fergus had been there. His belated arrival had caused a stir, having missed the wedding and the birth. When he asked Joseph to help him with his route, Maggie and Joseph were at odds. *It's easy ta see where Joseph gets his charm,* Maggie thought. *The children flock ta Fergus ta hear stories o' London an' Dublin an' all the towns an' villages in between. Joey would be no different. He's a farmer by circumstance — no' by choice. I see his eyes langin' fer the road. If I bind him ta this place, will he wither an' resent me? I haf' the power ta hold him here, but do I haf' the will? His mother watches me wit' suspicious eyes ta see if I will send her son away. If Joey doesn't work the land, it will go back ta the Annesleys fer rent an' back taxes. What will we do then?*

The peddler, a clever businessman, had a proposition for Maggie and her mother-in-law as well. He saw Maggie's work with tatting, knowing the extraordinary skill she possessed to create lace. If he supplied the fine bleached linen, and she created the lace trim, he could sell handkerchiefs and other items to order in London and all along the southern Irish coast. Now that the railroad had opened up those towns for tourists and the linen trade, he was sure of a handsome profit.

He delivered the mail to the circle of mountains where the railroad hadn't been successful. If she would be willing to teach the neighboring women of the area to make lace of her caliber, she could stand a goodly wage on her own. *I could do thet,* Maggie thought. *Especially nae the Annesleys dinna need my services as much.* The trunks were not coming as often and it was impossible to go to her mother's house since the baby had arrived. *If I kin make enough money ta pay fer the rent, an' Joey could pay the taxes, an' hire a hand or two ta work the land...? Missus Heenan would keep her land an' we would still fair well. We'll hafta discuss this later. We'll be at church soon.*

The flurry of activity switched the focus of their thoughts. Little Lizzie's red ribbon was retied high on her tiny leg, to be hidden by her baptismal gown. *Nae sense takin' chances with the old women's beliefs,* Maggie thought, chagrinned at mixing pagan and Christian traditions in the same ceremony. The tiny white gown was a testament to Maggie's lace-making expertise. She adjusted the tiny bonnet and wrapped her in a soft woolen blanket. Kissing her forehead, she held the child in her arms and waited.

Joseph was organizing the activities outside, getting the children and his mother in the back of the wagon with his uncle. When everyone was in their place, Joseph came back for Maggie and his youngest child. *How would I gae anywhere, if no' fer Joey takin' me? I'll hafta think on that aspect o' this whole proposition, won't I?*

At the crossroads, Maggie's mother and uncle were waiting to follow them to the church. As they turned into the road to Ballyward, Maggie waved at her mother and John. *I miss them sae much. What'll I do wit'out them* and *Joey?* Maggie shook her head in admonishment. *Turn yer thoughts ta yer little one, Maggie. This is her day.*

The child's godparents, Joseph's sister and her husband, were at the church before them. As they filed into the cold, dank sanctuary, Maggie looked at the bairn in her arms. Little Lizzie stared back at her with her calm blue eyes and her mother smiled. Joseph took the babe from her arms and gave her to the Reverend Mister McKay. Maggie barely heard the words of the service, but was filled with emotion. *This child is mine. She'll be my future an' I'll be hers. Where will ye gae? What will ye do? Who will ye be? Will ye haf' yer father's charm, yer grandfather's wisdom? Will ye be clever, headstrong, pretty?*

Startled out of her reverie, Maggie realized the service was over and Lizzie was given back to her. People were gathered around her all talking at once. Joseph picked her and the baby up and headed down the aisle.

"Mister Heenan? May I have a word?" The minister raised his voice to be heard.

"Yes?" Joseph turned and walked back to the tall robed figure.

"This gift was given to me to present to the child. There was no card with it, but it was brought by Mister Harden on behalf of the Annesleys. I'm to give you their best wishes for the child. Mister Harden had an urgent appointment to attend, but offered his heartiest congratulations to you both."

The small box was elegantly, if plainly, wrapped. Maggie could see Joseph's jaw working on the thought of the Annesleys insinuating their presence on this occasion. "Joey, 'tis only a gift ta wish her well. Dinna read anythin' else inta its meaning."

"Very well, open it. We'll not let anythin' disturb the celebration this day fer Lizzie's sake."

Maggie fumbled open the box. Inside was a tiny cup, with a cross and writing inscribed on the outside. "Elizabeth Jane Heenan, Born the Second Day of February, Anno Domini 1872.

"It's lovely." She slipped it quickly back into the box. "Thank ye, Mister McKay, it was kind of ye ta present it ta us."

Mother, father, and child quickly and quietly left the church. They hardly heard the cheer of the small group outside the church. The box weighed heavily in Maggie's hand, as if its weight had grown with the import of its meaning to Maggie. *Oh, Hugh, let this go. Don't keep my longin' fer ye alive an' out where Joey can see it. He's a good man. If I canna haf' ye, let me at least haf' someone who needs me.*

The festivities at the cottage did not lighten the spirits of the parents. They smiled and laughed, but quietly, as reluctant actors in a play. If anyone noticed their lack of frivolity, they didn't say anything to Maggie and Joseph. The box was relegated to the back of a shelf, unmentioned, unseen, but not forgotten.

In a few days, Maggie knew she had to address the peddler's proposal. It was not fair to discuss it without Joseph's mother, so Maggie, Joseph, and Missus Heenan sat at the table after the children were asleep. The peddler sat down to answer their questions. Maggie weighed her words carefully.

"If we're gaein' ta do this, we hafta ta come up wit' the rent an' taxes by April. I'll no' let yer mother lose her land. We should haf' most o' it by April if Market Days are good. My tattin' won't amount ta much coin, but if I kin teach it, I kin make more. Joseph will hafta make enough ta cover the rest, an' ta hire a man ta work the land. Is thet possible, Uncle Fergus? I will hold ye ta whatever ye say, so be cautious in yer answer.

Fergus looked in wonder at the woman before him. He never knew a woman with a head for business like this one. *An' wrapped in so a pretty a package at that.*

"Missus Heenan… Maggie," he said respectfully, "If Joseph is willin' ta work hard, I see a grand future fer him in bein' a travelin' salesman. It takes a bit o' coin ta make coin, though. He kin work with me a' first, I'll see he learns the ropes an' earns enough ta do as ye say. After, say…, six months, he'll hafta haf' his own proper mercantile wagon an' horse ta increase the territory we cover in a timely manner, ye see. I believe he's got the stuff ta do verra well indeed."

"Do the rest of ye agree wit' what we're sayin', then?" Maggie looked into each face for a sign of their thinking. One by one, they nodded.

"I'll write it up, Joseph. If we can agree on all the points, we'll all sign an' be bound by the contract. I'll be fair in the writin' an' I'll demand the same from each o' yer. If we canna fulfill the contract, we'll dissolve the alliance an' be done wit' it. Joseph, please bring me a pen, ink an' paper so I kin draft this properly."

Maggie was aware that all eyes watched her in amazement at her speech. They did not relax until she broke out in a grin. "Come along an' we'll start this adventure." Pen in hand, she began to write the terms she and the peddler laid out for them. The peddler and Maggie put their heads together and worked on the language of the agreement until all the points were agreed upon. The first part of the contract had to be fulfilled by a week before May Day; the second part, by a week before Tax Day in November. If each step of the contract could not be completed on time and to the satisfaction of all parties, the partnership would dissolve and Joseph would return to the farm. If they succeeded, the apprenticeship would dissolve when Joseph earned his own route with his own supplies and wagon. At that time, a new contract could be drawn to determine the fair responsibilities and division of profits, if they decided to stay in business together.

Maggie rewrote the final contract, had the peddler read it aloud to the group, and they each signed or placed their mark at the bottom. As Maggie signed, Lizzie awoke, crying in hunger. "An' now, ta the business o' motherhood, an unwritten contract that'll happily bind me fer life." The ensuing laughter broke the nervous tension at the table, and she wheeled herself to the wildly rocking cradle. She cheerfully instructed her mother-in-law to put the contract in a safe place and slipped into the other room to feed her bairn.

Fergus clapped his big hand on Joseph's shoulder and said, "Thet's a wondrous asset ye haf' in a wife, Joseph! Who woulda thought a man could haf' a beautiful woman an' a fearsome *barrister*, ta warm his bed a' night." Smiling, Joseph shook his head in wonder at the closed door hiding his wife and child from view.

When he went to bed that night, Joseph took Maggie in his arms and said, "Maggie, m' love, thank ye fer takin' care o' my mother this way. She ne'er woulda asked, but she is sae happy ta know her land is safe fer all o' us. I'll do my verra best ta make ye proud o' me, Maggie."

"Joey, yer tryin' yer best, I knae. Maybe this'll make yer happy," Maggie said. "When ye gae, I want ye ta take me ta m'mother's house. I'll haf' no way ta git around without yer, sae I'll take the baby wit' me, an' haf' John bring me back here ev'ry few days ta check on yer mother an' the children. I need ta continue the books fer the plants, if I'm ta help yer Ma wit' her land, an' hire a man ta work it. I need ta work in the office, Joseph. I'm no' much help ta yer Ma here, anyway."

Joseph sighed long and deep, "Sae, yer leavin' us already, 'twas too good ta be true?"

"No, Joseph, *you're* leavin' us. I'll come back here wit' yer, when ye return. I'll stay here, fer as lang as ye are hame. Afore ye knae it, Lizzie will be walkin' an' runnin'. Yer Ma has enough ta do fer' the first five o' yer children. Let m' mother take care o' this one."

"It's a strange life we're buildin', Maggie."

"I am, who I am, Joey. I'm no' lak' other woman."

"Fer sure an' ye aren't, Maggie. Yer a wonder," said Joseph, pulling her close. "I canna deny ye, m' love. Jes' come back ta me, when I'm hame, Maggie. I canna bear ta be wit'out ye."

"I'll no' be wit'out ye, Joseph Heenan."

The next morning, Maggie talked to Missus Heenan about her plan. She was surprised at the quick tears that filled the older woman's eyes. "Are ye already unhappy here?"

"Nay, mere, I haf' work ta do at the glasshouse. We wan' ta haf' the rent ready an' 'twill take all we can git, ta do thet. I canna ask my mother ta pay fer the tendin' o' this land as well. I'll come back here, when he's hame, I promise."

"Maggie, it's no' good fer mothers ta work, 'ceptin' ta care fer their families. The men should earn the money. The women tak' care o' the men an' bairns."

"I kin see ye thinkin', Ma. But mothers an' children are working in the linen an' flax mills ta care fer their families these days. I canna do the things mos' women can, sae I do other things ta earn m' keep. Joey understands. He knaes I'll be here with m' Heenans, whenever he's hame."

Maggie hugged her mother-in-law tightly. "Please don' think I'm unhappy wit' yer. I love yer an' the children. I will be countin' the days when I'll be back here ta be wit' ye all. I canna be more blessed ta haf' a family lak' this one."

Maggie prepared to make her journey home. When Joseph could put it off no longer, he loaded her belongings into the wagon. They said their goodbyes, and with the peddler's wagon behind Joseph's farm wagon, they were on their way.

Joseph brought Maggie and Lizzie into her mother's cottage. He asked to leave the wagon and the horse in the back until his return. A quick kiss for his baby and Maggie, a nod to Elizabeth and he was gone.

At her mother's look of astonishment, Maggie explained her plan. Elizabeth was delighted with the prospect of having her daughter and her granddaughter to herself for two weeks. "John will be delighted too. He's been concerned 'bout the plantin' this year, with ye gone."

"I'll be glad ta help him, Ma, but I haf' work o' my ain ta do, too. I'll hafta talk ta Tom Reilly about the glasshouse as well. I'll write a letter for John to deliver on Market Day. I have a note to send to the Annesleys as well."

Elizabeth heard Maggie's speech become more formal as it always did when she spoke of the Annesleys. *She straddles two worlds, one fer village an' family, an' one fer the high an' mighty Annesleys. When will ye chose, Maggie? When will ye make up yer mind it is no' the Annesleys ye belong ta?*

"Wha's this note ta the Annesleys, then?" she asked, suspiciously.

"They sent a gift fer Lizzie, Ma, a silver cup. They'll be expecting an acknowledgement."

"What bairn needs a silver cup? What use is thet fer folk lak' us?"

"It's wha' they do, Ma," Maggie sighed, impatient with her mother's naïvetéè. "It has her name on it. Never mind, it's no' important ta our lives."

"Well, it's nice o' yer, ta write a note," said Elizabeth, trying to appease her daughter.

At that moment, Lizzie woke up and all their attention shifted from their awkward discussion to the crying child.

Later in the afternoon, Maggie took the baby to the office and took out the little silver cup. She read the inscription, wondering what she would say in her note. As she turned it over in her hands, she read, *'Non nobis solum nati sumus.'* Maggie translated, "We are not born for ourselves alone." She felt her face flush in sudden anger. *How dare you visit our situation upon this child? If Joey knew what this said, he would forever doubt that Lizzie was his!* Even as she damned the nobleman's name, her heart beat faster with her memory of him.

With shaking hands, she carefully wrapped the silver cup and replaced it in the box. Hot, bitter tears of frustration coursed down her face as she stowed the cup in the back of the desk drawer. *I'll hafta be rid of it, but I cannot do it now. Not while Mother's in the house, and John not far away. Oh, Hugh! Why can't I rid myself of these memories of you?* Maggie sat back in her chair, hugging herself, remembering his arms holding her, indulging in the dreams that flew through her head.

Lizzie stirred and stretched in the middle of John's bed. Her tiny eyelids fluttered and closed again. *Sleep, my child. Ye needn't worry 'bout the foolishness o' yer Ma. Ye will live yer ain life, as ye please. I'll see ta thet. Ye will be strong o' will an' live by the say-so o' no man.*

Maggie took out paper and pen to write her note to Hugh.

To The Honorable Lord Hugh Annesley,

We are pleased to accept the engraved silver cup presented to us by The Reverend Mister McKay in your behalf, on the occasion of the Christening of our daughter, Elizabeth Jane Heenan, Saturday, February 10, 1872. Your thoughtful gift will be treasured throughout her lifetime.

Your humble and obedient servants,
Mr. and Mrs. J. H. Heenan

That should do it. Even if his mother looked over his shoulder while he read it, she could find no fault with that letter. She addressed the plain envelope with a steady penmanship, not too fancy, not too plain as was acceptable in his circles. She would hand it to Tom Reilly when next he was at the glasshouse. She carefully wrapped the envelope in a plain sheet of paper, so the gardener wouldn't have to worry about dirtying the envelope with his earth-stained hands.

Having accomplished this task, she returned to her books and her task of accounting for the plants from his latest journey. The work had piled up in the last six weeks while she was birthing and caring for her newborn.

Another two weeks went by, before Tom Reilly arrived. He had heard from Maggie's mother on Market Day that Maggie had returned home. "This is the first of the trunks from Japan," he crowed. "The master has gone clear 'round the world this time. I wonder what he's got fer us in this batch!" Maggie laughed at his excitement and found herself caught up in it as well. There were pictures of strangely costumed men and women with odd eyes and straight black hair. The embroidery on the clothing was fantastical, picturing dragons and wild birds. Among the pictures were notes in the handwriting she had grown to know by sight.

The few sentences were not addressed to anyone, but Maggie's heart claimed them as her own. "The land of Japan is wonderfully sculpted," he wrote. "Much of it is contrasting sharp peaked mountains dropping to the sea. It is like walking into a painting. The boats are like lanterns set adrift in the ocean as the sun sets blood red over deep purple landscapes. The plants are completely unknown to me. I tried to capture their image in bloom. I am too early for most of them. I sent photographs of Japanese drawings for them, so you might know what to expect. You will not believe the colors — amazing colors. The people are engaging.

Though I am not tall among men at home, I am a giant here. The people are very small and fine boned, interesting."

Maggie tucked the descriptive notes between the first pages of the Japan Catalogue. The other notes were the familiar jottings of Latin names, descriptive details, and the regimen required to preserve the plant before it was to be transplanted to Castlewellan. Maggie would check her geography book to see just where Japan was. She felt closer to him when she could put her finger on the land he was visiting. She read what small references there were in the books she had, and imagined what he was doing at that very moment.

The reality of what she was thinking brought her up short. *Maggie, you're insane, or will make yerself so! Don't torture yerself with these games. You have a husband and a child. You're not a little schoolgirl dreaming of her fabled prince. No good can come of this. Joseph will be home any time now and it is of he, you should be thinking,*

Resolved, she threw herself into the task of cataloging the plants from the trunk. As the pile of transcribed samples grew, the light outside grew dim and soon John came stomping clods of dirt off his boots. Lizzie woke from the sound and John reached over to pick her up. He sat on the edge of his bed, rocking her gently. "Hush, child, I mean ye no harm. Sh." Lizzie stared up at him, reaching for his moving lips.

"She knows ye voice, John. Keep talkin' ta her." As John murmured her name, Lizzie rewarded him with a lop-sided grin.

"Look a' thet, Maggie! Is there anythin' finer than a wee bairn's smile?" The sight of John's simple pleasure nearly burst her heart. "Shall I take yer an' the babe ta the cottage, Maggie?"

"Yes, John, we'll be havin' tea, soon."

"I'll take yer there, and then wash up good. It's nice ta haf' a bairn in the place, isn't? D' yer need anythin', Maggie?"

"Nay, John." She took Lizzie from him and drew her cloak around herself and the babe. The setting sun brought with it a cool, brisk wind. Entering the cottage proper, Maggie was grateful for the warmth, the tantalizing aroma of tea, and fresh biscuits. Immediately, Lizzie nuzzled against her for nourishment. Slipping behind her bed curtain, Maggie set Lizzie to nurse while raising her voice to speak to her mother.

"I'll only be a few minutes, Ma. I can't put her off any longer. She slept a lang time an' I was able ta get a lot done this afternoon. The new plants are lovely."

"I'm sure they are, Maggie. Ye should be nappin' when yer child naps, ye knae. Ye need yer rest ta make yer milk. Ye git up early an' stay up long afta dark, wit' hardly a bite in between."

"I need ta get this done afore I hafta gae ta the Heenans. Joseph should be here any day now, an' in the blink of an eye, it'll be rent day again."

"Ye will do as ye please, I'll warrant, but the child will haf' a say-so in the matter. She'll git wha' she needs an' she won't gif' a hang what ye think ye need ta do."

"Yer right about thet, Ma," the young mother replied. *If I haf' my way, she'll get all she needs from nae 'til I'm gone ta m' Maker.*

Chapter Thirteen

Just as Maggie's new routine gained a comfortable rhythm, the clopping of hooves, accompanied by the noisy jangle of peddler's wares, forced a collective dash to the windows of the little cottage.

"Joseph's hame," Maggie said, with all the enthusiasm she could muster. She was nervous, anticipating either good news or disaster, not knowing which she desired most. Good news meant he would be home with money, for only a day or two, then off again. Bad news meant he was home for a long time, but with no money, and back to the farming he hated.

The door burst open, and there he was, smiling like he was the happiest man on earth. He scooped Maggie up, and twirled her around, before setting her gently back in her chair. He sat jauntily on the stool, mouth grinning, eyes twinkling. "I'm hame, woman, an' I missed yer terrible. Let's gae ta m' mother's an' see what's a foot!"

"Joseph, tell me all about it. Leave nothin' out. We'll pack up in a minute. Did ye do well?"

"I did at thet, my darlin'. I did. Fergus says I am a natural salesman, born ta it, I haf' the knack. I'll haf' enough fer the rents come May Day, an' I'll haf' enough ta put away fer taxes an' rents come November, too. We'll be rollin' in clover, Maggie."

"Well, tha's good, Joey, but let's no' git ahead o' oursel's. As lang as I work on the catalogin', the taxes are paid fer, wit' a little lef' fer me. But, we still hafta git a farmer ta work yer ma's land, an' they don' work fer promises. So, yer work fer the next fortnight will hafta be as good, wan' it?"

"Oh, 'twill, Maggie. I kin feel it! Hello, Missus Coburn. Sorry fer the commotion. I'm sae glad ta be hame. Yer well, Missus? An' John, he's fit?" Maggie was happy he remembered to be polite to her mother.

Warily, Elizabeth offered him tea. She knew Maggie and the child would be off with him within the hour, and she sought to detain him as long as she could. She had gotten used to Maggie and Lizzie being there, and hated to see them go. She held back the sigh she felt coming. *Maggie looks sae happy to see him.* Elizabeth cautiously spoke directly to him, "Joseph, she's been workin' awful hard. See she gets a little rest while yer hame."

Seeing the shadow of worry cross his face, Maggie's eyes flashed a warning to Elizabeth. "Ma, I'm fine, really." Elizabeth ducked her head at the perceived rebuke, continuing setting plates on the table.

"I'll see she rests, Missus Coburn. I'll be hame fer three days an' I'll bring her back here again, fit as a fiddle. She's verra precious ta me too, ye knae. Fer nae, we should be goin'."

"Gae off wit' yer. I'll pack up the babe, an' bring her ta ye."

Maggie threw her tatting in a bag with a few things, and drew on her plaid. While Elizabeth was fussing with the child, Joseph sneaked a kiss from his bride. "I'll leave the peddler's wagon here, and take the other one hame, if thet's agreeable? I need a place fer the chair."

"O' course, Joey, switch the horses. I'll wait in here fer yer." *The travelin' seems ta do him good. I've no' seen him sae happy, no' fer a lang time. If he kin stay away from the drink an' women...,* she thought, *it may be a fair arrangement. Oh, I hope sae. Please God, let him stay happy, an' in yer care.*

Soon, they were on their way and nearing the Heenan cottage. The children were in the yard with his mother. "Pa! Pa! Maggie! Ye're hame!" Joseph hopped down. Grabbing each child, he swung them around joyously. Young Joseph, Ann, and Johnny had a thousand questions, and little Eliza just grinned and laughed. Joseph's mother could barely contain Baby James, bouncing in her arms.

When they were all inside, Missus Heenan looked at Maggie with all the questions she was afraid to ask. "Ever'thin's fine, Missus Heenan, we'll haf' the rent. Fergus is happy with Joseph, an' Joseph is happy wit' the work," she whispered. Joseph was busy playing on the floor with little James, not listening to the quiet conversation between his mother and his wife. Missus Heenan put her hand on her chest, and heaved a big sigh, letting out two weeks of worry.

"Joseph, where is Fergus? Is he staying at the pub? Or will he stay here?" Maggie asked.

"He's staying in Bainbridge, an' I'll pick him up on the way back. I think there's a lady he has his eye on," he said with a wink, "Quite a man with the ladies, thet one."

"Well, I'd better no' hear o' a man named *Joseph*, wit' an eye fer the ladies," Maggie said with a menacing tone.

"No, Ma'am. My heart belongs ta m' wife, ye knae. I canna even speak ta ladies. 'Less, o' course, they's buyin' company goods."

Maggie looked heavenward, and said, mocking him, "Keep yer eye on him, Laird. He'd better no' stray from the straight an' narrow way ta heav'n, or I'll be showin' him the punishment due him at the other place." Seeing the children's eyes grow large with concern, she laughed and said, "We're only playin' m' bairns. Now, come give Maggie a big hug." Five scruffy children ran to her, with arms open wide. She kissed each of them soundly, and hugged them together. As if on cue, Lizzie awoke and cried hungrily. *Could it e'er be better than this?* Maggie thought happily. *I canna haf' wha' isn't mine, but I kin be happy wit' what is, can't I?*

The next few days flew by, and it was time to leave again. The children cried, and Joseph's mother shed a tear or two, as they stood in the dooryard, waving goodbye. *Joey is sae good wit' them,* Maggie thought. *He's sae tender an' sweet wit' Eliza an' Ann, an' rough an' tumble wit' the older boys. He's sae gentle with Baby James. He holds Lizzie like she would break from the lookin' at her.* Maggie marveled at this man she married. She hadn't known *this* man. The last year had been a revelation to her. Her memories of him were of a rough, powerful young man, who took what he wanted and dared the devil to take it away. *He loves his children wit'out compromise.* Her thoughts took a sudden turn. *'Less he's drinkin', then nothin' else matters, no' me, nor his mother, nor his bairns. Oh Laird, watch over my man.* She smiled at this thought. *My man, thet's who he is nae, me ain man.*

Maggie turned in her seat, and looked long at him. His strong jaw, his impossibly red hair, and his firm full lips, made him so handsome. She was surprised at the pang of jealousy she felt for the road that would take him away — all that temptation on the road. The women and the public houses... *Stop! Yer assumin' the worst an' fergittin' ta enjoy him while he's here. Don't waste the time ye haf', by yer imaginin's!*

"What are ye thinkin', Lass? Yer got ye face all scrunched up, ready fer a fight, looks like. Did som'one hurt yer feelin's? I'll set him straight."

"No, Joey. I'm gonna miss ye, is all. How lang will ye be gone this time?"

"Don' knae, Maggie, love. He's takin' another route. I'll be back, soon as I kin. I'll be missin' yer too, ye ken. I wisht there was some way we could talk ta each other, whilst I'm gone. Kin ye imagine? 'Twould be like I was ne'er even gone, if I could jes' hear yer voice. I kin hear it in my dreams sometimes, but wha' if we could hear each other, anytime we wanted? Wouldn't tha' be grand?"

"Well, Joseph. They haf' telegraph with a code, but they've ne'er done anythin' with a voice. 'Twould be nice though. I knae! We'll read each other's thoughts, by lookin' a' the same moon." Maggie laughed at the fantasy she was creating. "Promise me, ye will look a' the moon ev'ry night, an' I will, too. I'll hear yer voice in the moonbeams."

Joseph pretended to be very seriously listening, but couldn't keep the laughter from spilling out. "Is it the *gift* ye haf', then? Ye've been listenin' ta the faeries, m' darlin'. Yer pretty mind is addled." He ducked as Maggie swung playfully at his head.

They pulled around the side of the cottage, next to the peddler's wagon. Before he jumped down, he took Maggie into his arms, baby and all, and kissed her soundly. Looking down, he saw Lizzie's eyes wide with wonder. "Hey, yer no' s'posed ta peek, young lady!" He wiggled her nose with a finger, and she grinned.

"Well, I'll tarry no langer, love. I hafta git ta Bainbridge afore dark, sae let's git ye inta the cottage an' settled." He took Maggie down, and into his arms, stealing a kiss, and another, as he turned the corner of the little house. They were laughing when they entered the doorway and met Elizabeth. She smiled, took the baby, and offered Joseph tea.

"Thank yer kindly, nay. I need ta be goin'. I appreciate ye takin' good care o' m' girls while I'm gone, Missus Coburn. I miss 'em already." Joseph impulsively kissed Elizabeth's cheek and stepped out the door.

"Hmph. He's a charmer, thet one," she said, with her hand on her cheek. Maggie could see a little smile playing around her mother's mouth, and that Elizabeth was not altogether displeased with her daughter's husband. *He has a lot o' makin' up ta do wit' Ma, but he's headed in the right direction, looks like.*

May Day came and went. There was enough for the rent, and taking Tom Reilly's recommendation, they hired a workman for the Heenan farm. Next year, Maggie was thinking to hire a boy to help the farmer. Missus Heenan's land was smaller than her mother's, but could be planted more wisely than it was. A portion was peat bog, and Joseph had cut the peats in the spring, and recovered the bog with heather turfs. Fuel for the coming winter was set, as evidenced by the stack at the northern end of the cottage. It was back-breaking, but satisfying work, as the number of peats thrown out to dry grew by his labor.

When they were first married, Joseph took Maggie to see the land his mother's leased and she was already thinking of how they could work the land more efficiently. She was distressed Joseph had no apparent interest in the land, or the work it would take to increase its value to the family. Now that he was otherwise occupied, her plans were more likely to be put into action. She would sit with her mother-in-law and the hired man in the winter, and present a new plan for the land. Maggie was excited with the prospects of bringing new life to this place. Perhaps she should discuss her plans for planting with Tom Reilly, and get his advice.

She remembered her father and Mister Heenan sitting by the fire for hours on a winter's day, plotting out spring farming. They had great respect for each other, and their love for the land. It felt good to be able to continue the caring of the land for both families.

As spring turned to summer, Maggie relied more and more on her mother, for the care of Lizzie. The child was more active and heavier now. She bore more watching than Maggie could spare. She couldn't reach her on the floor, and the child would fall if she were on anything higher.

Maggie was buried in her books, as new trunks followed the ones she had barely finished cataloging. The glasshouse was full, and Mister Reilly was at the cottage every week, to transport the hardier plants to Castlewellan. Maggie began to hope Hugh would come home, if only to slow the constant flow of work and new plants.

Mister Reilly brought his usual tatters of gossip back from the castle. Much to his mother's disappointment, what was to be a spring wedding for Hugh had fallen through, and he absconded to Japan. Tom thought the young master stayed so long there, because he wanted the heat of his mother's fury to dissipate a bit, before he faced her again. *Good Laird, I thought it was his brother, getting married, not Hugh,* thought Maggie. As if he could hear her thoughts, Tom said Lord William was ill, and could not be considered a marriage prospect. Lady Priscilla Annesley took her son to London, to more qualified doctors. In London, he suspected, there were better fashions, and more glamorous engagements, with an eye to find a suitable wife for Hugh, as well.

She knew Tom would be in serious trouble if anyone reported him for gossiping this way. However, Maggie was grateful for any news from Castlewellan, that hadn't been 'cleansed' by the Annesley family, as the local newspapers were. She knew she should stop him from carrying these tales, often dotted with his biased and sometimes outrageous opinions. She was often a guilty participant in the action, asking just enough questions to encourage his stories about the Annesleys. "Please, Mister Reilly, ye put yerself in peril, talkin' this way. Hush! Ye could be fired fer sayin' sech thin's," she said finally, whenever her guilt overcame her.

Hearing the now familiar wagon outside, Maggie hurried Tom out of the glasshouse, so she could greet her husband in earnest. If he knew she was eagerly indulging her fantasies, by studying the habits and mores of the Annesleys, he would not be pleased.

As the months and years past, Joseph seemed to love his travels and the work he was doing. He earned a fair and steady wage as well. Maggie was pleased he came home when expected and didn't seem to be indulging in his former youthful pursuits of drinking and carousing. He and Maggie slipped into a rhythm of comings and goings that, though unusual, seemed to work for them. His mother didn't complain. She planned out a schedule in which Joseph's sister watched the children, allowing her to go to Market Day with Young Joseph, to sell her wares.

The five children grew with amazing speed. Young Joseph did well in school and watched over John, Ann and Eliza. Missus Harden was replaced by a younger woman, who recently came to Legananny and took her work very seriously.

Maggie still took the students on the fall and spring outings, to explore the wonders of nature and plant life. She found she took away as much inspiration and knowledge, as she brought to the class. Their enthusiasm and questions, kept her searching for more items to explore for the next class. At first, it was her way to help Hugh fulfill his dream of an arboretum, to make it accessible and interesting for all of Ireland. After having taught the class so long, however, she knew it had become her own dream to inspire the children of the village to look more closely at the wonders around them and open the possibilities of higher learning for them.

Young Steven Magennis had gone to Dublin to study medicine, due in part to an introductory letter, Maggie sent to the Earl, shortly before he died. She had hoped something would come of it, but hadn't dreamed, he would provide a way for Steven to study at university.

Hugh became the 5th Earl of Annesley, Viscount Glerawly of County Fermanaugh, and Baron Annesley of Castlewellan, with his brother's passing. Maggie remembered the newspaper articles making a great to-do over his claim to the title and its granting. Hugh was still not married. *Much to his mother's displeasure*, Maggie knew. The 4th Earl never married, because he was so sickly. William never returned from England.

Lizzie was five years, now. "She's got the devil's red hair, but her ma's sweet temper, which will win out, d' ye s'pose?" Elizabeth said to John one day.

"She'll be a beauty, Beth. No doubt 'bout it. She's smart as a whip, too," said John, turning his gaze on Maggie, who was watching her child play in the dirt of the dooryard.

Elizabeth said cautiously, "The child needs ta learn how ta do the things thet matter, Maggie," said Elizabeth. "I'm too old fer raisin' children, but wha' else kin we do? She needs ta learn how ta work fer her keep."

"She's learnin' ta read, Ma. She's too little ta be much use ta ye, nae. Lizzie kin carry fer me, an' set the table. She's still a baby, Ma."

"When's yer husband comin' hame, this time, Maggie?" asked Elizabeth, changing the subject abruptly.

"Any day, I should think. I try no' ta pin down the day, so I wan' be disappointin' Lizzie. Should be soon, too late fer t'day though," she noted, as the shadows were lengthening, and the mountains were already turning deep blue. Maggie was hoping for that very day, but lately, Joseph had been staying longer and leaving earlier. She hoped it wasn't for getting in trouble. He had his own wagon now, and could plan his trips according to his customers, so she was worried, that he was finding other things to detain him.

"Da's hame, Da's hame," shouted Lizzie in the doorway. She pulled at the top of her apron in her excitement. With dirt on her face, her hair plastered to her scalp with early summer perspiration, she jumped up and down with joy. As the wagon ground to a halt, Joseph reached down to grab the outstretched arm of the little girl, and whisked her up in his lap.

"How's my little one? Did ye leave any o' thet dirt on the ground, Lizzie?" Joseph laughed at his own joke, and Lizzie giggled with him. Guiding the horses to the side of the cottage, he stopped the wagon. With Lizzie in his arms, he jumped down. Brushing the road dust from his clothes, he ducked through the doorway. "There's m' woman! How are yer, love?"

"Jes' fine, m' husband," Maggie said with forced cheerfulness.

"Hello, Elizabeth, John, I trust yer well?"

John and Elizabeth mumbled a reply, knowing something was up, but not wanting to change his outwardly happy demeanor. "Would yer like some tea?"

"No' t'day, Elizabeth, I hafta git these two back ta Leitrim afore full dark. I had a late start this mornin', an' a delay in Bainbridge."

Maggie rushed to gather some clean clothes, and her tatting. "Mother, could yer clean her up a bit? I'll change her apron. How can one child accumulate sae much dirt?"

"'Tis a gift ta be sure," laughed Joseph.

John silently stole from the room. He hated these days when Joseph would take Maggie and Lizzie away from him. It was always a rush of excitement followed by three days of loneliness. He guarded against wishing harm to Joseph, because he knew Maggie wouldn't like it. But still, he didn't like Maggie gone. Elizabeth hardly talked at all while Maggie and the child were gone. He found himself talking to his brother, James, a lot on these days. He dreamed more, too. Frightening dreams made him wake suddenly, sweating with fear.

The wagons switched and loaded, the family was on its way. "Maggie, there's somethin' I hafta tell yer, an' I'm gonna need yer ta help me tell Ma." Looking at the concern on her face, he said, "No' bad news, Maggie, *good* news."

"Sae, what is this '*no' bad'* news,' Joseph?" Maggie sighed.

"Maggie, the company owners invited me in ta talk. They said they liked my work, but they want me ta branch out fer them. It's a great opportunity, they said, wit' great rewards, too." Joseph stopped, trying to find the words to ease what he was going to say.

"Gae on, Joey," *He looks lak' he's about ta take a switchin' from Missus Harden*, Maggie thought.

"They want me ta go ta America, an' bring back more goods an' sell some o' our goods over there. It would take about three, four weeks, they said. An' they'd pay fer ever'thin' an' I'd get a c-commission on wha' I sell. They'll send another man along, ta show me the ropes. He'll decide wha' ta buy an' how much ta spend. He'll show me how ta sell wha' we haf'. I'll be learnin' how ta do it on my ain. I knae I kin do it, Maggie!"

"Oh, Joey, when do ye hafta tell them?"

"Maggie, I had ta tell them 'yes' or they'd give it ta someone else!"

"Joseph! Ye canna jes' gae off ta America wit'out thinkin' on it first. Wha' if somethin' happened ta the other man, or yer? Ye gotta *think* on it, Joseph." Maggie was horrified. She remembered the letters from her uncles, writing about Indians and people that hated all Scots and Irish. Suddenly, the picture of Hugh's black bear loomed up in her thoughts. *Who knaes wha' they <u>dinna</u> tell us!*

"Maggie, this is a chance fer me ta make m' mark, ta *be* somebody. It's the greatest opportunity I'll ever haf'! There's land there free fer the takin'."

"Let me think, Joey. Ye throw all this at me, an' I don' haf' a chance ta think! Promise me, ye won' say anythin' ta yer ma or the children until I think it through. Ye kin tell her t'marra afternoon, I dinna wan' her faintin' dead away on me. We hafta talk on this some more."

They rode together in silence, each afraid a single word would trigger a torrent of bitter words they couldn't take back. *How could he think I would welcome this? He hardly knaes wha' his family's doin', nae! He'll be gone three weeks, more likely, four. How many times will he gae? Will he e'en come back, this time?*

Lizzie looked from her da to her ma and back again. *Where did the happy faces go?* They were each looking at opposite sides of the road. It was like she wasn't even there. She could feel anger between them, taut and steamy. *Wha's this 'Merica? Ah, here's Mórai's cottage! Now we kin be happy.*

"Joey, we're almost ta yer Ma's place. Let her see yer happy ta see her. We'll talk when we are settled an' quiet," said Maggie.

"Yer right, I don' wanna upset her, if we don' hafta. Smile an' wave, Lizzie-girl!"

As the children and grandmother came out to greet them, Maggie found it wasn't difficult to be happy to see them. She missed them so much. Shoving the worrisome discussion to the back of her mind, she knew all the thinking in the world would not dissuade Joseph from his dreams of riches and adventure. She turned her attention back to the family and smiled broadly.

She acts lak' she's no' a care in the world, Joseph thought in wonder. *How's she do it? She's angry as a thunderstorm one minute, charmin' an' sweet, the next. I swear, I married one o' those chameleons from one o' them books she's always readin'.*

All better, thought the child with the red-gold curls. *We're all happy again!*

Chapter Fourteen

After supper, Joseph's mother and the children retired. He sat by the fire and watched Maggie tatting. She frowned in concentration, but bathed in the glow of the fire, she was the most beautiful woman he had ever seen. He'd seen women of all shapes and sizes on his travels, but none would hold a candle to her. "Maggie," he called gently.

"No' nae, Joseph, let me talk ta ye in the morning. I've too much ta think on tonight."

"Wha' e'er ye say, Maggie," he replied sadly. His earlier excitement was waning as he saw her struggling with the consequences of his prospect. *Doesn't she see I could make somethin' o' meself, if I did this? I could gif' her ever'thin' she wan's. We wouldn't hafta worry 'bout the rent or the taxes e'er again! We could own our ain land in America, an' ne'er depend on someone else's favor agin!*

They fell into silence until finally Joseph said, "I'm goin' ta bed." Maggie sat for a long time in front of the fire, her mind in a whirl of 'what if's and 'what if not's. She couldn't command a contract from the company. How could she ensure the scheme would work in their favor? *Who are these men who would drag*

Joseph half way 'round the world on an adventure wit' sae many snares ta befall him? She didn't have a good feeling about this. But his heart was set on it. Any venture carried some risk. *Is the reward worth the sacrifice in this perilous undertakin'? It won't stop there, either. Wha' will be the next prospect after this? Wit' Joseph, the best prospec' is al'ays over the next hill, or the next.*

Maggie drifted off to sleep in her chair, dreaming she was a little girl of eight again, crossing the Irish Sea on the dirty, smelly ferry. It was foggy and she could no longer see the shore. In her fantasy, she ran about on the legs she no longer possessed, crying, *"Da, where are yer? Where are we goin'?"* But only the wind answered her call. *"We're lost, we're lost."*

Out of the mist, her father picked her up and told her, *"It's an adventure, Maggie. We hafta cross this wild sea ta see the other side. We'll not knae 'til we land, where we'll be. It will be a grand place an' we'll haf' our ain land. Wait an' see, Maggie! We'll haf' a grand adventure."*

She woke with a start. Her tatting was on the floor and her neck ached from hanging down awkwardly. With a heavy sigh, she wheeled her chair to their little room and undressed. Joseph wakened and moved over, lifting the covers for her to snuggle in next to him. He wrapped his arms around her and his warmth lulled her back to dreams. This time, her da and Maggie disembarked on Ireland's shore. Then she was older and they danced at the harvest festival. Joseph and her mother were there, but her beloved da was gone. *"Where are yer, Da? What should I do?"*

"Follow yer heart, my lass," James Coburn's disembodied voice replied. *"Ev'ry man has one thin' God gives him ta do well. For me it's the land. Wha' does yer man do well, Maggie? What does his soul crave tha' makes him who he is?"* Then, he was gone. Her head filled with clouds, pushing out all conscious thought until in the cool morning light, she awoke to realize Joseph was gone from her bed. Her head was aching, her mouth was dry, and her

bedclothes were twisted about her until she could hardly move. *Poor Joseph, I must've been thrashin' about like a madwoman las' night.*

"Well, hello! Look who's awake. Lizzie was wondering when yer were gittin' up." Joseph sat on the floor by her head and brushed her hair from her eyes. "Ye had a wild night las' night. I'd think yer were in ye cups, if n' I didn't knae better, the way ye were lurchin' about. I'm guessin' ye were asleep, but maybe no', ye clouted me jaw in the night." Joseph grinned and kissed her nose. "I'm sorry fer givin' ye fits, m' love. It's no' easy, married ta a clod lak' me."

"Joseph," Maggie purred with half-closed eyes. "I've come ta decidin' ye should gae off ta America. Nae, afore ye commence ta hoopin' and hollerin', stay calm, 'cause I wanna tell yer Ma, while yer still behavin' yerself."

Joseph's eyes filled up as it occurred to him how difficult a decision this was for her. "God bless yer, Margaret Jane Heenan. I'll make yer proud, I will." He leaned in and kissed her lips sweetly, then deeply. He moved her over and slipped in next to her, taking her into his arms. She rested her head on his chest as he stroked her back and kissed the top of her head.

Raising her face to his, she said, "I love yer, Joseph Heenan." To her surprise, she meant it.

Suddenly, the door swung open and Lizzie said, "Da, ye said Ma was gittin' up! Breakfast is on the table an' Móraí's waitin' fer ye."

"Tell her we'll be there presently, but gae on wit'out us. Nae git, Lizzie, an' close the door."

Dismissed, Lizzie backed out sullenly and when the latch clicked, Joseph started tickling Maggie. "Hush! J-Joey, stop!" She beat him impotently with her tiny fists until his mouth covered hers and they were no longer laughing. She stopped struggling and returned his kiss. "Joey," she said, her eyes shining brightly, "We'll continue *this* discussion tonight."

When they emerged from the little room, hastily dressed and still aglow, Joseph's mother looked heavenward shaking her head, but smiling. "I'll be guessin' yer ready fer a *big* breakfast now," she said pointedly.

"Indeed, Mother. I could eat a horse, if it's no trouble, ta yer," said Joseph grinning unabashed, and winking at the children.

"Johnny, Ann, after ye finish eatin' breakfast, I'd like yer ta take the girls blaeberrying. Yer brother is busy helpin' in the fields. I need two big buckets ta make a pie fer t'night an' biscuits fer the mornin'. Kin ye do thet fer me?" The boy nodded, and said to his little sisters, "Eliza an' Lizzie, ye will hafta do as Ann and I say, nae. Did yer hear Maggie? Ye canna be eatin' all the berries outa the buckets, neither."

"Ye mind Johnny, nae. He's in charge." The girls groaned playfully, and rolled their eyes.

"Aye, Ma. But we don't hafta march like soldiers, do we?" asked Lizzie.

"No, darlin', ye don' hafta march." Maggie smiled as Lizzie whipped her head in Johnny's direction with her hands on her hips. *See?* she mouthed at her half-brother.

"Ye hafta stay close ta him though, Lizzie. I don't wan' ye wanderin' off," Maggie warned.

When the children left, Maggie and Joseph told his mother about the company's proposal. Maggie told her about the risks and the advantages. Since the arrangement of the past five years worked out, there was good reason to believe this new one would too.

"Did they say why they were changin' the way they're buyin' their goods, Joseph?" asked Maggie.

"They say the railway is able ta transport a large volume o' goods ta even the smaller towns in Ireland. They found they hafta sell more goods ta pay fer the transport from the factories ta the stores. Ever'thin' is sae much faster these days. Instead o' peddlers comin' ta the customers, ev'ry three weeks, the customers are goin' ta the stores in the villages anytime they please. The variety o' goods is greater in the stores than ye could e'er put on a wagon. It's the way o' the world t'day — people want more, an' bigger an' faster," he said.

"Well, I don' think *more' an' bigger an' faster* is ta my lakin'," grumbled Elizabeth Heenan. "I like slow, lak' its al'ays been. Gives ye time ta think on things."

"Don' think because ye prefer the old ways, it's gonna stay thet way, Ma," said Joseph. "I think we're gonna hafta gae wit' it, an' find out the best way ta make a livin' at it."

"Well, ye gonna do, wha' ye gonna do, son. I hope it's ever'thin' ye want it ta be." That said, she began to gather the dishes in her arms noisily, giving voice to the clamor of her thoughts.

"But, Ma . . ." began Joseph.

"Leave her be, Joey. Let her think on it. She'll come 'round," whispered Maggie. "Give her some peace fer awhile."

"Yer right, as usual, wife." said Joseph sadly. *Why can't women jes' be happy at good news? If it was rainin' gold coin, they'd hafta knae whose face was on 'em, 'stead o' jes' pickin' them up. They hafta* think *the joy outa ever' thin'!*

Joseph's mother was quiet the rest of the morning. She seemed to be arguing with herself. At times she was irritable, and at other times, hopeful.

Maggie had Joseph take her out to see the fields, so his mother wouldn't have to bear his watching her every move. Remembering how much Maggie loved to ride, he put her up on the horse and jumped up behind her. The fields were blossoming with early produce. They spotted the hired man down a row in a maize field. Maggie asked several questions, then asked if there was anything he needed.

"Well, 'ceptin' fer the harvestin', an' the tendin' I kin git it done wit' jes' Young Joseph here. He's sometimes reluctant, but I poke him along. I don' take him ever' day, cause the Missus needs him fer some o' the chores 'round the house an' fer the market. I could use his help more, but I don' wanna take him from yer Ma, ye understand."

"Thank ye fer yer truth, Mister Smith. Maybe we kin haf' Johnny help more wit' his grandmother an' give ye Young Joseph more time in th' fields," said Maggie. "It looks like yer doin' a fair day's work here. Come ta the cottage ta pick up yer wages an' join us fer supper, Mister Smith."

"Yes, Ma'am, I thank yer, kindly. Since my wife's been gone spring last, I don' git ta sit at table much anymore. It'll be an honor an' a treat fer me."

"Yer welcome, Mister Smith," said Maggie.

As Joseph turned the horse for home, he said curiously, "Ye wouldn't be makin' matches, would ye, Maggie?"

"Oh hush, Joey. Yer ma has a few years on Mister Smith, but they would both be grateful fer a little conversation an' a cuppa tea, don' ye think?"

"Maggie Heenan, yer a *devil* in woman's form," said Joseph, giving her a squeeze. "An' it is a very lovely form 'tis, too."

"She's no' likely ta be sae angry wit' yer if she has comp'ny, either," she said.

"I *did* marry the Deceitful One hersel', dint I, nae! I ne'er woulda believed it, had my ain ears no' heard it," he grinned. "Nae, wha' do ye say, we gae fer a real ride, Maggie girl?" He tightened his hold on her and kneed the horse to a full gallop.

I could ride lak' this ferever, thought Maggie. *No earthbound chair, jes' the warm wind an' Joey's arms 'round me, one ta let me fly, the other ta keep me safe.* She grasped the horse's mane and prayed it would never stop. But stop it did, at the cottage door. Joseph slid down and carried her into the house.

They told the elder Missus Heenan they had invited Mister Smith for supper and were pleasantly surprised that she was agreeable to it. "I'll be glad ta help, Elizabeth," said Maggie. "I'll fix the blaeberry pie, if ye will bake it fer me." Just as the words came out of her mouth, the children popped in with their buckets full of early blaeberries.

"An' some red raspberries too," shouted Lizzie.

"They're likely too tart," said Johnny. "I tol' her, but she doesn' listen ta anybody. The hulls are mostly gone, but jes' barely an' some are still there. Ev'ry one knows if the hulls are still there, they ain' fit ta eat. If she's sae smart, *she* kin haf' mine."

"I'll eat 'em, Lizzie. I won' mind if they're tart," spoke up Eliza, taking her half-sister's hand and pouting at her brother.

"Well, we'll just hafta look them over real good. If there aren't too many, we'll just use the good ones ta dress up the pie after it is cooked," said Maggie. "Thank ye fer bringin' 'em, Lizzie."

The squabble over the berries dispensed with, Maggie instructed the girls to bring her the ingredients for the pie. Joseph took Johnny outside and headed once again for the fields to lend Mister Smith a hand. Missus Heenan hummed to herself as she straightened up the room preparing for their guest.

It was the first of many evenings that Mister Smith came to supper. Young Joseph learned not to complain about working in the fields. Johnny, Ann, and Eliza helped their grandmother around the house. Lizzie adapted to the new arrangement by first staying with Eliza, then the next day going with Johnny, depending on how much trouble she was on a given day.

Soon, it was time for Maggie and Lizzie to go back to her mother's and for Joseph to begin his new adventure.

Lizzie asked Joseph so many questions, he finally turned to Maggie and said, "Did ye e'er hear sae many queries in all ye born' days? Lizzie, ye hafta wait until I come back ta git ye answers, 'cause I haf'n' *been* ta America yet. How kin I tell yer wha' it's like?"

"Well, Joey, hurry up an' gae, so I kin welcome ye back," laughed Maggie. "I'll be spendin' my time, missin' ye terrible, an' tryin' ta answer this child's questions, from mornin' till night."

Joseph packed up his wagon, changed the horses and set off for his journey in high spirits. Maggie thought, *I'm gonna miss him more than e'er this time. Is it 'cause he'll be sae far away or 'cause he's looks sae excited ta leave. Or, perhaps it's me who's changed? Will Joey al'ays feel trapped by his women? No' free ta choose his fate on his ain? Is any man free ta choose his fate?* She chuckled and thought, *No more than any woman, I 'spose.*

As the pattern of her life at home returned, Maggie told her mother about Joseph's journey to America for the company. Her mother stewed and fretted about Maggie losing her husband to the wilds of *'God-knaes-what-will-happen'*. Maggie had expected Elizabeth's disgruntled response as much as she had that of Joseph's mother. They each were raising grandchildren. It was not the natural order of things, and it was *she* who was failing her role.

"Maggie, ye spoil the child like English cream left ta the sun. She'll hae a hard lot ta work an' yer teaching her no skill. I'm much too aged fer the rearin' o' children, but who else is there? Joseph's gone, an' ne'er worth one English shillin,' by the by," Elizabeth spit out.

"Joey's gone ta America, Ma. I won't hate him for thet. If I could run off wit' him, I would, an' ye knae I would. He'll be back in less than two fortnights. We won' knae 'til then whether it was a wise or foolish decision fer him ta gae.

"An' Lizzie's barely five an' sae clever. Did ye hear her singin' this mornin'? Ye would haf' her as sour an' hateful as yer, afore ye knae."

Immediately, Maggie bit her tongue. Her ma didn't mean to be so bitter. Her lot was never an easy one. "I'm sorry, Ma. I don't mean ta be sae ugly." Her mother smiled at the expression her daughter used, she, who was so fair, strangers stopped to stare.

Maggie fought an overwhelming sense of guilt and loneliness. *Oh Joey, how selfish are we?* She resolved to talk to her mother about Lizzie's practical education. She learned to make candles and soap, to render lard, cooking, and washing. Later, her grandmother would to take her to market to learn how to trade, how to get a good price for her goods, how to choose a bargain. There were so many things she needed to learn if she was to live in this harsh land. *She canna learn it all at once, but she kin git started, I 'spose.*

So as the days went by, Lizzie was let in to the secrets of the household management as taught by her grandmother. They made biscuits, playing the game that Maggie played as a child. Soon, the child was baking them and brewing tea every day. When the time came for making candles and soap, Lizzie proved to be a capable and creative student. She was so interested in her new lessons, Maggie had to make sure the child had time to play.

Market Day came and Lizzie could hardly contain herself. She knew her half-sister had gone to market this year, and she was sure she would see her there. She missed her brothers and sisters. John used to take Maggie and Lizzie to the Heenan cottage for the day, while Elizabeth and John went to market. Since Lizzie was going to market with them, Maggie would stay home and work on her books.

Busily poring over her books, Maggie didn't hear the wagon pull up outside. A knock on the door frame startled her. "Maggie?"

The brilliant sunshine behind him obscured the figure in the doorway. "Mister Reilly? Tom?"

"Nae, Maggie. It's Hugh," he said quietly. Maggie jumped. It had been years since she had seen him.

"Wha's happened?" she asked before she could control herself.

"I had to see you, Maggie. To tell you," he said sadly. He stopped, as if he did not know how to continue.

"What is it, Hugh? What's wrong?" This tentative speech did not sound like Hugh, the Earl of Annesley. "Tell me."

He crossed the room and knelt in front of her. "Maggie, I'm getting married."

"I see," she said, slipping into the clipped, enunciated speech of nobility. "I'm happy for you. Why do you come to tell me this, Hugh? It's been six years since last I've seen you."

"I had to see you again before I married. I have stayed away out of respect for your marriage to Joseph Heenan, but you have never been out of my thoughts."

"Hugh, I am bound to my husband, my family. Why are you *here*?" Maggie dared not give voice to the feelings she held for him.

"I-I… Forgive me, Maggie. I shouldn't have come. I needed to talk to someone who would not betray me for a bit o' coin."

"Sit, Hugh. Tell me what's wrong."

"My whole life is wrong, Maggie. In less than two weeks, I'm being married to a child I hardly know, who has no feelings for me except what her mother tells her she should feel. She's nineteen years old and her greatest accomplishment is not dropping her fork at the Queen's birthday celebration dinner. She's lovely, but I don't know if she can even read. Mother says she will be a wonderful asset to me. I suspect that although the child is excited at the prospect of marriage, she is scared to death to find out what is under this mask. I'm 46 years old and I cannot even govern my own life."

Maggie laughed softly. "Poor Hugh, no one governs his own life. Not even the Queen. She is governed by the will of her people. As for this child-wife, you have an opportunity to teach her everything you want her to know. You can share with her the wonders of the world and show her places that I will never see." She reached for his hand. "If you remember, I was not much older when I fell in love with you and you with me. With her, you can share a life."

"I'm sorry, Maggie. I should not have come. I'm just treading water in an unfamiliar pond. You always know the wise thing to say." He picked up her hand and kissed it. "I guess I didn't want to add another wall that keeps me apart from you. I don't think I can ever love anyone but you."

Maggie took his face in her hands and said, "Hugh, what you and I have will never completely go away. We are matched souls. I have learned to love my husband in a way that is completely apart from the way I will always love you. You can learn to love and enjoy the love of your bride. I know this is true. I carry his child inside me and there is great joy in it."

He was silent for a moment, head hanging down. Looking up at her, the Earl smiled sadly, "I suppose it is wrong of me to be jealous of what makes you so happy. I want so much for you that I cannot give you. I imagine he does, too, each of us, in our own way, eh? If you ever need anything from me, just send word. I must go now, before I betray us both." He leaned forward, kissed her lips tenderly and reluctantly pulled away. Without another word, he left.

Maggie's arms wrapped around her body, trying to prolong the emotion the kiss had stirred in her. A single tear fell from her cheek and she brushed it away impatiently. *No! Don't start indulging your fantasies, again. This life is hard enough without dreaming of silly, romantic impossibilities. Joseph loves you. He's trying to build a new life for us. Don't befuddle your brain with your flights of fancy. You cannot have two men, so you might as well love the one you can. Come home, Joey. Come home, while I still remember I'm your wife and I love you.* A sudden sharp pain in her lower abdomen made her sit up straight and gasp for air. *Well, little one, am I to be punished for thinking of Hugh? You must be a boy, protecting your father so fiercely!*

Chapter Fifteen

Lizzie was enjoying her new status as Mórai's 'helper.' *I think Mórai's enjoyin' it too*, thought Maggie. *She couldn't teach me ta do these chores wit' my hands. We al'ays had ta figure out how I could do them from the chair. Some, I couldn't do at all. It must be verra satisfying ta do that kind o' practical work. I was lucky ta find somethin' I could do that was useful ta anyone. Were it no' fer my catalogin' books an' farmin' journals, I'd be utterly useless.*

Lizzie marched through the main room and picked up her grandmother's collection of irons. Watching Lizzie struggling under her load, Maggie asked if she could help. "Nay, Ma. I kin do it. If it's too heavy, *Mórai* says ta make two trips."

Lizzie adjusted the irons she carried in her apron and went out the door. Maggie felt a pang of jealousy as she watched her child become more independent every day due to her grandmother's teaching. *Joseph will be sae surprised. She had done none o' this when he left,* she thought. *I hope he gits back afore the baby shows. I wanna see his face when I tell him.*

She checked her journal where she had written the days since he was gone. It was almost time for Hugh to be married, *jes' two more days. July 4th. Joey should be back on the 3rd, but I don' dare* mention it. *If he's one day late, they will all think he's no' comin' back. They'll haf' him dead an' buried, scalped by Indians, or worse.* Maggie shivered. *I canna imagine what could be worse than that! Better git my mind off it. 'Tis no good fer the baby ta be thinkin' on sech things. He'll grow up ta be a child o' sorrow fer sure.*

I should haf' asked Hugh if he was goin' ta be travelin' afta he was married. If he stays hame, I won't haf' my books ta do an' the work will peter out. Well, don' git ahead o' the horse, Maggie. Wait an' see. Yer still haf' the greenhouse samples ta toughen up an' record their growth. Tom Reilly will be takin' those by August's end. The fields haf' almost been cleared o' the Japan shrubs an' bushes an' they've gone ta Castlewellan.

"Ma, kin ye hear me? *Mórai* says I kin put some good smellin' stuff in the soap this time. What should I chose?" Lizzie was bouncing up and down in her excitement with her new challenge.

"Well, wha' do we haf' the most of, little one? It takes a lot o' smelly stuff ta cover up lye an' lard. How about the rose petals ye've been gatherin'? It'll make the soap a funny pinkish-orange color, but ye might smell some roses in it. See what *Mórai* thinks." Maggie smiled as Lizzie ran off to consult with her grandmother.

Lizzie came back with bright eyes and breathless. The little girl putting her hands on her hips, shaking her head and mimicking her grandmother, she said, "She *saaays*, it's all right wit' me if ye want ta waste all thet effort ta make a wee smell o' flowers in yer soap. It's no' fancy parfumy, glyc'rin soap from France, ye knae."

"Make yer decision then, wee bairn. D' ye want ta use all yer rose petals fer soap, or did ye haf' some other purpose fer 'em? You did all the work o' gatherin' them, what do ye wan' ta do?"

Lizzie clapped her hands, "Use 'em in the soap. I kin smell it whenever I want. Besides, who wants smelly old yeller soap anyway?"

"Remember why yer making soap, Lizzie. It's ta clean, nae ta smell pretty," said Maggie, a smile tugging at her mouth.

"Why can't we haf' both, Ma? Cleanin' soap thet smells purdy?"

"We'll try. But don' be too disappointed if it don' cover up the smell as much as ye like," warned her mother.

"Nay, Ma, I won'." Lizzie dashed out the door with the huge cracked urn of her prized rose petals she'd been saving for months. Maggie sighed happily. *I wonder how many roses met an untimely death in that child's quest for the biggest collection o' rose petals?*

Lizzie returned to collect more supplies. "Ye gotta haf' vinegar, jes' in case if ye git lye on ye; an' salt, ta hurry the curin' stage; an' the big 'namel pot, *'cause ye don' wanna roon yer good pots.* Oh an' lard, *lotsa* lard will make the soap slipp'ry. She's cookin' down the rose petals nae. It smells like fairies breath, Ma. Kin ye smell it?"

"I kin smell it, Lizzie. I want ye ta do ever'thin' *Móraí* tells ye, an' don' git too close ta the pots. Be verra careful. The vinegar is in the cabinet near the fireplace. Take out one of the smaller crocks, not the big one. Thet one's not ready yet. Take yer time. You don' wanna break it."

Ma's enjoyin' this more than she lets on, I'm sure. One day, Lizzie will do this on her ain. When she taught me, she knew I'd ne'er do it on my ain. Ye waited a lang time fer sech a good student, Ma.

Finished with her morning chores in the main room, Maggie went back to the office. She made up John's bed and straightened up before she settled down to her books. She stayed alert to any new sounds that might warn her of any mishaps in the soap-making at the back of the house. It was difficult to stay out of the process of teaching her daughter these new skills. It was a role she always dreamed of when she was carrying the child. She could teach her the skills of the mind, but not those that required physical labor. It occurred to her how much her mother wanted to teach her those things when she was a child. She was too young before her legs became useless to her. After that, it was more practical to turn to more academic pursuits. A moment of self-pity overcame her. *Oh, my. Carryin' this baby's got me weepin' over ever' thin'. I'm sae touchy. Git aholt o' yersel', Maggie. Ye will haf' ever'one thinkin' som'thin's wrong wit' ye. It's more the truth thet som'thin's right.*

Maggie mopped up her face and decided that the sudden spate of tears was due to being overtired. *I'll gae back to my bed an' rest a while.*

As she went out the door, she was struck again with a series of sharp pains in her lower belly, then a deep unrelenting spasm that tore a scream from her throat. The chair fell on its side trapping her arm beneath her. Wild, swirling visions clouded her mind as the pain took over her body and threatened to tear it apart.

Maggie felt her head bouncing up and down as a roar deafened her ears. A kaleidoscope of faces and colors passed in her vision and her stomach lurched uncontrollably. Then, silence. She began to be aware of muffled voices growing louder and more distinct. *Joey... Ma... Who...?*

"She's coming around nae, Mister Heenan. Go easy wit' her. She won' know wha' happened."

"Maggie, Maggie, *a stór*. Welcome back." Joseph's face hovered over hers among a field of glowing stars.

"Wha's... Yer... Joey, yer hame," she whispered. As he finally came into focus, she thought she was still dreaming.

"Hush, m' love, ye should rest. Just close yer eyes and rest." Maggie did as she was told. She couldn't make any sense of what her eyes told her, Her ears felt like there were wads of cotton in them, and she couldn't trust her beating heart. *Yer dreamin', Joey's in America.* Her belly pain was duller, more generalized now, but hot. She slowly became aware of lying in a warm pool and a sweet metallic smell. Her stomach lurched again. This time she emptied its contents, thrusting her head to the side of her bed. She began to shiver. *So cold, sleep...*

Her mother cleaned her up and stripped the bedclothes from beneath her. She put a clean nightgown and blankets over her. When she made her as presentable as she could, Elizabeth brought Lizzie in to see Maggie.

"She's awful white, Móraí. Are ye sure she's alive?" Lizzie asked in fear.

"She's very sick, little one, but she's breathing. She'll come back ta us. Let's let her rest now."

"Joseph. Ye kin see her nae. She's sleepin', but she looks better. She might haf' a wee fever, but she's quieter now."

"Oh, Elizabeth, I couldn't take losing another. Maggie means the world ta me."

"Bite yer tongue. Don' even *think* it or ye will bring it down on us," Elizabeth said crossly.

"I'm sorry. I was jes' sae scairt. Missus Coburn, look, she's wakin'."

"Joey, how lang haf' yer been here?" Maggie struggled to sit up, barely speaking aloud.

"No, no. Lay still. Ye had quite a day, *a stór*." Joseph, ashen-faced, held her shoulder down. "I'm sorry, Maggie. Ye lost the baby. Ye hurt ye arm an' ye will be sore fer a while, but I think ye gonna be fine. Ye gave us all a fright, I don' mind tellin' yer."

"I dinna git a chanst ta tell ye, Joey. About the baby, I mean. N-nae he's gone." Tears began to roll from her eyes and she rolled toward him curling her body up. She gasped when she felt her arm seize with pain.

"Hush. Maggie. It jes' wasn' meant ta be, love." He leaned over and kissed her forehead. He stayed like that with his head on her pillow, brushing her hair back from her damp brow. "We are a family enough as we are."

"Lizzie made some tea fer ye, Maggie. Are ye up ta havin' some?" Elizabeth proffered the cup around the bed curtain for Joseph to take. "It might settle yer stomach."

"Thank her fer me, Ma. I'd like ta see her in a bit." Maggie's voice was raspy, but strong.

Joseph and Maggie sat up for awhile, Maggie sipping tea, he holding the cup steady. Her husband pulled back the curtain so Maggie could see Lizzie sitting at the table. "Come, Lizzie. Come see yer Ma."

"Gently does it, Lizzie. Yer Ma's feelin' a bit frail, right now."

"Well, Lizzie," Maggie said quietly, "Did yer finish yer soap-making, then?"

"We jes' got done when we heard the crash an' Da's horse. *Mórai* an' me came runnin'. Da took off fer Missus Callahan, the midwife, an' yer were all kinds o' crazy in the head. I'm glad yer back though."

"Lizzie! Yer kin say she was sick. Ne'er mind this *'crazy in the head'* expression yer usin'," admonished Joseph.

"Yes, Da." Lizzie hung her head. "I didn' mean she was *really* crazy, but she was talkin' crazy-like. I'm sorry, Ma."

"Well, thet must haf' been verra scary fer ye, little one. I'll be fine in a couple days though. Isn't it nice havin' Da hame?"

Lizzie threw her arms around her father's neck and said, "I'm 'specially glad he came hame, right when he did. I dinna knae what we'd haf' done wit'out Da."

"Lizzie's right on that score, Joseph." said Elizabeth. "I couldn't haf' gotten her inta the cottage, let alone inta her bed. Thank the Good Lord ye did come hame when ye did. Oh my, John will be hame any minute." Elizabeth went off to get the evening meal ready, bustling through cabinets, looking for ingredients.

"*Mórai* says the soap will hafta cure fer about a week afore we know if it has a good smell or a not-so-good smell. I'm hopin' it's gonna smell good. I'd hate ta think I used all my rose petals an' it still stunk o' yeller soap." Lizzie said, wrinkling her nose comically. Joseph snorted in mirth and tried to cover it up with a cough.

Maggie looked at her husband and smiled. *Maybe we are enough o' a family, this way,* she thought. *But oh, the child! I was already in love with him an' I hadn't even felt him move yet.*

Maybe she'll be all right nae Da's hame, thought Lizzie. *She dinna look sae good ta me. Móraí said she was peak-ed fer a couple weeks now. They won't let me see the dead baby. They said there wasn't nothin' ta look at. There musta been somethin' ta look at, if they were bent on hidin' it. Maybe it's bad luck ta look at a dead baby, I ne'er seen one. Ma's arm is all blue and purple. John will think Da's beaten her. I love him, but he doesn't like Da ... a lot.*

John arrived home at his usual time without incident. He looked in Joseph's direction while Elizabeth explained what happened. He ate his supper in silence and went back to the office.

"How's John doin', Elizabeth? He seems calm enough," asked Joseph.

"Oh, John's, *John,* he don't change any. We try not ta upset him an' he stays in the fields mos' days. I don't think he'll e'er be right, but he stays out o' trouble. E'en goin' ta Market doesn't upset him no more, lang as ever'body leaves him alone."

Lizzie was used to John being quiet and gentle. She'd never seen him be 'upset', but Young Joseph told her and Eliza he saw him wild as a banshee, long time ago. Lizzie remembered John carrying her on his shoulders, smelling of sunshine and sweat, but never heard or seen him be cross with anyone. He would even sit in the dirt and draw pictures of horses and goats for her. He didn't talk much, but she could be happy, being very quiet with him and not feel the need to talk. She could tell he had a lot on his mind from the way he moved his eyebrows up and down, looking mean one minute and scairt the next. Mostly, she thought Young Joseph and Johnny were just making up stories to scare her.

The next morning, Lizzie was up early, before anyone else. She saw Da slumped in a chair near Ma's bed. *Móraí* was still in bed sleeping, softly snoring. She dressed in her shift and apron. In her bare feet, she padded out softly to put the water on for tea. She stoked up the embers, drew water from the well and set the pot to boil. Turning away from the cook fire, she saw John by the shed, picking up his tools to go to the fields. "John? I kin make ye pail if ye want." Lizzie felt very grown up to be tending to the morning chores.

"Nay, Lizzie. I'll come hame in a little while fer breakfast. You gae inside like a good girl," he said.

"Hmph." Lizzie was disappointed that John didn't see how grown up she was. *What's he think, I can't make his lunch pail? All Móraí does is put yesterday's scones and a piece o' goat cheese in it. It don' take no cookin'. I knae, I'll set the table.*

Suddenly, John ran straight at her! He hit her back and grabbed her apron away from her body. *What's he doin'?* She spun around to see his hand on her apron hem, holding it tight.

"Ah-h!" John uttered, shakin' his hand. "Lizzie, child, ye canna stand too close ta the fire wit'out watchin'. Yer dress was on fire. Now it's all black at the bottom."

Lizzie's eyes were staring at John's hand, black with soot. Lizzie ran in the house. Wildly searching, she found *Móraí's* salve that was *good fer almost ever'thin'. Thet's what Móraí said.* She ran back to John who was alternating blowing on his hand and sticking it into the cool water from the well. "This will take care o' it," she said.

"Thank you most kindly, Lizzie Girl. That will do nicely," said John.

When Lizzie left the house to take care of John, the door slammed shut. Now, all the occupants of the cottage were in the window staring at the two in the yard. They were all talking at once. They saw Lizzie's burned apron and dress and they saw Lizzie, intent on spreading salve over the palm of John's hand.

Joseph swept Maggie up and carried her to her chair. Elizabeth checked Lizzie's dress and John's hand. "We'll catch our death o' fright, with yer actions, lassie! Ye could ha' been burnt up worst than John's hand here. A fire's no' ta be played wit', Lizzie." *Móraí's* voice was rising and increasing its volume with every word.

Lizzie burst into tears. "I-I was…"

John stepped in. "Beth! She's fine. She was tryin' ta make tea fer ye. She fixed my hand. Leave her be, Beth. She won' gae near the fire wit'out ye agin, will ye Lizzie?" John clumsily rubbed the child's shoulder with his other hand.

"Nay, I won' John. I *promise, Móraí.*" Lizzie's head hung down, until all Elizabeth could see was her red hair falling in curls around her head and tears falling straight down to the dry dirt at her feet.

Elizabeth was dumbstruck. It was the most John had said in a month. "Oh, Lizzie, I was jes' scairt ta death. Ye coulda been burnt up bad. John, come in, an' haf' some tea while I make yer pail." Turning to Lizzie, she said, "Go in an' tell yer Ma and Da yer all right, an' ye won' do thet again."

The little girl ran into the cottage where she was grabbed up by Maggie and Joseph, grateful she was not hurt. Between hiccoughs, Lizzie told them the story. "And I'll never, never, *never* do it agin!" she wailed.

Lizzie sat for a long time in her father's lap, while Maggie stroked her back. Elizabeth came in with the hot water and John followed, plunking himself down at the table. Lizzie reached out for John's good hand and held it. John smiled and kissed the tiny hand on his.

"Thank God, you were there, John." said Joseph. "Thank ye, fer catchin' her. She coulda been bad hurt."

John nodded and went back into himself again. He drank his tea, picked up his pail, and left for the fields without another word. "Bye, John," said Lizzie, calling after him. He raised his now bandaged hand in a wave as he walked away.

They don't knae you lak' I do, John. Lizzie thought. *Ye only talk when ye haf' somethin' ta say, don' ye? Ye haf' all these stories hidin' in ye head. Someday, if I listen lang enough I'll hear them. I knae I will. Until then, I'll be quiet wit' you as lang as you want.*

"Well, Lizzie, these dishes won' clean themselves will they, then?" said *Mórai*. "Don't take too many ta onct, mind yer." When the first dish clattered to the floor unbroken, the old woman clapped her hand over her mouth, shaking her head. When Lizzie looked up at her in shock at what she'd done, she could see *Mórai's* eyes dancing above her hand.

A few days later, Mister Reilly came with his wagon loaded with flowering shrubs. He was full of the news of the wedding and the Earl's young bride. "The newest lady o' the house loves ta travel. They are off ta the Mediterranean already. No need ta worry, Missus Heenan. There's plenty o' work fer both o' us," Tom Reilly assured Maggie. "In fact, I've brought plants from France, brought in jes' fer the wedding day."

Maggie felt a pang of wistful longing for the life Hugh's bride would haf', but quickly dismissed it. *It's enough that he has a wife who'll share his joys. You have a family o' your own, he should have one too, Maggie Heenan. You left him years ago. Can ye wish him any less than a life of his own and someone to share it with him?*

Except when the hours slowed, waiting for Joseph, time for Maggie seemed to pass in a blur of seasons. When did her children grow so tall and independent? Joseph and John, no longer scrawny little boys, were now almost men with broad backs and a working knowledge of farming. Anne and Eliza showed great promise with their handwork, tatting and crochet. James, quiet and slight, loved his books. Although only six, and the smallest of the tribe, Lizzie was a born leader, a problem-solver and practical thinker.

In the summer of '77, the Heenan children became ill. Truth be told, measles swept through the village like a summer storm, leaving children of all ages in varying stages of the ill health. Young Joseph and James were the first to complain of fever and headaches. Soon, all of the children were spotted with the tell-tale rash. By the time Young Joseph was feeling well enough to help care for the others, James was desperately ill and finding it hard to breathe. His raspy, barking cough suggested the croup had set in as well. The nights were the worst, while most of the children were resting, James' labored breathing required someone to sit with him all night. Maggie and Elizabeth were there, from the early signs of the measles, to spell Missus Heenan's constant trudging from patient to patient.

Within the week, most of the children were back on their feet. James, however, seemed to lose ground. At seven years, James Heenan slipped away in the night while Maggie held his hand. *Laird, how can I tell Joey? Sweet James, gone afore yer even growed. Yer sufferin' ends, whilst ours begins. We'll miss your quiet smile, your sweet voice. Gae with the angels, my love.*

Maggie searched James' face, the bruised hollows around his eyes, the bluish lips that had breathed their last. She picked up his cooling hand and pressed it to her cheek, already wet with tears wrenched from her broken heart. In the silence of the sleeping cottage, she carefully brushed his hair, wrapped him neatly in his blanket, and folded his hands across his chest. She took the cross from around her neck and placed it on his. *Goodnight, sweet prince, may flights of angels guard your sleep.*

Chapter Sixteen

Lizzie grew proficient in her chores and soon took over the smaller tasks of the household, relieving her grandmother of some of the burden that Maggie could not share.

She was an apt student at home and became equally adept with her school work. At ten and thirteen, the Heenan girls were easily at the top of their classes. The study in which one was weaker, the other was stronger, and they worked together to accomplish their lessons. Lizzie was becoming an expert laundress as well. She worked beside her aging grandmother, learning all the tricks of the trade.

Soon, it was Lizzie who went with John to Castlewellan to deliver the fresh linens, and set up the table at market while *Mórai* stayed home. Lizzie enjoyed, not only the feeling of importance it gave her, but the chance to be alone with John. Both her mother and *Mórai* warned her to avoid any excitement when she was with John.

"If you see any arguments or fightin' startin', get John away from the sit'ation right away. Ye don' wan' him upset. Ye don' know what he'll do. Jes' lead him away in a quiet voice an' tell him it's no concern o' yers," said Maggie. "Keep your voice verra calm, as if it were nothin' ta worry about, ye understand? No drinkin' fer him either. Tell him ye need his help an' he'll do as ye say."

One winter Market Day in mid-December, Lizzie entered the little cottage as if the wind blew her in. "Ma! *Móraí!* Ye'll ne'er guess! They's bin a *murder!*"

"Where's John? Lizzie, where's John!" both Maggie and Elizabeth both shouted back at her.

"Oh, he's puttin' the horse by. He'll be in a minute." The ten-year-old answered, her excitement gaining momentum as her words tumbled out. "But, there's a murder in Drumaroad. Alice McCartan's been run down by a ginger-ale cart! She's dead. Head crushed like a gourd."

"Slow down Lizzie. When John gits in here, I want ye ta talk quietly, an' don' be shoutin'. Ye hear, Lizzie?"

"Aye, Ma. I bin quiet all the way hame, but I've got ta tell somebody or I'll bust open like Alice McCartan's head!" The ghoulish delight in Lizzie's eyes was dancing and she was bouncing up and down as she spoke.

"Ma," said Maggie, "Bring John's dish ta the office an' let him knae it's there. This child will surely git him riled up, if she goes on lak' this in front o' him." Nodding her head, Maggie's mother did as she asked. Maggie put a finger to her lips to keep Lizzie silent for the moment.

After a minute, and a bit of bustling about outside, Elizabeth came in, shutting the cold wind out. She took off her plaid, settled into her chair and said, "All right, what's this 'bout a murder, little one?"

"Oh, *Móraí*, it's the most excitin' thin'! Alice McCartan o' Endarriff, *God bless her soul*, was killed on her way home from the shop there. She's Kezia McCartan's grandmere. I go ta school wit' Kezzie. The Market was all full o' the news t'day. She was walkin' alang, mindin' her ain, ye knae, an' she got hit with a cart goin' ta Castlewellan. They dinna even stop! Goin' like the *wind*, they were.

An' in their cups too, they said." Lizzie stopped, drawing in a breath for the next cascade of speech.

"They're 'restin' Will'em Valentine o' Castlewellan an' another fella. What a fancy name, Valentine! Sae anyways, they say he ran o'er her wit'out e'en stoppin' fer a by ye leave, an' went on their merry way, leavin' Ballynahinch an' the ol' lady, her skull cracked open like an egg, it was. *God bless her soul.* Her life's blood 'twas spilt all o'er the road ta Castlewellan."

"Aye," she confirmed, as she watched their eyes widen in the shock of her words. "An' they say she was deaf as a door post, couldn' hear a cannon blast from three feet. I brought yer the 'paper, Ma. I'm *no'* makin' it up. It's right there on the front page. It says she was knocked clear off her feet. They ne'er e'en found her scarf, an' one o' her *shoes* fell off! Young Joseph said her dress was halfway up her…"

Lizzie stopped, knowing she had gone too far. She looked at the amazed, but scowling faces of the two women in the room. "Sorry…, but that's wha' he *said*. She was real *ol'*, probably sixty, but she had almost no grey hair at all. Dark brown it was. Isn't thet the strangest thin'?"

"Yes dear, very strange. I hope you've got this out o' yer brain now, an' we kin calm down. What a dreadful story. Thet poor woman! Did anythin' else happen t'day? Ye delivered the laundry an' the banquet cloth? They were happy 'bout thet, were they?" Maggie said slowly, hoping to tone down the conversation to a reasonable level.

"Oh, ever'thin's fine," said Lizzie, hurt that they didn't want more details of her exciting news. "E'en Mrs. Callan at the Castle was talkin' about it. Not ta me, mind yer, but ta the kitchen help. They said the constable, Mister Davenport, is verra handsome an' smart. He'll throw thet Mister Valentine in jail ferever or e'en maybe *hang* 'im! Ye think we'll see a hangin', Ma?"

"Laird, help us wit' this child! If he hit her wit' a cart, don' cha think it was pro'bly an accident? I knae it's excitin', but if ye keep goin' on like this, it won' jes' be John havin' the night terrors t'night, will it?" said Maggie.

"Aye Ma, but if they left her there ta die, isn't thet murder? Besides, this is the first thing ta happen around here since ... *ferever*."

"Well, I knae wha' else hasn't happened around here Lizzie," said Móraí. "Gittin' supper on the table hasn't happened yet, *has it?*" Elizabeth was growling, but Maggie saw the light in her eyes that belied the sternness she showed Lizzie. "I suppose we'll hafta haf' a killin' a week ta keep ye happy?"

Lizzie looked at her grandmother, shocked until she saw the smile playing around her mouth. "Well, at least we haf' somethin' ta talk about besides how many peats we haf' fer the rest o' the winter an' how lang the apples will last us."

Maggie had a feeling of foreboding wash over her and shivered. *Poor Alice McCartan, an' poor whoever else thet was, whose body jes' gave up the ghost. Laird, help us in the strange times we live! Joseph's only hame e'er other month an' people are gittin' killed in the road. Orangemen an' Cat'lics are goin' at it every Satur'dy night seems. I kin hardly wait fer spring an' winter's barely here.*

Joseph had been gone for about a month on his latest trip to America. Business seemed good and he didn't ever seem to tire of the constant journeys back and forth. The trips took longer now that he had more places to go in America. Strange sounding names like Pennsylvania, Virginia. and Massachusetts fell from his lips with such ease. He relished the adventure and new conquests. Maggie wondered if the new conquests were all business ventures, or did his conquests include charmin' some company to wile away his time in a strange land.

Although he said he missed his family, his mind was away even when he was home. He talked about taking them all to America, but Maggie couldn't leave her aged mother, or her mother-in-law, to struggle on their own, and their growing children were needed to help with the land.

Young Joseph was sixteen and loved the land his father had abandoned. He resented his father's absence and the weight he and Johnny shouldered in his place. His Grandmother relied more and more on the sullen young man who looked so much like his father, but whose demeanor was quiet and withdrawn. His sisters could tease a smile from him, and a certain young lady could draw a hopeful light in his eye, but otherwise, he kept his own counsel and avoided any confrontation.

Joseph came home to a hero's welcome and brought presents to assure it would always be so. His daughters fairly worshipped him and Maggie greeted him warmly, if warily, these days. She wondered who caught his eye on each trip. It didn't seem to make her jealous, but she anxiously wondered if one day he would sail off and never return.

About two weeks after the murder, they heard the news. A letter came on Cartel, Kitteredge and Sloan Company letterhead, informing Maggie that her husband was killed in a ferry accident in New York Harbor. Watching her ashen face as she was reading, Lizzie asked what happened. Maggie threw the offensive letter from her hand and after a brief moment aloft, it fluttered helplessly to the floor. Lizzie snatched it up, her eyes tearing up as she came to the words that delivered the unexpected blow. A single word, "Nay," escaped her lips.

"Yes, my dear. Our fears are finally realized. He's gone."

Lizzie was astonished at the cold, grim utterance from her mother's lips. She suddenly realized the weeks of waiting had taken a destructive toll on Maggie's usually cheerful nature. It hit her like she had been thrown into icy water. *She's known this was gonna happen. She's been waitin' fer it.*

"How did ye knae this'd happen, Ma?" Lizzie asked quietly.

"When you play wit' the devil lang enough, he will take ye hame wit' him," her cryptic whisper sending a chill through her daughter's body. Maggie continued sadly, almost mechanically, "Some things, ye just knae. T'marra, we'll prepare fer a funeral or some kind o' service. Tonight, we hafta tell Missus Heenan, an' the children. Haf' John hitch up the wagon, Lizzie. We must gae as soon as possible."

"Maggie, stop," Elizabeth barked harshly. "It's late. Please, haf' a care. Wait fer the morning light. Only good news hasta be told immedia'ly. If ye canna make it better, then bad news kin al'ays wait 'til morning."

Maggie stared at her blankly, then realizing what her mother was saying, she spoke barely above a whisper. "O' course, yer right Ma. Hold on Lizzie, we'll wait. Let them enjoy the night.

"I'm gonna work in the office for a while. Please Lizzie, help *Móraí* wit' supper." Maggie threw on her plaid and wheeled her chair to the door. Lizzie ran to help her, opening the doors from the cottage and the office. "Thank you, Lizzie. I'm fine, now," Maggie said as she wheeled her chair to the desk. She gave her daughter a hug to which Lizzie clung for a long time. "I knae little one, to lose yer Da, is ta lose a large portion o' yer heart. Ye will hafta fill thet missin' part, wit' the bes' mem'ries o' yer Da. It'll keep him alive fer you." She straightened herself up and added sternly, "Nae gae, help *Móraí.*"

Dutifully, Lizzie left. Maggie opened her books and lost herself in the work she loved. Try as she might, her thoughts came back to Joseph's words. *"They don't much like the Irish there, but there's a barrel o' money ta be had fer anyone willin' ta overlook their poor manners. There's land west o' Pennsylvania, they're givin' away free fer the takin'. We could be richer than Croesus,*

Maggie. We wouldn' hafta be apart e'er agin." Well, nae ye've done it, hafn' yer? Bein' apart is nothin' new, but this time it's final, ain' it? The tears finally came, unbidden, washing down her face, splashing on the page below. Disgusted with her self-indulgence, Maggie coerced the torrent to halt. Carefully, she blotted the tear-splattered ink. With a linen handkerchief, damp from drying her face, she cleaned the edges of the ink until they were no longer apparent. Patiently, she blew to dry the page. After there were no more signs of dampness, Maggie retraced the letters she had destroyed. *There. No sense in arousin' idle curiosity wit' evidence o' childish emotion. Hugh will hear soon enough, I'm sure.*

As she settled once more at her task, it occurred to Maggie there would be wages for her to collect from the company. She would have to figure out how to do that, and soon. She would have to reread the letter for details on whether Joseph would be returned to Ireland, how to secure his wages and if there were any expenses involved. She sighed. *How will I break the news ta his mother, an' his children t'marra?*

Lizzie came in the office. "Supper's ready an' John's hame. Let me help ye inta the cottage." Evening had come and Maggie hadn't realized the passage of time. She looked at her daughter, pale but strong, *determined ta take care o' all o' us. Poor Lizzie, we take sae much from her. I'll hafta gif' her more o' my time. It's sae easy ta just let her take on the whole o' our care. She's only ten, she needs ta be a little girl fer a few more years. We need ta give her som'thin' ta look forward ta. Until nae, it was her da's return, she hung on ta. Nae, what? What will her heart hope fer, nae?*

As they sat at the table, the mood was somber, each with their own thoughts clanging in their heads. John's eyes darted from one downcast head to the other, wanting to offer comfort, but having no sense of loss for Joseph Heenan. He was sad for them who loved him, but had no love fer the man himself. *Better ta be quiet, than ta upset 'em further*, he supposed. "I'm goin' ta bed." he stated matter-of-factly. He stood up, knocking his stool to the floor, catching his sleeve on his cup, sending cup, dish, and knife after the stool, in a resounding clatter. As he tried to catch the falling cup, he stepped awkwardly onto his dish, and slipped across the rough boards into a heap. The two startled women screamed at the commotion. "John! Are you all right?" they shouted in unison. Lizzie began to laugh, hysterically. John roared, laughing on the floor among the scattered tea and dishes. The infectious mirth spread until everyone was caught up in helpless spasms.

Finally spent, Elizabeth rose and picked up the dishes. "Imagine how funny it'd be if he broke a leg," she said acerbically. The three remaining dissolved off into gales of uncontrollable laughter again.

"Lizzie, help *Móraí*. John, ye no' hurt, are ye?" Maggie struggled to put her voice in control. "We canna be seen like this, once the others knae about Joseph. They simply won't understand." She averted her eyes, not daring to look at the others for fear she would start in to giggling again. She took a deep breath and said good night to John.

She took out paper, ink, and pen to write a list of chores for the coming days. By the time she finished, Lizzie and her grandmother had cleaned up the tiny room and gone to bed. Maggie retrieved the letter from the shelf and read it again.

"My Dear Missus Heenan,

It is with great sadness that we inform you that your husband, Joseph Heenan, of our employ, has suffered a tragic accident which claimed his life, falling from a ferry in New York Harbor, December 16, 1882. Though many attempts were made to revive him, they were of no avail.

There is a matter of some wages due him as an employee of Cartel, Kitteredge and Sloan Company. Be assured that the release of his wages will be expedited for your convenience. These wages will be held for you at the Castlewellan Customs House, Office of Commissioner, Mister Samuel Smithson, Esq., until such time as you present yourself to claim it. He is instructed to answer any questions you may have at that time.

The body of said Joseph Heenan of Legannany, Drumgooland, in County Down has been requisitioned by the State of New York, United States of America for the duration of the investigation regarding his untimely demise. A Certificate of Death will be issued at the conclusion of the investigation and sent to you and authorities at Bainbridge, County Down, Northern Ireland. Unless there is any petition for the body by his direct heirs, he will be buried in a place determined by the State of New York, in the City of New York.

Please accept our sincerest condolences in the untimely passing of your husband. Joseph Heenan was a valued employee of our company and a friend of all who knew him.

Sincerely,

Mister John Cartel, Esq."

Carefully, Maggie folded the letter and put it back on the shelf. Tomorrow, she would put it away in the desk in the office, after she went to Missus Heenan's cottage. She knew it would be difficult to face Joseph's mother. *The sun rose wit' the liftin' o' Joey's head, an' the troubles o' the world disappeared as he kissed his mother's cheek. He could ne'er do wrong in her eyes, an' nae he's gone. The world will be a drearier place fer her ta live in.*

She sat for a while in her own thoughts, finally weary, she went to bed, her dreams fraught with dark thoughts of Joey.

The storm tossed the heavy-laden ferry, dark against the sea. The shadow of a lone man fell, flailing from the top most deck into the icy waters below. "There goes another drunken Irishman gone to meet his just end." The lights on the ferry flickered out and the passengers mourned its loss. The black of night blinded Maggie's eyes and she woke to rain splashing against the window panes. Drifting back into slumber, she saw the solitary figure falling again into the icy waters below. The scene played out over and over, until the morning light startled her awake, and she arrived panic-stricken in her own bed. Blankets twisted around her, she clawed for purchase, frantic to free herself from her bonds.

Lizzie, hearing her struggle, ran to her. Maggie, coming to her senses, grabbed her daughter in a fierce hug, clinging wildly. "Oh Lizzie, my precious, I was dreaming. Did it rain last night?"

"Oh, yes. We had a wild rainstorm early this morning." She searched her mother's eyes and finding no words to form the questions flooding her brain, she said, "I'll bring yer basin fer you."

"Thank you, dear. I'll be up in a minute. Is *Móraí* up?"

"Oh yes. She's been up an' breakfast is on the table. Better hurry, afore it's cold." Lizzie ducked behind the curtain and closed it tight.

Laird, jes' lemme git through this day! Maggie dressed, slipped the letter in the pocket attached to the arm of her chair. *Perhaps 'twould be better ta haf' Lizzie tell her brothers an' sisters. I will send them outside fer a walk if it clears. I'll decide when I git there how ta tell them. Missus Heenan's sorrow will be colored by her fear of how they will survive wit'out Joseph's money comin' in. Mister Smith is gittin' too old fer farmin', but he hangs on wit' the boys' help. She pays him next ta nothin', jes' food an' a little fer his ain rent an' taxes. If he had fam'ly ta feed, he couldn't afford ta work fer her. No matter, I'll figure out somethin'.*

Breakfast cleared, John hitched up the wagon, then headed back to his room. Lizzie, Elizabeth, and Maggie went to the Heenan cottage. The air was cold, but there was no snow on the ground, and the wind was calm. Bouncing over deeply chiseled ruts, the women clutched the seat of the lurching wagon for fear of falling. Their pace was agonizingly slow, to prevent the horse from slipping in the half-frozen puddles from the night before. A thickly overcast sky gave no respite from the gloom, the dusk-cloaked countryside belying the mid-day hour. *How appropriate ta the news*, mused Maggie.

Upon reaching the Heenan cottage, the three riders were thoroughly chilled. No one ran out to see them. Lizzie ran to the door to announce their arrival. Opening the door, she saw young Joseph, Eliza, and Missus Heenan engaged in a heated argument. "Hello! Ye haf' comp'ny," she shouted. The three turned in unison to stare at her.

"Joey, help me wit' my mother, Lizzie ordered. Softening her tone, she added, "Please, Joey."

"Of course," he said, striding to the door, the anger and confusion on his face, unspoken.

Eliza, John and Missus Heenan stood gaping at Lizzie, each with their own questions held in thought. Galvanized by the shutting of the door, Missus Heenan said to Eliza, "Put the tea on, girl! They must be half froze." She hastened to put cups on the table with a few biscuits from breakfast.

The door flew open again, with the young man carrying Maggie, and her mother following. "*Mórai*, Maggie kin use the big chair. No sense in bringin' in her wheel chair." His stepmother was impressed with his commanding tone and his maturity.

"Thank yer, Joseph," she said, carefully omitting the 'Young' from the name that chaffed him now at fifteen. "Ye did thet verra well. This chair will do nicely."

Bearing it no longer, Missus Heenan began a torrent of questions. "Maggie, Elizabeth, what brings you here on this nasty cold day? Is Joseph hame? No, he would be wit' ye. Haf' ye heard from him? Is there som'thin' wrong, oh Laird, there is, isn't it? Somebody tell me!"

"They will, *Mórai*, if ye gif' 'em half a chanct," interrupted Joseph, crossly.

"Elizabeth, yer right, it is sad news. I haf' a letter from America, an' it's no' good news." Maggie bade her sit down at the table with her and watched her face as she broke the news that her son was dead.

"Was it the savage Indians? Oh Laird, tell me no!"

"Nay, Elizabeth," said Maggie, cutting her off. "He fell from a ferry in New York Harbor. Joe, you can read the letter aloud to her, if you wish."

Although Joe had never been a great reader, he welcomed the chance to impart important news to his grandmother, who did not see him as the man he felt he had already become. His hands trembled holding the letter, his mouth seemed to stumble over the strange words at times, but he forged on in his role as head of the family.

When he finished, Maggie continued, "I will see the Reverend McKay in the morning, unless you'd rather I saw Reverend Crane of the Presbyterian Church?"

"I've no' much use fer thet man," said Elizabeth. "Neither did Joseph, so let's be done wit' him."

"Very well, do ye wan' the wake here or at our cottage?"

"Here, if ye don' mind. Ye ken use the back room fer yersel's. Ye won' hafta gae back an' forth the whole time," answered the old woman.

"Very well, it was here he stayed when he came hame, so's it's right enough," said Maggie. With a few other matters tended to and the obligatory tea consumed, Maggie bid farewell to the family and asked Joe to take her to the wagon. Johnny, Ann, Eliza, and Lizzie followed them out the door. Joe tied his horse to the back of the wagon and gently took the reins from Elizabeth. He expertly turned the horse into the cold gray road toward the Coburn cottage.

Chapter Seventeen

Maggie instructed Joseph to put her chair in the office, then bring her there. He stoked up the fire and turned to leave. *John must be walkin' off his memories*, she thought. Joseph was stern and brooding, his clouded face betraying his thoughts.

"I don't mean ta be unseemly, Maggie, but did you love my Da?"

"Yes, Joseph, I did. Why do ye ask?" Maggie answered cautiously.

"He was away from hame all the time, how could ye stand thet, if ye loved him?" he asked.

"It was the work he could do best, Joe. He was no farmer an' the Sweet Laird knaes, he tried. He would haf' withered away, resentin' me if I dinna let him gae. Ye hafta do what's best fer the ones ye love."

"But I hated him fer it!" Joe blurted out, vehemently. "He left us wit' nothin' but hard work an' bein' alone. Wha' makes me miss him sae much?"

"Poor Joe, of course ye miss him terrible, an' ye will fer a lang, lang time. Ye kin hate wha' a man does an' still love him fer who he tries ta be. He loved yer, an' was verra proud o' yer, Joseph. He had no feel fer the land lak' ye do. The sun on yer back, an' the dirt on yer hands, feeds *yer* soul. It took yer da's spirit away ta be apart from people. He needed the kind o' work thet fed his soul, too."

"My da was a farmer, did ye knae?" Maggie continued. He loved the land an' taught me ta love it. In Scotland, they made him a shepherd an' it nearly killed him. Feed yer spirit, Joe. Stay on the land ye love, but don' think ever'one is suited ta work it."

The revelation on his face showed Maggie she said the right thing. His face crumbled and he turned away from Maggie, embarrassed at the show of emotion. She tugged on his sleeve and he knelt in front of her, his head in her lap. She smoothed his mahogany hair until his emotions calmed.

"T-thank ye, Maggie, yer sae smart. Yer the best ma I coulda had. I mean, I miss my ma, but I'm glad Da married yer."

"I'm glad too, Joe. Yer a good son. Take good care o' yer grandmere, an' yer brother, an' yer sisters." Maggie whispered humbly, moved by his speech. "Ye best gae on hame now. I'll see yer *t'marra*."

When the boy left, John stepped out of the shadows where he was hidden. "Yer a wise woman Maggie, I didn' much lak' Joseph neither, but I knae he loved yer. An' a boy needs ta haf' somethin' he kin respect in his da."

The next day, John and Maggie went to the Church of Ireland in Ballyward to confer with the minister there. Mister McKay left John in the kitchen where he would be warm, and took Maggie into the parlor to talk about a service for Joseph.

"Was it only ten years ago, Missus Heenan? It seems like it was yesterday one minute, and a hundred years ago, the next. I'm getting old. My wife died last year and I'm quite lost without her. She was my memory. Every time someone would come to call, she would give me a quick history on them before I met with them, so I would not confuse the names. Now, I am found out. Most names go right out of my head, I'm afraid. Well, be that as it may, you didn't come to hear me ruminate about getting old, did you?"

The Reverend McKay patiently listened to Maggie's petition for a funeral service, and her explanation that there was no body to bury, nor any chance there would be one later. In the end, they decided a simple memorial service would suffice for the mourners and perhaps, at a later date, a plaque of remembrance to mark the life and death of Joseph Heenan would be appropriate. He mentioned it was not unusual, in cases with no recovery of the bodies, such as with sailors lost at sea, or soldiers lost in battle. It gave the families a focal point for remembrance.

On the way home, John made a stop at a public house to announce Joseph's death. Several men came out of the shop to express their condolences to Maggie. "He was a good man, thet Joseph," they mumbled shyly, with their hats in their hands. "He'll be sorely missed." John jumped up on the wagon again and they continued their journey home.

"Ye kin take me ta the Heenan cottage, then gae hame if ye like, John. I ken ye haf' no likin' fer wakes." Maggie didn't haf' to add, *especially Joseph's.*

"All right, Maggie, if yer sure ye will be fine."

"Young Joseph will take care o' me, John. It'll gif' him a chore ta keep him busy an' out o' mischief. He's feelin' a bit touchy right nae, bein' sae angry wit' Joseph, an' missin' him, all at the same time."

Neighbors had already gathered. *Missus Heenan's stayin' occupied, takin' in all their attention,* Maggie thought uncharitably. She saw Lizzie and Eliza huddled in the corner, whispering to each other. *I should check on them ta see they are bein' polite. It wouldn't do ta haf' them gossipin' and makin' jokes at a wake.* Shaking her head, she wheeled her chair to the two young girls. When they saw her approaching, they stopped talking. Maggie warned them not to be talking inappropriately and to remember why they were there. She received a satisfactory, "Aye, Ma." from each girl as she wheeled away.

In the early morning of the memorial service, a discrete knock on the door was answered by Lizzie, who invited Tom Reilly into the Heenan cottage. He went straight to Maggie and said, "There is a carriage outside ta take the family ta the church, complements of Lord an' Lady Annesley, Ma'am. They wish ta express their condolences on the loss of yer husband."

Maggie, amazed at the speed at which the news traveled to Castlewellan, remembered their stop at the public house. She thanked Mister Reilly, offered him tea and a warm place by the fire. "I'll be glad ta drive yer, ma'am."

"An' I'll sit wit' yer up top, if I may," said Joe, shaking the man's hand.

When it was time to go, Joe took Maggie out first and set her in the carriage. Mister Reilly strapped her chair on the back where the luggage was usually carried. Soon, they were all loaded into the carriage with Joe and Tom Reilly in the driver's seat. Mister Smith rode his horse behind.

On their way, Maggie watched the girls admiring the carriage, and she remembered the stories her father told about their trip from Scotland, and all the questions she had for Mister Harden. *Dear Mister Harden.* He and his wife had moved to Castlewellan years ago. She still missed them both. She marveled at how the time passed so slowly as a child and so quickly after the coming of age. *Sae much has changed. Sae much will change. These two young ones will do things o' which we dare not even dream.*

In the empty church, the little group seemed noisy, with every tiny sound echoing loudly. In his deep resonant voice, the Reverend McKay conducted the solemn service hardly above a whisper, yet every word was clear. A sudden draft went through the small congregation as the massive door swung open to admit a late penitent. Sitting at the side of the front pew, Maggie picked up her head at the disturbance.

There in the back, in a long black cape, was Lord Annesley. He met her eyes over the bowed heads of the parishioners. *Hugh!* No one but Maggie seemed to notice the added presence in the sanctuary. She bowed her head, quickly. Her cheeks aflame and her heart racing, she gripped her handkerchief so tightly she thought it would tear. She raised her head again and saw Lizzie's eyes studying her, questioning her. Quickly, she focused on the minister, trying to hear his words. All she could hear was the relentless pounding in her ears and chest. She became aware she had stopped breathing. Slowly, she practiced taking air into her lungs. She was light-headed, afraid she would faint. *Are you an emotional schoolgirl, then? Maybe they'll think I am overwrought wit' grief.* She clung to that hope as her hand gripped her chair, trying to breathe her way to calm sanity again. She felt like every person in the room was staring at her, knowing her every irreverent thought.

Lizzie! Lizzie will give me away! Oh, Lizzie, wait until I kin explain...

Suddenly, it was over. He was gone. The minister was speaking to her. Having no idea what he was saying, she merely nodded and took the hand proffered her.

As they were leaving, Lizzie was still staring, watching her face. Maggie looked at her and shook her head slowly, hoping she would not ask until they were alone. Lizzie sat beside her on the way home. "Who is he?" she whispered.

"No' nae, Lizzie," Maggie whispered back. "Later."

Sparks flew from Lizzie's eyes. Thoroughly intrigued, Lizzie knew she couldn't insist, or she would never know. Her mother was nervous and agitated, trying to appear calm. *There's a mystery here!* She thought gleefully. *She'll hafta tell me or I'll ask ever'one 'til she does. Whoever thet old man is, he's verra important an' he's rich! She hasta tell me!*

Maggie's stomach churned. *What'll I tell her? She's smart. She won't jes' accept any story I give her. But I can't tell her the truth, either. Damn it, Hugh! Why couldn't ye jes' stay away? But it was sae good ta see ye again!* Maggie used the ride to the Heenan cottage to think about what she could tell Lizzie. Then, it occurred to her, what if Lizzie tells her sisters and brothers! *Oh my, this had better be a story fer all o' them.*

Maggie could feel Lizzie's eyes on her all the way home. Tom Reilly stopped at the Coburn cottage first and unloaded Maggie and her chair. Elizabeth and Lizzie followed them inside. As Elizabeth busied herself making tea, Lizzie looked at Maggie expectantly.

"We will gae ta the office after tea," Maggie whispered pointedly. "I will tell ye about the man at the service. Please be patient." She had decided what she would say.

Later, after tea as promised, they went to the office. "Lizzie, when the Earl of Annesley was a young man, my uncles had chanct ta save his life. He was a soldier in the Crimea who was very seriously wounded."

"Is that why he wears that black mask, Ma?"

"Yes, dear one. It's a patch to hide his injury. He wanted ta repay them, so he brought *Mórai* and *Daideó* (grandfather) from Scotland ta this place. Yer grandfather was a farmer wit' no land an' the Earl made this land possible fer him. I, too, haf' land as a security. He is the one for whom I keep the books o' plants. It is my land on which we grow his plants from his travels."

"*He's* the Earl? I saw him afore, but I dinna knae who he was! I 'member, he was at the castle when I brought the laundry. He smiled at me, lak' he *knew* me!"

"He knows who you are, little one. But you mustn't ever disturb him. He is an important man with a great many responsibilities to attend."

"Ma, ye sound like yer a lady! How come ye sound lak' him? E'en Missus Donavan doesn't sound as proper as ye right nae!"

"I suppose when I think of him, I think how I would talk if I was among his family. It's just a game I used to play as a child."

"But why would he come ta Da's service? Did he know Da, too?"

"The Earl knows all his tenants, Lizzie. He has to know who the people are who tend his land. He's a good man, Lizzie. Now enough, I want ta git some o' this work done."

Lizzie's keen ear heard the change in her mother's voice and knew the story was over for the moment. She had a lot more questions yet to be answered, but she was wise enough to hold them for now. *Wait until I tell Eliza! She won' knae what ta say! The Laird o' Annesley saved from the edge o' death by Mórai's brothers! Johnny will spit on the ground when he hears!* Lizzie hugged herself, then impulsively threw her arms around her mother's neck.

Maggie smiled, knowing she hit the right chord in telling the story. *When a child asks a question, you kin gie her the truth wit'out givin' her the whole history o' the world 'round it,* she thought. *Ma always said thet, an' she was right. That'll keep her fer nae, but Lizzie will be back ta squeeze more out o' this old rag.*

Lizzie skipped out the door and Maggie turned to the desk. She opened the drawer and reached into the back of it. Retrieving the cup, still wrapped in its box, she opened it, as she had so many times before. The silver tarnished, like the memory of the day she received it. She remembered how angry she was that day. *Leave us alone, Hugh. Don't torture us with dreams which stir up our wants. I've seen the sadness behind your eyes. You have children now, as I do. It's not as easy to dream and want now, without hurting other hearts. They have naught to do with what we are to each other, but they will be injured still, by our selfish indulgences. Leave my thoughts, Hugh. Each time I see you I open my heart to destruction, yet again.* She tenderly wrapped the cup, placed it in the box and returned it to its hidden recess. Involuntarily shaking her head, she returned to her work.

Lizzie delighted in telling her story to Eliza when next she saw her. Her half sister's eyes grew large with the intrigue of Lizzie's words. Together, they made up stories built on the premise of Lizzie's uncles, as daring soldiers, rescuing the Earl's brother. It gave them fuel for an entire winter's occupation.

Johnny pretended he was not impressed, but wished he could ask his stepmother for the real story of her family and the Earl of Annesley. *Pro'bly nothin' ta it, Maybe Joey knaes,* he thought. *Lizzie's jes' a silly girl makin' stories out o' stuff an' nonsense. She still believes in faeries and ghosties. What could she know o' earls an' soldiers?* Still, a part of him wanted to believe a nobleman by circumstance, could be, beholden to a common man enough to grant a wish or two.

As the five Heenans grew, they left this fantasy for more exciting adventures. Ann was married with a child on the way, the boys were still tending the farm, and Eliza, shy as ever, took care of her aging grandmother. At fifteen, Lizzie was fair and fine-featured, with wild, bright red hair falling near to her waist. The sun caught the gold lights of the tresses around her face, and her blue eyes captured more than one Celtic heart that thought it was immune to her charms. One such heart was Will Wright. His father was a publican, with a small piece of land.

Will wasn't much for books, so he drove a supply wagon for the public house, sold herbs on market day for his mother and tended the tap when called upon. Will was quiet and easy going as a rule, but would allow no one to interfere with Lizzie's wishes. Lizzie found this surprising at first, then amusing.

The town was abuzz with news of the Queen's Golden Jubilee approaching. The celebration was slated for mid-June and young people were making plans to go to Castlewellan, Bainbridge, or Belfast to watch the festivities.

Lizzie's mother and grandmother were holding steadfast against the children participating at night so far away. Joseph, now twenty, could do as he pleased, but the girls would not be going, and that was final. Johnny was not interested in the goings on of the Queen he said, and no amount of finagling or cajoling would change his mind. He found it amusing that Lizzie and Eliza suddenly found his company desirable, if only as a chaperone.

Hoping to gain some favor in Lizzie's eyes, Will offered to take them up to *Slieve Croob* to see the celebration from the mountain. Lizzie was determined to join the fun some way, so she broached the subject again to Maggie.

"Ma, we'll be properly supervised an' no harm kin come ta us if Will an' Johnny gae wit' us. Half the town will be up there. I beg o' ye. *Please*, let us go." Lizzie pleaded.

Maggie watched her daughter's animated face dancing in front of hers and remembered the same petition she made to her parents so long ago. "Johnny an' Will are goin' ta be wit' ye, then? I want ta see them before yer s'posed ta leave. Only then, will I allow it." She smiled, letting Lizzie know it was possible she struck the right bargain this time.

"Oh Ma, thank ye, thank ye. 'Twill be fine, I promise." Lizzie danced around her mother's chair with joy.

"Remember, I hafta see each one o' them afore I'll let ye go," warned Maggie. "Eliza, too. Does she haf' a boy she wants ta see there? I'll hafta talk ta him, too."

Maggie sat back and reminisced of her day on *Slieve Croob*, of Joseph, her wild ride up there, seeing Joseph and Mary, her near catastrophic accident, and Hugh's arms around her. The flood of pictures in her mind ended with Hugh's kiss. Her face was flushed and her dreamy eyes made Lizzie ask, "Ma, are ye all right?"

"Oh yes, little one. I am jes' fine." she replied mysteriously. "Just remembering ye Da, in days lang past, an' wanting ta go up the mountain ta see wha' I cud see."

"Wha' was it lak', Ma?" asked Lizzie, eagerly.

"Yer Da was young an' handsome. He took me up on a horse an' we rode like the wind, we did. It was wonderful. I had ne'er been on a horse afore."

"Did ye love him, then?"

"No, child, no' yet, but I was *likin'* him, jes' fine," Maggie answered in a dreamy voice. *The story will come in small pieces, Child. Don't press fer more.*

Staving off more questions, Maggie said, "Lizzie, why don't ye take the horse, ride ta the Heenan cottage, an' tell Johnny an' Eliza I want ta see them when they kin come. If ye should see Will, away from the public house, ye kin tell him, too."

Lizzie jumped up and was out the door in a blink of Maggie's eye. Short minutes later, she could hear the horse at a quick trot on the road. "I see ye didn't tell her the whole tale, Maggie," said her mother quietly, looking up from her mending.

"No, Ma," Maggie sighed. "That's a tale I'll keep ta myself, an' may ne'er tell. I was safe in the palm of God's hand thet day."

Later, while she was working in the office, Johnny and Will came to her door. She bade them sit on the edge of John's bed while she talked to them.

"Lizzie and Eliza want ta gae up the mountain ta see the celebration. I'd like yer in charge, Johnny. Will, ye may gae along ta keep them safe, but ye will take ye cue from Johnny. Headstrong an' foolish is a dangerous combination, 'specially fer girls. Do I haf' yer word ta keep them out o' harm's way?"

They both nodded seriously. "Say it! I want no doubt as ta wha' yer swearin' ta," Maggie demanded.

"I-I'll keep 'em safe, Maggie. Ye knae I will," answered Johnny. He was wondering why Maggie even considered *him*, and not the always reliable, steadfast and true, Young Joseph.

"Yes, Missus Heenan," echoed Will.

"Does Eliza haf' her eye on any boy, I don't know about, Johnny?"

"Well, lately she's been moonin' o'er young Patrick Morgan, but I don't think *he* knaes it."

"Well don't let things get ta more than talkin' before ye step in, Johnny. I'm holdin' yer ta thet. Lizzie kin stay at yer cottage thet night, jes' make sure it's nae too late when ye git there. Yer grandmere will worry. An' yer don' want thet. I'm done wit' ye, Will. Ye kin step outside while I talk ta Johnny."

"Yes, Ma'am," Will scurried out the door.

"John, there's no need ta start an argument wit' yer sisters if things aren't goin' as ye think they should. Just distract them if it looks like it's gettin' serious. Is there anyone yer fond o' yerself?"

"No' at the moment, Maggie. No' since Sally ran off an' got married," Johnny answered with a lop-sided smile.

"Well, ye've time enough, John. Sally dint know wha' she was missin'. Just don't forget who yer takin' care o' t'night," said Maggie.

"I won't, Maggie," Johnny said. "I think Sally jes' wanted ta git out o' Legannany."

"Ye are better than mos', Johnny-boy. Let them come ta you for yer *ain* sake. The right one will come along when ye least expect it."

"Thanks, Maggie. Don't worry 'bout the girls. They're safe wit' me. An' Will is an all right boy-o fer Lizzie. She's much more darin' than he is. Maybe he'll slow her down a bit." Johnny's crooked smile let her know he was sure of that.

Chapter Eighteen

Queen Victoria's Golden Jubilee, June 20, 1887, was celebrated in all British dominions throughout the world. In Legannany, the young people of the village climbed *Slieve Croob* and watched from a distance, the celebrations of several cities and the Isle of Man.

"Look, Lizzie. There's Peter an' Margaret. Let's go sit wit' them on the other side o' the fire. Come on, Eliza, there's a certain Mister Patrick Morgan over there wavin' at us, too." Johnny was enjoying his role of guardian and orchestrator of this party.

Lizzie tossed her hair over her shoulder, hitting Will square in the face. He pretended to be stunned by the blow, reeling back and moaning in pain. "Oh stop it, Will." Lizzie swatted at him, causing another feigned reaction of being mortally wounded.

"Ye oughta take better care o' yer suitors, Lizzie. Yer running out o' candidates," Johnny said, teasing her. Lizzie mugged an astonished face at him and ran at him with fist raised.

"Oh, *yer!*" she protested.

It was early evening and the sun was just beginning to disappear behind the hills. The bonfire was glorious with flames reaching for the deep purple sky, sparkling with thousands of blinking stars. The edges of the sky, as it met the Mournes, were an azure blue, melting into a pale yellow rim. Families nestled pots of soup in the embers for their supper, and bits of meat stuck on green sticks, spit and sputtered in protest of the heat.

Lovers and friends sat on blankets near the edge of the flat to watch the anticipated show. Before dark, they had a clear view of the Irish Sea and the Isle of Man, parts of Belfast, and looking south, Castlewellan. Now, as darkness enveloped them, they saw the lights of the city emerge and fireworks start to erupt.

"Look! Look at the Isle of Man. They're lighting the tar barrels." Johnny shouted amid cheers of the onlookers. Very faint at first, then brighter as more and more barrels were lit around the island. Soon the island was ringed with tufts of fire, first on the beaches, then in ever increasing heights, until the whole island seemed ablaze. The crowd was hushed at the spectacle, until one man heard the fireworks start at Castlewellan. As one, the assembly looked southward toward the castle.

While the crowd was rapt at the display, Will stole a kiss from Lizzie. Johnny saw, but was silent. *I wish ye good fortune, Will. Thet one knaes wha' she wants an' it's doubtful she'll settle fer the polite boy ye are. 'Twill take a strong man ta hold the wildfire in thet heart, boy-o. She may play wit' ye fer a while, but she'll surely break ye heart. Eliza, though, runs deep an' the man who gits her heart will haf' great solace fore'er. Me? I'll hang m' heart on my sleeve in hopes someone will take it hame ta keep.*

Soon, the families with young children were heading home. Johnny sat in the warmth of the fire watching his sisters and the boys, look dreamy-eyed at each other, when a girl sat down next to him. "Johnny? I didn't see yer here before. Where haf' yer been?"

Startled, he stammered, "I-I've been here all the time. I must no' haf' been payin' attention." Shyly, he made room on his blanket.

Lizzie looked over Will's shoulder and whispered, "Don't look, but I think Johnny's gonna be too busy ta insist we gae hame right nae." Will turned his head, saw the couple talking low and nodded smiling.

"Janie will keep him occupied fer a while. I told her he had a likin' fer her, but he was too shy ta talk ta her," Will whispered back.

"Ye are shameless! When did ye git sae smart, Will Wright," teased Lizzie.

"I must haf' caught the smart disease from you, Lizzie, girl. 'Cause I ne'er had it afore." Emboldened by her compliment, he kissed her again. Just as he did, he saw Johnny rise from his position on the ground and walk toward them. "Uh-oh, it was too soon."

"Lizzie, Will, pack yer stuff up, we're leavin'." He winked at Will, so he'd know there were no hard feelings. He strode over to Eliza and Patrick giving them the same message. Having done his duty, he went back to where Janie was sitting. She took his hands to stand and they walked to where her parents were gathering their blankets. Lizzie watched them in confusion. "Wha's he doin' Will?"

"I imagine he's askin', nice 'n polite, ta walk their daughter hame. But, he'll make sure *we're* hame first. He's a lot smarter than me, Lizzie. It'll take him a lot longer ta git hame wit' his new girl. Shy, m' *foot*," said Will, wryly.

The little group filed down the narrow pathway to the main road, where Janie's family split off and Johnny's group headed to the Heenan cottage. Johnny and Janie waved from the front door as Will trotted home on his horse.

Johnny and Janie rode his horse slowly to her home. He couldn't believe his fortune, his arms around this lovely girl, rocking back and forth to the rhythm of slow, measured hoof beats in the moonlight. *This chaperoning job isn't nearly as bad as I thought. I may offer my services from nae on.* He thought, smiling.

Soon, they were approaching Janie's cottage. Johnny turned the horse into the side yard and kissed the brown-haired girl he hadn't really noticed before that night. He slipped off his horse, and as he took her down, kissed her again. He took her hand, led her to the door and said goodnight.

All the way home, he thought, *I'll hafta remember ta thank Will fer a lovely evening. An' Maggie, too, for knaein' it would happen sooner or later.* That night, he dreamed of a brown-haired girl with deep brown eyes and a winning smile of which he couldn't seem to get enough.

"Sae, Johnny. How was yer ride hame with *Janie* las' night?" asked Lizzie devilishly, reaching over to pull his sleeve at breakfast. "Ye seem ta fancy the lass more than a bit."

"Ah, Lizzie, m' girl, that's fer me 'n Janie ta knae," James winked back.

"Woo hoo, Johnny. *Thet* good, was it?" Lizzie enjoyed teasing her brother.

"Twas all quite proper, young lady, an' don't ye be sayin' otherwise. Janie's a verra sweet lass," Johnny tried to say very sternly, but a radiant grin burst on his face, "A verra *lovely* lass."

"Oh no, he's smitten. There's no hope fer him," Eliza cried, her wrist to her forehead in feigned sorrow. The two girls looked at each other and giggled conspiratorially. "Will's got a good eye fer this matchin' business, don't he, Lizzie?"

"Enough. If ye wan' ta go ta Blaeberry Sunday, ye will keep yer tongues from waggin'," laughed Johnny. He was quite enjoying himself.

"C'mon, children, ye haf' work ta do an' Lizzie's goin' hame this mornin', sae hush yer noise, an' git ta eatin' ye breakfast." Missus Heenan winked at Johnny letting him know there was no bite in her bark. She was happy to see her often troublesome grandson having a connection with a calming influence.

Taking her home, Johnny asked, "Lizzie, how is it with you an' Will? Are ye serious wit' him?"

"Hea'ens, no," said his half sister from her perch in front of him. "Will is verra nice, but I'm no' lookin' ta git *tied* ta the lad. I haf' a lang list of thin's I wanna do afore I choose a man ta spend m' life wit'."

"That's good. Yer too young fer thet, but Will's upside down o'er yer, an' ye should no' lead him too fer on, afore ye let him knae he hasn' a chance ta reach the end o' it."

"I keep tellin' him, but he don' care. He says he will follow me ta the bitter end, if I jes' look his way onct in a while. He's hopin' I'll change m' mind one day an' he wan's ta be there when it happens. Wha' should I do wit' thet, Johnny?"

"Keep tellin' him and smile at some other poor lad when ye kin, I s'pose. Be careful ye don' break him while yer at it, Lizzie. He's a good lad."

"I *knae*, Johnny, I wisht Joe went wit' us las' night. He's been chasin' after the Steele sisters, an' canna seem ta make up his mind. Margaret is too much like him and Mary's too much like me. He needs a lass that will make him dare ta do stuff. He's too stern an' sober fer his ain good." Lizzie whipped her head around to see if he agreed.

"Ach, thet hair o' yours," Johnny sputtered, pulling a strand from his mouth. "Can't ye cut it off or tie it down, somehow?"

"Who would favor me then, Johnny?" Lizzie laughed. The bright curling flames of red hair were tied with a ribbon and covered with a kerchief. Still the fiery tresses escaped, wild in the summer wind. She pulled the long ends down over her shoulder, away from him. She yelped in surprised delight when Johnny heeled the horse into a gallop along the empty road.

They arrived at the cottage, breathless and laughing, to see Maggie sitting in the shade with her needlework. Her smile of welcome lit up her face and Johnny thought, *It's easy ta see why Da loved her. Janie's smile is like thet, a candle on the darkest night. Oh, listen' ta me, nae I'm a poet! Watch it, lad! Yer gittin' too close ta the sirens, ye will lose yer wits.* Janie's face loomed in his thoughts, all smiling and sweet.

"John Heenan! Are ye listening?" Maggie's voice broke into his dream state. "Johnny, do ye think ye haf' time ta help Mister Reilly load his wagon?"

"He's dreamin' o' his new-found love, Ma. He canna hear a thin'," laughed Lizzie, musically.

"I hear, o' course I'll help him, Maggie," Johnny said, scowling. "I'll help him."

He took the horse around back, where Tom Reilly was sorting out the plants to go to Castlewellan. Daughter and mother looked at each other, grinning. "I'll tell ye all about it, Ma." She plunked herself down on the grass beside her mother and began to tell of the events of the night before.

Life in Legannany went on as it usually did in small villages, with one day following another in rapid succession, until the people wondered where the time went. Days turned into years, with barely a change in the tapestry of their lives.

On occasion, unexpected events seem to rend a hole in that fabric. In the early spring of 1891, events in the Annesley family conspired to do just that.

The Fifth Earl of Annesley and his wife, Lady Mabel Annesley, were summoned from London to Donard Lodge, Newcastle to find his mother gravely ill. Priscilla Annesley was 84 years old, and had been in surprising good health, until a malady overtook her. Hugh was shocked to see his usually robust and commanding mother in such a state. He knelt by her bed only moments after his arrival, holding her frail, bony hand. To his horror, he watched helplessly as her life simply ebbed away.

He fled from her room, demanding to see the doctors. After speaking with the triumvirate of medical experts attending her, without another word, he turned on his heel and went to his bedchamber. When his wife followed him, she heard the key in the lock, barring her from the room. She was frantic. He had never refused her comfort. His young wife was startled when she heard a crash resound from behind the door. She pounded on the door relentlessly until she heard him stride toward it. She stepped back, frightened. The door opened. The servants that gathered around his wife were shocked when he grabbed her arm and pulled her roughly into the room. The door slammed and all was silent. The servants looked at each other, wondering what to do. One by one, they cautiously took their leave, as no other sound emanated from the chamber.

The next day, when the Earl emerged, he sent a maid servant to clean up a broken vase from the floor and to tend to Lady Annesley's day gown. Not a word was spoken of the night before, not even among the servants. The days of the funeral passed and the couple returned to Castlewellan.

The newspapers reported the death of Hugh's mother with all the pomp and respect due her station and reputation. Lizzie could see her mother was visibly distracted, and saddened. *Surely she doesn't knae this woman. Why is she sae upset by the account in the newspaper? Móraí says it's a sad thin', but Ma's on the verge o' tears all the time! Wait, oh, wha' if it's the Earl she's sae sad fer. There's* more *ta the story than she was tellin' when Da died. But she was only a little girl when she met him. Why is she sae over-sad fer him? Ach, maybe it's no' because o' him a 'tall.*

Lizzie filed her thoughts away to ask her mother at another time, a time when she was not so obviously upset. She carried Maggie's formal letter of condolence for the family to the post.

Barely three weeks later, another newspaper report of an Annesley death was reported. This time, it shook the entire county. This was not the sad but expected death of an elderly noblewoman; it was the untimely death of a young vibrant mother of two, and the wife of the Earl of Annesley. The whole of County Down was reading the tragic account of Lady Mabel Annesley, who fell from a horse while riding one day. She died from a broken neck sustained in the accident.

This time, Maggie did not try to hide her tears. She dealt with the emotions as she usually did, by shutting herself in the office and burying herself in her work. She wrote another, thicker letter of condolence to the Earl, imagining it was one of hundreds from his colleagues, officers of the court, members of the House of Lords, and his many social contacts in London and around the world.

A week later, on Market day, as she was working in the office, there was a knock on the door. Startled, Maggie knocked her pen and papers to the floor, hit her knees on the desk and nearly tipped her chair over. The door opened before she reached it.

The Honorable Hugh Annesley, Earl of Annesley entered the room. Maggie looked around the spare room, for a place for him to sit. There was nowhere but John's bed. He didn't seem to mind as he strode to it and sat across from her. She wheeled her chair over to him and took his hand.

"Oh Hugh, I am so sorry."

He hung his head. "I am too." he declared simply. "She was so bright and sweet. She was such a surprise to me. I loved her, Maggie, and I didn't think that could be possible. She wanted everything I wanted, except for you, of course. I was even able to tell her about you." When Maggie turned her head to hide her tears, he said, "She didn't begrudge the place you have in my heart. She seemed to understand. What a blessing she was for me! And now... she's gone. I'm staggering around blind, Maggie. I'm lost."

"I'm so glad you had her, like I had Joseph. I learned to love him too. Is that strange? Are we so fickle as to just go right into another's heart as if we didn't know each other?"

"I'd like to think we loved them more, because we couldn't have each other. How generous of them to love us in spite of who we are," he said.

"I never told Joseph, you know. It would have broken him. He knew I loved you, but not how much, how long." Maggie was crying in earnest now. Straightening her posture, she tried to break the sadness that surrounded them. "How are the children doing, Hugh?"

"About as you'd expect. They can't believe she's gone. They're afraid to laugh because they think it's a betrayal of Mabel. I tell them laughing is a good way to remember her, but I don't think they believe me. God forgive me, Maggie, I shouldn't be here, but I couldn't stay away." He took out his handkerchief and dried her tears.

Maggie smiled, "Another handkerchief, Hugh? I seem to collect them from you. This will make three." They laughed together, memories flooding back. Maggie sighed.

"You should go, Hugh. Your children need to see you laugh, so they will know they will be all right. Thank you for coming to see me."

Hugh touched her chin, and kissed her forehead. "I will go. Promise me, Maggie. If you ever need anything, come see me. Or send for me. I will come."

"Thank you, Hugh." As she spoke those words, the door opened again and Lizzie burst into the room.

"I-I beg your pardon, sir!" she stammered and dipped to a small curtsy. "I dinna knae anyone was here."

"This must be the charming Lizzie," smiled Lord Annesley. "I'm pleased to meet you. I do beg your pardon, Miss, but I must be on my way." He nodded his head and left Lizzie with her mouth hanging open.

As soon as he was gone, Lizzie fired questions at Maggie. "It's him, isn't it? Lord Annesley. Wha's he doin' here? Wha'...?" She kept looking from her mother to the door and back again.

"Lizzie. Please. Sit down. Let me tell you about my friend. First, you must pledge to keep this to yourself. Promise me. It is important that I can entrust you with this story. You are not to tell anyone. Do you understand, Lizzie? Promise me."

"I promise, Ma. Not even Eliza?"

"Not even Eliza. Maybe after I am dead and buried. But no, do not tell Elizabeth, nor Joseph, Ann or Johnny, *Móraí*, no one. This story is just for you and me, Lizzie," Maggie whispered.

Maggie told her the events of that Blaeberry Sunday, but not about stopping on the way home. Not about the kiss or the conversation. She told her about seeing him on occasion at the glasshouse, and going over the books and photographs, but not about their intimate moments. She tread a fine line between surface fact and the whole truth. "He is my friend. He has always been my friend."

Lizzie looked at her mother shrewdly, "Do you love him, Ma?"

Maggie looked her straight in the eyes, as she knew she must, "As a friend, Lizzie. He is an honorable man. He just lost his wife. He came to me as a *friend*."

"Well, good," said Lizzie. "He's sech an *old* man!"

Maggie smiled. "Lizzie, he misses his wife and he loved her dearly. His children are so sad to have lost their mother."

"Sae why does it hafta be a secret?" asked Lizzie.

"Because he is an important man, and people love to make up stories about important people. If you tell someone, they would tell someone, and so on. The story gets changed and exaggerated every time it gets told and his honor would be challenged. I don't want that to happen to him and he would not want that to happen to me."

Lizzie seemed satisfied with that. "I *will* keep yer secret, Ma. But promise me, ye will let me talk ta yer 'bout it, 'cause I'll burst if I can't say anythin' ta anyone!"

"Very well, you can talk to me, but only if we're alone. Don't make any comments ta me about it in front o' anyone else. Do ye understand?"

"Aye Ma," she said with her hand on her heart.

After a few days of frustration, Lizzie found she could set the story aside and keep her promise. She stopped asking questions of Maggie when she discovered she would not learn anymore about the subject. Life began to go back to the way things were in Legannany, one day much like the next.

Will Wright finally found another's heart, a lass more ready to settle down. Lizzie flittered from lad to lad, each one vying for her attention. Eliza shyly followed her sister with no one special to capture her attention.

John and Janie were in love. John was cautious, wanting to build the farm with Joseph before he married. Janie was anxious, wanting to build a family. Farm prices were dropping every year and the Heenan farm had to produce more volume to make up the difference and meet the expenses.

One day, Missus Heenan became ill. The elder Elizabeth Heenan never complained. The once stout woman became thinner and thinner. A rasping cough disturbed her sleep and contributed to her pallor. Before long, she took to her bed. Maggie's mother brought various remedies, but they offered no real help. The girls took turns sitting with her, seeing to her needs, and reading to her when she was awake. Finally, one cool autumn night while they were sleeping, the coughing stopped, and so did the life of Elizabeth Heenan.

Mister Smith clapped his hand on Joe's shoulder, and said, "I'm sorry, son. She's gone an' so am I. I only stayed fer her sake, ye ken, but nae I'm moving on. I'll git m' things."

"Mister Smith, you knae ye will al'ays haf' a hame wit' us. Ye don't hafta go."

"M' daughter's been afta me fer years ta go live wit' her, sae nae, I guess I will. Thank ye Joe, fer all ye kindness."

"She loved yer, Mister Smith. She al'ays spoke well o' yer. God bless you," said Eliza.

Watching the old man walk away, she turned to her brothers with her eyes brimming with tears and said, "Wha' will we do nae?"

Joseph spoke slowly, deliberately, "We'll take it a day at a time, fer a while, Eliza. It'll sort itself out by spring. We've enough fer the taxes an' rent. We'll gae on as we've always done, then a plan will present itself when we can look at it coldly."

"Yes, Joe." Eliza did not sound convinced, but she had nothing else to offer, so she was silent.

Lizzie, her mother, and grandmother came to help with the wake. Elizabeth Coburn, now frail with age, let Maggie take charge. Lizzie, John, and Elizabeth followed her orders, relieved to leave the decision-making chores to Maggie. Joe stayed in the fields, plotting their future.

Maggie let her mother's shaky hands fix candles in their holders and fold napkins from the linen chest. Watching her mother smooth out the cloths gently, almost reverently one by one, Maggie thought, *she's rememberin' the old days when she was strong an' her family surrounded her. It must be sae sad ta see her whole generation fadin' away, old friends an' relatives taken one by one, an' waitin' fer her time. She said the other day, she was no' afraid ta die. She misses them all. The names an' faces are fadin' from her mem'ry, but she still feels their arms around her, their laughter, their tears. How lonely she must feel wit'out her contemporaries, those who knae her history! I must get Lizzie ta slow down, ta sit wit' her, ta listen ta her stories. She needs ta knae who her grandmother is, before she too, is gone.*

Maggie stopped her reverie, giving her attention to the business of the wake, the notifications, the funeral, and the manner by which mourners move through the process. *John kin fend fer himself fer the next few days. I'll haf' Joe check on him t'marra. Joe needs ta be part of this, too.*

The funeral done, Maggie remembered her wish to have Lizzie sit down with her grandmother. She took Lizzie aside to explain her quest.

Lizzie tossed her head. Callously, as young people often do, she said, "While you were busy with yer books an' *Mórai* was teachin' me how ta cook an' sew an' make candles an' soap, wha' do ye think we talked about, Ma? We talked 'bout Lanark, where she grew up, an' how my grandfather was a farmer wit' hands sent from God. We talked 'bout her brother who died as a child, an' how her mother was burned in the fire. Ma, I knae more o' *Mórai*, than I do about *yer*."

Maggie snapped her head back as if Lizzie had struck her full in the face. Her hands flew to her flaming cheeks at this chastising statement. *Haf' I made her feel this way, lak' she was no' part o' my life? God save me! She thinks I didn't wan' ta do those thin's? Ta teach her the things no' found in books, thet I wanted nothin' more than ta do them wit' her?*

Seeing the effect of her careless tongue, Lizzie immediately ran to her mother. "Oh Ma, I am sorry. Please forgive me. I knae you couldn't do those things an' I am grateful thet *Mórai* was able. She told me about her life over time, only because I asked question upon question. Ye were busy writin' in yer books, sae I asked her. When I wasn't working wit' *Mórai*, I was off playin'. It's yer, I didn't ask about. Can ye forgive me?"

"Lizzie, in wantin' ye ta do everythin' I couldn't do, I drew away from yer. I'm the one who needs forgivin', no'*yer*."

"Stop, ye are a fine mother. Ye taught me wonderful thin's about books an' the world. Nae, I think ye should teach me... about *yer*."

The young woman in front of her was a strange new creature, one Maggie didn't recognize. This girl-woman had taken ownership of her hurtful words and given her mother a graceful way to come back to her. Maggie drew herself up and calmed her emotions before she spoke again.

"I knae ye ask verra hard questions, my girl, but I will try ta accommodate ye. Still, I may no' be generous wit' answers I'm still sortin' out. Since I haf' apparently missed more time wit' yer than I realized, *ye* must teach me somethin' about ye, fer everythin' ye learn about me. Do we haf' a pact, Lizzie?" Maggie smiled to let her know she bore no ill feelings about the outburst Lizzie was now trying to soften.

"We must shake hands on it, if it is ta be a contract, isn't thet right, Mother?" Lizzie teased her.

"I think I'll seal it with a kiss. Come here, child." Lizzie leaned toward her mother to receive her kiss and gave her a hug in return. *She's al'ays the gracious one, an' I'm sae clumsy wit' my words,* thought Lizzie. *Will I ne'er learn ta say the right thing? Poor Eliza, I'm fore'er hurtin' her feelings; nae Ma, the las' person I want ta hurt! I seem ta haf' a gift fer it! Joseph an' Johnny jes' git mad at me an' stomp off. An' Will finally jes'... wen' away. I am nineteen years old, am I al'ays gonna be this horrible person?*

Maggie could see her daughter's mind whirling with self-recrimination. "Lizzie, you're a good girl. You al'ays speak the truth, as you see it. But, sometimes thin's are no' as easy fer others ta hear. People dinna tak' yer words lightly. Ye mus' choose yer words well, an' al'ays speak them wit' love. Ye canna go far wrong ta do thet. If they choose ta be hurt when ye do thet then, it's they, doin' the choosin'. I was hurt, because ye spoke God's ain truth, an' I wasn't ready fer it. T'day, ye taught yer mother a thin' a two. 'Twas a worthy lesson child, I thank yer fer it."

Lizzie looked into her mother's eyes. *Does Maggie al'ays knae wha' I'm thinkin'? I swear she's got the gif'!*

The next day, Maggie brought Lizzie into the office and sat her down. Gathering up her courage, she said, "First question, Lizzie."

"Tell me of the journey from Lanark ta Legannany, Ma. *Móraí* already told me wha' she remembers, sae tell me how *ye* saw it." Lizzie lay back on John's bed while Maggie told her what she could remember of the trip. In turn, Maggie asked her about the last Blaeberry Sunday, what was it like, who was there, and what did she feel.

From then on, Maggie and Lizzie would take some time from their work, to talk about the family stories. Some days, it was only facts and times. Other days, it was stories and events. Maggie welcomed their times together as she learned about her daughter's world and talked about her own. She feared the day would come when Lizzie demanded to know more about Hugh. But Lizzie carefully stepped around those questions for a long time, because she didn't want the stories to end.

Chapter Nineteen

On Sundays, the boys and Eliza drove the wagon to church, stopping for Maggie and Lizzie on the way. Maggie's mother stayed home with John. *Mórai* said she was already shaking and didn't need the cold, damp air to help her do that.

In early January, after an evening of fresh snowfall, Maggie stayed home from the services while the young people went to the church by themselves. Lizzie loved to get to church early to look around at the decorative carvings, listen to the organist warm up the pump organ, and see the other parishioners file through the vestibule to the sanctuary. The people coming in for morning worship were buzzing about the new rector, the Reverend Mister W.J. Coburn. Mister McKay was going to retire soon and the new minister would ease the transition. *Mórai* said he was the nephew of Lizzie's grandfather and her Uncle John from Scotland. Lizzie was daydreaming, trying to find the young man's relation to her. *Sae is he Mother's cousin? An' his son Andrew, is he my cousin?*

The service began in its usual way, and as the new clergyman entered from the side of the altar, Lizzie sat straighter in anticipation. The younger minister made an astonishing announcement from the pulpit. He invited any young men and young ladies from the congregation, of eighteen years of age or more, who were interested in relocating to America, to see him after services. There was a great rustling through the audience and several angry whispers heard from the congregants. Lizzie and Eliza looked at each other, and Joseph just stared straight ahead as if he hadn't heard. Lizzie yanked on his sleeve. "No' nae!" Joseph whispered angrily. "Pay attention ta the service." Lizzie and Eliza looked at each other excitedly.

Lizzie was thinking feverishly. *Perhaps this was the answer fer all o' them, a chance ta gae ta America! Joseph an' Johnny haf' been sayin' the farm wasn't payin' enough ta make a decent livin'. Mister Smith's gone an' Joseph said he dinna haf' enough ta pay him anyways. Maybe Joseph could sell back the lease, sell the rest o' the goods, an' start fresh in America!*

Lizzie was lost to the rest of the service. She couldn't wait for it to be over. She thought her heart would leap out of her chest and run away. Finally, he pronounced the benediction. *This new minister kin find more words ta say! Amen. C'mon, amen!*

Six young people stayed after services, looking nervously at each other while Mister McKay and his younger cleric shook hands with the departing parishioners. One angry woman came back in, grabbed her son by the ear and dragged him out. "Ye are no' eighteen years, Mister Callahan. Ye will gae hame an' stay there, until I say yer are."

Johnny raised his eyebrows and grinned. "Ye knae there'll be no' warm reception ta this when *we* git hame, neither. Maggie's gonna pitch a fit, if this is wha' we do. We don' even knae wha' 'tis they're offerin'."

"Hush! Here he is." All eyes followed the Reverend Mister Coburn to the front of the room.

The new minister motioned for the listeners to come forward and sit in the front pew. He clasped his hands together and said, "I have received a letter from a congregation in America." Reaching in his pocket, he pulled out an envelope. "My Dear Mister Coburn and so on... Ah, here it is. If you have young women wishing to gain passage to America, we can offer them safe and respectable positions in our community for one year, as house servants in reputable households. Young men are also needed to work as laborers for a local government business, in return for passage, room and board, also for one year duration." W. J. Coburn looked up to see his rapt audience and smiled.

"At the end of the one year indenture, there are many opportunities for industrious, hard working young people. There are lands for homesteading in the west, free for those who would claim it and work the land. There are great cities with industries needing hard working men and women." At this point, the minister continued reading, but his congregants had drifted to dreams of riches and fertile lands. When he finished, the young people burst into excited conversation. "Joseph, this is heaven-sent! We've got ta gae! After a year, we kin do anythin' we wan' ta make our fortune."

"Now, children," Mister Coburn said raising his voice to be heard. "There are precautions to be observed here. You must weigh all the pros and cons of this opportunity, carefully. We are not talking about streets paved with gold, or opportunity without price!" He could see the flights of fancy his distracted listeners were taking. "You must also consider the ones you leave behind. You must not just run off thinking there are no consequences to your impetuous decision. Think about it, ask questions, and talk it over with your families. You are not born alone, my young friends. You are responsible to your siblings, your parents, your elderly relatives. Consider how they will be cared for, how they will survive without you. Talk to them and tell me if you are still interested next Sunday. There will be forms to fill out and arrangements to be made. Take these forms home with you. I will see you after services next week. Are there any questions?"

Joseph stood, "Mister Coburn, sir, if we do this, how soon would we leave? When would we be in America? Would we be met by someone there? Do we hafta haf' money wit' us?"

"All good questions, Mister Heenan, from what I understand, you would be required to leave at the end of March, you would arrive 'twixt the tenth and the fourteenth of April. You would be met by your sponsor or his representative at the port of entry and travel to the place of your indenture. As far as money, it will be provided for you as part of your indebtedness to your sponsor. The period of indenture will be one year from the date of your first day of employment."

"Read the contract very carefully. I will answer any other questions next week, when you return the papers to me. Let us pray for guidance, children." The Reverend Mister Coburn bowed his head and Lizzie grabbed the hands of Johnny and Eliza tightly.

When they were dismissed, Johnny said to Lizzie, "There is nae doubt yer strong enough for the job, girl. Ye've rendered Eliza an' I fairly crippled in the hands ye've crushed with yer enthusiasm!" Lizzie grinned at his teasing.

Lizzie chattered all the way home about the prospect of going to America. Finally, she quieted when she noticed, Eliza wasn't saying anything. "Eliza, wha's wrong?"

"Oh Lizzie, *Mórai* is gone such a short time. I gae 'round the house, touchin' her thin's ta remember her by, an' I don't know if I kin gae without her thin's around me. I miss her sae much. If I gae off ta America, I won't haf' her things wit' me. It'll all be different."

Lizzie saw how sad and torn her half-sister was. In her excitement, she forgot how lonely the Heenan cottage must feel without Missus Heenan. Lizzie slipped her arm around Eliza and laid her head against hers. "We'll hafta make sure ye kin bring somethin' o' *Mórai's* wit' us. Her teapot, her tattin', maybe her shawl ta wrap around yer. I'll need somethin' o' my mother's and *Mórai's* too, Eliza. Ye will al'ays haf' me, but tha's no al'ays a great thin', is it? I need yer ta remind me o' the quiet comforts though. I'm sae awful sometimes."

Joseph looked over at his sisters. *Like night 'n day, they are. Lizzie is all sunshine and heat, bustin' through life lak' ever'thin's easy all the time, al'ays dreamin' o' t'marra. Eliza is quiet 'n deep. She knaes enough ta run scairt when there's danger. She holds her mem'ries dear, an' is careful o' another's feelin's.*

"Aye, ye are *awful*, tha's fer sure." Johnny teased Lizzie, breaking into Joseph's thoughts.

Joe realized, *Lizzie does show us the possibilities, though. She charges right ahead an' damn the consequences. Someday she'll fall hard an' the world had better be on the lookout fer the shards a-flyin' thet day!*

Lizzie swatted Johnny impotently on the arm of his heavy, if over-patched coat.

She grew thoughtful, trying to plan how she would broach the subject of America to Maggie. *We were jes' gittin' along good, too. Mórai will haf' her hands full carin' fer both John an' Ma. Oh Laird, please let me go!*

It shocked Lizzie to know why she wanted to go so badly. *I don' wanna be stuck here! I don' wanna hafta stay hame ta take care o' my mother an' grandmother an' John fer the rest o' my life. Even if I should marry, I'd be stuck wit'out e'er climbin' out o' this quagmire o' near poverty. Scrimpin' an' savin', scratchin' fer a livin'. Like the girls in the mill, with no husbands or whose husbands haf' left them fer greener pastures. Am I sae selfish? I jes' wanna git away from here. Ta make my ain way. Is it sae wrong ta want somethin' better? I don' want somethin' fer nothin', but I don' wan' nothin' fer all m' hard work, either!*

Soon, they were at the Coburn cottage. When she noticed Maggie was in the office, as usual, she asked Eliza an' the boys ta come in wit' her ta see her mother. *It'll be easier if I haf' Joseph wit' me,* she thought. *She'll stay calm if he's there. I need her ta stay listenin' while I give her the facts. She'll carry on weepin' an' wailin' later, an' I kin handle that, if she will listen in the first place.*

Maggie raised her head, startled at the entrance of the three young people and the cold air chasing them through the door. She shivered, looking at each of them with suspicious eyes. "Wha's happened? No' thet I'm no' happy ta see yer."

The two girls turned to Joseph and waited for him to speak. He looked up at the ceiling and sighed, knowing he would have to do all the talking. He looked crossly at Lizzie then began. "Maggie, the new minister, Mister Coburn had a talk wit' us afta church t'day…."

As Joseph gave her the facts, Maggie's eyes narrowed and darted a look at Lizzie. *So thet's why Lizzie had ta haf' reinforcements. She's afraid I will say, "Nay, never. Ye hafta stay wit' me."* Lizzie flushed and returned to studying her boots. *Eliza is scairt an' sad. Joseph is keepin' his mind open, but is seein' the inevitability o' failure here. Johnny doesn't knae what ta do.*

"How lang 'til ye hafta decide, Joseph?" she asked quietly.

"Jes' the week, Maggie, we haf' the contracts," Joseph said nervously watching Maggie's cool demeanor. *She's no' showin' any o' the feelin's I expected. It's eerie.*

"I'll take a look at it. I haf' some things ta think about. I may haf' some questions fer ye, since ye seem ta be the spokesperson fer this project," said Maggie, looking around at the group.

Joseph flushed, opened his mouth to object and snapped it shut, not knowing what to say. He looked at Lizzie, angrily.

"Ma, I pushed him inta it. It was me," blurted Lizzie.

"I knae thet, Lizzie, I jes' wanted ta see if ye'd own up ta it, an' no' leave him swingin' in the wind." Maggie took the contract Joseph offered and turned back to the desk, dismissing them.

Outside, Lizzie apologized to Joseph for leaving him to break the news to Maggie. "Ne'er mind thet, Lizzie. Why's she actin' sae strange? I expected anger, or sadness, weepin' or wailin' maybe, but not this cold *acceptance*."

"I don't knae, Joseph. It scares me. It's like the faeries took her." Lizzie's eyes were wide with wonder.

"Oh, posh, don't be silly, Lizzie. Somethin's off though. It's no' like her," Johnny said.

Eliza looked shrunken into herself. Pale and fragile, she had not said a word. She turned and climbed onto the wagon, anxious to go home.

Joseph divided his attention between the silent Eliza and the vociferous Lizzie. "I'll find out what's goin' on, Joseph. She may be more willin' than we thought. Gae nae, I'll talk ta ye t'marra if I kin git away."

"Lizzie, I want ye ta knae, I am no' goin' ta America. This may be the las' favor I'm doin' fer ye," said Joseph, sullenly climbing the wagon. "It woulda been nice, if ye asked me if I were o' a like mind afore ye made me yer speech maker."

Lizzie jumped up after him and hugged his neck. "I thank ye heartily, Joseph. I'm sorry fer puttin' ye on the spot. Please, forgive me."

She looked so contrite, he smiled and kissed her cheek. "Ye knae I can't stay angry wit' yer. Ye need a thrashin', ye do." He laughed as she jumped down, and grinned wickedly at him.

Lizzie watched the wagon as it drove out of sight, her mind bouncing from one scene to another trying to reconcile Maggie's strange behavior with the news of America. Slowly and deliberately, she went into the cottage to prepare for the Sunday meal.

Maggie was still in the office, making plans. *I have to talk to Hugh. I'll send word to him by Tom Reilly tomorrow. He may be still in London. The queen conferred a posthumous medal on his mother for charitable works. That was in the newspaper. Maybe he's back in Castlewellan by now. If mother is having a good day, I could have Tom bring me to Castlewellan and back. I need to talk to him about this. He's been there.* Even as she was thinking this, Maggie knew it was only an excuse to see him. *How devious is the heart when it wants someone it cannot have!*

Almost without knowing, Maggie reached for the comfort of the cup hidden in the desk drawer. Carefully unwrapping the treasure, the tarnished cup seemed to glow with meaning. *I will have to give it to her. It is after all hers, not mine.* Emotionally, she clutched it to her breast. *It won't have as much meaning for her, but she will always know she's loved by more than just her family.* She touched her face and was surprised to find it wet. She held the cup briefly to her lips. Sadly, she rewrapped the gift and tucked it back into its hiding place. *Not yet, Lizzie, but soon.*

The next morning, Maggie put on her best clothes, hoping her plan would come to fruition. If Lizzie thought it strange that her mother was so carefully dressed up, she didn't say anything. Maggie waited in the office for Tom Reilly to arrive.

"Aye, he's at Castlewellan fer the day," said Tom when he came. "T'marra, he goes ta Dublin and back ta Parliament. The man gits no rest, but these days, he's no' desirin' any. 'Tis sad, he is, wit' his wife an' mother gone last spring. They's some talk o' him gittin' married agin, ta some pretty young thing from London. Beggin' y' pardon, Ma'am. I know ye don' wanta hear 'bout gossip."

"Tom, I wan' ta gae ta Castlewellan ta meet wit' the Earl. I want ta bring his catalogues an' git his advice about somethin'. Would yer please take me there in yer wagon? I kin return late in the afternoon, if I kin meet wit' him today."

"I'll be glad ta do it, Ma'am. But, do ye think he'll see ye wit'out an appointment? It's takin' an awful chanct, ye know. He's a busy man."

"I'll take thet chance, Mister Reilly. It's important. If I can't see him, I'll make an appointment ta do sae. We'll have ta leave straight away an' bring my chair wit' us. Is thet agreeable, Mister Reilly?"

"Aye, Ma'am. I wish ye the best. It is verra cold, sae if ye pardon m' advice, ye best dress warm an' bring a blanket."

Maggie put on her hat, cloak and gloves, grabbed the blanket she had prepared and wheeled to the door. "Mister Reilly, Tom, please let Lizzie at the cottage knae we're leavin' an' thet we'll be home by late afternoon."

"Aye, Ma'am." He settled her on the wagon, and tied the chair in the back. Knocking on the door of the cottage, he waited for Lizzie to answer. When she did, Lizzie's eyes were wide with surprise to see her mother on the wagon. Mister Reilly gave her the message and left. Closing the door, Lizzie leaned against it, adding this mornin's strange behavior to a growing concern surrounding her mother.

"Sorry the wagon is sae rough, Ma'am. It's no' meant fer passengers, ye know."

"And I'm sorry for disrupting your schedule today, Mister Reilly. I hope it doesn't set ye back too much. Most o' the plants in the greenhouse are transferred already, an' I think the others are no' hardy enough ta travel." She often wondered why he always came every Monday, whether it was summer or winter. In warmer times, he came to the office three days a week, because the plant growth and the Earl's travels warranted it. However, in the dead of winter, when nothing grew, and he had no trunks to deliver, he came every Monday, good weather or bad.

"Mister Reilly, ye really don't have to come in winter, if ye hae no work ta bring me. I won't hold it against yer," said Maggie, smiling.

"Missus Heenan, Ma'am, the Earl insists I keep m' schedule a' least on Mondays e'en if there be no trunks or books ta haul. He says Mondays he should start off the week knaein' his cataloguer is all right an' his plants are healthy. I don' mind, I git paid the same if I come here, or I stay there. An' truth be told, it's a lot easier takin' the trip, than stayin' in harm's way, wit' the women o' Castlewellan decidin' how I spend m' time." Tom slapped his knee, laughing.

Maggie laughed with him. "Ye'd rather *I'd* tell ye wha' ta do, Mister Reilly?" she teased.

"They's only one o' ye, ma'am, an' seven o' them! Then, I hafta decide who's got the most power in the house. I don' e'en think the Earl knaes *thet*, ma'am! They's the head housekeeper, the housemistress, the head laundress, an' the head cook. She's the strongest an' will deck ye fer bein' late. Then, they's the butler, the footman, 'n the blacksmith, wit' all the ones under them. I kin hide in the fields all summer, but the winters are terrible. Ye gae inside ta keep warm 'n they's all got another job fer me ta do. I'll do anythin' fer the Earl. He's a right man, but them others, I can't figure 'em out. They think I got nothin' ta do."

The cold wind blew her blanket off her shoulders and Mister Reilly snatched it back and set it around her again. Maggie pulled it tightly around her, trying to block out the cold January blast. The dark thick cloud cover looked ominous, but the air was dry. The snow from the day before was almost gone from the rough rutted road. By the time Maggie was losing faith in her decision to travel, Castlewellan loomed ahead. She was surprised at the number of people in the streets, hurrying from one place to another. The courthouse held a steady stream of petitioners on its steps, and the marketplace had a number of would-be sellers of merchandise, huddled up to their little fires. The knife-sharpener spun his wheel and held a partly-rusted knife against the platen with his fingerless gloves. His assistant stoked the fire as his employer barked orders at him. Beyond the town, the imposing castle stood upon the hill. It wasn't the bitter wind that caused the chill that ran through Maggie.

She tried to remember when she was here last. Eight years, she was, catching the nervous energy flowing from her mother and father. At forty-six, she was no more calm viewing the servants' entrance of the huge edifice. Her mother had been here many times over the years, finally winning over the respect of the head laundress. Even Lizzie was known to them for her superior ironing skills, pressing the stylish shirts of Victorian menswear. Maggie felt very small, as Mister Reilly carried her to her chair at the top of the stairs. He answered those who called out to him, with a nod. He seemed very popular among the staff, and proud to bring them a mysterious stranger. They knew he would have a story of intrigue when he at last sat down to supper among them that night.

"If ye please, ma'am, wait here, whilst I talk ta the houseman ta see if the Earl is here an' if he'll be seein' ye." He removed his hat and left her in the corridor outside the kitchen. She marveled at the number of servants scurrying back and forth, each with their own purposeful errand.

A young scullery maid asked if she wished a cup of tea. Maggie thanked her but declined. She was intrigued by the accent of the young girl. The sound of it was neither Irish, nor Scottish, nor English that she could tell. She found her answer in the sharp rebuke of the cook. "Git yer little Welsh bum in 'ere an' stop gawkin' at the lady. She'll think yer dim-witted an' she wan' be wrong by half!"

Chapter Twenty

Maggie saw Mister Reilly and the houseman hurrying toward her.

"He'll be happy ta see ye, Missus Heenan. Barnaby, the head houseman, will bring ye ta him, straight away," Mister Reilly said, breathless from his exercise.

"If you'll allow me, madam," said the tall servant. Barnaby guided her chair carefully, if speedily, along the corridor. Having seen the flurry of activity just moments before, she was surprised that no one stepped in front of them along the way. All motion stopped, clearing the way in front of her chair. She saw stairs ahead and wondered what would happen when they reached them.

Just short of reaching the stairway, a burly man stepped from an intersecting hallway. Reversing the direction of the chair, the houseman lifted the back of her chair upright up the stairs, while the man below grasped the seat of the chair to raise the wheels above the steps. This was accomplished smoothly and without so much as the slightest jarring motion. Upon reaching the top step, they set her chair down. Maggie grinned at the brawny young man who made the journey seemingly without effort, and thanked him.

Maggie spoke to the houseman who was hurrying down yet another corridor. "He seems a pleasant young man."

"Yes, madam, I suppose he does," Barnaby replied stiffly. "The Earl will see you in his private chambers."

A little boy of about eight with wild, blond curly hair, came running out one of the adjacent doorways, and down the hall, away from them. Quick on his heels was his chubby young governess, her frilly white bonnet askew, and her dove brown straight hair, slipping out of its bun, flying in all directions. She stopped short when she saw the houseman and Maggie, and hastily curtsied, saying, "I beg your pardon, Ma'am, Mister Barnaby." She turned on her heel and ran after the boy whom she cornered at the end of the hall. She grabbed the youngster by the ear, ignoring his complaints, and pulled him into a side room.

When Maggie entered Hugh's private chambers, she was grinning from ear to ear. Barnaby wheeled her to the center of the room, and said, "Begging your pardon, M' Lord. Shall I send for tea?"

Standing at the massive window, Hugh said, "Yes, that will be fine, Barnaby. Leave it in the hall. When I hear you knock, I'll get it myself. We are not to be disturbed for any reason." Barnaby bowed in her direction and left. Hugh stood with his back to her until the door closed.

How cold and unlike him, thought Maggie, nervously. *Perhaps I shouldn't have come. I presumed too much on his tenderness toward me.* Hugh turned finally, strode to the door and locked it. He went out another door and she heard another door lock. When he reentered the room, he smiled warmly and said, "Maggie, you have no idea how welcome your visit is." He came straight to her, picked her up from her chair, and carried her to the long, white lounge near the fireplace. He took her hat and gloves, then her cloak, rather awkwardly, since she was sitting on it. "Oh dear, I didn't hurt you, did I? I have never learned how to do that gracefully."

"Neither have I, Hugh," she laughed. Looking around, she commented, "What a beautiful home you have. It just occurred to me, when I was here last, it was in the old cottage, not the castle."

A discreet knock on the door drew his attention. Standing military straight, he opened the door, and brought in a tray of a large assortment of pastries, and a sparkling tea service with linens. "I used to do this for my mother," he said wistfully. He set the tray on a low table next to the lounge. Sitting on the floor, he poured two cups of tea. "Sugar, milk? Oh, please excuse me." He rose, went to the door again and relocked it. Coming to her side of the table, he lifted her legs onto the lounge and sat facing her. "The tea was for mother. This is for you." He cupped the back of her head and gently kissed her. His smiling blue eyes bore into hers, mocking himself, he said, "I am at your service, Madam."

Maggie marveled at the contrasting behavior she was seeing in him, cold and businesslike in front of Barnaby, young and warm when he looked at her, sad and childlike when talking of his mother, protective and secretive when tending the door. He becomes so many people responding to ordinary circumstances. *When is he himself? Is the one he is with me, who he really is? I don't envy his life of privilege when I think of who he must be for so many people.*

Maggie touched his mask tenderly. With a deep sigh, she stared at him for a long time. She couldn't stop smiling. *He looks tired*, she thought. *He must be sixty, still handsome, still Hugh. I'm still his. He's talking. I should listen. I can't.* Instead, she kissed him. She laughed at herself. *I am a wanton woman when he is near.* A warning thought tickled the edge of her emotions. *Protect yourself, Maggie. You cannot have him to yourself.*

"This is very nice, Maggie," Hugh said gently, "But is this why you came here?" He grinned at her pretty blush.

"No, but it is as good as any reason I could conjure," she replied impishly. Sitting up and directing him to sit across the table from her, she reached for her tea. "But to business. I need advice from a world traveler." She smiled at the baffled reaction on his face.

"My children, Lizzie, Eliza, John, and possibly Joseph are asking to go to America. I have a contract I want you to look over, and I need you to advise me what to do. I am so ignorant of anything outside Ireland and need to know what they can reasonably expect out there."

Hugh stood, pacing across the room and back. "First, what is their situation here? Are they unhappy? Is something driving them away?"

"No. Well perhaps, yes. Joseph's mother died last fall. The farm is not doing well. I don't know if Joseph or Johnny want to leave, but they won't have the girls go alone. Eliza will go wherever Lizzie goes. Lizzie is the spearhead of this adventure, I'm sure. I think she sees her life as a trap, and this is her way to have a better life. She has a romantic nature, building her fantasies from her uncles' letters from Canada, and her father's stories of America. Do they have a chance to do well there?"

"Ah. Let me read the contract." Still standing, he read, scowled, then brightened, turned on his heel and continued to pace. He stopped near the window. In the light of the winter sky, he stood tall, as handsome as ever to Maggie. His sideburns long, his hair streaked with gray, he brushed them back with his hand, as he scrutinized the paper he held. He paused and stared, unseeing, out the window, deep in thought. Maggie was content to see him in his element, the lord of his manor, of his land. This was a man she had not seen before, the judge, the parliamentarian, the lawmaker, the baron. She was right to come here. She was right to ask his advice.

He came back to her, sitting at the far end of the lounge. He asked many questions. Are they hard workers? How did she feel about them leaving her? Could she survive without them? Did she trust their judgment in difficult times? Had she considered going with them?

"Me? Go to America? I could not. My mother is ill with the shaking disease. My uncle needs someone to keep him out of trouble. I have no sponsor or fare. I cannot earn my way. My land is all I have, Hugh. How could I leave it?" Her emotions obvious, her frustration keen, her green eyes filled with quick tears. *How could I leave you?*

"Maggie, I need only to know how you feel. I want you to have what *you* need. The land is yours for your lifetime and a day. Now let me tell you what I think and you can tell me what you will do.

He went on, "Lizzie's dreams are painted on a large richly-colored canvas. From what I have seen of her, she is of good character and has a brave countenance. She is exactly the sort of person upon which that country is built. She will need to be strong to make her way. Eliza will be protected by her and her brother. She is not afraid of hard work, but she is lead by strength, so she will have to stay close to them. Joseph is strong like Lizzie, so? John seems a little foolhardy, but is sensible and cares deeply for his sisters. John and Joseph will watch over them. Doesn't John have a young woman he is interested in? What will she do? What about Ann and her husband?"

Maggie was amazed at his portrait of her five children. Her eyes narrowed, "How do you know so much about these children, Hugh?"

Unexpectedly, his face flushed. Chagrinned, he said, "I am found out. Tom Reilly cannot keep a word to himself. I confess, he tells me everything about your family, Lizzie, you and your step children. At first, he didn't want to tell me for fear I would recriminate him for his betrayal. I needed to know how you were, how your children and your husband were faring. I shamelessly pressed him for information you told him in confidence. He is a natural storyteller, our Tom is. Never tell him anything you don't want me to know. I apologize if I offend you. I could not bear *not* to know about you. It's like water or air to me, to know you're well and happy." Hesitating, he said, "But, I *will* remove him if that is what you want."

Maggie sat with her mouth agape at the shock of his confession. "No," she said. "Don't remove him. Don't tell him I know, either. We have a conduit of information neither of us has a right to, except that we love each other. Do you think he doesn't tell me about *you*?" she laughed. "We are the fools, Hugh. He has it all. He is our secret messenger. On the one hand, I admonish him for a gossip, on the other, I too, press him for details about you." Shaking her head in amazement, Maggie bit her lower lip coyly.

Hugh cleared his throat, and said quietly laughing, "Hung by my own rope. He hasn't been talking to the children, has he?"

"I'd think not, but you may want to warn him. Lizzie is very inquisitive and is very interested in 'that strange man who comes to funerals, but doesn't stay to speak to the mourners,' and that 'mysterious man' she saw coming out of my office. She has a very romantic view of you. I told her you were a friend and she wasn't to discuss you casually with anyone. You were not to be a subject of idle gossip."

"Oh Lord. She is an intelligence that bears reckoning. She is a beautiful girl, Maggie. How could she not be, as your child? Dare I ask….?"

"No, Hugh. She is *Joseph's* child. When I first carried her, I wasn't sure. The midwife said she was early, tiny, and underdeveloped. Moreover, she is *my* child. Joseph was gone so much of the time and so were you. Neither of you could claim her as their rightful daughter. Even if you were, I would not tell her." Maggie hung her head, trying to hide the range of emotion she felt.

"All this time, I dared not hope, dared not interfere, lest I destroy the life you made for her. In my heart I wanted her to be mine, but knew I couldn't claim her, unless you wished it." He blew out a breath as if he had held it for a long time. "When you married so soon, I thought she must be mine. Can you forgive an old narcissistic fool?"

"There's nothing to forgive, Hugh, truly." Wanting to escape the heavy emotional charge in the room, she said, "Now, tell me about America."

"Ah yes, America." Hugh seemed to struggle with the change of thought. "America has many opportunities for people from many countries. The Irish especially so, it seems. The Irish are not always welcomed warmly, I must warn you. Perhaps it is only because they don't know how things are done in America. The class structure there is built only on money and how long they have been in the country. Other than that, it seems any man can make his own way, if he is willing to work hard and take the chance he will succeed."

"If they are permitted to go, the greatest danger will be on the dock before they board the ship. I have heard terrible stories of passengers being cheated out of their tickets, robbed of their fare, or pressed into service against their will. They must stick together and not talk to strangers. They must keep their tickets inside their clothing, if possible, and not in a purse or their bags. It is a rough place and much jostling goes on, to confuse the innocents. Joseph will be of great service as protection for the lasses. I don't mean to frighten you, but I need you to understand the hazards. Your uncles were robbed and forced into service on the docks.

He went on, "The journey itself will not be comfortable in steerage. It should be over in eight to ten days, however. They will go through a series of examinations when they land, to make sure they have all their papers, are healthy, and have a sponsor or money to support them. The children will have sponsors, so they will be met at the immigration entrance building. From there, they should be transported to their living quarters for the next year. According to the law over there, the only ones who can offer work to immigrants for passage are government officials and the clergy. Reverend

Coburn has a clergyman in America to sponsor them?" Maggie nodded, showing him on the paper where Mister Coburn would sign if the contract was to be binding.

"Excellent. Although it must be difficult for you, I truly believe they will do well there. The girls will be protected by the office of the clergy for the first year. They will have a place to live and will have time to find a situation after they have been freed of their obligation.

"The boys will work at a government sanctioned job for a year. If they choose to and have done well, they probably could make a living at it. Now, Maggie, tell me what you are feeling about all this?"

"I want what's best for them, but I also want to keep them near me. How do you expect me to feel?" she said plaintively.

"Maggie, I can only tell you what I know. I cannot decide this for you." Hugh said softly, taking her hand.

"Of course Hugh, I don't mean to heap my dreadful duties on you. I know what I must do, though it wrenches my heart."

Unbidden, her eyes freshened with tears. She reached in her purse and pulled out a handkerchief. "You see, Hugh," she said wryly, "I *do* know to carry a handkerchief."

Hugh smiled at her attempt to lighten the moment.

"It's yours, of course," she said, waving it for him to see. She dabbed her eyes daintily, and peered over the square of linen at Hugh. Her eyes were bright and dancing. "It looks like I'll never return it."

"It is and was always a gift." He sat again beside her on the lounge and held her, playing with the tendrils surrounding her face.

The nearness of him confused her senses. The smell of the starch in his collar, the deep blue of his stylish silk tie, the woolen texture of his dark gray coat, were all heady contributions to the ever more dizzying state of her emotions. She saw the graying sideburns as they disappeared beneath the black leather patch on his cheek.

She nuzzled her head into his neck and his arms tightened around her. The quickened tempo of their breathing seemed to come from one source. Her wildly beating heart strove to match his.

As if she suddenly was aware of what she was doing, she shuttered and gasped, "Hugh! There's someone at the door."

"Sh-h. They are not to disturb us. They will go away." Maggie realized he was right. The soft knocking stopped and footsteps retreated. They were entirely alone. Maggie was awestruck with his ability to command his privacy.

"That is indeed, a pleasant privilege to have Hugh, but much has happened to bring us to this circumstance. We have both lost much. I am no longer the impetuous child willing to abandon my moral path for a wanton hour with you. As much as I love you, we cannot be thinking of only ourselves. My children and yours would have deep feelings about this. *'We are not born for ourselves alone.'* Isn't that what you engraved on Lizzie's cup? Can we be so callous that we forget the ones who saved us from our own impossible destinies? The memories of Mabel and Joseph deserve more than this."

Hugh heaved a great sigh and smiled sadly. He kissed her forehead, rose, and stood by the window again, thoughtful but resigned.

The war in her sapping her strength, Maggie laid her head back and drifted into a light sleep. He glanced at the clock on the mantle, calculating the time he could allow her to nap. He covered her with a light robe from the other room and straightened his clothing. True to his military training, he set the tray near the door and tidied the little table. Going into his dressing room, he brushed his hair, and checked his attire. When he was certain he was back to his previous impeccable appearance, he returned to Maggie.

She slept like a child, her arms wrapped around her middle, her hair loose, over the lounge pillow. He sat in an upholstered arm chair just watching her serenely. *My God, how precious a gift she is to me! How can she still love me? Oh, how I would long for the life of a tenant with tattered clothes and rustic living, if I could have a treasure like her beneath my roof as solace for life's cruel jokes. Joseph, how could you bear to leave her? Maggie was your wife. How could you abandon her? You demented fool!*

When it became time to wake her, Hugh walked to her side and gently shook her. She turned her face away with a moan. He turned her face back toward his own. Slowly her eyes opened wide, realizing where she was, realizing he was so close, and she was so vulnerable. Awake now, her hands flew to her hair. "Oh my," she gasped, embarrassed at her state of dishevelment.

"Hush, dear. It will be fine, Maggie," Hugh said in a calm, soothing voice. He picked her up and carried her to the dressing room. Perched at the vanity, she combed her hair and replaced the combs he rescued from the sitting room floor.

"I am so embarrassed. How could I have fallen asleep!" she said with a self-deprecating grin. "I hope I can pass inspection of the twenty servants I met on my way up here."

"The only thing they will see different is a certain glow to your cheeks that did not come from the cold air." Hugh said, amused. "My servants are discreet, silent, and well paid, Maggie. They will protect their livelihood, their position... and *mine*. Now we must get you home."

He managed to get her cloak and her into the chair without too much entanglement. When she placed her hat on her head and pulled on her gloves, Hugh handed her the purse with her papers safely tucked inside. He walked to the wall, pulled a cord, and presently Barnaby showed at the door.

"Barnaby, the lady will use my private exit. Tell Terry you will need his assistance and Tom Reilly should bring my carriage to the side entrance. I will accompany her home. We will wait here until you are ready."

"Very good, sir," Barnaby replied. He bowed, leaving to see to his arrangements.

While he was gone, Maggie asked, "Hugh, the little boy I saw in the corridor when I came in. Is he your Francis? What a beautiful child."

"Yes, he is. His sister is studying with her French tutor, I believe. Their mother's death last year has been very trying for them. While Francis seems to be taking it out on his governesses, Mabel has thrown herself into her studies, pretending it doesn't affect her at all."

"Every child grieves in their own way, Hugh, just like their parents. If you are patient and keep them close to you, they will survive it." Maggie said softly, mindful of Barnaby scurrying back with Terry in tow to bring her down the stairs.

The houseman assisted Lord Annesley with his cloak and handed him his hat and gloves. Terry grinned shyly at Maggie, and took her chair to another corridor, and a wider stairway. As before, Terry stood at the lower step, while Barnaby guided the chair from the upper stair.

"We're thinking of putting in a lift from America, but we haven't decided just where yet." said Hugh cheerfully. "It will be much easier for our visitors … and me as I grow old." Maggie just smiled and nodded. Among the present company, she didn't know how to reconcile her own familiarity with the Earl of Annesley and her social standing equal to his rigidly class-conscious servants. She wanted to offend, neither Hugh nor his servants, and felt if she opened her mouth, she would certainly do both.

Once down the stairs, she thanked both men enthusiastically and accepted a lift into the carriage. The chair securely tied to the back, Mister Reilly urged the horses to begin their journey home.

Alone once more, Hugh took Maggie's hand in his. "It is so strange and so wonderful to see you again, Maggie. You're the air I breathe, the blood in my veins. I don't seem to exist without you here. I don't want to be without you again."

Maggie sighed, "Pretty words Hugh, and I know you mean them. But the man I love is also another man: a father, a nobleman, and the responsible guardian of all he sees. By your hand, the grandest arboretum in Ireland will live beyond our century and the next. It is all destroyed if we are together for more than a casual meeting."

He stared sadly out the window of his opulent coach, knowing she was right and frustrated with the truth of it. *Yes, I'll probably have another socially acceptable marriage to ensure my family's name and to perpetuate my obsessive arboretum. At what cost?* The darkness that shaded his face made him look brooding and angry.

Hoping to erase that look from her memory of the afternoon, Maggie said, "Hugh, thank you for today. I will live a long time happily remembering this day. One day, Lizzie will know how much you mean to me."

"Then I'll not waste this ride with wanting more." Hugh said, his mood brightening. He removed her glove and tenderly kissed the hand he held. Uncharacteristically, his military bearing foregone, he slumped back on the seat, drew her head to his shoulder and smiled wistfully.

"Maggie, promise me you'll call me, for even the slightest favor I can do for you. Promise?"

"It will be our only vow to each other," she replied. Smiling, she laughed softly, "God bless Tom Reilly, gardener, and spy. Thank you Hugh, for making time for me today."

Chapter Twenty-one

Lizzie ran to the door when she heard the carriage drive up. She threw her plaid around her shoulders and ran out just as Tom Reilly alit from the driver's seat.

"Go inside, Lass. You'll catch yer death. I'll bring her in. Gae!"

Reluctantly, Lizzie did as she was told. Peering out the frost-covered window, she could only see shadows of the figures moving about the carriage. "I knae it's Tom Reilly an' mother, but there's someone else, too!" Lizzie reported excitedly to her grandmother.

"Lizzie! Put the kettle on. They will be wantin' hot tea ta warm their bones," said the old woman. "It's cold enough in here, let alone out there. Push up the fire, too."

Meanwhile, Maggie was urging the men to come in to warm up before their journey home. Lord Annesley, seeing his driver shiver, agreed.

"Lord Annesley," Maggie said formally, "why don't we go into the office? I can show you the new catalogue I've started. Mister Reilly, please go into the cottage and send Lizzie to the office. My mother will make you tea and you can warm yourself at the fire. We should only be a little while."

Tom brought Maggie's chair to the office then, hesitantly, went next door. His intense curiosity was evident on his face, but he could not do but what he was told.

When they were alone, Maggie said, "Before she goes to America, I want Lizzie to meet you. I'll decide how much to tell her about you when I write to her. For now, let me give her a real introduction. Is that satisfactory to you, Hugh?"

"Whatever you wish, Maggie. I want to meet her, but don't want to disturb your family." He sat on John's bed, holding her hand. Smiling in surprise, he said, "I believe I am a little nervous at the prospect."

At that moment, Lizzie entered with a gust of icy wind. She noticed their hands spring apart and her mother's eyes reluctantly pulling away from the distinguished gentleman, toward hers. "Yes, Mother?"

"Lizzie, may I present Lord Hugh Annesley. It is he, who owns the lease on your grandmother's land, and by whose benefit I own mine. Lord Annesley, my daughter, Elizabeth Jane Heenan."

Amused, and endeared by the obvious wonder in Lizzie's eyes, Hugh said, "I am most pleased to meet you, Elizabeth. I've heard many good things about you. I understand you are very interested in going to America."

Catching her breath and looking him defiantly, she said impetuously, "I am, sir. If I am not too bold, may I ask why it should concern you?"

"Lizzie!" exclaimed her mother, embarrassed by her impudence.

Hugh raised his hand, to forestall the rebuke from Maggie. "And well you may, Lizzie. Your mother asked for my insight as an old friend and a traveler, as to whether I thought her children would do well there. I was able to assure her I thought you would. I also told her of a few pitfalls of which I thought you should be aware before your journey. It is, of course, your mother's decision to make, and your decision if you wish to take the advice. I have no right to have an opinion, except as invited."

Chagrinned at his gracious reply, she implored, "Please forgive me, Lord Annesley. I have been told I often speak before I have considered the consequences." Lizzie, her face flushed deep red, looked at her mother, begging her forgiveness as well.

"Sit down, Lizzie. Hugh, perhaps you could explain these 'pitfalls' to her. She is aware you are well traveled, having helped me with your catalogs for many years."

Lord Annesley spoke softly, reiterating the cautions concerning the docks, how to protect their papers, and the procedures for immigrants, both in Liverpool and New York's Ellis Island. "I do not know exactly how the system will work now, because it is a new facility and they may have made many changes. However, you should be able to meet your sponsors there and they will take you in hand at that time. You've never been on a ship?"

Lizzie shook her head, subdued now that she understood his presence was for her behalf.

"It is not as simple a feat as you may think, to maintain your balance in a water conveyance. The strongest of men often look like marionettes, completely undone by the motion of the water. If you feel your balance is slipping, look directly at the horizon. It is sometimes the only thing you'll find that is not moving against you. The horizon will settle your stomach and reestablish your equilibrium. It took my whole first journey to reconcile that in my mind. I was seasick the whole way to Africa. I was just about your age at the time. Of course, I knew it all. I did not heed the advice about the horizon however, and I soon learned I was not as brilliant as I previously thought myself to be." He laughed at the memory.

"When you are below decks, try to seek a venue where you can see the horizon for as long as possible each day. Immediately when you get off the ship, seek the horizon again. Your feet will think you should still be swaying, and the ground beneath you will be rock solid. You will see even the strongest men, falling helplessly on the dock after eight days of moving over the water."

Lizzie was won over and fascinated by Lord Annesley's instruction. He looked out the window at the darkening skies and said, "I must be back in Castlewellan soon, so regretfully, I must take my leave. Let me bring you back to the cottage Maggie, and apologize to your mother for my abrupt departure. Lizzie, would you bring her chair?"

"Of course, Lord Annesley, thank you so much for your advice and the stories." Lizzie was astonished at how her speech mimicked the Earl's, like her mother's when she spoke to him. *Strange, the mere presence of a Lord causes an ordinary woman to speak as a lady!*

Back in the cottage, John stood in the shadows until they were all seated, then eased out of the room to the office. Lizzie's grandmother was flattered by the Earl's attention. She offered him a cup of tea which he sipped to please her. When he spent enough time to satisfy polite convention, he and Mister Reilly took their leave.

Before the hoof beats were out of hearing, Lizzie fired pent up questions at Maggie. "Mother, ye were gone all day! What took sae long? What's the castle like inside? Did ye meet his children? What are the upstairs servants like? What do they wear? Did he knae ye were comin'?"

Maggie put both hands up in mock defense of the barrage. "Lizzie, one question at a time; I'll answer every one, but one at a time." They pulled their chairs to the fire and the two women listened to Maggie's tale of the castle. Lizzie was rapt in her mother's story, keenly aware of her mother's tender references to the Earl. *She speaks of him like a lover, not a friend. If she's wants to pretend he's naught but a friend, let her. Da has been gone almost ten year now. She has no interest in any man but the Earl.*

On his way home, Lord Annesley had time to reflect on the day's events. *What a lovely child she is,* he thought with a small stab of jealousy. *She's so full of fire, bright, and determined. What a shame for all the Annesley advantages in society; we put a damper on that fire in our children with our lessons on genteel etiquette, duties of their position, and the proper conduct we demand. I will have to make sure my Mabel doesn't get too civilized. I want her to be strong and have some command of her life. Francis will be able to choose a life within more generous parameters. Mabel should have a life of substance. I would not like her to become a shallow, court-driven, lady-in-waiting, whose only purpose is to make a good marriage.*

Lizzie, though, will take what she wants wherever she goes. She's the mirror of her mother, but for that wild, gold-sparkled red hair. Oh, to be the faerie on her shoulder as she tears her way through life! Good fortune is yours, Lizzie. You have but to take it.

That night, Lizzie went to bed with her head full of dreams. Sea monsters carried her to strange lands, hoodlums stole her purse, and the Lord Mayor of Castlewellan made her sweep the streets clean. Several times, she woke with a start, running from one monster to the next. Finally, nearing dawn, she lay awake in the dark gray light, thinking of the story she would tell Eliza about Lord Annesley, her mother, and the tales they told. Her greedy curiosity wanted more. Was it friendship? Were they lovers? Nothing fit. Close up, he looked younger. That leather patch on his face, intriguing. *The lines in his face only add ta how handsome he is. His wife was verra much younger than he. Accordin' ta the paper, more than ten years younger than mother.*

Today, I hafta fill out the papers and git Joseph, John, and Eliza ta do the same. We'll bring them to Mister Coburn and the die will be cast! We're goin' ta America!

Guilt overtaking her, Lizzie rationalized her absence. *Mother will have John to help her care for Moral. They will be fine without me. Jennie Claren can help them too, if they need her. Enough of this daydreamin', better git up. I wonder if Janie will want ta gae? Johnny won't gae without her, I daren't think.* Lizzie went through the motions of getting breakfast, but her mind was miles away.

Maggie saw her setting the table and wondered what it must be like for her, to think about leaving everything she knew to go to America. *Ah, she's young. She only looks forward, no' ta what she may miss when she's gone. It's we older folk who look back an' reminisce. Oh Laird, this little cottage will miss her flittin' about. Moraí will miss her sorely. I'll miss her even more. I was jis' gittin' ta knae her,* she thought regretfully.

Later that morning, Maggie asked Lizzie to come into the office with her. Lizzie looked at her curiously, but asked no questions. Maggie reached in the desk for the cup she had polished a few days earlier. Still in the box, wrapped in a handkerchief of her own, the cup lay waiting for this moment. With solemn care, Maggie opened the box. Unwrapping the cup, she handed it to her daughter. Lizzie's eyes snapped from the proffered cup, to her mother's eyes in unspoken questions. "It is yours. Now that you've met the man who gave it to you, I think you should have it."

Lizzie slowly turned it in her hands to see the inscription. "*Non nobis solum nati sumus.*" She slowly translated, " '*We are not born for ourselves alone.*' That's what Reverend Coburn was sayin'. But wha' does the Earl mean by it?"

Maggie took a deep breath before replying. "Lizzie, it means that we've responsibilities to those who came before us and to those who'll come after. We must carry the things we learn and teach them to our children, and they must teach them to their children. It is the same in our circumstances, as it is with the landed and powerful families the world over."

Lizzie's head was spinning with questions that she could not voice. Her mother could have kept her silence and never given her the cup. Lizzie did not want her to regret her choice to trust her with the revelation of this secret. It was wiser, she thought, to allow her the gesture and ask her questions later. *I wonder wha' Da thought o' the cup?*

"Thank ye, Ma. It's a treasure. I've been wonderin' what I'd bring wit' me ta America. This'll be the first thin' I put up. When I look at it, I'll remember you, an' meetin' Lord Annesley."

The rest of the week bore a flurry of activities, all pointing to America. The Heenan children scarcely slept for all their imaginings. They were irritable and forgetful, snapping at each other, regretting their behavior instantly. Lizzie was the most verbal in her abusive behavior. Just when she wanted to be sweet and loving, it seemed she'd become possessed with a demon of a forceful, demanding nature. She would fly into a rage over the smallest frustration, then recriminate herself with guilt.

Finally, just before she was to leave, Maggie took her aside and said, "Lizzie, it's all right ta be scairt, or saddened by leavin'. *Moraí* an' I are, too. Try ta make these last few days a memory you kin recall wit' pleasure, not angry an' heated. We *want* ye ta be happy, child."

Oh, Ma, I'm happy ta be goin' an' sad ta be goin', too. I've sae much I want ta say an' I'm wastin' my time snappin' at the ones I count most dear. I'll write yer often as I can, ta let ye know I'm fine an' happy an' I miss ye terrible."

"Let me knae the truth o' it, Lizzie. Without pretence, tell me everythin', the good an' bad. We'll miss yer sorely an' need ta hear yer stories. Now, ye haf' yer papers tucked in the inside pocket I made in yer cloak. Ye will be able ta git them quickly when ye need them, but they should be safe 'til ye do. Mister Denison will be takin' yer ta the ship, then?" At Lizzie's nod, Maggie asked, "What's this Mister Denison like, Lizzie?"

"He's just a man, Ma. I don't know. Hafn' e'en talked ta him, really. If Mister Coburn say he's gonna be his assistant soon, he must be a good enough man fer him."

Maggie shook her head wryly at this less than detailed description of the man who would take charge of her children's journey. "Well, I'll meet him soon enough, I ken. He'll be here in the whisk o' a horse's tail, so git yer belongings together an' see if ye kin carry your load. I don't knae how ye kin carry them irons an' still have strength fer yer other things."

"The Laird will gif' me the strength ta carry what I need, an' the rest will hafta stay here. I'll be a laundress when I'm done with my sponsors, won't I? I hafta have my irons, isn't tha' right, *Mórai*?"

The old woman chuckled with pride at her granddaughter. She had given Lizzie the irons she had rescued from the fire that took her own mother. It was her legacy and now Lizzie's. *Morai* stole a glance at Maggie to see if she did the right thing. Maggie never used them like Lizzie had. Maggie smiled, understanding her mother's reasoning, and nodded in agreement. Lizzie had earned her right to the irons and Elizabeth could no longer use them. *She has her silver cup an' her irons ta tell her from whence she came; the clothes on her back and an' a change in the bag; her tickets ta America an' a letter from her sponsor. Wha' more could she need? Our hopes, our wishes, an' our prayers, go wit' yer, Lizzie. The Laird puts dreams in yer head ta follow, Lizzie. I pray he'll give ye a penny fer yer pocket, a place ta lay yer head, an' keep ye safe in the palm o' His hand. An' if we ne'er see yer again, think on us kindly, Lizzie Heenan.*

Maggie listed the items they needed to be ready for the journey, hoping to calm her nerves. "We'll have a pail fer ye ta take t'marra, an' add some biscuits ta yer bag fer later. Ye will leave afore dawn ta git ta the ferry? Mister Denison will be here verra early an' ye will be off. Joseph, John, an' Eliza will drive the wagon here, then ye'll all gae t'gether. Matthew Mahoney will git the wagon in a day or so. Are we fergettin' anythin'?"

"Ma, I'll have all night ta think about it. I won' be sleepin' anyways. It's a shame Joseph an' John won' be goin' ta America. Janie won' be persuaded, an' he won't go wit'out her. Ah, she waited a lang time fer Johnny, sae maybe it is fer the best."

"No' ever'one can pick up an' leave fer sae fer away," said *Mórai*.

"Well, it is no' our bus'ness, is it? Joseph will find a girl soon, I hope. He doesn't wan' ta leave the land," added Maggie. "I hope he doesn't regret stayin'. But I'm sae glad he is. I wouldn't wan' ta lose *all* my children."

"Lizzie, ye should try ta git some rest, e'en though yer mind is runnin' on. T'marra will be a very lang day, goin' ta Belfast an' gittin' the ferry in the mornin', then takin' the train ta Liverpool. I'm sae glad the young minister is goin' with ye ta Liverpool. Yer da's brother's son, James, is goin' over too, sae ye will have a cousin on the ship wit' yer. Thet's one less worry we'll have, 'til we hear from ye. I knae ye will do yer best ta please yer sponsor. Remember, he's a minister, sae mind yer tongue, Lizzie. He may no' be sae understandin' as the ones who love yer."

"*Aye*, Ma," she replied in a way that Maggie knew she was giving too much advice. "I'm goin' ta the office ta see if I kin say goodbye ta John. I don' wan' him ta think I didn' think o' him," said Lizzie. She was quiet now, realizing it was her last night. She slipped out the door and looked out at the stars. *T'marra, I'll be on my way. I'll see these selfsame moon an' stars from a different place. I hope the skies are clear sae I kin see them. I'm really goin' ta America! Ever'thin' will be strange an' different an' new.*

She tapped on the office door, listening for the familiar deep voice in reply. The door creaked open and John's face lit up to see her standing there. "Kin I come in a minute, John?"

"Come, Lizzie," he said, opening the door wider. "Wha's wrong?"

"Nothin', John. I just wanna ta tell ye goodbye, is all. I'm gonna miss ye terrible." She stepped close and put her arms around his neck.

"I-I'll miss ye, too, Lassie." John clumsily patted her shoulder. "It wan' be the same."

She held him tightly for a long moment, taking in all that she could of her uncle: the smell of his shirt, his curly gray hair, the rough grizzled beard. His tall, skinny frame seemed slighter than she remembered.

"'Member, Girl, how much ye ma loves ye. An' don't trust no strangers. 'Member, how much yer Ma loves ta git letters. Don' gae near them Injins, neither. I hear they's bad ta wee lasses. 'Member, too, wha' *Mórai* taught ye. An' onct in a while when yer feelin' blue, think on ye Uncle an' how much he's missin' yer."

Lizzie stepped back, and looked at him, memorizing his face and how special he was. "Goodbye, John. Remember me, too. I'm the star jes' left o' the moon. You tol' me thet when I was a jes' a wee lass." With a flash of a grin, she left him standing there before he could see her eyes fill up with tears. *I am gonna miss ye sae much, John.*

Mórai had gone to bed by the time Lizzie came back to the cottage. Maggie was sitting at the table in the middle of the room, just waiting for her. *It's the last time I'll be waitin' fer her.*

She thought. *She's full grown an' I canna hold her here anymore. This arrow is shot in the air an' I may ne'er see it again. She'll see things I'll ne'er see. I hope they are good things, child. Oh Laird, keep her safe.*

The daughter sat across from her mother. Sensing her thoughts, she took her mother's hand in hers, tracing the fine veins on the back. Lizzie thought, *her hands are soft an' fine. Mine are broad an' rough, used ta harsh work an' weather. Hers are delicate an' do fine needlework. Her writing is beautifully formed, an' mine is plain. We are sae different. She is always kind. She thinks before* she speaks. She should haf' been a lady. I've no patience fer fine work an' niceties. I'm clumsy an' awkward an' talk too loud.

Maggie studied her daughter. Unexpectedly, a single tear splattered on the table in front of her. Maggie's green eyes were filled to overflowing. "Ye should git some rest, Lizzie. Yer new life's comin' in the mornin' an' nothin' kin stop it nae. You're sae much braver than all o' us. Yer Da would be sae proud of yer. Take care o' Eliza an' Cousin James."

Lizzie walked around the table and kissed her mother. "I will, Ma. There are none cleverer, or braver than ye are. When I look at all the new things in America, I'll be lookin' at them fer yer, too. I'll write as often as I kin, Ma, an' tell yer all about it. When I make my way in America, I'll be sendin' fer yer, sae ye kin see it too."

Maggie sat up long after Lizzie went to bed, and would wake her early the next morning. She drew Joseph's pocket watch from her apron, opened it, heard the reassuring tick-tick and placed it on the table before her. Yes, she had remembered to wind it and check the time with the sound of the bells from the village church at vespers. By the flickering light of a candle, she composed a letter to her daughter, on her last night home. She would hide the note and the watch at the bottom of Lizzie's bag, with the little silver cup.

She wrote:

To My Dearest Daughter,

I write this epistle on the occasion of your departure to America. Although I find it difficult to organize my thoughts, I shall endeavor to express them clearly. I am excited for your adventure and want for you the best of all you wish.

You have been, as I expect you always will be, a good and obedient daughter. I hope you will accept my humble assurances that your experiences to this day will stand you in good stead in your new home. Trust in God and your own counsel to guide you in all that you endeavor. You are strong, brave, and intelligent. Keep yourself modest in appearance and speech. Be ever watchful for anything that seems too fortuitous. The best reward for hard work is the satisfaction of having done your best. Remember, good always follows good.

Save your money carefully. Endeavor to owe no one. Conduct your life in such a manner as to allow people to think well of you. Be polite to everyone, even the most disadvantaged. Kindness is never earned. Give it freely, especially to those who deserve it least. Cultivate friends who are worthy of your company. Do not be too familiar with those who are above your station, but be helpful whenever possible.

There will be many new things to learn in America. Be studious in all parts of your life. Listen more than you speak. Attend diligently to your assigned tasks. Do more than you are asked in every instance. Do not stand about, waiting for your next task. Read and write as often as allowed.

I do apologize for the commanding tone of this letter, but I fear I have been neglectful in your raising and did not foresee this journey. Remember always, that your mother, Moraí, and your uncle will keep you in their constant prayers. We pray for your safety, good health, and happiness every day, now and forever. God bless you always,

    Your Proud and Loving Mother,
    Margaret Coburn Heenan

As she hid the letter and the watch among Lizzie's things, she smiled ruefully at what could be perceived as pretentious advice. *What knae I o' oceans, indentures an' America? How I envy yer spirit, Lizzie, an' yer innocent faith thet all things work out fer the best.*

Peeking in at Lizzie, she saw her daughter frown in her sleep, then restlessly turn away from her. Maggie smiled, remembering her journey from Scotland so long ago, recognizing the wild anticipation and fear in her daughter's dreams.

Fly, my angel. Soar ta the ends o' the earth, if ye will. Though tempestuous seas divide us, may yer heart e'er feel the winds o' County Down, where the blue Mournes touch the sky.

The Truth and the Fantasy

Because this is a collection of stories based on real people, real events, and real circumstances, it is incumbent upon me to tell what is true, and what is merely creative license connecting those people and events. In all cases, the timeline of published events of all the characters of the book have been carefully preserved to the best of my ability. Descriptions of private events were extracted from family lore set in the culture and times they occurred.

Hugh Annesley, 5th Earl of Annesley (1838 —1908)
His journal of the Crimean War, letters and newspaper articles supplied the true events found in the Prologue. He was indeed a contemporary of James and Elizabeth Coburn, and Maggie. He was an amateur photographer. He served in the Kafir wars and the Crimean war. The Frazer boys also served and were injured at the Battle of Alma, where Lord Annesley was shot. There is no proof they were in contact with each other, or that the Frazers mentioned, were relatives of Elizabeth Frazer Coburn of Scotland. Hugh Annesley was later the landlord of the Coburn holdings, as well as most of County Down, and portions of several neighboring counties.

Although the Coburns undoubtedly knew who he was, and the Earl knew who they were from a bookkeeping standpoint, it is improbable they had intimate contact with each other. It is reasonable that the Coburns went to Castlewellan on Monday Market Days to sell their wares. Family lore says Elizabeth and Lizzie did ironing for the "high and mightys" of Castlewellan, and their guests from London. Hugh Annesley was a magistrate at the courthouse in Castlewellan at the time, later serving in the House of Lords in Ireland. He lived at the castle with his brother, the 4th Earl of Annesley.

Any personal interaction between Hugh and Maggie is romantic conjecture. Hugh Annesley did build a fine arboretum, largest in Ireland, and third largest in the United Kingdom. I visited it in 2011 and was impressed. He held public office and I have adhered to the timeline of events in his family's life, and that of the Coburns. The letters and quotes mentioned in the Prologue contain direct quotes from his letters on file in the family archives, or as published in newspapers: *Details from the field of Battle, Nelson Examiner and New Zealand Chronicle,* Volume XIII, Issue 711, 17 February 1855, page 4, retrieved from *paperspast.natlib.govt.nz/cgi-bin/paperspast?,* Nov. 30, 2013. Several articles with excerpts of his letters were published in County Down and London newspapers.

He married first, a young lady of the court, twenty years his junior, 4 July 1877. His wife, Mabel, traveled extensively with him. In 1891, his mother died and less than a month later, Mabel died in an accident. He remarried to a very young cousin in London, July 1892. He spent the rest of his days at Castlewellan, much to his wife's disappointment. She was a notable hostess in London for many years. He wrote a small book about the arboretum in 1906. He died 1908. Again, the romantic story between Margaret and Lord Annesley, with apologies to both families, is fiction. Many of the papers, photographs, leases, and diaries researched to accurately portray his life and times, are located in the Public Records of Northern Ireland (PRONI).

James Colburn (Cockburn) (ca. 1828—?)

James is said to have been from Scotland and my research places the majority of the Coburns (Cockburns in Scotland) in

Lanarkshire and neighboring areas. We have yet to locate any documentation that links James and Elizabeth, and Margaret in Scotland. His name is on a plot plan of Drumgooland, Ireland, listed on Griffith's Valuation (1863) in Legananny as #1, with Margaret Coburn's plot as #2. (This Margaret may have been James' sister-in-law, who inherited the land from her husband. For the purposes of the story, I made it Maggie's land, but it is unlikely.) James Coburn also had tenancy in a neighboring townland, Slievnaboley, adjacent to the land in Legananny. Maggie was only 8 years old at the time, so it is unlikely *our* Margaret had a lease on the land, regardless of the spin I have put on it. I have put his emigration to Northern Ireland at about 1858, when the lairds of the Lanarkshire area were converting their farms to sheep and wool production. For the most part, the lairds of that time did make it possible for their former tenants to find employment in larger factory towns, and in some cases, arrange for them to continue farming in Northern Ireland.

Hugh Annesley had a number of colleagues who served with him as Scots Fusilier Guards, who were lairds in Scotland. The notion that Hugh Annesley and James Coburn's laird cooperated in granting James a land lease in Legananny, is completely imaginative conjecture.

We did find in the Valuation Revisions of 1878-9, that the names of James Coburn and Margaret Coburn were taken off the land, and replaced by John Coburn. It could be that James or Margaret died at that time, but it could have been much earlier. John Coburn was likely much younger than his brother, James (if they were brothers). John appears as a farmer, never married, in the 1911 Census at 85 years old. After 1914, another name replaces his on the Valuation Revisions.

Elizabeth Jane Frazer Coburn (Cockburn)

It is likely Elizabeth Frazer was born and married James near Lanark, Scotland. Their daughter, Margaret Jane, stated she was born in Scotland (shown on the *S.S. City of Chester* manifests 1892 in Liverpool and New York). Owing to Margaret's invalid state, Elizabeth raised her granddaughter and namesake, Lizzie. My grandmother, Lizzie, did not mention her grandfather, except that his name was James. They lived in a cottage with two rooms (according to the 1901 and 1911 censuses). Griffith's Valuation describes it as a cottage and office. My father, Raymond MacNeill, said they did all their cooking outdoors, maintained a few sheep, a milk cow, spun wool, made candles, soap, and raised crops. There is an Elizabeth Coburn who died in a workhouse in Belfast in 1895 at 94.

Margaret Jane Coburn (Cockburn) Heenan
(1845 -after 1893)

Margaret Coburn was said to be an invalid. Family lore says she stopped walking at an early age *(that story may have stemmed from my having been born with dislocated hips, which were not discovered until I developed a limp at age five. The defect is hereditary.)* Margaret was reputed to be very bright, but unable to care for her child. Her mother, Elizabeth, raised Margaret's child, Lizzie.

I decided to write the story as the research at that time seemed to confirm. Joseph Heenan was probably the father of her child, but it is not proven. The circumstances of the conception are purely fictional, as is the relationship of Maggie and Hugh. At this time, we do not know why Maggie *(and her child Lizzie)* stayed with Elizabeth Coburn after her marriage to Joseph (if indeed, they *did* marry), but as an invalid, she would have made a poor wife to a farmer and his brood of children.

Someday, perhaps we will find the true story and no doubt it will be even more interesting than the invention I have given it here.

Margaret did come to visit Lizzie in America, but was not detained at Ellis Island. She was an invalid and as such was never classified as an immigrant. She traveled on a non-immigrant ship and was probably issued a temporary visa. She probably left the United States within six months.

Joseph Heenan (about 1850-?)

Joseph Heenan, son of Elizabeth Heenan, #20 on Griffiths' Valuation of Legananny, County Down, Northern Ireland, is most likely the father of Lizzie Heenan. It is not proven that he ever married Maggie. We know he was married first to Margaret Steele. *(I called her Mary to lessen the confusion of names.)*

In later research, I found the person who drowned in New York Harbor was not Joseph, but probably his nephew, James. In early genealogy findings, we supposed that *James Heenan* was the name of Lizzie's father, and he was the one who drowned in New York Harbor. In the story, I have Joseph traveling to America when Lizzie was still a child, and the family receives word that he died there. Research revealed, after the story was written, Joseph likely remained a farmer in Ireland all his life. It was James Heenan, possibly his nephew, who drowned. Joseph and his first wife (Margaret Steele) had five baptized children: Joseph, John, Ann, Elizabeth, and James. This James died at about six years of age, so the James Heenan, 24, who sailed on the *City of New York* with Eliza and Lizzie, was probably a cousin whose presence allowed the young women to make the trip, and is a more likely candidate for the Heenan who died in the ferry accident. Instead, I contrived to have him involved in the Oklahoma Land Rush.

Elizabeth Jane Heenan MacNeill (1872-1964)

Lizzie was described by herself (as quoted by her son, Raymond H. MacNeill) as "an only child of an only child, raised by her grandmother, tough as smithy's nails." Her mother called herself

Margaret (*nee* Coburn, Cockburn) Heenan and as an invalid, turned the child over to the care of her mother, Elizabeth Jane Fraser Coburn. Lizzie had a half-sister, Elizabeth Ann Heenan, daughter of Joseph Heenan and Margaret Steele, according to Church of Ireland records. We are still untangling the Heenan family lines at this stage. One theory is, Margaret Steele (*Mary*, in the story) was Joseph's 1st wife, and Margaret Coburn had Lizzie out of wedlock. On Elizabeth Jane Heenan's (Lizzie's) birth certificate, Joseph's name does not appear as her father. The mother's name appears as Margaret *Heenan*, and the eyewitness to the birth was Elizabeth *Heenan* (Joseph's mother). The certificate was signed with her mark. With four Elizabeths (the child, her half-sister, and both grandmothers), the record could have been distorted many ways. More research is needed to prove the marriage of Margaret Coburn and Joseph Heenan and their resulting issue, Lizzie Heenan. The last child of Joseph and Margaret (Steele) Heenan was James Heenan, born 1 JUN 1871, *eight months* before Lizzie. Margaret Steele is not mentioned after this birth. I have not found baptism records to support Joseph as the father of Lizzie. The records I was able to find from the Anglican Church of Ballyward, stop at 1871. Lizzie was born the following February.

Elizabeth Ann Heenan (1868 - ca. 1956)

Lizzie's half-sister, daughter of Joseph Heenan and Margaret Steele, is called Eliza in the story to separate her from Lizzie, but our father said his mother and his aunt were both named Elizabeth and both called *Lizzie*. She is listed on the Liverpool and Ellis Island passenger manifests as *Eliza*. He said they visited several times, once in Malden and a few times in Middleborough. They were Aunt Lizzie and Uncle Charlie to our father, and their children were double cousins, because his mother (Lizzie) and Aunt Eliza were sisters and his father (William) was Uncle Charlie's brother.

Other People Mentioned in the Story

Other names of real companies and persons are included, but their characters are romanticized, such as the aforementioned Earl Hugh Annesley and his family. The ministers, their families, and their landlords are all true persons who lived in the area and had contact with Lizzie and Margaret. The Reverend Mister Williard Crane, is the only exception. His name, demeanor, and physical appearance are fictional. The story as told by my grandmother did not include his name, but explains why they had a falling out with the Presbyterian Church and switched to the Church of Ireland.

With four Elizabeths, two Margarets, two Josephs, several James and others, the entanglements are overwhelming. It is my hope to have described the individuals with such clarity as to keep them separate characters in the reader's mind, without having to resort to renaming all of my ancestors.

I offer my apologies to those who may have suffered a poor characterization by my hand. Events retold from generation to generation are often so greatly distorted, as to resemble the childhood game "gossip".

When my grandmother, Lizzie, heard some of her grandchildren were researching her family in Ireland, she said, "Ye kin do all thet if yer wan' ta, but ye might no' like wha' ye find."

ACKNOWLEDGEMENTS

I would be remiss if I did not express my gratitude to the many friends and family who put up with my endless prattling about the characters in this book.

My sister, Joyce Presley, who came to live with me during the final stages of this book, was my greatest help. She gave me quiet time to write, slipped food in front of my keyboard, reminded me of four o'clock eye drops, and took messages from the phone calls I ignored, while I worked.

I also thank my super cheerleaders: My sister, Janice Hammond, my brother, David MacNeill; friends: Mary Ann O'Connell, Beverly Bifano, Roni Herlihy, and my sister-in-law, Evelyn Dupont; all of whom were instrumental in keeping me focused on my goal.

Special 'thank-you's go to Joe Dutcher, who opened my eyes to the possibilities of digital publishing and to Cathy Voci, who poured through this book, line by line, searching for mechanical missteps in my writing.

It was my father who challenged me to write this series of books, so that the stories he gave us would not be lost to the next generations. Thank you, Dad, for teaching me to never let the lack of proof stand in the way of a good story, and allowing me the license to make sense of the disparate facts, however unlikely. We may never know the whole truth, but the known facts were lovingly arranged in their best light, so the generations that follow would think well of their ancestors and perhaps seek out the missing parts of the story as it really happened.

ABOUT THE AUTHOR

Dorothy MacNeill Dupont is a new writer, an amateur genealogist, a graphic designer, a water color artist, an avid traveler and an active volunteer at a local charity and her church. Recently retired from the advertising world, she makes her home in a small town in Massachusetts. She misses her husband George, the love of her life, every single day. She has two wonderful sons, Thomas and Anthony, of whom she is proud beyond words.

The Winds of County Down is the fictionalized story of Margaret Jane Coburn, the author's great-grandmother. It is the first of the *Legannany Legacy* series.

The second of the series, *The Self-same Moon and Stars*, is the story of her grandmother, Elizabeth Jane Heenan. This book is scheduled to be published in spring of 2015. The series includes five generations of women from 1828 to 1970.